CHAOS THEORY

CHAOS THEORY
INITIATION

AUBREY BALLARD

This book is a work of fiction. All places, people, businesses or events are a product of the author's imagination and any resemblances to actual places, people (living or dead), businesses or events are completely coincidental.

Visit us online! TheAubreyB.com

Cover and book design by Victoria Ross.

Printed in the United States of America
First Edition, 2019

ISBN 978-1-7337877-0-3

This book is dedicated to all who have lived through heartache and were brave enough to make something beautiful out of it.

Love is a story, and the world needs yours.

PROLOGUE

I was there when the first Chaos occurred...well, the first attack on American soil, at least. I guess that is where I will begin my story. A time that seems so long ago, I refer to that period of my life as *The Before*. Before my naive bubble of reality burst, before I knew about the U.D. and their Kronies, before the world turned upside down, before I lost my family and found myself, before Rome.

It's unnerving to think how "normal" everything seemed back then...when my biggest worry was the Economy test on Monday or what All-Mark outfit to wear to the movies. We were all oblivious to the global anarchy growing right under our noses. Oh sure, we saw clips of destruction on the nightly news and read the ever-increasing death toll as we scrolled the Internet. But that was in Europe or Asia. Not in America, and especially not in Oklahoma City, the center of nothing.

We were not concerned in the least about a Chaos starting in our backyard. We didn't even know it had a name at that time. If there were to be an attack, surely it would happen somewhere of importance: New York, Los Angeles, Chicago. I often wonder how different things would have been if I had not been directly involved...if I lived in a different city and was able to watch the whole thing unravel through the safety of the television screen. But I was right in the middle of it all. So, that is where I will start; the day *The Before* ended and my new life began.

CHAPTER 1

CHAOS ONE

"Eve," my mom called from the other room. "I'm heading to All-Mark to pick up a few things. Want to come?"

I had just sat down to binge watch the last season of *Great American Dream*, my favorite show. I was getting a late start and couldn't waste a minute if I was going to catch up to my best friend, Natalie. Annoyed, I paused the hologram on host Gavin Starling's gleaming white smile and trademark purple glasses. "Um, I'm kind of in the middle of something. Ask Connor."

Mom's small frame appeared in the doorway. "Your dad is taking him to his indoor soccer tournament. What's so important anyway?" she asked as she swept her soft brown hair out of her face.

I motioned vigorously toward the television. "Tomorrow is the groundbreaking season twenty premiere! It's going to be epic! I have to prepare."

Mom rolled her eyes and put on her white, fuzzy coat. "You can do that later. Come on, it'll be fun. We'll grab dinner at the food court before we leave."

"Every other family doesn't go on shopping trips together. Why do we have to?" I whined.

I recited Mom's answer with her. "Well, we aren't every other family."' It was one of her "go-to" phrases whenever Con or I complained about scheduled family time. The truth was, I actually liked being around them, as long as no one from school found out.

"Don't you like hanging out with your mom? Aren't I hip enough for you?" She threw her hands above her head and shimmied her hips in a way that couldn't be unseen.

I couldn't help but laugh at her failure. "Actually, you're too hip for me. But in all seriousness, tomorrow is the premiere! That leaves me with approximately twenty-eight hours to watch the entire last season, behind the scenes footage, and the *Where Are They Now* recap!"

Mom crossed her arms, unmoved and unamused.

"Uuuggghhhh, fine," I moaned as I dragged myself off our new surround sound couch. I grabbed a coat and threw my long hair into a messy bun as I slunk toward the garage. It wasn't that I didn't like going to All-Mark; a mega-store with everything you could ever want. "Your one-stop shop for *All* your consumer needs at a price that hits your financial *Mark*," according to the advertisements. The problem was that the trip would eat up my entire afternoon. It was utterly impossible for my mom to spend less than five hours in the store. I would need to be on my A-game to hurry her along. Thankfully, All-Mark was only five minutes away. The faster we arrived, the faster we could leave.

As our self-driven car purred quietly through the streets, Mom reviewed her list of items: milk, eggs, socks for Connor, blah, blah, blah, a new Insta-cook. Suddenly, Mom reached across me and pointed to the highway. "Upper! One point for me!"

I gazed longingly at the shiny black SUV as it passed out of view. Our family always played the "Upper game." One point for seeing an Upper Class vehicle or person, which was pretty rare in Oklahoma. I had no shot of winning, but that didn't stop me from gawking out the windows as we took the dedicated exit and joined the mass of excited Saturday shoppers. All-Mark was the highlight of most people's week.

We pulled into the parking lot and I marveled at the sight of the beautiful building. The entire base level of the four-tier spire was made of the highest-grade projection screens proudly displaying the newest in All-Mark fashion and trending electronic gadgets. The building spiraled upward to the newly constructed addition that sparkled with glass and lights. It seemed like every week, OneGlobal was making the place bigger and better. Despite my initial sentiment, I found my anticipation growing. Going to O.G. establishments almost made me feel like an Upper.

The OKC All-Mark had been established for almost ten years. The government started opening them in major cities twenty years ago and, like most things, it took some time for the trend to reach my boring sector of the country. I vaguely remembered shopping at disgusting old "malls" as a child but I tried to block that from my memory.

Places like All-Mark started after the *Economy Crunch* of 2074 when poverty ravaged the world. My parents were only kids then, but don't think for one second I didn't know every detail. The message was preached to us starting in third grade; the story of how large corporations jeopardized every industry by competing with each other to raise prices. The public suffered from inflation and people barely had enough Credits to eat, let alone afford entertainment and luxuries. These companies destroyed the economy, forcing the government to step in and take over their businesses and standardize everything. There were protests at first, but once everyone realized the government could provide food for their family at a "price that hits your financial mark," the protesters shut up.

The government was able to afford these provisions from contracts with OneGlobal: the revamped economic and business version of the United Nations. Established in 2075, OneGlobal "provides tax-free trading for countries striving for a better world." They basically saved the planet. If it wasn't for the O.G., I'd be living in a cardboard box, drinking dirty water and trying not to die from the common cold.

Plus, they made everything affordable. Before the foundation of OneGlobal, over eighty percent of the country lived below the poverty line. This led to horrible diseases like the Decimus plague which wiped out almost half of the world's population. Thankfully, OneGlobal developed a cure and allowed every law-abiding citizen the right to health care, cable television, and fast food. They didn't just save our country; they saved the world. They optimized every aspect of society. I should have known all the details from my eighth grade OneGlobal class, but all you really needed to know to pass was that OneGlobal is amazing. Stay loyal to the O.G. and the O.G. will take care of you.

Anything economic or political bored me to death.

I worked under the philosophy that, if it makes life simpler and I didn't have to worry about it, then *carry on big government!* I would have bet most of the nation felt that way about our world. OneGlobal boosted the American economy so much, why not let them run everyone else's too? Slowly but surely, the O.G. became the chief governing body of the rest of the world. Local businesses had to shut down in the process, but there were news stories every day about how the old mom-and-pop shoe store barely staying afloat now designed sneakers for people across the world. The technological and medical advances were astounding, but what I loved most about OneGlobal is what it did for reality TV!

They took the best show ideas from around the world and combined them into the most amazing, dramatic, and entertaining programs in the history of television. Every person I knew religiously watched *Great American Dream*, where everyday people are able to develop their talent and become superstars! Entertainers, artists, chefs, scientists and even industrialists, were chosen from the normal class, trained in their respective field and given the opportunity to work for OneGlobal. Of course, each week America voted for their favorite and some poor loser is eliminated from the competition. The winner from three seasons earlier became an executive for All-Mark and one time a cook from Oklahoma made it to the semi-finals. She ended up as the head chef for *Burgerz*, the only hamburger chain left in America. My mom had told us stories of her younger days about how there were several different hamburger restaurants. It was hard for me to believe because *Burgerz* was the only place I'd ever known. Plus, why have lots of options for the same thing when you can just have one that is the best? And it wasn't like OneGlobal controlled our lives. I could still choose between tacos or spaghetti for dinner or decide which All-Mark shirt goes best with which All-Mark skirt.

I really could not understand the problems they were having in Europe. We didn't hear much about it, but occasionally there would be a thirty-second blurb on the evening news about some crazy radicals, the "Universal Defiance," overtaking some government-run building. OneGlobal forces always stopped them within minutes and the anarchists were usually ex-convicts who escaped from some small prison. But nothing like that had ever happened in America and I didn't see why it would. Sure, older people were paranoid that the attacks would cross the ocean, but I wasn't worried in the least. Our country was invincible with OneGlobal leading us forward.

"Brrrr. I hate winter," Mom said as we hurried through the large, glass doors of the south entrance. "Let's start with getting Connor new socks. I swear he goes through at least a pair every week."

The atrium flashed with large holographic advertisements of the weekly specials and clearance items. Interactive video boards previewed the evening's television programs mixed with public service announcements from OneGlobal. "Help yourself and help the world," one of them chimed. "Follow your Department of Compliance. Please report any suspicious behavior and obey all security personnel. Protect OneGlobal so we can protect you." We usually spent thirty minutes in that room alone, but a holographic sneak peek of the *Great American*

Dream premiere reminded me of my mission. I grabbed Mom's arm and made a beeline for the entry tunnel.

The north and south atriums were connected by a long, cement tube lined with vending machines and restrooms on the outer wall and one directional exits from the store on the other. My friends and I nicknamed the area the "echo tube." When All-Mark first opened, the empty area allowed your voice to carry the entire length of the tube. We would stand at opposite ends and see who could make the funniest sounds before security would run us off. When I say "we", I mean my friends would do it while I stood as a lookout. I was always too scared of getting caught.

Our games were put to an end when All-Mark installed a ginormous jumbotron in the middle of the tube, welcoming shopper to the solitary entrance to the actual store. The crystal clear picture and deep, booming sound demanded our attention as we walked toward it in a trance. The three-dimensional screen was the most impressive form of technology I had ever witnessed. I sucked in a breath as a giant, high-definition Gavin Starling illuminated the tube.

"Happy New Year! Are you ready for tonight? Do you have your favorite snacks? Upgraded to that next level sound system? Invited your friends to your virtual watch party? The countdown is on. Only twenty-seven hours and thirty-six minutes until the premiere and, trust me, you do NOT want to miss a single second. See you soon!"

Gavin winked through his glasses and my heart fluttered. "Let's go get those socks!"

After several unnecessary pit stops, we finally made it to the boys' clothing. I was in the middle of recalculating how many episodes I could go through in one night when a deep voice called out my mom's name.

"Angie! Hey, Angie!"

We whirled around to see a large man half jogging, half waddling toward us. He looked like a normal shopper, a fitted black shirt and bulky gray jacket, but the clear earpiece slightly protruding from his right ear suggested a security guard of some sort.

"Dave! It's been forever!" Mom said, smiling as she reached out for his hand. His giant paw engulfed hers. "Dave, this is my daughter, Eve. Eve, Dave and I went to high school together."

"Nice to meet you, Eve," he panted as he shook my hand enthusiastically. "Your mom and I go way back!"

"Oh, high school wasn't *that* long ago," Mom joked. "What's new with you? We're just making a small shopping run."

"I work for All-Mark now," Dave beamed. "Security. Undercover."

"Is that so?" Mom asked, one eyebrow arching.

"Yep." He leaned in as if to tell us a secret and whispered, "I pretend to be a shopper, but I keep an eye out and notify the Department of Compliance, a.k.a. the D.O.C., if I notice anything suspicious."

I couldn't help but smile at the guy's enthusiasm. You would have thought he had achieved his life's dream.

"Fascinating," Mom said, attempting to keep a look of seriousness on her face. "Well, we appreciate you keeping all of us safe. I bet the increasing crowds make your job more difficult."

"They don't make it easy," he said, giving me a wink. "But, I'm not complaining. More overtime means more Credits. Once they finish the east wing, it won't feel as crowded. You're not going to believe how fancy it's gonna be. All the bells and whistles. They are pushing hard to double my department by next month *and* there's a chance I could get promoted."

"Good for you." Mom said warmly. She was one of the kindest people I knew. She genuinely cared about everyone. "You've got to love living in a stable economy. How are Sierra and the kids?"

"Sierra is good, still working in quality assurance. Maddy is in fifth grade now and Mark is in first. Can you believe they are starting Economics in the first grade now? The homework that kid brings home looks like the stuff I did in high school!" Dave chuckled.

"I know what you mean. My son, Connor, is in eighth grade and has homework that I couldn't even begin to understand. But, I don't blame them. I'm sure OneGlobal wants the next generation to keep making improvements and finally stop all that craziness that's going on in Europe." Mom turned to me. "What do you think, Eve? How's the homework of a seventeen-year-old?"

"Uh, sure. Brutal," I agreed, apathetically.

A small beep emitted from Dave's jacket. "Duty calls. I've got to get back to work. It was nice seeing you, Angie. You guys take care." He turned and huffed away.

"You, too!" Mom called as she returned her focus to the socks. "I could have sworn he had a son your age. Weird that he didn't mention him."

My phone buzzed in my pocket. It was Natalie: "ONLY 26 HRS TIL THE PREMIERE!!!!! WHAT EPISODE ARE YOU ON?!?!?"

I texted back my sad tale of shopping through emojis. *Ugh, why does my mom always need a shopping buddy?* Natalie didn't even talk to her parents. Sometimes, I just wanted to be the typical teenager. Deep down, my family meant the most to me, but in situations that interfered with my social life, I didn't know if I was lucky or cursed.

The rest of the afternoon proceeded with checking off the list one agonizing item at a time. Natalie continually sent me updates on her progress in the G.A.D. binge. I was about ready to throw my phone through the display case in front of me when I recognized the man on the screen. I froze and grabbed my mom's arm.

"Mom, can I please buy this new album? Please, please, please?" I begged.

"That's funny," Mom said as she scrolled through her phone. "I don't remember seeing new music on my list."

"Oh, come on. If you insist on me not being on social media while you drag me around All-Mark, the least you can do is buy me this very special album. Please, I'm your favorite daughter." I gave her my cheesiest smile.

"For one, you're my only daughter. Two, rules are rules. Three, what's so special about this very special album?" Mom asked.

Since she asked about the album, I knew I had a shot. I took a deep breath and prepared my argument. "*Pop 2112* was recorded by *two* artists! One of which is my absolute favorite: last year's winner of *Rock the Mic*, Rembrandt! Usually, the winner only provides music for the year they were crowned champion then never heard from again. But Rembrandt was so popular they let him contribute to this year's album. And I just love his name. It's so unique, I don't know how he came up with it. Don't you agree?"

Mom rolled her eyes but nodded. I pulled her into a bear hug then scanned the display with my phone. The album loaded automatically. Mom reached over and took one earbud and we danced our way through the aisles.

"Alrighty. I think that does it," Mom said as she scanned her list for the twentieth time. "I don't know about you, but I'm starving."

Eleven restaurants encircled the massive food court in the center of All-Mark. Mom ran off to find the healthiest option, while I took advantage of my alone time by checking my social media as I waited for sushi. A message flashed across the screen that my order was ready. I slid my phone into my back pocket, grabbed my tray, and turned directly into the chest of a guy my age.

"I'm so sorry!" he exclaimed as he bent down to pick up the carnage. He handed me the tray. The roll was contained inside its box, although thoroughly deconstructed.

I bit my lip as I tried to come up with something to say. "It's fine. It will taste the same." My cheeks burned hotly as I avoided eye contact. *Taste the same? That's the best you've got, Eve?* I had zero skill when it came to boys. Thankfully, Connor wasn't present to announce my fumble to the entire food court.

I worked up the courage to look up at my crash victim, but he was gone. I stood motionless until I noticed Mom waving me over to a table in the center of the room. I dropped my tray on the table and sat down.

"I still don't see why you like that stuff. Is it supposed to look like that?" Mom asked as she wrinkled her nose at my plate.

"Yes, it's the new sushi salad. But you wouldn't know because you never try anything that's remotely out of the box," I quipped.

"Hello, kettle. It's me, pot," Mom retorted.

I rolled my eyes. "I'm willing to try new things...I just like to follow the rules, like a good citizen. Isn't that what you want? Or would you prefer for me to be more like Connor and have to worry what trouble I'll get into next, just counting down the days until I'm labeled Noncompliant."

"Eve, don't joke like that!" Mom hissed. She looked around to see if anyone had heard. "I'm just giving you a hard time. You know how much I appreciate your good behavior. Keep up your Compliance record and you're bound to end up in a rewarding career."

I played with my jumbled food. "Don't get your hopes up."

"Eve, you need to be more positive about yourself." Mom said, dropping her fork as she stared into my soul. "You are a smart, thoughtful, beautiful, young lady with a bright future ahead of you. You'll have a great match and a great career."

I blushed and shoved a piece of sushi in my mouth. I didn't like to talk about my future, mostly because I was nervous about my career path. Aptitude tests weren't until the following senior year, but I always choked on test day. Mom had high hopes, but I was a realist. With my luck,

I'd be scrubbing toilets for the rest of my life.

I collected our dinner trash to take to the waste incinerators when I noticed a man racing toward our table. It was Dave, only he had changed into his full security uniform and looked terrified.

Mom spotted him too, "Dave? Is everything alri—"

"You both need to leave the store now," he whispered, his voice shaking.

Mom darted her eyes from me to him. "Is something wro—"

"I don't have time to explain. Get your things and get out of here!" he interrupted, pointing toward the exit.

I looked around, embarrassed. An elderly couple sitting next to us stopped eating to take in the drama. Dave noticed and moved to block their view. He put a hand on Mom's shoulder and strained in a hushed tone, "You have been in the store too long. Store policy declares this as suspicious behavior and we ask you to take your purchases to the check out immediately."

Mom shook her head, her brows furrowed. "What are you talking about? We've only been here since four this afternoon. We can't possib—"

The elderly woman stood up. "Is something wrong?" Her loud voice only drew more attention.

"Everything is under control. Please remain in your seats." Dave turned back to Mom. "Ma'am! Do not make me call for backup! Do you want the Department of Compliance to get involved?" Many shoppers stopped their meal to watch the drama. Dave looked completely stressed out. Sweat rolled down his temple and off his quivering jaw. "Angie," he pleaded. "Please listen to me. Take your daughter, checkout, and go home."

Mom looked from me to the growing number of onlookers. "Um, okay. We will leave, but I want a good explanation later this evening."

Relief spread across Dave's face as we stood and gathered our belongings. "Thanks," he murmured, then turned to race back in the direction he came from.

"I wonder what that was all about. It wasn't like we were loitering or in an unauthorized area. I've never seen him act like that before. Oh, well," Mom pondered as we pushed our cart toward the wall of checkout chambers at the front of the store. "You know...when I was little..."

"No! Don't go there!" I laughed.

"When I was little, we didn't have these fancy checkout chambers that scan your entire cart. We had to go through each item separately. It took forever. In fact..."

I put my fingers in my ears and pretended to not hear the speech my mom gave *every* time we checked out at All-Mark. I smiled to myself as the shopper in front of us walked into the small room, leaving us next in line. It may have freaked me out a little, but thanks to Dave's little meltdown, I was almost home free. I could hear the theme song for *Great American Dream* calling my name.

I felt a tap on my shoulder

"Excuse me, miss?" It was the elderly lady from the food court. "What did that security officer want? Why was he acting like that?" There was something like panic in her expression. She seemed nervous and spoke a little too loud.

Mom stepped beside me. "No, I was just telling my daughter I had no idea what that was about. I—"

The lady interrupted, her pitch rising. "Why did he want you to leave? Is something going on here like the other places?" Other customers began to notice the woman's theatrics.

"Is something going on?" a woman with two young kids in the adjacent line asked.

"No, nothing is going on!" Mom tried to explain.

The old lady became more hostile. "Something *is* going on and these people were warned. Tell us if we are in danger!" she yelled.

I had heard rumors of elderly people "catching paranoia." We even had a lesson over it in health class but I had never witnessed it firsthand. The news reported that the attacks in Europe had acted like a triggering agent to set off certain older people. Some even required hospitalization to calm them back down.

People crowded around us and joined the jumbled conversation. I felt like we were on the cusp of a riot. Thankfully, the chamber door in front of us opened and we pushed our cart through the gate. The door closed behind us, silencing the commotion.

"What is going on?" I asked Mom as the automated cashier machine scanned our cart.

"Your guess is as good as mine," she said, looking worried. "Those people were acting crazy!"

"Yeah…what was it she said? Something about being in danger?"

"I don't know, but I say we take Dave's advice and get

out of here. ASAP." Mom wrung her hands nervously. I'd never seen her look so scared.

The cashier chimed happily overhead. "Two-hundred and fifty-four Credits will be deducted from your account, Mrs. Price. Enjoy your day and thank you for shopping at All-Mark."

The exit door slid open and we hurried into the echo tube. I immediately sensed something was off. The sound of metal carts being pushed to the exits reverberated off the walls. A palpable tension filled the air as I looked around to see what was different. That's when I realized why the hall was so quiet. "Mom, look! The jumbotron isn't working. That's never happened before. Something isn't right."

"Maybe it's down for maintenance," Mom replied casually, but she started pushing the cart faster.

I kept her pace while trying to convince myself everything was normal. *Just think, ten minutes from now you will be back at home, watching G.A.D.* I sighed in relief when I saw the familiar glow from the advertisements in the atrium indicating our immediate exit.

We were ten meters from the doors when a loud screech stopped us in our tracks. Glass shards busted through the atmosphere as a body flew through the doors and landed at my feet. The man moaned, rolled onto his side and spit out several teeth. Blood poured down his face as he looked up at me. I held onto Mom for balance as my dinner attempted to make a reappearance. I looked past the man to see hundreds of people flooding the entryway. Instinctively, I grabbed Mom's arm and ran in the opposite direction. We darted into the nearest restroom and peeked our heads into the hall.

We watched in horror as our cart disappeared when several explosions took out the rest of the entrance. Smoke filled the area as teenage boys roared through the opening. Some ran screaming into the store while others strolled in, carrying baseball bats and large guns over their shoulders. *I didn't think guns existed in America!* Some wore dingy, tattered clothes while others wore Designer athletic gear. Some wore masks, and others elaborate face paint. One boy carried a large boom box on his shoulder that played some weird type of deafening music.

I covered my ears as Mom pulled me to the ground. I couldn't tear my eyes away from the destruction. Systematically, they demolished every checkout chamber exit and raced into the store. Through the damaged chamber door directly across from me, I could see terrified shoppers scatter as the boys decimated everything in their path, pushing over shelves, smashing TVs, even setting off fireworks and other small bombs. An older boy walked into my line of sight. He carried a megaphone in one hand and a shotgun in the other. His shaved head contrasted his thick beard. He sounded a police siren and all the boys froze in place.

"WHO'S READY FOR A LITTLE CHAOS?" he screamed and fired a gun into the air. "KRONIES... EMERGE!"

Suddenly, hundreds more gushed into the tunnel. Boys fanned out in all directions, completely taking over the store. The noise was deafening. I thought my heart would beat out of my chest.

Mom pulled me deeper into the restroom. I had to yell

over the sounds of the store imploding. "They have guns! Real guns! What do we do? We have to call the D.O.C.!" I patted myself down and realized I had dropped my phone somewhere in the bedlam.

Mom looked as terrified as I felt. Her hands shook as she reached inside her purse and pulled out her phone. "I have no signal. That's never happened before. We can't stay in here. If they come in, we're trapped. It looked like they were all coming from the south and going into the store. Our only chance to make it out is to reach the north entrance before they do. It's a straight shot down the hall. Stay low and go as fast as you can. No matter what happens, keep running. If we get separated, meet at home. Okay?"

I tried to speak, but no words came. All I could manage was a nod. The lights flickered on and off. Mom grabbed my hand and we edged to the doorway. It appeared that most of the group was inside the store, while a few stragglers hurried inside from the south entrance. The rest of the hall was devoid of life.

Mom pulled me into a bear hug. "On my count. One. Two. Three!"

We raced out of the restroom and toward the opposite end of the store. Mom led the way and pulled me behind her. I couldn't get my shocked body to work correctly. It felt like I was running through honey. Mom looked back at me to see what my hold up was when a grown man slammed into us. The three of us crashed to the ground. I moaned and pushed myself to a sitting position as the room spun.

The man scrambled to his feet and leaned over us.

"Do you want to escape alive?" He appeared not to have showered in some time. His matted beard stuck out in all directions. His breath reeked as he yelled at us again. "I said do you want to get out of here with your lives?"

"Yes!" Mom yelled back at him as she stood protectively in front of me.

"Then act insane," the man said matter-of-factly.

"What? What do you mean?" Mom breathed. I crouched behind her, terrified.

"Act like you're out of your mind!" The man squatted down and mimicked a chicken. "They sent me in here to warn people...to give them a chance to get out. That's how you escape. You don't get lucky. You make a fool of yourself and if it's good enough they let you go."

I peeled my eyes away from the man to survey the store. I noticed part of the ceiling was missing and more boys repelled down. It sounded like the war movies shown in school about the *Pre-OneGlobal Era*: screams mixed with gunshots and broken glass.

The man turned to leave, but Mom grabbed his sleeve and screamed above the noise. "Don't go! Help us get out!"

He yanked his arm out of her grasp. "I'm just a messenger!" He barked like a dog then ran toward the middle of the store.

I stood in complete shock, as the only person who had some idea of what was going on disappeared from view. The lights flickered and snapped me back to reality.

Mom pushed me in front of her. "Keep going!"

We were halfway down the tube when hundreds of customers came screaming into the hallway from the checkout chambers. I felt Mom's hand rip from my grasp as people flooded in around us. I frantically searched the sea of faces with no sight of her. I spun in a slow circle. "Mom!" I screamed, as desperation built in the back of my throat. Bodies pushed me in all directions as they rushed toward the exits. Suddenly, someone grabbed the back of my shirt. I turned in relief to see Mom, tears streaming down her cheek.

A loud metallic pop directly above us halted our reunion. I looked up to see the jumbotron sway dangerously from side to side. I stood in horror as the screen screeched ominously.

"Eve! Run!" Mom cried as the last cables holding the screen gave way. All I could do was close my eyes and brace for impact. A force slammed into my shoulders and threw me backward. A thunderous crash filled my ears as I gasped to replace the air that had left my lungs. I rolled to my side to see the smashed jumbotron just centimeters in front of me.

"Mom!" I shrieked, as I struggled to my feet. Frantically, I scanned the wall of debris. *Don't panic. She can't be under there. She's fine. She has to be.* The shattered screen stretched all the way from the checkout chambers to the outer cement wall. There was no way to get to the other side. I would have to go into the store to find her.

"Eve?"

I froze as my heart skipped a beat. *Was that Mom?* I ran toward my name and climbed up the side of the debris to a tiny crack between the wall and screen.

"Eve? Are you okay?" I could barely hear her over all the noise.

"Mom!" I yelled back. "I'm okay! Wait right there. I'll

find a way to get to you!"

"No! Go home! There is a hole I can climb through over here to get outside. Get out of here and run home. I will meet you there."

I bit my lip as I weighed my options. Half of me wanted to follow my mom's advice and get out of the store as fast as possible. The other half wanted to fight my way to my mom and make sure we were both safe. After what felt like an eternity, I decided to follow Mom's instructions. *Who knows if I could even make it to the other side?*

"Okay, I'm leaving. I'll meet you at home." I turned around and immediately froze. A boy with a clown mask stood below me. He wore a vest and tie, with no shirt and faded jeans. His head cocked to the side and a shotgun slung lazily over one shoulder.

"Well, Dupe, that was a close one. Now, let's get you down from there before you mess up that pretty face," he said as he stepped closer and reached for my hand. I had no choice but to let him help me climb down the pile. Once at the bottom, he offered me his arm like he would escort me to prom. I hesitated.

"I don't have all night, sweetheart."

I gulped as I slowly slid my trembling arm into his. He interlaced his fingers with mine. Never in a million years did I picture my first time holding hands with a boy to be in the middle of a terror attack.

"See, this isn't so bad," the clown chided. "Too bad normal rules aren't in play or this could have been a great evening for us." He walked me all the way to the north atrium. I could see the cars in the parking lot, past the shattered advertising displays. The clown abruptly dropped my hand.

"You're so close! You may just make it out of here." He pointed the gun at my face. "Or maybe not."

The smelly man's words raced through my memory. *Act crazy.* I had no idea if it would work, but it was my only option. I started my own version of a ballet routine and did a pirouette. I slowly backed away, right into a trashcan. The receptacle and I both tumbled to the ground.

The clown let out a mirthless chuckle. "I see one of our informants has told you a little about us. Keep dancing, sweetheart."

I slowly stood to my feet as the clown watched, never lowering his gun. I spun and weaved my way through the broken glass to the exit. In the atrium, two young boys that looked to be about Connor's age sat perched on top of a cracked monitor. They eerily stared at me as I twirled through the exit.

"Thanks for shopping at All-Mark," I heard one of them say.

Tears streamed down my face when I stepped into the parking lot. I'd never been so happy to leave All-Mark in my life. *I made it out!* Freedom had never tasted so sweet. The brisk evening breeze seemed to kiss me on the cheek. From where I stood, everything looked completely normal, except for the five school buses crashed into the other entrance of the building. *I need to find Mom.* I sprinted toward the area where we were separated. I reached the middle of the building when I realized there was no hole in the wall. I ran my hands across the solid structure in disbelief. *What? Mom said there was a hole. What if she's still inside?* It was suddenly more difficult to breathe as a new batch of tears filled my eyes. My heart tore as I debated running back inside to find Mom or running home to safety. A loud squeal interrupted my thoughts. I turned to see a beat up, old car screech to a halt right in front of me.

The car windows rolled down as the driver smiled at me. The bright lights of the parking lot cast a shadow across his face as he took a drag from what appeared to be...a cigarette? *Those haven't existed for decades.* He looked me up and down. "Need a ride?" he asked. I could tell from the deepness of his voice he was several years older than me.

Two guys in the back of the car started laughing. One of them stuck his head out of the window and yelled, "Looks like you're almost home free, Dupe. But that's where we come in. The cleanup crew!"

I closed my eyes. *Act insane.* I tried to cluck like a chicken but I was so terrified my voice wouldn't come to me. I weakly flapped my elbows up and down but all I could do was focus on the sound of the rattling engine. *This is it. This is how I am going to die.*

"Nice try, but we don't have the best reputation of following the rules," the deep voice said. "Sick her, boys."

My legs finally gave out as I sank to the ground, covering my tear-stricken face in my hands. I heard the car doors open and I peeked through my trembling fingers. All three boys jerked from my vision as another car plowed into theirs. Both vehicles skidded to a stop in the next row. An angry middle-aged man jumped out of the second car.

He turned toward me. "Don't just sit there. Run!"

For the first time that night, my body responded appropriately. I ran. I ran and ran and didn't stop until I reached my front porch.

CHAPTER 2

FALLOUT

I made it home that evening in an exhausted mess of tears. My lungs burned as I expired frigid air in puffs of smoke. I pressed my hand against the access pad, but sweat and debris made my palm unrecognizable. I banged my shaking fists against the door, hoping my dad and Connor were back from the tournament.

Dad opened the door and shock swept over his face. "Eve? Wha—What happened? Are you okay?"

"There was an attack!" I sobbed as I crashed into his chest and hugged him tightly. "An attack...like they have in Europe. Guys everywhere...destroying All-Mark."

He pushed me back and looked into my eyes. "Are you hurt? Where is your mother?"

"I'm fine but I don't know where she is! We were separated and, and..." I wept uncontrollably as the reality of the evening hit me.

"Connor, get in here!" Dad yelled, as he directed me to the living room couch. "Listen to me, you and Connor are going to stay right here and wait. If your mother shows up call me and let me know."

"Where are you going?" I asked, unable to comprehend my father leaving me.

"I'm going to go look for your mom. Whatever happens, do not leave this house." He was out the door and into the car before I could beg him not to go.

I didn't want him to head into danger, but more importantly, I didn't want him to leave us. I needed my family beside me, holding me together while the outside world crumbled.

Connor sauntered into the living room. Even though he was four years younger than me, he was nearly as tall. His mop of brown hair shot out in every direction. "What's the big fuss—good gravy, what happened to you?" A mixture of surprise and disgust crossed his face. I must have looked horrible.

I sighed heavily, fell onto the couch and smashed a throw pillow onto my face. "I don't even know where to begin."

Connor pulled up the computer chair and sat on it backward. "Lay it on me, Sis." He placed a hand on my knee. "Wait, before you start, did Mom get my socks?"

After recounting my story to Connor, he stared at me in with his jaw hanging open. "This is the craziest thing that has ever happened in the history of ever! This changes everything! I'm sure Mom's fine. She has to be. Let's turn on the news and see what's happening."

"I didn't even think to turn on the news! Maybe we could see Mom and Dad!" I fumbled the TV remote and turned it to News1, "America's Only 24/7 News Station." The anchor happily chirped about how scientists were making breakthroughs on genetic engineering and how modifications like changes to eye and hair color may soon be affordable to the general public.

"Why aren't they showing anything?" Connor complained.

I shook my head. "Well, it just happened. Maybe the reporters are getting there now. It's seven forty-eight. They show breaking stories at the top of the hour. I'm sure it will be on then. Try calling Mom."

Connor dialed her number. "No answer. I'll try Dad... nothing. Voicemail."

It drove me nuts that all we could do was sit and wait. My parents were in danger and I was completely useless. Eight o' clock came, and nothing happened. The top stories focused on OneGlobal making strides in free energy, who may be invited to the President's OneGlobal Gala and a preview of the next day's premiere of *Great American Dream*. We sat with our eyes glued to the TV waiting for a special report to break in at any moment, but still, nothing happened.

Connor paced the floor. "The local news is on at nine. It *has* to be covered then."

At exactly nine o'clock, the local news anchor started reporting on the high school's virtual basketball victory over Tulsa. Story after story appeared on the TV with no mention of the attack.

"This. Is. Insane!" Connor yelled at the TV. He flopped down on the couch beside me. "They have to know what's going on...maybe we should go up there."

"Absolutely not! Dad said to stay here until they get back.

What if Mom comes home and no one is here?"

"Then you stay here and I'll go look for them," Connor stated matter-of-factly.

"No way! We stay together no matter what. We have no idea what it's like out there. I'm sure OneGlobal has it under control by now. Try calling Dad again."

Connor picked up his phone. "I can't call anybody. The lines must be down. That never happens. It must be from the attack."

For the next twenty minutes, we sat in silence, growing more restless by the minute. Then Connor's phone buzzed.

"Is it Dad?" I asked.

"No, a text from Isaac."

"Great. I'm glad we can't get ahold of our missing parents, but you can still get texts from your BFF." I started toward my room.

Connor jumped up and ran to me. "Eve, look at this. He says there's a website with a video of Mom on it."

I grabbed the phone out of his hand and scanned the text. "DUDE, IS THIS UR MOM? HelloAmericanChaos. ud/videos." I shook my head. Isaac was obsessed with anything that even resembled a conspiracy theory. Therefore, he loved all the craziness in Europe and monitored the web for any morsel of information. Being a technological genius was the only reason he hadn't been busted for his research. All websites that did not end in .OG or .US were prohibited. We risked major fines, Noncompliance marks, or even prison time for visiting any other site. "That's an illegal website. We can't even access that."

He shrugged. "Isaac jailbroke my phone. I can go to it if I want."

"Jailbroke your phone! You know how much trouble you can get into if—"

"I'm going to it," Connor said, as he grabbed for the phone.

I held it out of his reach. "It's *ILLEGAL!* It's not worth it. What if it's nothing and it goes on our record? Noncompliant acts like that can follow us forever."

"What if it *is* something? If we can find out some information on Mom, it's worth it. Information is our friend. The more we have, the more likely we can do something with it. Plus, I'm still young enough to play dumb and get away with it."

I didn't like it, but Connor had a point. I was so desperate to know if Mom was okay, I was willing to risk it. "Fine…but if we see anything suspicious, exit out immediately." I handed the phone back to him.

He clicked on the link. A red cartoon skull appeared in the middle of the screen with the words "Enter the current Chaos" underneath. Connor touched the skull. An insane laugh echoed from the phone as the screen faded into four boxes, each displaying a different person.

"There's Mom!" I yelled.

Connor clicked the picture labeled "Madam President." A video showing Mom standing in the sporting goods section of All-Mark filled the screen. She looked like a mummy; wrapped head-to-toe in toilet paper. She wore a toilet bowl lid around her neck. I noticed her hands and feet were bound together as she struggled to keep her balance. Four boys stood around her, wearing black security suits and hockey masks.

"Shut up, everyone," yelled a voice behind the camera.

"We're filming. Alright, ladies and gentlemen. We have a special guest tonight, *the* President of America."

One boy stepped into frame and put a sign reading Prezident Mendax around Mom's neck. Several chuckles could be heard as the camera shook gently.

The gruff voice continued, "Please state your name for the camera."

"Victoria Mendax. President Victoria Mendax."

"Well, well, well...the First Lady of America is gracing us with her presence tonight. How are you doing today, President Mendax?" the guy asked.

"I'm a little tied up at the moment," Mom replied.

Several boys guarding Mom shook with laughter. Through her tears, Mom attempted to make funny faces like someone who was trying to entertain a baby.

Connor asked, "Why is she doing that with her face?"

"She's staying alive," I whispered.

The video slowly zoomed to her face. "Now...tell me, Madame President, what is wrong with this country?"

"We are!" Mom yelled.

"And who is this 'we' you speak of?" asked the gruff voice.

"We the government; OneGlobal! We prey on the small-minded that blindly follow. We prey on the public that is too busy being entertained to see what is really going on." A loud boom sounded in the background. The camera panned over in the direction of the explosion. In the foreground of the smoke, I noticed a younger boy with cue cards kneeling in front of Mom.

The camera snapped back to Mom. "And what is really going on?"

"We have a plan, a master plan. We..."

A new voice interrupted Mom. "Hey, it's time to get out of here. Docs up front." Police sirens echoed in the background.

The picture zoomed closer onto Mom's face. The gruff voice screamed, "Spit it out! What's the master plan?"

Mom was crying so hard she could barely speak. "The, the, the master plan is to..." She broke into sobs.

"Kronies! Out! Now!" someone yelled.

The camera zoomed back out. "I'm so sorry, President Mendax, but we have to cut our interview short. Now, one last task and I believe you earned your freedom."

Continuing to make awkward faces, my mom soiled herself. She fell to her knees and then the screen went black.

We stared at the phone for several long seconds until it slipped from Connor's grasp and fell to the floor. I looked at Connor. Tears silently trailed down his face. I hadn't realized I was crying too.

I breathed in deeply as I wiped the tears away. "This...is a good thing. It...it means she is fine. You heard what the guy said. She earned her freedom," I stammered, trying to keep the panic out of my voice.

Connor nodded and picked his phone up. The screen flickered to white then a message appeared: Website forbidden. A report has been filed with the Department of Compliance. "This is way more serious than I originally calculated."

A loud knock made us both jump. I hurried to the door while Connor peeked out the window.

"Who is it?" I asked.

"The car says...Department of Compliance." He ducked

below the window. "It's the Docs!"

I froze. I didn't know if I should be excited or scared. I had just broken the law for the first time in my life and five seconds later a Doc shows up at my door. On the other hand, maybe they were just there to take us to Mom. It was ingrained in my bones to always trust a government official. They were the good guys.

A second pounding on the door brought me back to reality. I shook off my fear and told myself to do the right thing. Connor stood behind me as I opened the door to reveal a tall, middle-aged man in uniform.

"Are you Evelyn Price?" he barked.

"Yes, I'm Eve." My eyes darted to his badge. It read Officer Green, OKC D.O.C.

"We have reason to believe you were present during the attack on All-Mark tonight."

"Do you know anything about my mother? Is she okay? What's going—"

"Miss, we need you to come with us downtown. We can explain everything once we get to Central. Now, please come with me."

I hesitated and looked back at Connor. A strong grip wrapped around my arm and pulled me toward the door.

"Wait!" I yelled. "My brother! I can't leave him here alone. Not with everything that's going on."

The officer paused and surveyed Connor with an annoyed look on his face. He grabbed the communicator on his shoulder. "Central, this is 72509. I have the suspect. Her brother is with her and she doesn't want to leave him alone at the house."

After a few seconds, the communicator beeped. "Roger

that. Bring them both downtown."

"Ten-four," he looked back to me. "Alright, both of you, into the patroller. Quickly, please, and may I remind you that anything less than one-hundred percent Compliance is a felony."

"Of course, Officer. Come on, Con, grab a jacket." I silently hoped he was smart enough to leave his phone so they couldn't take it for inspection. Thankfully, I knew that if I had thought about it, then Connor was already a step ahead of me.

After climbing into the backseat with Connor, I repeatedly asked about my parents to no avail. Eventually, the officer rolled up the soundproofing window so he would no longer be bothered by my nagging. I sank back into the seat and chewed on my lip, feeling completely helpless.

"What do you think is going on?" Connor asked. He looked at the officer then whispered, "Are we in trouble? Do you think it's about the vid—"

I pinched him hard and shook my head. Something in my gut told me not to mention the video. Maybe it was how I didn't like being referred to as "the suspect." *Don't think like that. You need to be as cooperative as possible to help Mom.*

The rest of the ride passed in silence. As stressed as I was, I couldn't help but smile as we drove into the bright lights and flashing signs of downtown. The area was always a hotspot for points in our Upper game. Secretly, I loved walking through the skywalks connecting the huge buildings pretending to be on assignment for some important

Upper. Although, that didn't happen often since I didn't usually have a reason for being there and didn't want to be charged with a loitering violation. Downtown housed the main offices for all the major industries of the city. Since OneGlobal slimmed down the "open market", having everything in one location was incredibly efficient and convenient. The utility company was right next to the news station, which was next to the recreational sports offices. It went on and on.

The outside world felt like a normal evening until we arrived at Central. I didn't even know that many patrollers existed in Oklahoma. We drove past the front entrance and pulled into the alleyway between Central and the hospital. A long ramp sloped under the building to a hidden parking garage. We stopped in front of a pair of large, glass doors with bright electronic letters reading "RESTRICTED ACCESS".

A Doc from inside headed toward our car and opened my door. His pressed suit matched the crisp lines of his haircut. I had the feeling he was a no-nonsense type of man. "I'm Detective Larkin. Please come with me."

Connor and I followed the man into the building. The only time I had been inside Central was during a school field trip in third grade. Back then, we started in the main atrium that opened up all the way to the fifteenth floor. We ended the tour with the Noncompliant holding area. The small, clear containment boxes used to detain criminals scared me so much, I vowed to never do anything to risk going back. Yet, there I was, walking into the great underbelly of Central. The feel was completely different than the sterile yet inviting atrium. The small entryway funneled to a large, metal gate and check-in station. Beyond the gate, I could see a round lobby encircled with elevators. The low ceiling made me claustrophobic. It didn't help that the place was swarming with Docs. I'd never seen so many of them in one area. I knew their excessive presence should have made me feel safe, but it only added to my already high anxiety level. Detective Larkin escorted us to the main security desk.

A large screen displayed a life-sized video of an uniformed older woman. "Phones against the scanner," she stated as she looked down on us.

I showed my empty hands. "I lost mine tonight, during the...attack." I didn't know what else to call it.

The woman frowned then looked to Connor.

He shrugged. "I left mine at home. We were in a rush."

I thought the woman was going to reach out of the screen and smack him. "Young man, you know it's illegal to be caught at any time without proper identification. Especially, wh—"

"I'll vouch for them, Shirley," Detective Larkin interjected as he scanned his phone. "We're in a bit of a hurry."

The older woman scowled. "Place your hand on the scanner." We followed her instructions. Below the scanner popped out two silver badges with our names and most recent school identification photos. "Wear these at *all* times."

We attached them to our shirts as the metal gate beside the display opened. Larkin ushered us into the circle then directed us to an elevator.

The doors opened to reveal two Docs standing at attention. They hovered behind us then followed when we arrived at level three. Larkin picked up speed as we walked down the narrow, white corridor.

Central felt even bigger on the inside, like a never-ending maze of hallways and offices. I hoped an officer would escort us back out. There was no way I could ever find my way around the place. We stopped at three different security checkpoints, each with its own set of passwords and locking doors. With each access point, I felt more and more like a prisoner.

Connor leaned into me. "If I don't make it out of here, give Isaac my StarStryke system."

"Shut up," I hissed as I punched him in the shoulder. "You'll be fine. Just cooperate. We didn't do anything illegal. Remember?"

Connor looked over his shoulder. "Yeah, but I have a history. Remember that time I hacked the school website to change the mascot to a unicorn?"

I stifled a giggle. "A unicorn pooping on our rival's mascot."

Con shook his head. "That's beside the point! The Docs don't take well to repeat offenders. I'm sure I have Noncompliant risk written all over my files."

I rolled my eyes. "You were six years old. You'll be fine... just don't voluntarily bring that up. Plus, they don't keep files with stupid stuff like that. You weren't there tonight. So, just stay quiet and let me do all the talking."

Finally, we arrived at a large, black door labeled Interrogation. We were buzzed through and entered a small, bright hallway with doors lining each side. Detective Larkin stopped, opened Interrogation Five and motioned me inside. I entered the small, white-tiled room, filled with only a white table and two chairs. I turned just in time to see Connor ripped from my view and shoved down the hall. I dove toward him, but a hand on my shoulder held me back. Connor's screams stopped as the door slammed shut.

"What is going on? Where are you taking him?" I yelled.

Detective Larkin ignored my question and sat down at the small table. He took out a pair of glasses from his jacket pocket and synced them with his phone before fitting them across his nose. "Please sit down, Miss Price and I will explain everything."

I debated whether to follow his instruction or demand an answer. "Where is my brother?" I asked, hesitantly.

Detective Larkin shook his head and sighed. "We question everyone individually. Trust me, I've been doing this since long before you were born, and it is easier to split up siblings suddenly. We apologize for any discomfort this may have caused you, but you will be reunited shortly. The Department of Compliance thanks you in advance for your cooperation and understanding. Now, can we please get started?"

I slowly sank into the chair. "Connor doesn't know anything. He was at a soccer tournament when this happened. You can let him go." I bit my lip, as the image of my mom on Conner's phone flashed through my mind.

"Great. If he doesn't know anything then he will be done in no time. Therefore, the sooner we finish this interview, the sooner you will see him." The sarcastic smile on his face gave me a queasy feeling in my stomach. As if reading my mind, the smile vanished. Larkin put a hand to his ear as he stared into space. He nodded slightly then focused back on me. "Oh, and we have your mother in custody. She is receiving all the proper medical care. You should be able to see her as soon as she is cleared."

Tears filled my eyes as I relaxed into the seat. It felt as if a huge weight had been lifted off my shoulders. My mother was alive. We were all going to make it out together. My heart filled with gratitude. The detective was back in my good graces.

"There, there." Larkin handed me a tissue from inside his jacket. "No one should have to go through what you and your family have gone through tonight. We want to put an end to these, so called, 'Chaos' attacks and you can help us. It is your duty as a OneGlobal citizen to help in any way you can. Will you help us stop these criminals and bring back safety to this community?"

He was right. I needed to help in any way possible. I wiped my eyes and nodded in agreement.

"Splendid. Let us begin."

For the next six hours, I sat at the table with Detective Larkin and rehashed the entire evening: beginning to end, over and over. He stopped me periodically to ask for more details or to speculate on the attackers' motives. The detective paid particular interest to Dave, the security guard. How did my mother know him? Why did he warn us? Who told him about the attack? Then we switched to the topic of my phone. When did I notice it was missing? Did I drop it? Did I ever see anyone else with it? Larkin seemed to grow more and more frustrated with every reply of "I don't know."

At one point, my brain became complete mush. I couldn't think straight and started to mix up facts. Larkin stopped my answers and had an officer bring me a cup of coffee. After only a few sips, I felt completely re-energized. I remembered small details I had previously forgotten: the boys' outfits and how tall they were, what type of weapons they had and how many of them I encountered. I felt like I was really helping the cause. Even Larkin seemed to pep up a little. I hoped that the better I did, the sooner I could leave.

After debating with myself, I chose to leave out the video of my mom. Although I desperately wanted to ask what it meant, I didn't want to put an unwanted target on Connor. And more importantly, I didn't want to say anything that would keep me in that room longer than necessary.

"I have one last question for you, Miss Price." The detective took off his glasses, leaned forward, and peered into my eyes. "Why do you think they let *you* go?"

"I told you, I acted crazy. That is what the weird man told me to do. So, I danced around and made noises and they let me go."

Larkin's gaze did not falter. "What if I told you that other people who did this exact same thing, this 'acting silly,' were not so fortunate and did not make it out alive? What would you say to that?"

I felt like he wanted a certain answer, but I didn't have it. "I don't know. I'm just lucky, I guess."

Detective Larkin stared at me for a few more seconds then smiled dryly. "Thank you very much for your testimony, Miss Price. Your country thanks you and the world thanks you. OneGlobal will not forget your service." An officer entered the room and handed me a fresh cup of coffee as Larkin continued. "Now, I know you are anxious to go be with your family, but I feel you are owed some information. Of course, I cannot tell you everything, but hopefully what I can tell you will help you move past this horrible experience." I felt more at ease as I sipped the hot liquid.

"We believe this group of delinquents are a copycat of the groups that have been terrorizing other countries of the world. They have no real connection to the 'Universal Defiance' and pose little threat to us in the future. They call themselves Kronies and do nothing more than cause as much destruction and chaos as possible. We have a large portion of the boys involved tonight in custody and will apprehend the rest in the next few hours. While we regret that you were involved in this situation, the important thing is that you are safe, your family is safe, and this will not happen again, partly due to your help tonight. You did the right thing."

By the end of his speech, my heart was so filled with warmth I could not hold back the tears. I felt silly in my earlier mistrust of the D.O.C. They had everything under control. Detective Larkin stood up and motioned toward the open door where Officer Green stood at attention.

"Oh, and one last thing, Miss Price," Larkin grabbed my arm. "Due to the sensitive nature of this subject, we ask you not to share this information with *anyone*. We will be releasing a report to the media when we have more information, but bear in mind, most facts will be withheld from the general public for their own protection. You will be given my personal contact information before you leave. No one outside of the Department of Compliance should be contacting you for interviews. If anyone does, notify me immediately. If you remember any other details, please let me know." He paused and moved his hand from my arm to my shoulder. "I can't emphasize it enough, but refrain from discussing *any* aspects of tonight…even with your family. I know it will be hard, but studies show that lingering on these events may cause increased stress, undue trauma, or even permanent damage. With everything you and your mother have gone through tonight, I would hate for anything worse to happen. It is best to move on and get back to normal." He gave me one last squeeze, a little too hard for my liking, then let me leave the room.

Officer Green escorted me through another maze of hallways. We moved across a glass skywalk and I realized we were headed into a completely different building. The sun rose over the tall buildings of downtown as I watched the steady stream of morning traffic pass below me. *Was I really here all night?* After several more minutes of walking, we entered a large, warm atrium. An elderly woman in pink manned the check-in station.

"Evening, Dorothy. I have Miss Price to see her family," Green told the receptionist.

"I'll let them know." She busied herself on the computer. "Please follow this gentleman." Seconds later the door beside the woman opened and a young male orderly walked out. He escorted us down a hallway and opened a door labeled Waiting Area 3.

Officer Green placed a hand on the doorframe, blocking my path. "Remember, everything about this night is classified. Discussing *any* information is an act of Non-compliance, and therefore, a punishable offense. We will be keeping a close eye on you."

Frustration kept up inside me. Did they really need to remind *me* to follow the rules? I only nodded my agreement to keep from smarting off something I may regret. Officer Green lowered his arm and I walked into the room.

My dad paced the floor as Connor slept in a chair. "Dad!" I yelled as I ran and threw my arms around him. My shout woke Connor, who joined the embrace. "When did you get here? Where's Mom? Is she okay?" I asked.

Dad released me. "Thankfully, the D.O.C. tracked me down around midnight. I couldn't get within a kilometer of All-Mark. First responders had the area locked down. That explosion must have been huge! I'm so glad you're safe."

"What about Mom?" I asked again, nervous about his response.

Dad smiled weakly. "She...is doing okay. Medical said she needs to stay for a day or two. We should be able to see her once her interview is complete."

I couldn't believe the Docs were still questioning Mom after all she had gone through, but I was too tired to ask about it. I guessed they just wanted the information as soon as possible to catch the remaining boys. I collapsed into the nearest chair. Every muscle in my body ached. It felt like I hadn't slept in weeks.

Dad sat down across from me. "What happened tonight? Connor told me some things, but you were there. I want to know everything."

Reliving the night, yet again, was the last thing I wanted

to do. I leaned my head against the wall and noticed the camera in the corner of the room; a small orb, barely noticeable. I wanted to test my theory, so I stood up and began pacing the room. The orb moved slightly, following my movements.

I sat back down and bit my lip. Detective Larkin's words echoed in my mind. I didn't need to hurt Dad with the gory details of the evening. I decided it was better for him not to know.

I chose my words carefully. "Dad, I really don't want to go through this again. I just spent hours explaining every detail. The important thing is that we are all safe. Let's just move on."

Dad started to object but nodded grimly. I sighed and tried to get comfortable in the chair. I looked to Connor. "How did your interview go?"

He gave me a discreet thumbs up. "No unicorn sightings."

I smiled, watching him sprawl out over three chairs and fall asleep almost instantly. The kid could sleep anywhere. I felt an overwhelming need to protect him from the chaos of the world. I closed my eyes and made a promise to do everything within my power to protect my family. I didn't remember falling asleep.

I woke to my dad tapping my shoulder. "Hey, it's time to see Mom."

I jolted up and rushed to the hallway, but no one followed. "Where is she? Aren't you coming?"

"One visitor at a time. Connor and I already saw her. I thought you could use the extra sleep," Dad said.

Frustrated, I stood in the hall wondering where to go. An officer guarding our waiting room pointed to my right. "All the way down the hall. Last room on the left."

I started off down the hall in a sluggish sprint, angry with my dad for not waking me. I needed my mom like never before. I just wanted her to tell me it was going to be okay and—

I slammed into a laundry cart that appeared suddenly from a linen closet. Freshly pressed surgical scrubs flew through the air as the woman pushing the cart apologized profusely.

"It's my fault," I confessed as I pushed myself off the floor. "I wasn't paying attention." I helped her pile the clothes back onto the cart and then continued on my mission. I froze when I saw my mom through the large window of her room. She rested peacefully in her bed as tubes and wires traveled across her body. I ran inside and wrapped her in a bear hug.

"Not so tight!" she yelped.

"Oh my gosh, I'm so sorry. I was just...excited. I didn't know if I would ever see you again." I wept as I buried my face in her arms.

Mom stroked my hair. "Shhh, it's okay. We are fine now. Everything is going to be okay."

Her words warmed my heart but other concerns surfaced in my brain. "Mom, I saw a video..." I whispered as I looked into her face. She wasn't looking at me. She was looking at the officer standing in the corner of the room.

"A little privacy please?" I asked the man.

He didn't move. "I'm sorry. I know this isn't the most ideal situation. But policy states that all citizens be under guard for their own protection while in the custody of the Department."

"We understand. Thank you for your service." The gratefulness in mom's voice was sincere. She grabbed my hands. "Eve, I need you to listen to me, okay? What we went through was a terrible, terrible ordeal. But that is over and done. I don't want us to get stuck in the past. We must move on and continue to do our best as productive members of our global society. We will be cooperative and help out in any way possible. Agreed?"

I nodded. "Of course, Mom."

She wrapped her arms around me and whispered in my ear, "Don't ever mention that video. It never happened."

CHAPTER 3
AFTERMATH

Dad took us home after my visit with Mom. A physician informed us it would be three more days before she would be stable enough to return home. It drove me nuts that I couldn't visit or even call her. But her neurologist insisted giving her space would allow her body and mind to heal more quickly.

I still couldn't wrap my brain around what I experienced, but I hoped hearing about the event from the media would bring some closure. Before, Connor and I had never shown much interest in the news, but that evening we gathered around the TV fifteen minutes early to see what the local headlines would be. Dad reluctantly meandered into the living room. He made multiple comments that we should return to our normal lives, which didn't include the nightly news. The second the clock hit nine, the familiar tune of the local news chimed.

The lead anchor appeared, his cheery smile dazzling in the bright lights. "Tonight's top story, the OKC All-Mark suffered massive damage after an expansion project accidentally dissected a gas line. Construction crews were working to add the much-anticipated east wing. The mishap is estimated to add another six months to the project. Several patrons and workers were injured in the mishap, but are all in stable condition. All-Mark released a statement saying 'they look forward to serving the community again tomorrow when they reopen.' In other news..."

I looked over at Dad. His brow furrowed as he suddenly became very interested with his phone. Connor stared at the screen with his jaw hanging open.

I stood up and walked closer to the screen in disbelief. "Are. You. Freaking. Kidding me? What the heck was that all about?"

"Eve, calm down," Dad said.

"Calm down? They called it a 'mishap.' Several people injured? I was there! People died!"

Dad stood up. "Now, Eve. Didn't Detective Larkin tell you they would only release limited information to the public?"

"Limited information isn't changing the facts. They lied! This is not okay! People need to know."

"Why?" Dad snapped. "Why do they need to know all the terrifying aspects of that night?"

My brain raced. "Well...well, because people should be warned...in case it happens again so they can be on the lookout."

Connor's eyes ping-ponged back and forth between us.

Dad put a hand on my shoulder. "Eve, I understand your frustration. You went through a horrible trauma. But pause for a second and imagine you weren't there.

Would you want to know all the gory details?"

I shrugged. "Maybe not all the details...but I would want to know that *something* happened so I could keep an eye out for a lunatic with a bat about to beat my face in."

"I would agree with you *if* there was still a threat. You know what the Department of Compliance told us. The situation is under control and it will NOT happen again. So what's the point of freaking everyone out and possibly starting a panic when there is no possibility of recurrence?" Dad sat back down and flipped through the channels.

"Because...uh..." I paused, not able to come up with a good answer. "Well, I guess I just don't think people should be lied to."

"Is it really lying if they are doing it to protect people?" Dad asked.

I thought hard. "Well, technically it's still lying, but... I guess that would be okay if it kept people safe. "

"See, that's what they are doing. Protecting us. They really have our best interest at heart. They don't want some little old lady trying to run away from Connor and his friends and break a hip. Now, I want both of you to listen to me. You have information about this situation and that is a *privilege*. I expect you to do the right thing and keep it to yourself. Do not tell anybody...not even your best friend." Dad focused on Connor, who held up his hands in innocence. "When Mom gets home, do not bring this up. Not one word. I don't want her to have to relive that night. Is that clear?"

We both nodded. It did make sense, even if it felt weird. Frustrated, I went to my room, grabbed my reader, and slumped onto the bed. Maybe my textbooks had something to say about the situation. For the first time ever, I read a school book voluntarily.

I clicked on The History of OneGlobal text and searched for "chaos." The only hit was in a chapter on disaster preparedness. I figured that was as good of a place to start as any. The introduction was full of statistics about how disasters were virtually extinct. "The Shared Knowledge and Information Act even led to meteorological advances making it possible to predict and pinpoint the path of tornados. LOCAL FACT: This greatly protects the people living in Oklahoma." The only section I found remotely helpful was the policy of "greater good." It stated that OneGlobal governments would give information to the public on a need-to-know basis following the principle of the greater good. Whatever is in the best interest for the most people will dictate what the O.G. will do in the rare instance of an actual disaster.

A knock at my door interrupted my research. I turned off my reader and hid it under my pillow. "What?"

Connor popped his head in. "Hey, a drone just dropped off your phone. They found it in the debris." He tossed the phone on my bed. "The drone said it had to be completely reset, so it won't be functional again until tomorrow... you okay?"

I rolled onto my stomach. "I'm fine, Con. Just ready for Mom to be home."

"Me too." He lingered in the doorway for several weighty seconds before leaving.

I massaged my temples in an attempt to relieve the pressure in my brain. I didn't know what to think or who to believe. I didn't like the idea of the government just glossing over the attack, but I also agreed with Dad. Why cause unnecessary panic? I decided not to worry about it until the next day. Maybe someone at school was at All-Mark during the Chaos…and lived.

I woke to the sound of my "you're late" alarm on my phone (a.k.a. backup alarm number two). I grabbed it and let it scan my wide eyes for ten seconds to shut it up. I considered just staying home and linking in for virtual class, but I really wanted to be face-to-face with other people to get a read on them. I threw on a pair of jeans and my favorite "Rock the Mic" t-shirt and ran out the door. Days like that made me wish I could just drive myself to school. Dad told me stories of grandpa driving at age sixteen, but then the legal driving age moved to eighteen to decrease pollution and accidents. I didn't understand why, since all cars drove themselves anyway. I made it to the stop right before the bus pulled away. I climbed in and found a seat in the back.

"I was wondering if you were coming to class today." Connor popped his head over the seat behind me. "Hey, are you going to ask any of your classmates about…you know?"

"No. I'm not, and you shouldn't either. Just act dumb, that should come naturally for you."

Connor rolled his eyes. "Whatever, if I'm so dumb then why have I scored higher than you in like…everything?"

"You know I was teasing," I said. Connor was smarter at age five than I would ever be. He even had the potential of choosing whatever career he wanted on Revelation Day. I would have been lucky to test well enough to have more than two options.

Connor moved to sit next to me. "But seriously, Isaac and I have been doing some critical thinking and I think we are onto something big."

I rolled my eyes. "Critical thinking" was their code word for scheming. I knew nothing good could come of it. "Let me stop you right there. You can't research this type of stuff. I don't care what you've found. Just drop it." Connor looked at his feet, defeated. I grabbed his chin to force him to look me in the eyes. "I'm serious. Don't mention anything. Promise me."

"Don't get your undies in a wad. I promise." He hopped back into his seat.

I popped in my headphones and listened to Rembrandt until we arrived. Since virtual school was so popular, Oklahoma City only needed one campus. Each grade had its own auditorium or "learning theater." I waved goodbye to Connor and headed to the junior hall.

I took a seat toward the back. Not that it mattered, since no real teacher was present, but it made me feel more comfortable seeing the whole room in front of me. I pulled out my tablet and scrolled through the latest local news. Still nothing.

"Oh. Em. Gee!" a voice squealed right next to my ear. "I am so glad you are here today! I tried to get ahold of you all weekend! Did your phone fall off the planet or what? We have to talk about everything! Tell me every single thought that passed through your brain."

A gorgeous brunette with flawless makeup plopped down in the seat beside me. Most All-Mark fashion was basic in color and design but Natalie could combine them to look like she belonged on a runway instead of a classroom. We were designated partners in fifth grade for an economic evaluation project. We spent so many hours talking about how much we hated the assignment, we became best friends.

I let out a huge sigh of relief. "You have no idea how happy I am that you are asking me," I whispered back. "I want to hear your version first. I may go crazy if I don't hear about it from someone else."

"Okay, well, first off…I did NOT like the model. Shocker! I know that's very catty of me to say, but she was just so smug like she already had it in the bag. I liked the baker, his backstory was so amazing. Anyone who can survive a kitchen fire and get back to cooking gets extra points in my book. The entertainers are always going to make it to the next round so I don't pay much attention to them. But—"

"Wait, what are you talking about?" I asked, confused.

"What do you mean, 'what am I talking about'? The *Great American Dream* season premiere! Did you lose your mind and your phone? Anyway, who is your fave?"

I slid down in my seat like a deflated balloon. Tears welled in my eyes as I covered my face with my hands.

"Eve, are you alright?" Natalie asked, as the lights dimmed and the holographic professor flickered into view.

"Good morning, class. Glad you could tune in today. If you would please stand for the morning pledge."

It took all my strength to pull my disappointed body upright. I placed both hands over my heart with the rest of the class. "I pledge allegiance to OneGlobal and to uphold the ideals of its foundation. To seek the unity of all mankind, to be committed to the greater good, and strive to be a productive member of the international society. I devote my life to the well-being of the world and will put its needs before my own, no matter the cost," we all recited.

The professor nodded in approval. "Very good. Please pull up page one-hundred and sixty eight in your Historical Reader and we will finish our discussion over the golden age of OneGlobal relations. Now, in two thousand eighty-seven, the OneGlobal Headquarters moved from America's capital of New York City to..." I didn't hear anything else for the rest of the class.

The day dragged on forever. All I wanted to do was go home and crawl into bed, but I forced myself to smile and nod as Natalie recounted every detail I missed on G.A.D. I counted nine times that she said, "I can't believe you forgot it was on!" By the end of the day, I vowed to only attend virtual classes for the rest of the year.

I slunk down into a seat on the bus, grateful that Connor was at his StarStryke club and wouldn't be able to bug me. My phone buzzed. It was a text from Dad. "MOM WAS CLEARED EARLY. SHE'S HOME. REMEMBER TO GIVE HER SPACE AND LET HER REST."

After the longest ride of my life, I rushed off the bus and ran through the front door as fast as I could. Mom reclined on the couch, covered in blankets.

"Mom!" I wrapped my arms around her. "I've missed you so much. How are you feeling? Can we talk? About everything? I've been wanting—"

"Hush." Mom looked at me with kind eyes. "Eve, I'm fine. Who knew you could still get the flu? We are safe and together. That's what matters. Now, what do you want to order for dinner? I was thinking sushi."

I took a step backward. "The flu? Mom, I'm talking about—"

Dad stepped into the room and cleared his throat. "Eve, let your mom get some rest." He put a hand on my arm and gently escorted me into the hall. "I told you to give her space. The physicians said bringing up the past will only slow her recovery. She's been through so much. You don't want to hurt her again, do you?"

I shook my head. "No, I just wanted to talk to her."

"I understand, but it's truly best if we forget this whole ugly mess and move on with our lives." He pulled me into a hug. "It's our duty to our family...and our world."

I rolled my eyes and pulled away from him. "I'll do it for Mom, but I highly doubt this makes a difference for the world."

"Don't talk like that," Dad scolded. "Now, I need you to set the example for your brother. When he gets home, it's your responsibility to make sure he doesn't disturb Mom. Why don't you unwind in your room for a while and I'll order us some food? We'll get back to our normal routine." He patted me on the shoulder and headed back to the living room.

Dinner was an awkward affair. Isaac invited himself over, as usual. The best term I could use to describe the scrawny kid was eccentric. With continually unkempt hair, shifty eyes and scattered freckles, he gave off the impression of a young, mad scientist who drank too much caffeine.

He bounced into his seat and gave me a knowing smile. *I knew Connor couldn't keep his mouth shut.*

Mom and Dad attempted to make normal conversation while Connor and I exchanged sidelong looks. Although Mom decided she actually liked sushi after trying it, I couldn't even finish my meal. I noticed Connor and Isaac weren't eating either. "May I please be excused?"

Dad shook his head. "You know the rules. This is family time."

I looked around the table and chose a safe defense. "Natalie's family never eats dinner together. They barely even talk."

Mom patted my hand. "We aren't like every other family, and I don't want us to be. I want you to know how much I love and care about you. I enjoy every moment we get to spend together."

Isaac leaned back in his chair. "I couldn't agree with you more, Mrs. P. It's like I always say, the family unit is the most important stone in the foundation of emotional and mental stability."

Mom nodded slightly. "That's very…profound." She turned back to me. "Please, stay until we are finished."

I gave her a weak smile and fiddled with my chopsticks. I felt like an invisible wall had formed between us. *Was she different or was it me?* As weird as it sounded, Mom was one of my best friends, but I couldn't even tell her what was really on my mind. I couldn't tell anyone what was on my mind. I had never felt so alone.

That night Connor snuck into my room and sat on the end of my bed. "Can we talk?" he whispered.

"Go to bed, Con. You know we can't talk about...what happened."

He didn't move. "I can't get it out of my head. Who were those guys?"

I knew I should have insisted on him leaving, but I had to talk to somebody about the attack or I would lose my mind. My willpower dissolved and I lowered my voice. "I don't know. The detective told me they were just a bunch of Universal Defiance copy-cats who just wanted to cause destruction."

Connor shook his head. "You really think hundreds of guys would come together with an organized strategy just to damage an All-Mark?"

"What are you getting at? I know you. You probably have some crazy theory."

He held a finger up to his lips, then winked conspicuously. Suddenly he bellowed, "Oh, I'm sure it's nothing... it's better just to move on like they said. I won't bring it up again. Goodnight, Eve."

I was scared his loud statement would wake our parents, but Connor grabbed my phone and reader and shoved them under my mattress. "What are you doing?" I hissed.

He threw a pillow at me. "Shh!" He sat down next to me and leaned in close. "We have to whisper very softly. You can't tell to anybody what I'm about to say. Not Mom or Dad, not Natalie, and especially not the Docs. Promise?"

I eyed him suspiciously. "Promise."

His voice was barely audible. "Okay, I don't think they were copycats. I think they were the real deal, *the* Universal

Defiance associated with the groups in Europe. I've been doing some research and that website they posted was—"

"Wait a minute. Research? Have you been going to illegal websites again?"

"Don't worry about that. I made sure they can't trace my activity and left a safe, yet believable goose chase on my school account in case they get nosey. Anyway, Isaac and I have this secret notebook. I'm talking about an old school paper and pencil notebook."

"How did you get that?"

"Don't worry about that either. Anyway, we've been keeping track of everything we find. You wouldn't believe the anti-government claims these guys are making. The scary thing is that they make sense, but that's not the big news...we think they are going to strike again. They call their attacks 'Chaos' and they want to overthrow OneGlobal."

I massaged my temples as my mind exploded with all the possible ways he could get in trouble. As much as I wanted to know more about the boys who hurt Mom, I couldn't let him go down that rabbit hole. I couldn't play into his delusions. I had already risked too much by talking to him at all. "Con, don't you think the Docs will know all that and more if two eighth graders figured it out? This isn't your responsibility. Plus, it's dangerous to search for that stuff on the Internet! Viruses, tracers...not to mention it's *illegal*! If you get busted with that notebook I guarantee you'll be labeled as Noncompliant. That would ruin your entire future! Think of what that would do to Mom and Dad." Connor scratched his head like he hadn't imagined getting caught. I ruffled his hair. "OneGlobal is on top of this and they will protect us. You need to stop worrying about it. I probably don't want to know, but what were you going to do with all this information?"

"I don't know," his shoulders slumped. "I just thought you should be in the loop. Keep your eye on the news and if you see anything suspicious, let me know." He slid off my bed and walked out the door.

Guilt filled my stomach. I knew I had hurt his feelings by not acting interested, but I needed to keep him grounded in reality. The last thing I wanted was for my family to be torn apart by the Docs carting him off as an online criminal.

On the outside, the next two months flew by as if nothing had ever happened. On the inside, however, the memory of the attack constantly haunted me. I put on a good front, but I felt so alone. Some days I wondered if I had dreamed the whole incident since the only physical evidence I had was the small crack in the screen of my phone. Well, that and Connor's obsession with the news. Occasionally, I would catch him late at night scribbling in his antique paper notebook. I gave up telling him to stop.

I broke my vow and started going back to school. Natalie was more than happy to rewatch the episodes of *Great American Dream* I had missed. Slowly, I started to feel normal again. I helped Natalie work on her application for a dating profile and promised her I would *think* about applying. I went to Connor's soccer games and got back into my old routine. I did, however, refuse to step foot inside All-Mark. Mom didn't understand my hesitation but Dad agreed I shouldn't go. Overall, I decided it really was in everyone's best interest to act as if nothing happened.

The Friday before spring break, I took a trip to Tulsa with Natalie's family to watch her older brother compete in a StarStryke tournament. Natalie found the sport boring and begged me to tag along. Dad thought it was a great idea for me to get out of OKC, so it was decided.

I tried to enjoy the change of scenery, but riding in the FasTrack always made me nauseous. After my third trip to the restroom, I felt my stomach was sufficiently pacified... and empty. I took my seat next to Natalie. "I think I'm good now. Next time I promise to bring my nausea pills."

Natalie automatically held out her closed fist with pinky extended. I mimicked the motion and we locked fingers to seal the promise.

I readjusted my simple ponytail, envious of Nat's perfect curls. "Explain what your brother plays again."

"Jeff is a defender for the Tulsa Comets, a StarStryke team," Natalie chirped proudly as she flipped through the game's program on her tablet.

"StarStryke? Like the online game Connor plays?"

"Yeah, but instead of playing on a screen they play in full holograms so we can watch the action live. If they win tonight, they go to the finals in New York. I've already begged my mom to go, but she said the Travel Bureau is way behind on requests. We should have applied for passes months ago. It is my life's goal to go to New York. If they do this good next year, I will not make that mistake again."

I wonder if that has anything to do with the attack. I pushed the thought away, trying to pretend the incident never occurred. "How does his team win?"

"Oh, Eve. Don't you know how StarStryke works? I hate video games and even I know that. The teams take turns attacking or defending a star. The battle map changes after each round. First team to ten points wins. But honestly, the gameplay is so fast I can never keep up with it. I just like the holograms. It's beautiful to watch. Oh!" She inhaled sharply, dropping her tablet in her lap. "Did I tell you that Emma Swanson, you know the really tall girl who graduated last year, told me that she matched with Erikson Mendax! I say she's a big fat liar. Like anyone from Oklahoma would match with the President's son! Oh, and get this! Elizabeth Adam's dating application was denied. What if that happens to me?"

The rest of the trip consisted of me reassuring Natalie she would be accepted. The very idea of Natalie being denied was laughable. She was easily the most beautiful person I knew, made decent grades, and had a spotless compliance record.

Once she calmed down, the tables turned and Natalie worked on convincing me to apply. "You have to apply by May! Anyone who doesn't apply by their eighteenth birthday just looks weird and will never get a good match. That only gives you two months! Oh, Eve, this is serious! Let me do some research." She typed furiously on her tablet.

We had promised each other we would apply together the second she turned seventeen and a half, but there was no way I'd be ready by the next week. Ever since the Chaos, I couldn't imagine adding that stress to my life.

My stomach dropped at the very thought of talking with a guy, much less dating one. Besides, no one ever had a True Match until long after professions were decided at the end of our senior year. Anything before that was just practice.

After the FasTrack pulled into the station, we headed straight for the OneGlobal stadium of Tulsa. The cool air brushed my face as we entered the gigantic egg-shaped arena and found our seats. Natalie pointed out the players sitting in large, metal cockpits at the base of the dome. I sat in awe watching the teams warm up with practice maneuvers in holographic ships that raced around the arena. I took in the enormity of the room. There must have been at least ten thousand people filling the stands. Suddenly, a ship flew right up to us, centimeters from our faces. The shield of the vehicle rose, and there sat holographic Jeff! He waved at us, then flew back to his teammates.

I was pretty pumped to watch my first StarStryke competition, especially since we looked up each team's roster and picked out the hottest players. Of course, I was rooting for the home team, but I would keep an eye out for number twenty-five of the Dallas Cosmos.

The pregame clock counted down to zero and the ships lined up at their respective ends. A light show, like I've never seen before, brought everyone cheering to their feet. I looked at Natalie and smiled. She was right; the stadium sparkled beautifully. It really felt like we were sitting in the middle of space. For the first time in months, I felt like life was completely back to normal. I could finally let my guard down, move on, and enjoy the show.

"Ladies and gentlemen," the announcer yelled. "It's time to welcome your Tulsaaaaaaaa Coooooomets!"

The crowd's cheer was deafening. Then, the music stopped, the lights went out, and the second Chaos began.

CHAPTER 4

CHAOS TWO

We waited in pitch black for several long moments. The murmurs of the crowd created a soft hum. I tried to choke down the rising panic in my throat.

Natalie's face lit up from her phone. "I cannot believe an event this big has a technical malfunction. This is ridiculous. I'm posting about it now. Eve, are you okay? You're moving the entire row."

My legs shook uncontrollably as I sat on the edge of my seat. *Not again. It can't happen again. This is just a coincidence. You're overreacting. Just breathe.*

A single spotlight lit the middle of the arena, where a lone boy stood. He wore a tuxedo with the sleeves ripped off and a black top hat. Red and black paint streaked across his face, which appeared on every screen. His voice boomed throughout the stadium and a hush fell over the crowd.

"Good people of America…Please allow me the honor of introducing the moment you've alllll been waiting for," he paused and bowed dramatically, "your first Chaos."

My biggest fear was coming to life right before my eyes. The world moved in slow motion. It felt like my brain had been dunked in glue. I knew we had only seconds to react and have a chance of reaching safety. Every cell in my body screamed, "GET OUT!"

"Natalie, we have to leave! We have to leave right now!" My voice cracked despite my efforts to sound calm. I grabbed her arm. "Natalie! Move! We need to get out of here! If they catch you, act crazy."

The deafening music I remembered from the first Chaos started as a new light show began. In the dim light, I could see Natalie, her family, and everyone in the near vicinity gawking at me like I had lost my mind. The boy in the middle of the arena started talking again, but I was too preoccupied with saving our lives to hear him. I stood and spun around, searching for the way out. Thankfully, the emergency exit sign glowed in the distance. I pulled Natalie down the row.

She yanked away from my grasp. "Eve, what are you doing? Have you gone mental?"

"I know this sounds crazy, but we have to get out of here now. Our lives depend on it! Please! I'm begging you. Just...come on!"

Natalie furrowed her brow and didn't budge. Tears clouded my vision as my rising panic gave way to full-blown terror. I faced an impossible decision: save myself and leave my best friend to possibly die, or continue to unsuccessfully convince her to leave when she thought nothing was wrong.

That's when it hit me. She needed to know something was seriously wrong...the fire alarm! If the emergency exit still worked, then hopefully the fire alarm functioned too. I turned from Natalie and raced up the stairs toward the orange glow. When I reached the hallway, I could see a small box on the wall labeled FIRE.

I sighed in relief and continued toward the alarm. Five meters from my rescue, I stopped dead in my tracks. A large boy had walked around the corner, a baseball bat slung across his shoulder.

"Well, hel-lo. I'm sorry, Miss Dupe, but you picked the wrong time to take a bathroom break." He shone a bright light in my face, blinding me. "Now, I'll give you three seconds to go back to the show."

I couldn't see anything, but I knew I only had one chance. I tried to envision the exact location of the alarm on the wall. I squared my body toward my best guess and sprinted forward.

"What the..." the boy moved his flashlight from my face to the wall, illuminating my target. I was veering left. I corrected my course and gave it all I had. Realization filled the boy's face as he cursed, threw down the bat, and raced toward the alarm.

I was one meter away when I saw the boy in my periphery and realized he wasn't going for the alarm. He was going for me. I stretched out my arms and I threw my body toward the wall. My fingers grazed the box just as the boy collided with me. I curled my fingers around the handle as the impact jerked me to the ground.

My head bounced off the concrete floor and my vision wavered. It took me several seconds to realize the ringing in my ears wasn't just in my head. It was the fire alarm! Water sprayed from the sprinklers and small floodlights lit the way to the exits. A loud, automated voice filled the hall. "Attention. Attention. Fire alarm activated. Please proceed to the nearest exit in a calm and orderly fashion. Attention. Attention..."

I looked toward the arena and anxiously held my breath. Suddenly, people flooded the hallway, racing toward the exit. I rolled to my back and laughed with relief...I had done it. I saved us from the Chaos. As I buried my face in my hands, two strong arms jolted me to my feet.

"Now you've done it!" the boy screamed into my face as he slammed me against the wall. His eyes gleamed with rage. "You ruined everything. You're dead. You know that, right?"

He leaned down and threw me over his shoulder. I tried my best to wiggle out of his grasp, but he was too strong. I looked up to see the emergency exit fading from view. I screamed for help until a bodycheck into the nearest wall emptied all the air from my lungs.

My captor pushed his way through the frantic crowd, working his way deeper into the arena. Several people told him to turn around, but he shoved past them. He stopped to kick open a door and we headed down a flight of stairs. The silence in the stairwell was deafening compared to the roar of the exit route. After several twists and turns, I realized the guy had the building memorized. I squirmed randomly in an attempt to catch him off guard, but nothing worked. Finally, we entered a bright room, and I was dumped onto the floor.

"This is the Dupe who pulled the fire alarm!" my captor yelled.

I groaned as I rolled to my side. Sweat instantly broke

across my forehead from the heat of the room. Smells of fried wires and melting plastic filled the air. I looked up to see a group of at least twenty teenage boys peering down at me. They weren't dressed all crazy as they had been in the All-Mark attack. Most wore black OneGlobal Stadium uniforms with headsets and sat in front of computer monitors The rest wore All-Mark clothes that could have blended into any crowd. It felt as if a flurry of activity had suddenly stopped and awkwardness settled in its place.

One of the taller guys stepped out from the back of the room. He appeared to be in his early twenties, tall and lean. He rubbed his hand across his shaved head and down to his short beard. He ignored me and looked at my captor. "So, there wasn't a glitch? Someone activated the system. What did you see?" he asked in an eerily calm voice.

The boy who carried me panted heavily. "I was walking…to my post after the lights went out…then, I saw her running toward the fire alarm. I tried to stop her but she was already there."

The tall guy sauntered toward me and bent down, centimeters from my face. He scratched his chin and looked directly into my eyes. "DO YOU REALIZE WHAT YOU'VE DONE?" he roared.

I scrambled backward, but my captor grabbed the back of my neck and held me in place. I stared in horror as the guy, obviously the leader, moved toward me. He looked vaguely familiar, but I couldn't help but gawk at the large vein popping out of his forehead.

"You ruined everything! Years of planning! All for nothing! Aahhhhh!" He reached for the nearest computer and threw it to the ground. He paced across the room for several moments, then stopped, threw his hands behind his head and yelled again at the ceiling. He turned to me and sighed calmly. "Well, what do you have to say for yourself?"

I didn't know how to react to his violent mood swings. Then, something triggered a memory of my mom in the All-Mark. I recognized the calm, gruff voice. He was the guy who tormented my mother and started the insanity. I slowly stood to my feet and glared into his eyes. He smiled menacingly and crossed his arms.

Rage boiled in my blood. Standing three meters from me was the guy responsible for hurting my family, endangering my life and wreaking havoc in my community. I wasn't afraid anymore. I was beyond afraid; I was pissed.

"I was there in Oklahoma City," my voice quaked. "I almost died that night, along with my mother. I saw the destruction you caused and I couldn't let that happen again."

Several boys shuffled around, looking at each other. The leader's eyes grew large, as a concerned look came across his face. "Really? Ha. What are the odds?" He hopped up to sit on the desk behind him and swung his feet. "I'm sorry if we inconvenienced you, but if you only knew the damage *you* did tonight, I think you would realize that the scales don't tip in your favor. *You*, Dupe, are in debt to *us*. Now, the question is: how will you pay?"

"I don't owe you a thing. I'm glad I ruined your plans. Anything to stop this, this...whatever this is, was worth it and I'd do it again if I could." I balled my hands into fists, overwhelmed with a confidence I'd never before experienced. I contemplated lunging at him and ripping the smug smile off his face.

"Well…if that's how you really feel." He stood, pulled a gun from the back of his waistband and pointed it directly in my face.

All the confidence I thought I had immediately left as gravity suddenly became twice as strong. I couldn't move. I couldn't think. Looking down the barrel of the gun, I knew I was about to die.

"Gage, no," stated a small voice to my right.

I looked over to see an older guy casually leaned forward in his chair, hands clasped, watching the events unfold. His fitted white shirt made his large, tan muscles stand out, dwarfing the other boys' arms. The long, dark blonde hair on the top of his head contrasted the buzzed back and sides. He stood up and slung a backpack across his broad shoulders. I couldn't help but notice his expensive looking jeans and black Designer shoes. He looked at his watch. "Let's just get out of here. The Docs will be here soon."

"She deserves it!" Gage screamed back, not moving the gun.

"I don't disagree with you, but this is *not* how we decided to handle things. We're wasting our time." His voice was firm and authoritative.

This seemed to agitate Gage even more. For a second, I thought he might run over and attack my defender, but then he regained his composure. He nodded his head and licked his lips. "You know what, Roman? You're right. We are wasting our time."

He cocked the gun and I held my breath.

"Coverture," Roman said.

"What?" Gage glared at him. "You can't be serious."

"You heard me. Coverture. Now, let's go." Roman walked to me, gently grabbed my arm and ushered me toward the door. I had no idea what was going on but was willing to go with whoever could get me away from trigger-happy Gage. We started down the hall at a brisk pace.

"What is going on?" I hissed.

"Not now. No time. I'll explain in the van." He didn't look at me as he spoke. His eyebrows furrowed as if he had a headache.

Suddenly, I didn't care that the guy had just rescued me from certain death, because when I was five years old, my mother taught me never to get in a vehicle with a stranger, especially a van. I planned on bolting at the first opportunity. I mentally prepared to run as soon we made it upstairs with the other evacuees, but instead, we went down, deeper into the arena. After navigating several more corridors, I decided Roman had the place memorized as well. He led me into a large underground parking lot.

"This is where the employees enter the building, and it's how we will get out," Roman said, as we walked through countless rows of vehicles. He pointed to a black van. "That one's ours."

I bit my lip. *It's now or never.* "Is that the D.O.C.?" I pointed behind us.

As soon as Roman turned his head, I ran. My muscles screamed as I sprinted between two lines of cars. I made it maybe ten meters when Roman caught up and scooped me into his arms. "You're only making this more difficult on yourself. We don't have time for this."

Struggling was pointless. His strong arms locked me

in place as the van screeched to a halt in front of us. A skinny, pale guy flung open the back doors. His long, black hair was held back by aviator goggles. "Woah, looks like Roman caught himself a lady friend. You sure do know how to celebrate."

Roman tossed me into the hollowed out van. "If you only knew the half of it, Gideon. I need a tracker kit."

I pushed myself off the floor as Roman, along with two other boys, hopped in behind me and slammed the doors shut. Roman crouched in front of me. "I know this is overwhelming for you and you have no reason to trust me, excluding the saving your life bit. I promise I will explain everything later, but I need you to roll with me for the next few minutes, okay?"

My eyes darted around the van. I counted five boys. *This isn't good.* I scooted backward into the corner of the van, worried I would hyperventilate.

Goggle boy flashed a light in my face. "She's terrified. What did you do to her?"

"Shut it, Gid." Roman sighed loudly and scooted closer. "There is a tracking device in your arm. It was placed there when you were younger. I need to take it out before we can leave. I will numb the area so it won't hurt, but we need to do this immediately."

I stared into his piercing green eyes in disbelief. "What? A tracker? You're crazy! I would know if I had a tracker."

Gideon handed Roman a small satchel. He emptied the contents into his lap. A knife reflected in the light.

I freaked. "No! There's no way you're touching me with a knife!" I covered my arms with my hands.

Roman sighed again. "First of all, this is a scalpel. Second,

I would be more than happy for Gideon to do this. He has more experience, but either way, it's coming out."

The van came to a jarring halt. I realized the vehicle was much older than it appeared on the outside. The guy up front was actually driving the van. The driver yelled back, "We're at the exit. That thing needs to come out before we leave. Ditch the tracker or her body. Makes no difference to me."

Roman reached for my arm and I pulled away. He shook his head as he stared at the floor. "You're really starting to get on my nerves, and I'm already regretting my decision. So, unless you want your family wondering how you were run over in the parking lot during a fire drill, I suggest you give me your arm."

I bit my lower lip and stuck out my left arm.

"Other arm. This is going to sting." He grabbed my right arm and stabbed my shoulder.

I screamed as fire spread across my arm for ten seconds, then numbness took its place. Roman rubbed a small screen across my arm. One spot appeared red. He marked the area. "I advise you to look away."

I did.

"What's your name?" He asked.

I hesitated. "Uh...Natalie."

He chuckled. "What's your real name? I'll find out in a couple hours anyway, but I thought we could start with proper introductions."

"My name is Eve," I said as I continued to avert my eyes.

"Nice to meet you, Eve. I'm Roman. Hold out your left hand."

I followed his instructions and a bead about the size of a

pea fell into my hand. I looked at it in disbelief. "This isn't a tracker, you psycho. It's a hormone dispenser placed by a physician when I turned ten."

"You are correct." He handed me a metal tube as big as my palm. "But, it is also a tracker. Put it in the tube and push the ends together," he instructed as he gently wrapped my arm with gauze.

I hesitated to follow his instructions but saw no alternative. I slid the ball into the tube and tried to crush it, but nothing happened. Someone giggled. Roman grabbed the device and squeezed. Crunch.

"We're ready," Roman called to the driver.

I was hurled to the floor as the van accelerated, tires squealing. I pulled myself upright. "How fast are we going?"

"Pushing ninety-five right now," the driver said over his shoulder.

"What? That's impossible! Cars can't go over forty-five."

All the boys laughed. One said, "She may not be the brightest screen on display but at least she's good looking."

I didn't know whether to be offended or flattered. Gideon patted me on the shoulder. "Kid, you've got a lot to learn."

I looked at Roman. He leaned back against the side of the van with his eyes closed. The speed of the vehicle had no effect on him.

"Where are we going?" I asked.

"Back to the Asylum," Roman replied, not opening his eyes.

"What's that? Who are you guys? And what's a Dupe?"

Roman looked at his watch for several seconds before replying. "I'll explain everything when we get there. Until then, can we please just have a quiet, peaceful ride, so I can reevaluate my life?"

Gideon shook his head. "Guess the shoes weren't lucky after all. I'm taking them back."

Anxiety rolled over me from my lack of control. *Stay calm, Eve, just think. You're a smart girl...somewhat. You can figure a way out.*

I felt a familiar buzz from my back pocket. *My phone!* I had completely forgotten about my phone, and, by some miracle, I had put it on vibrate before the game. I weighed the risk of taking it out or waiting for a better opportunity. Another buzz interrupted my thoughts, then another and another. Someone was blowing up my phone. I couldn't risk the boys hearing. I shifted my weight, turned my back to them and casually reached for the phone to sneak a peek.

It was Natalie. "WHERE ARE YOU? WE ARE WAIT-ING BY THE ENTRANCE GATE...CALL ME!!!"

I kept my head up to avoid suspicion while my fingers typed wildly from memory. "I WAS KIDNAPPED. SEND HELP! USE THE SIG—"

Before I could hit send my phone buzzed loudly as Natalie's picture appeared on the screen. Fear gripped my stomach. *How can she call at the worst possible moment?* I immediately hid the phone under my hip, but it was too late.

Some boy pushed me over, took the phone, and looked at the screen. "She's hot," he commented as he passed it to Roman.

My rescuer-slash-kidnapper pulled out a pocket knife, popped the screen off, and yanked out the internal memory. It snapped in half with a small pop. He tossed the remains to the floor, closed his eyes, and returned to his meditation.

I looked around. All the guys, except Roman and the driver, were staring at me. I turned my back to all of them and curled my knees to my chest. I didn't want them to see me cry as my spirit broke worse than my phone. *How could this possibly be happening?* I hid my face for the rest of the long drive.

After an hour or two, the van slowed. I peeked through the front window to get a look at what would be my new home...the Asylum.

CHAPTER 5

THE ASYLUM

We pulled through the barbed wire wrapped gates of the compound as empty guard towers peered eerily down on us. The moon cast long shadows on what appeared to be an old abandoned factory with scattered warehouses and silos. We drove past the larger buildings to an inconspicuous shed in the back. The driver flashed his headlights, but I could see no entrance into the metal box. After several seconds, the entire side of the building rolled up and the van squeezed inside.

The door creaked shut behind us, plunging the room into total darkness. I resisted the urge to grab the nearest person and clung to myself instead. A terrible metal screech jolted through the silence. The van shook gently, and I realized we were descending into the earth. The room was some type of large elevator.

After several minutes, the movement stopped and light flooded the van as a door in front of us opened. We entered a large parking lot filled with vans, cars, trucks, and even several buses. We pulled into an empty slot and the boys piled out of the van. Gideon hopped out last, leaving me with Roman.

Gideon smirked. "I guess I should leave you two alone to get to know each other. Brown chicken, brown cow."

"Shut it, Gid." Roman had not moved, nor opened his eyes since the beginning of the trip.

Gideon turned to me before leaving. "But in all seriousness...it's gonna be rough for you, kid. Keep it together and you'll see it's all worth it."

"I'm not a kid!" I yelled at him. Gideon looked my age at most. My gaze focused past the open door of the van to the empty elevator shaft. From my previous failed attempts, I figured that moment was not the most opportune time for another shot at escape. I dropped my head into my hands. *How did I end up here?* It was surreal.

I turned my attention back to Roman and my breath caught in my throat. In the dim light of the van, I realized just how drop-dead gorgeous he was; the type Natalie and I would daydream about all day in class. My stomach clinched instantly, but I tried my best to relax. *Breathe. Even if he looks like he belongs on an E-billboard for Designer jeans, he's still a part of the crazy cult who just kidnapped you.* There was nothing I could do but try to remain calm, stay focused, and wait. The fact that I was alone, in a dark van, with a male model did not help.

Roman brushed his hair out of his face and took a deep breath. "We're at the Asylum. This is the home base for the Oklahoma division of the American U.D. We are about forty-five kilometers outside Oklahoma City—"

"U.D.?" I interrupted, my mind flashing to the news blurbs of anarchy. "Like the crazy people in Europe causing all the destruction?"

He finally opened his eyes and shook his head. "The Universal Defiance isn't what you think. Don't believe anything you hear in the media. We are the good guys. We are the Kronies that will save this world. You're a part of this now and—"

"I'm not a part of *any* of this! I'll never be a part of this and I don't want to be here!" I whined.

"I don't care where you want to be," Roman barked. "If it wasn't for me, you'd be dead right now. I didn't plan on this happening so I'm figuring it out as I go. But if you want to remain in the living state, I suggest you quit interrupting me and listen!"

I bit my quivering lip and stared at the floor.

He continued his reprimand. "I don't know if you are aware, but you kind of ruined everything tonight. It's only a matter of time until word gets out that *you* pulled the fire alarm. So, I suggest keep your head down, your mouth shut, and do what you're told. Now, come on."

He jumped out of the back of the van, but I remained huddled against the wall. I had no idea what to expect in the Asylum, but it didn't look promising. I desperately wished to rewind the clock and never step foot outside my house.

After several long moments, Roman sighed and leaned against the van door. "Hey, I'm sorry I snapped at you. I know you were just trying to do the right thing in your eyes, but tonight was just...big. I'll try to make your stay with us as tolerable as possible, but we really need to get you to my room before the rumors spread."

I could hear the rumble of the garage elevator. As much

as I didn't want to be compliant in any way, shape, or form, I sure didn't want to be around when more Kronies arrived. Roman leaned forward and offered me his hand. I lifted my chin, ignored his gesture and hopped out of the van. Unfortunately, my left foot caught the bumper and I crashed to the ground.

I heard Roman stifle a chuckle. "You okay, graceful?" He offered his hand again, and again I ignored it.

"I'm fine." I pushed myself back up to my feet.

Roman shook his head. "Follow me, stay quiet, and keep close...please." He started toward the doorway at the end of the lot. I had to jog to match his large strides.

We walked down a long hallway with metal walls and ceiling. Our footsteps echoed off the concrete floor as some of the hanging lights flickered. The creepy ambiance made me want to move closer to Roman, but I refrained, determined to maintain a strong appearance.

At the end of the hall, we came to a set of double doors. Roman pressed his watch against a box on the wall. The scanner beeped and turned green. He pushed the doors open and we stepped into the Asylum.

We stood in a large open area, with several tunnel entrances jutting around the perimeter. I looked up the three-story high brown, brick walls to see countless doors connected by narrow walkways. Large, round lights hung from the ceiling, and I realized there had to be hundreds of boys, maybe a thousand, meandering through the compound. Their shouts and yells bounced off the walls. As we walked through the middle of the open area, some younger boys threw a toy back and forth, pushing each other down in an effort to catch it. We crossed the dirt floor to a staircase on the other side of the clearing.

When the boys noticed Roman, they would stop and stand at attention. When they noticed me, their eyes would widen and they would whisper to each other. I got the feeling Roman was someone of importance. We climbed the stairs, Roman taking them two at a time, and reached the second floor. I looked over the railing toward the open area. Almost all of the boys had stopped to watch us. I hurried after Roman as he led me to a small alcove. A young man with dark skin leaned against a door. His shaved head reflected the dim light.

Roman walked forward and stood centimeters from the guy's face. "Move."

The bald guy stood at attention, but with a smirk on his face. "Gage would like to see you."

"I bet he would," Roman sighed. "Now, move."

"I guess I didn't make myself clear. Gage wants to see you...now!"

"Tell Gage he can go..." Roman paused and looked at me. "Tell him I will be there shortly. Is there anything else?"

The man glared at Roman for a few seconds. "No, sir." He shoved Roman with his shoulder then spat on the ground by my feet and mumbled something under his breath.

"Ignore him, he's just Gage's puppet," Roman said as he scanned his watch on the panel of the door. It clicked and he held it open for me to walk inside.

The dark room was small, only half the size of my room at home. It didn't take long to take inventory: an unmade bed, a small set of drawers, a sink and mirror, desk and chair, and a door at the far end of the room.

Roman turned on the desk lamp. "You can stay in my room for now." He pointed to the door. "There's a bathroom through that door. Sometimes there's hot water."

He looked around the room, a small amount of pink filling his cheeks. "Um, I didn't expect to bring anyone here. I apologize for the mess. Anyway," he flopped onto the bed, "I have about five minutes before Gage really gets upset, so what questions do you have?"

His relaxed demeanor caught me off guard—no trace of the frustration I saw before. I stood against the wall and racked my brain. I had thousands of questions, but I tried to think of one that wouldn't make me look like a baffling idiot. I decided to go with my most pressing concern. "Where are you going to stay?" I asked, hoping my face didn't look as hot as it felt.

"I'll bunk with Gideon. If you'd be more comfortable, you can stay with the others in the Commons. That's a big area where most of the lower level Kronies bunk. I just don't want anyone giving you a hard time or Gage sending someone to mess with you. You should be safe here. Next question."

"How long will I be here?"

Roman shook his head and ran his fingers through his hair. "You probably wouldn't like the answer. So, let's just say…until we get this big mess sorted out and by 'big mess' I mean the whole overthrowing the government thing. But let's not focus on that now. Let's try another route. What's a term you've heard that doesn't make sense?"

I ignored the rock that had settled in my stomach. "Um, what's a Dupe?"

A smile spread across Roman's face. "That's easy. It's

our term for the typical global citizen because you've been duped by OneGlobal; a person who unquestionably believes anything the media tells them. We call ourselves Kronies, official members of the Universal Defiance. What else?"

I had to stop myself from rolling my eyes at his anti-government propaganda. I hugged my arms around my chest and felt the bandage. "Okay…what was that whole tracker thing about? I would know if the government put a tracker in my arm."

"Didn't you say it was a hormone regulator?"

"Yeah, but that's not a tracker. They would have to get permission from my parents to track me."

"The government does things without permission all the time, but in this instance, they actually did get permission." He sat up and perched his elbows on his knees, new energy filling his voice. "First of all, the government requires you to get the regulator. You think it's a choice and it's just something all ten-year-olds do so they won't get acne, but the government makes sure every girl gets it for two reasons, one: to track you, and two: so you don't get pregnant without the government approving." I felt myself starting to blush. Thankfully, he rushed on. "The male version decreases testosterone levels. That's why boys around here may seem…less docile. Anyway, when you went to the physician for the regulator placement, your mom had to sign a huge stack of papers with all the risks and benefits. There is a statement allowing the government to track you in there. I don't remember how it's worded, but it's in there. You'll learn all of that during re-education."

"Re-education?" I asked, glad to be off the topic of

hormones and pregnancy.

"The class you'll start taking tomorrow. Every girl who arrives at the Asylum enters the re-education process. You go through the history of the U.D., what we stand for, and all the ways you've been lied to your entire life." He looked at his watch. "Shoot. I gotta go to Command before Gage blows a fuse." He smiled to himself. "He's so mad at me." He stood and walked to the door.

"Roman, wait," I blurted, not wanting to be left alone. He paused in the doorway. An awkward silence filled the room. I tried to think of another question, some other word I didn't know to break the tension. "What was that thing you said to Gage so he wouldn't kill me?"

Roman looked at the ground and kicked at the floor. "Coverture...it's another policy we operate under. It basically means you're under my protection. No one should mess with you, but under the present circumstances, we shouldn't take any chances. Coverture also means you're my responsibility and under my authority while you're here."

"What does that mean?" I asked.

"How can I put it in terms you'll understand...if you are *noncompliant* according to the rules of the Asylum, I have to answer for it. So, if you keep on track with your recent history, I'm going to be in a lot of trouble." Roman's watch beeped. He stared at it as a look of anger spread across his face. "Speaking of trouble. I'll see you in the morning. Goodnight." He clicked the door shut.

I didn't know what to do. It felt like I was treading water in a sea of hopelessness. I sank into the chair at the desk. *How am I going to get out of this mess?* I turned to find a tablet staring me in the face. My eyes widened as I tapped it furiously. *Maybe I can send a message to my family and the D.O.C. could save me!* The screen slowly lit up to display a message: Please scan band to activate.

Locked. *I should have known. I'm not that lucky.* I buried my face in my hands, mentally and physically exhausted. *Don't give up so easily! There has to be a way out.* Maybe all the boys were at Roman's meeting and I could sneak out undetected. I jumped to the door but couldn't figure out how to open it. There was no handle. I pushed against it to no avail. I reared back and threw my body into it but only hurt my shoulder. I was trapped.

I dragged myself to the bed and sat down. It felt weird being in a guy's bed, so I stayed on top of the covers and curled into a ball. I couldn't believe how my life had completely changed in a matter of hours. To think, that morning I was hanging out with my best friend, talking about our favorite TV shows, and debating which guy on the starting lineup was most attractive. If I could have talked to Natalie, she would be more concerned about the fact that I was in a guy's bed than kidnapped by an anarchist cult.

My attention turned to my family; I couldn't even imagine what they were going through. Not only was my mom humiliated during the first Chaos; the second Chaos took away her daughter. Just thinking of her made my heart hurt. *I have to escape. I have to get back home.*

I told myself that the next day, I would figure everything out. I would devise a plan and if all else failed, it was only a matter of time before OneGlobal broke in and rescued me. The O.G. always saved the day. The good guys always won, and I was definitely on the good guys' side.

CHAPTER 6

RE-EDUCATION

I awoke the next morning to a knock on the door. I bolted upright. For a few glorious seconds, I thought I was home and overslept for school. My head ached as a tidal wave of memories from the previous day crashed into my consciousness. I staggered over to the mirror. *Yikes.* My hair was a hot mess, mascara streaked across my face and my shirt was smudged with dirt. I knew I should have worried about a million other things, but all I could think was, *I cannot let Roman see me like this.*

"Just a minute!" I called as I washed my face in the sink. Behind the mirror, I found toothpaste and squirted it into my mouth. I then tried, unsuccessfully, to detangle my hair with my fingers. I did the best I could...which was pretty pathetic. I walked to the door and took a deep breath. *Remember, he kidnapped you. There's no reason you should worry about what he thinks about you.*

I reached for the door handle but remembered my dilemma from the night before. "Um, how do I get out?"

I heard a beep and the door unlatched. To my

disappointment, a pair of aviator goggles stood in front of me with a tray of food.

"What are you doing here?" I asked.

"Well, good morning to you too. You look....well-rested. We haven't officially met. I'm Gideon. Rome had some business to take care of this morning, so he asked me to help you get situated. May I come in?"

I shrugged. "Yeah, I guess."

Gideon waltzed into the small room and slid the tray onto the desk. "We don't have the most glamorous of food options, but it's edible."

The tray contained some type of meal bar, an apple, and a sports drink. My stomach released an audible growl.

"Here's your wristband." Gideon held out a thick, black bracelet. "This will grant you access to places like Roman's room, the rec center, the cafeteria...and, not surprisingly, not give you access to places like...oh, say, the exits." I held out my arm and he locked the ends together with a small, magnetic bead.

Gideon motioned to the desk. "Please, go ahead and eat. Don't mind me. We have some time to kill before class. I was planning on giving you the grand tour, but that's probably not the best idea right now."

"Why not?" I asked as I chowed down on the meal bar.

"Hmm, how do I put this delicately?" Gideon sat on the bed. "People hate you."

"What? Why? People here don't even know me."

Gideon sighed. "Yeah, that came out harsh. Let me rephrase. *Most* people hate you. I don't hate you. I think what you did was brave and I understand why Roman stood up for you, but other people don't see it that way."

I felt the need to defend myself. "I was at the first Chaos. I knew what was about to happen. All I wanted to do was get people out of there so they wouldn't be murdered."

Gideon held up his hands. "You don't have to explain yourself to me. The fact that you were at the first Chaos was...an unforeseen complication. But try to see it from our perspective. Months and months of planning went into this Chaos. You had no way of knowing, but it wasn't going to be like the first one. No violence. Craziness, yes, but no hurting people, just truth. And, FYI, no one was murdered during the first Chaos. Injured, maybe, but... well, that's a long story we don't have time for."

I nearly choked on my drink. "What do you mean people weren't killed? I saw all the guns and weapons. People died."

"Hate to burst your bubble, but no they didn't, at least not from us. That's Rome's rule: no death. Think about it. Did you actually witness someone dying?"

I thought back to that night. "Well, no. But the Docs told me people didn't make it out. They also told me what you guys really are. Just a bunch of copycats looking for attention."

Gideon smirked. "Lesson one, kid: the government lies."

Frustration crept up inside me. The more I found out, the more questions I had. I wasn't making any progress in understanding what was going on. I tried a different approach. "You know, the D.O.C. must be close to finding me by now. I'm sure they've launched a full-scale investigation. Are you guys sure you want this whole operation discovered just because of me?"

Gideon scratched his head. "I'm sure the Docs are

searching for this place but I doubt they are that interested in you. No offense. I'm sure you're a great person and all, but OneGlobal doesn't give two Credits if you're safe or not. Have you ever heard of a search for someone who wasn't an Upper?"

He had me there. "No, but that doesn't matter. They know I was at the first Chaos. Won't it look suspicious that the only citizen at both attacks was kidnapped?"

"Kidnapped sounds so barbaric. I prefer involuntarily recruited. You do bring up a good point. I'll keep a close eye on our radars, but I'm not too worried. We've been outsmarting the Docs for years and it's only a matter of time before the first domino falls."

I shook my head, "I don't understand. What's the point? Why are you keeping me? Why are you doing all of this?"

"That, my friend, is probably the most important question of all. You'll have your answer today at re-education."

"What's with this education class?" I asked as I started on the apple. "You can't seriously tell me a bunch of rebel boys still go to school."

"Yes and no. We 'rebel boys' don't go to class, we go to training. Only the girls go to school."

"There are other girls here? I didn't see any yesterday."

"Yesterday wasn't a normal day. But to your credit, there aren't many chicks here…unfortunately. You'll meet all the other noobs at class." He recognized the confusion my face. "Noobs—ya know, newbies—new people to the U.D. Anyway, time to make like a drone and buzz off."

Gideon headed toward the door while I crossed my arms and remained at the desk. "I'm guessing I don't have a choice in going to this class."

"Of course you do. Here in the U.D., we are all about the freedom of choice. However, all choices have consequences, so I highly recommend you go. It wouldn't look good that Rome's Coverture didn't attend class." He scanned his wrist at the door and disappeared down the hall before I knew what happened.

I chugged the rest of my drink and hurried to catch up. "Your bracelet let you out of his room. Do *you* have access to everything?" A plan formed in my brain. *If I could somehow get his bracelet off then I may have shot at the exit.*

"First of all, we call them bands, not bracelets, and I have access to what I need to have access to, nothing else. Same as everyone here." We made our way to the central area. Gideon pointed over the railing. "This open area is called the field. It's where we play football every Monday night."

"What's football?"

Gideon stopped in his tracks and turned around. "Oh, sweet mama. I forget you Dupes don't know what that is… uuugghhh. I don't have time to explain all the intricacies of the beauty that is football. Alas, we must continue. Down this hall is your class and on the floor below are the Commons: open dormitories where most of the guys stay. Only higher ranking officers have their own room." We stopped in the middle of the hall.

"So, Roman is a high-ranking officer?"

"Ha. You're kidding, right?" Gideon asked with raised eyebrows. "Oh…you're not. Well, I guess you could say he is high-ranking. He's *the* guy in charge of this *entire* Asylum. On that note, I'll let you get to class, straight ahead through that open door. Think you can make it?"

"Yeah, I'll be fine. Thanks."

Gideon swiveled around and left me standing alone in the hall. *Woah, Roman is in charge of everything? Interesting.* I looked around and debated what to do. It was my first time being alone and not locked in a room. I could use the opportunity to try to escape or I could follow the rules and go to class. Searching for an escape, while still my number one priority, was full of uncertainty. Plus, I wasn't sure I wanted to find out what *consequences* could result. I went with my natural inclination and headed down the hall. I needed to avoid anything that added to the already large target on my back. I had no idea what to expect, but maybe I could learn something that would help the D.O.C. once I made it out. I took a deep breath and walked through the open door.

The tiny room was unlike any classroom I'd ever been in. Four rows of desks filled most of the area, with a larger desk in the front. Six girls already sat in the front two rows. Their chatter ceased as they turned to peer at me. I dropped my head and walked quickly to the third row. I'd prefer to sit in the very back, but I wanted to blend in as much as possible.

There was a faint smell of mold. I looked around to see where it was coming from and couldn't believe my eyes. The entire back wall was filled, floor to ceiling, with books. I had never, in my entire life, held an actual book in my hands. I didn't even know they still existed. I wondered what could possibly be the purpose of having all of them. Seemed to me like a big waste of space when the information could just be uploaded to a tablet.

I turned forward to evaluate the girls in my class. Most of them looked to be around my age, but one of them was younger, probably in Connor's grade.

The girl in front of me turned around and stuck out her hand. "Hi, I'm Stevie."

"Hey, I'm Eve." I said.

Stevie smiled brightly. Her dark yet flawless makeup stood out against her fair skin. "Eve, I like that. Is that your birth name or your Defiance name?"

"Um, birth name."

"Lucky." Stevie tossed her long, blonde hair over her shoulder. "My birth name was Stephanie and I hated it. When they told me I could choose whatever name I wanted I was thrilled. Tomorrow, I'm gonna chop my hair off and dye it red. Start fresh, like a real Kronie. Don't you love it here? There's so much freedom!"

Stevie seemed just a little too excited to be there. I gave what I thought would be the correct answer. "Yeah, it's great."

"You missed the introductions. This is Becky, Adriane, Charli, Heather, and our youngest noob, Hannah. Did you get here last night? My brother's been a part of the Defiance for years. I've been waiting for this for-ev-er. I'm just happy I was able to find him before that idiot pulled the fire alarm."

My stomach hit the floor.

Stevie continued. "Who would do that? I heard a rumor that it was a girl and she's actually here in the Asylum! I don't know if I believe it though. If they caught her she's probably dead or in confinement. Anyway, how did you end up here?"

"I...uh...I..."

Thankfully, our instructor walked into the room.

However, my gratefulness was short-lived. Upon seeing our professor, I was thrown off for several reasons. First, she was a she; a girl at least a few years older than me. I assumed whoever taught the re-education process would be one of the older guys. Second, she was beautiful: tall and slender, with long, silky black hair and mocha skin. She looked like a model with her ripped jeans and bomber jacket. The third thing I didn't expect was her attitude. She walked in with such confidence and authority; everyone immediately knew she was in charge. The final thing that surprised me was my instant distaste for her. I wasn't exactly sure why. Maybe it was just a female jealousy thing, or maybe it was the fact that when she hopped on the desk to face the class, she was glaring directly at me.

"Good morning, class," she spat, still scowling at me. "I'm in a bit of a bad mood today. I'm running on zero sleep. I wasn't approved to push this class back until tomorrow. We ran out of coffee AND, yesterday, *somebody* decided to ruin months and months of hard work. However, we must trudge on." Her eyes finally unlocked with mine. My face felt like it was on fire. I hid behind Stevie's head.

The teacher stood up and paced across the room with her arms folded. "Welcome to your first re-education class. My name is Professor Emily Gray. I will be your instructor for the duration of the session. We will meet every day, zero nine hundred to twelve hundred, then I'll escort you to the cafeteria for lunch. In the afternoon, you'll have time to study on your own, take a training course over whatever interests you, or, once you become more acclimated, help out around the Asylum.

"The goal of this class is to open your eyes to that which

you are blind. Hopefully, I will help you to free your mind to the possibilities of life. The world in which you lived is a mere shell of its former glory. This 'society' lies to you, deceives you, and forces you to bend to its will while providing the illusion of choice." She paused, surveying the room. "The purpose of the Universal Defiance is to show people the truth and give back their freedom, their rights, their lives. For, from Chaos, revolution is born."

"Now, some housekeeping." Professor Gray walked bent down behind her desk and grabbed a small stack of books. She strolled through the rows, placing one in front of each girl. "These are your new member manuals. They state our rules and regulations, but more importantly, they explain our history, purpose and beliefs. We will go over some of this in class, but I encourage you to read through this entire handbook as soon as possible."

No, thank you.

"Along the back wall are actual books. These are old textbooks used in schools before the OneGlobal education takeover. You are free to borrow and read them at your leisure. They are very old, fragile, and extremely valuable, so please handle with care. Anyone responsible for damaging or losing a book will answer to me." I could feel the threat behind her words.

"Usually after a Chaos, we have a much larger class; however, somebody..." she paused as she reached my desk, holding my manual slightly out of reach. "...really screwed things up last night." She dropped the book onto my desk, making a loud *smack*.

Professor Gray returned to the front of the class. "We are all dying to know, so please enlighten us." She turned around slowly. "Eve, why did you pull the fire alarm?" Someone inhaled sharply. All eyes converged on me. Stevie spun around, her mouth hanging open. "It was you?" she whispered with a slight tone of disgust.

Every trace of bravery I had when facing the boys disappeared. I looked down at my desk, wishing I could melt into it. Professor Gray tapped her fingers as the seconds ticked by. I wished I was a better liar since there was no way I could tell the truth. I didn't think Professor Gray wanted to hear why I did "the right thing," or what I really thought about their whole operation, or what she could do with her re-education class. I chose silence.

Professor Gray sat down behind the big desk. "Mmm-hmm. Well, I'm sure we will get to that *fascinating* part of the story when we get to Chaos later. For now, let us start at the beginning."

Thankfully, the girls' focus returned to the front. Stevie's gaze of betrayal lingered on me for several seconds before she turned around.

Professor Gray absentmindedly played with a metal bead on her necklace as she began her speech. "We can all agree that the world was a very different place before OneGlobal. Countries operated under their own separate governments. I know you've been indoctrinated with the belief that this caused the world crumble. War, famine, and disease ravaged the earth. Society as a whole was on the brink of collapse, but then, lo and behold, the answer to everyone's problems arrived to save the day: OneGlobal. I'll give them some credit; they did create a façade of peace and stability. They facilitated the sharing of technological and medical breakthroughs. Great solutions were birthed from this new community. But at what price? What did we sacrifice in order to receive these advancements?

"OneGlobal was founded out of the fragmented remains of the United Nations. At first, many people were skeptical, but everything seemed to run smoothly. The world didn't change all at once. Like a frog slowly boiled to death, minute alterations were made in the government. You would be shocked at what people will overlook in trade for instant gratification and laziness. Over the years, OneGlobal gained control of every aspect of society. By the time anyone realized what was happening, it was too late. Although most welcomed the blindness, the few visionaries became the Defiance.

"The U.D. was founded in Europe. In the beginning, it was just a group of people who wanted to keep their country's identity separate from OneGlobal. But after their investigations, they discovered the true darkness lurking behind the pristine exterior. When they noticed that some of their more outspoken members were mysteriously disappearing, they decided to go into hiding and formulate a plan to overthrow OneGlobal. Over the decades, the U.D. has grown into an underground community spanning the world. Finally, at this point in history, we have the power to expose OneGlobal's corruption to the public and shut them down." Professor Gray's eyes gleamed victoriously.

I think she expected a standing ovation, but no one made a sound. *What corruption?* I shook my head. One-Global was a near-perfect system. I couldn't think of one reason to complain about the way they ran things. It was a waste of my time even trying to imagine one. I wondered if anyone was buying into her propaganda.

"Let's start with some examples." Professor Gray scanned the room. "Stevie, what grade were you in?"

"I was a sophomore."

"Okay, so you were finished with most of your required education. Tell me something that you learned in school. Anything in detail, but it can't be related to OneGlobal."

Stevie started to say something, then stopped. I couldn't come up with an answer off the top of my head, but it wasn't a fair question. I hated school. Didn't every teen? It was just one of those things you had to endure before you could begin your real life.

Stevie finally came up with an answer. "Math, I learned math."

Professor Gray nodded. "I'm sure you can do basic math. But did you learn anything higher? Algebra? Geometry? Calculus? Trigonometry?"

"Heck, no," Stevie laughed. "Those classes were only for the crazy smart people."

"Alright, what about science? Biology? Chemistry?"

"Well, I liked science and I was able to take one biology class, but I never tested high enough to continue."

Professor Gray surveyed the room. "Think about it. You've spent ten years in public education and that's the best you can do? Doesn't it astonish you how little you've actually learned that's not related to OneGlobal? Isn't it unfair that certain subjects are taught only to the top ten percent, while the rest of you go to only basic required economic courses that sing O.G.'s praises? Why is this?"

Professor Gray tapped on her foot, waiting for an answer. The younger girl raised her hand. "Well, the goal of going to school is to find out what you're good at. That way the government knows which career you're best suited for and they can prepare you for the correct job."

Professor Gray clapped her hands slowly. "That is a perfect answer, Hannah. Another way of saying it: so the government can choose your career for you. The government tests you because they don't want to waste their time or resources on what you care about. They want the biggest bang for their buck. They educate whoever tests highest and brainwash the rest into unquestionable devotion. What if I told you that before the 'standardization of education,' students had the right to pick whatever classes they wanted? A variety of basic classes were required, but after that, the choice was up to you. If you liked science, you could take all the science courses your heart desired. Today, your history classes are completely devoid of truth and do not get me started on what they took away...poetry, art, choir, band, drama. Anyway, what would you think about choosing your own classes, Hannah?"

The younger girl shrugged. "I guess that would be kind of cool."

One of the older girls raised her hand. Professor Gray called on her. "Yes, Charli, but you don't have to raise your hand here. I like to maintain an open format."

"It doesn't make sense to let people choose their own classes. What good is it going to do for someone like my dad, who's a chef, to focus on biology and physics?"

"What if your dad didn't want to be a chef? What if he wanted to be a physician?"

"It doesn't matter what he wants, it's about contributing to society in the best possible way," Charli quipped. *I like her.*

Professor Gray nodded enthusiastically. "Precisely! That's exactly the way they've programmed you to think! They want you to believe that by giving up your choice of career, you are helping society as a whole. But in reality, they just want to decide your destiny. They won't put any resources into someone who doesn't repay with interest. There is a Career Class book in our library. It's an entire book focused on helping students choose the right field of study. It discusses several considerations like, your strengths, your interests and how to channel that into a satisfying career that *you* will enjoy for the rest of your life. It's a very interesting read, and enlightening to imagine what it would be like to choose your own career."

I found myself shaking my head again. *What a nightmare!* It stressed me out to decide what to wear to the movies, let alone pick my career. I didn't see why the government choosing our profession was that big of a deal. It just made life easier. Plus, most people got two options and smart people could do anything with OneGlobal's approval. I wasn't buying it.

Professor Gray resumed, "Let me give you another example. Bear in mind, these are simple and superficial illustrations. We won't get into the deeper horrors until the later weeks."

Weeks? I tried to keep my panicking heart rate steady. *You'll be long gone by then.*

"A tracker was removed from each of you prior to your arrival at the Asylum. If even one was left activated, this place would be shut down within a matter of minutes. Some of you may wish that was the case, but take a step back. Do you think it's right for OneGlobal to have the ability to trace your every step?"

Again, I didn't see what the big deal was. I would have loved for the O.G. to track me down at that very second. Plus, if you had nothing to hide, what did it matter if OneGlobal knew where you were.

Professor Gray's voice carried across the room. "But it's more than that! They have access to every text, video, private message, phone call and email you have ever sent or received."

Uh, oh. There were definitely several messages with Natalie regarding our perpetual crushes I didn't want anyone to see.

"OneGlobal has spent billions of Credits developing bots to detect any malice towards the government. Have any of you ever spoken of OneGlobal in a negative way? I can answer that for you. No. Because if you had, you wouldn't be sitting in this room...I'm here to show you the truth. It's up to you to accept."

For the next few hours, Professor Gray continued to give examples of the government taking our freedom away. I kept my mouth shut and didn't participate in any of the discussion, even though I really wanted to say something when she talked about music. I mean, how was it even possible to create hundreds of songs every year in different genres? One album a month was plenty of music for me and everyone else in the real world.

Professor Gray looked up at the clock behind her desk, 1217. "That's enough for today. Tomorrow, we will go over Chaos Theory and Coverture. Your homework for tonight is to read through section one of your handbook, 'History of the U.D.' We believe in embracing our heritage, the good and the bad, unlike the current regime. Now, please follow me."

She walked out the door, and everyone in the room fell into step behind her. I purposely left my manual on my desk, hoping Professor Gray would get to the classroom early the next day and see it there. I wanted her to know I wasn't buying her crazy theories, even though I'd ponder them all night.

I trailed behind the group as we headed to lunch. I thought about sneaking off to Roman's room for the rest of the day, but isolating myself wouldn't help me escape. Plus, I didn't want to cause more trouble for Roman. Only a few boys played in the field as we walked by. I wondered what they did during the day if they didn't go to class. I wondered what Roman was doing. *Stop thinking about him and focus on a way to get out.* I shook my head and tried to be more aware of my surroundings.

We made our way through the north tunnel. Professor Gray stopped in front of two large, metal doors. A boy ran out from the cafeteria and a dull roar escaped behind him.

"Breakfast is served from zero seven-hundred to zero nine-hundred, lunch is eleven to thirteen-hundred and dinner is seventeen to nineteen-hundred. At all other times, these doors will be locked, since teenage boys are always hungry and like to sneak food from our limited supply."

She turned and led us inside. The large room was packed with mismatched tables and chairs gathered around a central drink station. *No wonder there were no boys on the field.* They were all crammed into the cafeteria. I scanned the crowd for Roman, but I knew my chances of seeing him were low with hundreds of guys milling about. Professor Gray escorted us through the bedlam as the entire room stopped to notice us. Whistles and cheers came from every direction. I hid my face and hoped they didn't already hear I was the one who pulled the alarm.

A row of windows lined the back wall, and above each, a screen displayed a different meal option. Professor Gray stopped in front of one and yelled, "Pick your meal, scan your band and find a table. The boys know you're new, so they shouldn't bother you, but anyone giving you a hard time will answer to me. I'll see you in the morning."

She turned to leave, but not before giving me one last frown. As she walked to the exit, boys around her bowed their heads in respect. One almost tripped as he ran to open the door for her.

I turned back around. All the girls had picked a line. I chose the nearest window without looking at what it offered. To my surprise, a girl manned the booth.

She gave me a sympathetic smile. "The first week is always the hardest. Keep your chin up. I promise you will come to love it here." She slid a tray into my hands.

I thanked her and walked away. She seemed nice, but I didn't plan on being there long enough to make friends. Anyway, she probably didn't know who I was. If she did, she would hate me like everyone else.

The other girls had grouped up and pushed two small tables together. I had a decision to make. I could pull up a chair and squeeze my way into the girl table. *Pass.* I could join a table with some boys. *Double pass.* Or, I could walk around the edge of the cafeteria to an empty table on the far side of the room. I ducked my head and chose option three.

I slid into the chair, thankful no one had noticed me. I surveyed my tray: turkey sandwich, banana, and a bag of chips. I gazed at the drink station in the middle of the room, a long walk through a sea of boys. *Guess I'll just go thirsty.* I sighed as I stared down at my lunch without much of an appetite.

"So, how's the first day of class?" The voice startled me. I looked up to see Gideon sitting across from me.

"Gideon," I breathed. "You scared me."

"Sorry. I was just checking on you, kid. How's it going?"

"Oh, great! The whole 'welcome to our cult, everything you know about society is a lie' speech was quite inviting," I quipped.

Gideon laughed. "I know you hate this place, and with good reason. We kidnapped you, took you away from your family, destroyed a local establishment in your hometown. But…" He slid a bottle of water in front of me. "If you give us a chance, you'll see we aren't that bad."

"Thanks." I smiled slightly as I took the water. I tried to pinpoint why I felt comfortable around Gideon. It probably had to do with how he always seemed so mellow. Even at that moment, when he was sitting with the most despised person in the entire Asylum, he looked like nothing in the world could stress him out. Or maybe it was as simple as the fact that he was nice to me.

"The one thing I ask," Gideon said, "is that you keep an open mind. I'm sure you want to believe that every word that comes out of our mouths is a lie from the pit of hell. But just try to decide for yourself what you believe. Not what someone has told you in the past, but what you personally think is the truth. What did you talk about this morning?"

"We went over all the ways the government controls us and doesn't let us make any choices, like with music, television, fashion, and the career placement program. Blah, blah, blah."

Gideon nodded thoughtfully. "Career placement is actually what got me involved here."

"What? How?"

"Well, ever since I was a little kid, I was fascinated with technology. I loved the idea of creating something out of wires and batteries to detect when my sister came near my room. So, when we started classes involving anything related to engineering, I ate it up. Unfortunately, I have horrible test anxiety. For some reason, knowing that some other person is going to judge how I answer really freaks me out. Not surprisingly, I bombed every exam. I scheduled 'private' tutoring sessions, which were really only online repeats of the same school lessons. But nothing helped to boost my scores enough to land a career as a technological engineer. When my eighth-grade class assignments came in and I saw nothing except remedial classes, I had a mini breakdown. I scoured the Internet for ways to change my career path, but all I found was O.G. site after O.G. site saying the government knew what was best for me and to trust them for a 'Compliant and satisfying life.' I still tried to study anything about engineering, but my fate had already been determined. Eventually, they locked me out of my favorite textbooks. I stopped going to school and became a hermit. Then the U.D. found me. So..." He leaned back in his chair and spread his arms open. "Here I am. Head of the Engineering Department, doing what I love, with people who support my dreams."

I definitely related to his test anxiety but had never considered skewing my school experiences to get a certain job. While no one wanted a bad career, we all just accepted whatever field we were best suited for, and that was the end of it. I didn't know how to respond. "I'm really happy for you."

"Ha. Your tone betrays you. This place may not be for you, but at least recognize that it is the right place for some people. Roman, Gage, Emily...we all have our reasons for being here."

His comment spurred a question. "So, this morning you said Roman is the leader of this Asylum."

Gideon nodded. "Yep."

"Then why did it seem like Gage was in charge at the Chaos?"

"Technically Gage outranks Roman, but he's had a bit of a tough time gaining respect. Rome's been the head of this Asylum for about a year and a half. After the decision was made to have the first Chaos in Oklahoma, our headquarters sent some of their people to help out. Gage and Emily were involved in multiple Chaoses in Europe. Since everyone is so young around here, their experience is invaluable."

I scanned the room. "Yeah, why are there so many kids here? Where are all the adults?"

Gideon laughed. "Most of the adults are at the headquarters and have higher rankings in the Defiance. We focus on recruiting younger people for several reasons. They've had less time to be brainwashed by OneGlobal, are more creative in seeing the possibilities, and are literally the future of our society." He looked at his band. "Well, it's time for me to get back to work. Oh, I forgot to tell you some cool features about your band."

He slid into the chair next to me. "First, it's a watch. Just tap the flat part on top and it displays the time. I already set an alarm for all the girls an hour before class. It can also send messages to anyone in the Asylum. I preprogrammed Rome, Emily, your classmates, and me. Tap the screen, say 'text Gideon' to use the voice control, or use the holographic keyboard." He stood and started for the exit. "Oh, and please don't try to break it. They are fairly durable, but they aren't cheap. I doubt you want to be scrubbing toilets for the next ten years to pay for it. Catch ya later, kid."

I watched him leave the cafeteria and looked around the room. The group of girls sat at their table chatting, but there was still no sign of Roman. One boy did catch my eye; he reminded me of Connor. The thought of my brother made me homesick. I wished Con was there. He would know what to do. In fact, he probably would have already escaped while simultaneously managing to shut down the entire Defiance.

I noticed the younger girl from my class walking toward me. She nervously played with a strand of her wavy hair as she approached. "Um, hey. Would you like to sit with us?"

I felt bad turning her down, but I didn't have the energy to put on a fake exterior for the girls. "I appreciate the invite, but I just want to be alone right now."

She shrugged. "Well, my name's Hannah. You can sit by me if you change your mind." She turned and walked back to the girls, who had all stopped eating to watch the interaction.

I twisted in my seat and faced the wall. It was nice of Hannah to go out on a limb to talk to me, but I wasn't ready to be sociable. I made a mental note to look her up on social media after I escaped. I snacked on my bland lunch and waited until most of the crowd left before sneaking back to Roman's room.

I'm not very good with directions, but finding my way back to Roman's room was surprisingly easy. I paused at the door. *Should I just go in or knock?* If he was there, would he leave? Was he mad at me and that's why he sent Gideon to look after me? There was only one way to find out.

I bit my lip, knocked on the door and waited. No answer. I knocked again and counted to thirty in my head. Nothing. I took a deep breath, scanned my band and pushed. The room was empty and I let out a disappointed sigh. *You shouldn't look forward to seeing him. He's part of the Defiance, just like everyone else. He's the enemy.*

I flopped onto the bed and stared at the ceiling. I had to think of a way out. I examined my band. Maybe I could somehow trade it with a Kronie without them noticing. I twisted and pulled but it didn't budge. I needed more information for the only plan I had developed. I tapped the screen. "Text Gideon: I can't get my band off and I need to shower."

After a few seconds, my wrist vibrated slightly and the word "message" flashed on the screen. I tapped it. "GIDEON: IT'S WATERPROOF...AND THEY DON'T

COME OFF."

My only strategy disintegrated into thin air. Since I was permanently wearing a black bracelet, I wondered if it was the Defiance's way of tracking me. "Text Gideon: So, I traded one tracker for another?"

He didn't reply. "UUUUGGGHHHH." I punched Roman's pillow several times, frustrated the Defiance would know if I even came close to an exit. *Pull it together, Eve! You can't give up. You have to keep thinking.* Maybe a shower would help me calm down and think more clearly. I did a smell check. *Yep, I definitely need a shower.*

I rummaged through the dresser to find a towel. They sat in a neatly folded stack beside a mass of socks and boxers. I blushed just imagining Roman walking in to find me going through his underwear drawer. I grabbed a towel and slammed the drawer shut. Once in the bathroom, I realized it didn't have a lock. *This is going to be the fastest shower ever.*

It certainly was one of the worst showers I've ever taken. The water was lukewarm at best, and I came out smelling like a boy with only men's body wash and shampoo available. I hated putting my dirty, old clothes back on, but that was my only option.

I tried to think of other ways to find out more data on the Asylum. Information was my friend. The more I learned, the more likely I would be able to figure a way out. *Maybe I should have taken my handbook with me after all.*

I could try to hack into Roman's tablet. That was my best chance at information, but when I opened the bathroom door, I noticed it was gone. *Was it there when I got back from lunch?* I couldn't remember. Roman must have grabbed it sometime during the day.

I sighed. Another failed plan. I was either really bad at successful ideas or really good at horrible ones. I resolved to do something productive, so I explored the tiny room. The dresser contained nothing of interest, just more clothes and a ridiculous amount of shoes. Behind the mirror were normal toiletries, toothbrush and toothpaste, floss, some cologne (that smelled amazing), a razor and shaving cream. I considered taking the razor, but in reality, I was more likely to cut myself than anyone else. I moved on to the desk. The top drawer was mainly empty, just paper, pens and pencils. *Where did he get this archaic junk?* In the second drawer I found some round, silver disks that seemed useless. I opened the third drawer and froze. A piece of paper read,

Have fun snooping, but you won't find anything.
If you're bored, here are some of my favorite books.
Be back soon.
— Roman

I picked up the note and reread it several times. I didn't know how to feel. I was mad that he assumed I would be snooping, and a little ashamed that he was right. But what was I supposed to do after being kidnapped by a bunch of crazy teenage boys? The note did mean he was thinking about me at least, but I was disheartened that my "protector" would be gone for an undetermined amount of time. *I wish Natalie was here to decipher this.* I looked at the small stack of books. I had never heard of any of them. I put the note back on top, hoping it looked like I never opened the drawer.

I moved my attention to the bed. I bent down to my knees and reached underneath. I swept my hand back and forth, feeling nothing at first. Then, my fingers grazed something leathery. I pulled out a brown, oblong ball with white stitches. I tossed it aside and reached under again. I slid my head and shoulders under as much as I could until I touched the wall. I stretched to the far corner and felt something move. I struggled for a minute but finally grabbed the item and pulled out a small brown box sealed with duct tape.

I bit my lip, debating what to do. If I tore open the box, he would know I looked inside. I gently shook the box. Something rattled. I sat on the bed and placed the box on my lap. *What if it's something to help me escape?* I had no choice. I had to open it.

Slowly and carefully, I peeled off the tape, wincing every time part of the box ripped. After several agonizing minutes, I lifted the lid up just enough to stick my hand inside. I felt something flat, like pieces of paper, only glossy. I grabbed ahold and pulled out a stack of pictures. I had never seen pictures that were printed on paper. All our family photos were displayed on digital screens. My phone alone could store more pictures than I could ever take. I wondered what was the purpose of having them on paper?

I shuffled through the stack. Most of them were group pictures with a younger version of Roman. *It must be his family.* His dad was tall and serious with dark, shaggy hair. His mom looked full of energy with a trendy short haircut. He had an older brother who was slightly taller than

Roman but much skinnier. I flipped through more family vacation photos, then the scenes changed to his brother in a hospital bed, giving the camera a weak thumbs up. Suddenly, I felt guilty, like I was viewing something sacred. I put the pictures back into the box and tried to reseal it as best I could. I slid the box back into its hiding spot and collapsed on the bed.

Day one recap: I had no idea how to escape, my teacher hated me, along with most everyone in the Asylum, I was being tracked, there was nothing useful in Roman's room, he was gone AND I smelled like a boy. *Perfect, great progress.*

I wasn't hungry at all. I decided to skip dinner and go to bed early. I laid in bed and stared at the ceiling. *How am I possibly going to escape this place? There's no way I'm smart enough to do this. I did absolutely nothing today. What would Mom tell me right now? Be positive and tomorrow you'll figure something out. What would Connor tell me? You just need to think of a new approach, an unusual tactic they wouldn't expect.*

I silently thanked them both and vowed to myself I would do better. I had to get out for them. I cuddled under the blankets and fell asleep.

CHAPTER 7

STRATEGY

I woke up the next morning to an annoying beep vibrating my wrist. My band read 0800. I stretched across the bed as my stomach rumbled. The last thing I wanted to do was to go to the cafeteria by myself. I hoped Gideon would bring me breakfast again or I would just tough it out until lunch.

I looked at myself in the mirror. On the positive side, I looked better than the day before. On the negative, I still looked horrible. I opened the mirror and grabbed the toothpaste. I hesitated when I noticed the toothbrush. Nope. *Crush or not, I am not using his toothbrush.* That was just gross.

I paused, toothpaste glob hanging midair, in the realization of what I had thought. I closed the mirror and pointed at myself. "You do not have a crush on him, Eve! He kidnapped you and is the leader of this insane cult. It doesn't matter that he saved your life or that he's stupid hot or that he's the first boy you've had an extended conversation with. Your only priority is finding a way out of here, nothing else."

I nodded at myself. *Good pep talk.* I used my finger as a toothbrush then sat back down on the bed. I looked at my band: 0804. *Great, almost an hour to kill.*

I spent the time trying to devise an escape plan but only came up with a few plausible ideas. My best option was to somehow get a message to the outside world. There had to be a phone somewhere, or someone's accidentally unlocked tablet. I made a mental note to keep my eyes open. The other option was to somehow be escorted aboveground, then make a run for it. It wasn't that great of a plan since I didn't have the slightest clue how to make it happen. Plus, I had already discovered I wasn't good at running.

At 0858, I decided to call it quits. *Ugh.* I did not want to go to class, but my odds of escaping did not increase by sitting in Roman's room all day. *Information is my friend.* I chanted to myself.

I made my way to the classroom and walked in at exactly 0900. Everyone, including Professor Gray, was already in their seats...and staring at me. I hurried to my chair, and couldn't help but notice that Stevie had followed through with her hair. It was chin length and flaming red with a few black streaks in the front. The room was silent for a few long seconds.

"Good morning, class. I'm sure *allll* of you did your reading assignment last night." Professor Gray paused and several girls giggled. Apparently, everyone noticed my abandoned manual. "We will start with some of the leadership in the Defiance. As I told you yesterday, the U.D. was founded in Europe and that is where our original headquarters still resides today. Unlike One-Global, the U.D. encourages individualization. We believe every country has its own unique people, resources, and problems. Therefore, each country should have its own separate policies and practices. The American chapter of the U.D. runs independently of the British U.D., which operates independently from the Russian U.D., etc. We are all united with the same purpose: overthrowing One-Global and restoring power to the countries.

"In America, our headquarters, called the Cerebrum, is located in Washington, D.C., where our nation's capital resided prior to the O.G. takeover. Once upon a time, each state had its own set of laws and separate governing body. We want to reinstate that structure, so the American U.D. operates in the same way. Each state has at least one Asylum with its own truly elected leader. Unlike One-Global, who assigns its leaders based on corrupt loyalty, but that's a whole different topic. This Asylum's leader is Roman Dilis. When it was decided that Oklahoma would be the site of the first Chaos, the Cerebrum sent some of their top officials, like Gage Levison, to oversee the preparations."

The girl with long, black hair spoke up, "Why Oklahoma? We are in the middle of nowhere. Wouldn't a more populated area have a bigger impact?"

"Excellent question, Charli." Professor Gray stood up and strolled across the room. "Oklahoma was chosen for several reasons. First, we wanted to do a smaller Chaos to see how the government would handle it. Would they cover it up or expose the U.D.'s presence in America? It also allowed us to see how easily the government could track us. If the Oklahoma chapter of the U.D. was compromised...no offense to you Okies, but it wouldn't be the biggest loss. And most importantly, was for recruitment purposes. We hoped to gain strong recruits once word of the U.D. spread locally after each Chaos. Historically, people in the central area of the country had more 'anti-big government' values. Oklahoma was one of the last places to accept the OneGlobal conglomerate."

"Figures," Stevie said. "We're the last ones to get on board with anything." Several girls giggled in agreement.

"Most of you didn't get to experience a true Chaos since yours was cut short, but let me explain to you the reasons behind it. Has anybody ever heard of chaos theory?" Professor Gray waited, gazing across the silent room. "I didn't think so. In short, it's an area of mathematics that proposes that small events happening now can have huge impacts in the future. In essence, the butterfly effect. Let me show you an example. Charli, will you please come up and assist me."

Charli walked to the front of the classroom where Professor Gray handed her a ping-pong ball. "This orb represents the path our society is on. Charli, I want you to drop the ball from wherever you would like, but do not move your hand after releasing."

Charli, who was tall already, reached as high as she could, and dropped the ball. It bounced around the room before settling beside the door.

"Now, this orb represents the path of society with the Defiance involved. Drop it in the exact same fashion," Professor Gray instructed.

Charli repeated the action. The second ball bounced

toward the back of the room, then rolled to a stop against the bookshelf.

"You may have a seat. Thank you. The orbs ended up in completely different areas of the class with minimal changes to the beginning circumstances." Professor Gray gathered the balls as she continued. "Under perfect circumstances with no changes at all, you would expect both of them to end up in the exact same location. Charli did her best to replicate the same result, but minute changes greatly impacted the destination of the second ball. This is the principle we stand behind. We believe the small changes we are making now can have a dramatic influence on our future. Out of Chaos, revolution is born. Most of you lived mere kilometers away from the first Chaos and never knew it happened. However, I bet Eve would agree it completely changed the lives of her and her family. And all of you are forever impacted because of the second Chaos. We believe these humble beginnings will eventually bring OneGlobal to its knees."

Stevie leaned forward in her desk. "How is that possible?"

"OneGlobal survives off predictability. They believe they know the future because they can anticipate their citizens' behavior. They depend on people remaining ignorant, mindless drones, who blindly do as they're told. The more random variables we can interject into the equation, the more likely we will derail OneGlobal off it's present course. What Chaos intends to do is empower citizens to think for themselves, therefore destroying the predictability OneGlobal thrives on."

I couldn't take it anymore. I had to say something. "Why the violence?" I blurted. "Why kill and hurt people?"

"What makes you think the U.D. kills people?" Professor Gray asked me. She wore a slight smile that made me think I was walking right into a trap.

"I've seen it!" I remembered Gideon telling me Roman's no death rule but the Defiance was much bigger than him.

"Where?" Professor Gray challenged.

"It's all over the news, OneGlobal told me and I saw it WITH MY OWN EYES!"

Professor Gray played with her necklace for a second, then crossed her arms. "Let's address one issue at a time. First, the more well-known topic. I'm sure all of you have streamed reports on the U.D. 'attacks' in Europe and Asia. To put it mildly, the media has not portrayed the Defiance in a positive light. I would concede that Kronies in other areas of the world are more violent, but not like the media would have you believe.

"Every single second of media that you have ever witnessed on television was scripted and approved by OneGlobal…everything. Every news report captured from a particular viewpoint. Every reality show filtered through their writers. Every song orchestrated with an agenda. They don't tell you the truth, they tell you what they want you to believe. The U.D. has actually become a scapegoat for OneGlobal. They use us to keep their record sparkling clean. If there is a random radiation plant catastrophe, they blame the Defiance, even though we had nothing to do with it. What's worse, we have intelligence that shows OneGlobal has even caused some of the destruction themselves."

"That makes no sense! Why would they do that?" I interjected, trying to keep my temper in check.

"To silence people who have discovered something that shouldn't get out, or murder someone questioning OneGlobal. I'm sure you think all of this is ridiculous, but a little part of you thinks it's possible because you've seen how the media works firsthand. The fact that the government told you we killed people carries absolutely no weight. Again, they tell you what they want you to believe and blame their mistakes on the Defiance. So, let's get back to the seeing 'with my own eyes' bit." Professor Gray used air quotes and mocked my voice. "You were there during the first Chaos. Please share your experiences with the class."

Everyone turned toward me. I swallowed hard. "I was at All-Mark with my mom a few months ago and..."

"Wait!" Hannah interrupted. "That All-Mark explosion in OKC was a Chaos?"

"We will come back to that," Professor Gray hushed. "Please continue."

"We were about to leave when a dead body was thrown through the glass doors. Then all of these boys ran inside. They had guns and bats and started destroying everything." Finally being able to talk about the attack to other people was both cathartic and stressful. For months, I had been dying to share my story, but I had never imagined doing so with the very group that caused the Chaos. "A man came up to us and said if we wanted to survive we had to act crazy. We were racing to escape when the jumbotron fell from the ceiling separating my mom and me. I was on my way to the exit when a boy with a gun stopped me. I danced like a ballerina so he let me go. Some more boys almost attacked me in the parking lot, but a stranger rammed them with their car. I ran home, my dad went to find my mom and my brother found..." I stopped. I didn't want to talk about the video of my mom. It was too personal. "He found it better to stay home with me."

"You saw a dead body fly through the glass? Could you tell if he was he breathing? Did you check his pulse?" Professor Gray asked.

I remembered the man looking up at me but I didn't share that tidbit of information. "No, but he was beaten to a bloody pulp. If he wasn't dead already, it was only a matter of time. Plus, gunfire was everywhere. There were explosions. People were screaming. The jumbotron almost crushed us!"

"But did you actually witness any deaths? Someone missing a head or anything where you could say, without a shadow of a doubt, that someone was murdered by the Defiance?"

I couldn't recall anything specific, but I felt certain people had died. "I...well, maybe I didn't see anyone die, but people must have."

"That's all of your proof?"

I racked my brain and came up blank. "Yes, but I know *my* life was threatened, several times. I honestly thought I was going to die."

"Sometimes fear for one's own life is the only thing that will force people to open their eyes and reevaluate their circumstances. Some Kronies believe this more than others, but either way, the body you witnessed thrown through the door was a known OneGlobal agent patrolling the area...and not just any normal agent. We had more dirt on him than I would care to share in the presence of younger students. We needed to take him out first or jeopardize the entire operation. People did die from the Chaos, but not from the Defiance. I'll come back to that." Professor Gray paced. "Eve, what happened after you made it home? Did the Docs come to speak with you?"

"Yes, they came and took my brother and me downtown to Central. They questioned me about everything, then took me to see my mom in the hospital. The Docs *rescued* her from the store."

"So, they questioned you for hours, then let you go home." Professor Gray sat on her desk. "Did you tell anyone else what happened?"

I could see the direction she was taking me. Part of me wanted to lie and protect OneGlobal. But the other part wanted my story to be heard. "No, I didn't."

"Really? Your entire world was just rocked. Your city was terrorized. Your mom was hospitalized, and you didn't mention it to anyone? Not even your dad or your best friend? Why?"

I balled my hands into fists. "They asked me not to."

Professor Gray played with her necklace. "Asked? Hmm. I'm not buying. What could they possibly say to convince you to keep quiet?"

My first thought was of my mother in her hospital room, when she hugged me and told me to pretend like nothing happened. I remembered the fear that resonated in her voice. I pushed the memory aside and went with my dad's response. "They told me it was better not to cause a panic. The situation was under control and the boys were in custody."

"Well, obviously that was a lie." Professor Gray chortled.

"Did anybody hear any mention of the U.D. when they heard about the 'accident' at All-Mark?"

Several girls murmured no.

"Eve, didn't you find it odd that the entire Chaos was covered up by the government? Consider this: from your perspective, you witnessed a group of savages run into a community building, cause all sorts of destruction, murder countless people, and then the media covers it up. Why?"

Stevie exclaimed, "Because they didn't want to admit to the Defiance's presence in America!"

"Precisely. Just think—if they are willing to cover that up, what else are they hiding from the public? I did say that people died in the Chaos, but not from the U.D. That night the Department of Compliance took everyone found at the scene into custody. They interrogated everyone, as they did with Eve. Anyone who did not agree to keep the secret was silenced."

Her statement hung heavily in the air for several long seconds.

"You mean, like, murdered?" Hannah asked.

"Some, yes. OneGlobal killed the ones wouldn't go along with the charade, or showed any sympathy to the Defiance. They also kept tabs to make sure you complied. So, Eve, every phone call you made, every text you sent, and every website you visited for the weeks following the Chaos were closely monitored."

My thoughts flew to Connor. He was doing his own research on the Defiance. *If the government really was tracking my activity, would they be tracking his too?* My stomach dropped.

"There's no way the government is murdering civilians.

That's not possible," I asserted, mostly to myself.

Professor Gray scoffed. "Why not? You think the lives of some negligible non-upper citizens matter compared to the O.G. saving face? If I proved it to all of you, would your opinion of the world change? And believe me, I have way more proof than the feeble arguments of Miss Price."

It was time to fight fire with fire. "What about when Gage pointed a gun in my face and almost pulled the trigger?" I thought I had her.

"You're still alive, aren't you?" Professor Gray said as she folded her arms across her chest. "Well, that covers chaos theory and the first Chaos. I want each of you to think about what the government told you and what really happened. What do you think is right? I don't think we have time to get into the second Chaos so we will save that for tomorrow. Now, let's go over more housekeeping business: rules and expected behaviors in the Asylum."

I didn't pay attention to the rest of the lesson. All I could think about was the safety of Connor and my family. *Could all of that be true?* I didn't know what to believe. Professor Gray could have been lying. She seemed to enjoy anything that would make me squirm. I mentally muddled through the possibilities until my stomach rumbled. I looked at the clock: 1235, almost twenty-four hours since I last ate.

Finally, Professor Gray wrapped up her monologue. "Looks like that's all for today. One last thing, who is Covertured?"

Most of the girls raised their hand. I noticed Stevie was one of the two that did not.

Professor Gray continued, "There are two, actually three, ways to enter the U.D. First is through voluntary recruitment. You seek us out or we seek you out and you willingly join the ranks. Not surprisingly, this is a very extensive process. We can't go up to every person on the street and ask them if they would like to join a movement to take down the government. When you are recruited, you automatically receive the right to become a Kronie once you prove your worth. The second way is via Coverture. This is when a member of the U.D. claims you as his own and takes you as his charge. This policy is based off an ancient English principle that, when a woman marries, or to put it in terms you'll understand 'True Matches', her rights and obligations are that of her husband. Basically, he is responsible for you and you are under his direction. Your Coverture will have a vital role in deciding your involvement and assignments in the Asylum, as well as determining if you will be offered membership as a Kronie. It's a big responsibility for a Kronie to take a Coverture. If the Coverture does something to get in trouble..." Professor Gray looked at me. "Then, the Kronie will be the one to deal with the consequences. He, in turn, will determine the Coverture's punishment. Coverture can only be used once. If a Kronie uses Coverture, they may not use it again. The third way to enter the Asylum is as a prisoner. In this case, you have no rights and you are at the mercy of the Defiance."

My stomach flipped as I realized what Professor Gray's statement meant. *Roman could only use Coverture one time and used it on me!* No wonder Gage was shocked when he did it.

Stevie straightened in her chair. "Can a woman take a Coverture?"

"Yes, but it's rare. Most females enter Asylums via Coverture and are unable to take their own until the one who claimed them dies. Also, you must be a Kronie and that's a little more difficult for women."

"That's messed up!" Stevie exclaimed. "Why is it harder for girls?"

Professor Gray opened her mouth to speak but hesitated. "The Defiance does not actively recruit women. The main reason being that having a large number of teenage boys and girls milling about distracts from our mission. Covertures may become Kronie, but, as you can imagine, that is a much slower process. We can dive into that tomorrow. Now, head to lunch before the cafeteria closes."

The class stood up and headed out the door. Professor Gray remained seated at her desk. I grabbed my manual and purposely avoided looking at her.

When we arrived at the cafeteria, most of the lunch crowd had already cleared out. Only two lines remained open and my stomach roared at the idea of food. I chose the closest line and grabbed a tray.

The girls gathered around a large table. As much as I didn't want to, I decided to join them. *Information is my friend.* I snagged a drink and was relieved to see an empty seat next to Hannah.

I sat across from Stevie, who was facilitating an intense conversation. "The first two were nothing. This next Chaos is *the* big one. The government won't be able to cover it up, and what's even more exciting is that Kronies from this facility will be chosen to help out."

Out—the word set off bells and whistles in my head. It was my chance to escape! A new strategy began to piece together. Somehow, I needed to be chosen for that Chaos. *If I could get everyone to believe I switched sides, there may be a possibility. Perhaps I could use Roman's position to my advantage. I needed—*

"Eve!" Stevie snapped her fingers in my face. "Are you with us?"

"Yeah, yeah. Sorry."

"You were completely zoned out."

I focused on my new strategy. "So, you were saying something about another Chaos. When is that happening? And where?"

Stevie eyed me suspiciously. "Why should I tell you anything, fire alarm girl? You're the one who ruined the last Chaos. Speaking of which, I don't want to wait until tomorrow. Let's hear the story, now."

I looked around the group. Once again, all eyes anxiously focused on me. I contemplated how to incorporate their attention into my plan. I needed them to accept me, especially Stevie. She seemed the most assimilated into the Defiance.

"Okay," I swallowed hard. "We were at the OneGlobal Center, watching the warmups, when the lights went out and the guy in the middle of the arena said a Chaos was starting—"

Stevie interrupted, "We were all there for that, remember? Get to the part where you screwed everything up."

Everything inside of me wanted to smart off to her, but somehow I was able to keep my cool. I smiled politely and continued. "You heard my story about the first Chaos. That's what I thought was happening again. I didn't want anyone to get hurt. So, I ran into the hall and noticed the fire alarm. A Kronie realized what I was doing and tried to stop me. He tackled me right as my fingers grabbed the lever. Like I said, I just wanted to get everyone out. If I had known it was going to be a peaceful Chaos, I wouldn't have done it."

"Don't feed us lies," Stevie scoffed. "You don't regret pulling that alarm one bit."

Too strong. I thought to myself. *Ease into your change of heart.*

"Well, if I hadn't pulled the alarm I wouldn't be here right now. That seems like a big enough reason to regret it." I smarted back.

Hannah spoke up, "How did you end up here?"

I looked around the table at my captive audience. Each girl gazed upon me with anticipation, even Stevie. If I was wanting to make some allies, I had my opportunity. "After I pulled the alarm, the guy who caught me threw me over his shoulder and hauled me down to the basement where everything was being coordinated. He dumped me on the ground and told everyone I was the one who pulled the alarm. Gage started screaming at me, but I stood my ground and yelled right back. It got pretty heated. Then Gage took out a gun and held it to my face. He was about to pull the trigger but I was Covertured."

"Ha!" Stevie exclaimed. "Who is the idiot who Covertured you?"

"Roman."

Stevie froze midway through a bite of her sandwich. Her eyes widened as she leaned forward. "Roman...Dilis? The guy in charge of this place?"

I nodded.

Stevie threw down her food. "You've got to be kidding me. The person who ruined everything was saved by the most important slash hottest guy in the Asylum. No wonder Roman's been in so much trouble lately."

"What do you mean?" I asked, already feeling myself getting defensive.

"Roman and Gage don't see eye to eye on a lot of things. But I heard that recently, there has been even more tension. I guess *you're* the reason why. I'm sure he's really regretting his decision," she smirked.

I couldn't stand the thought of Stevie judging Roman for his actions. "It's none of your business, but Roman saved my life. Gage was about to kill me!"

"Well, maybe Roman should have let him!" Stevie snapped, her volume rising rapidly. "People like you are the reason the world is screwed up right now. You're just another mindless government drone. I should have picked up on it immediately."

"E-Excuse me?" I stammered, shocked at the sudden turn in the conversation.

"I bet back at home your life revolved around TV and daydreaming about the Upper Class. In school, you're happily dumb because that's right where OneGlobal wants you. I bet you don't have many friends because you don't have the ability to carry on an intelligent conversation since you're unable to make any decisions for yourself." She stood to her feet, breathing heavily.

I couldn't believe her accuracy. "Hey! What is your problem..." I tried to raise my voice to match hers, but my throat dried as my vision blurred.

Stevie continued her diatribe. "You're the very thing we

are up against; idiots who want to remain idiots. That's the sad part. You have the opportunity to see what's really going on and you're choosing to stay blind. You mope around here thinking 'poor, pitiful me.' Well, you know what? It's true. You are poor and pitiful, but that's your own fault. Roman deserves better than you. He absolutely wasted—"

I jumped up from my chair and ran toward the exit as tears flowed down my cheeks. I wanted to go home so badly I could barely stand it. I hated the Asylum. I hated Stevie. I hated Professor Gray. I hated everything. I raced through the halls to Roman's room. I wanted to scream and cry, then dig my way out of that place with a spoon if I had to. I scanned my band and shoved the door open.

I collapsed onto the bed and sobbed. It felt good to cry. Everything I had been holding inside since that first Chaos, since I thought I'd lost my mother, since I was taken, rushed out from a broken dam. The fear, the grief, and the hopelessness I had been shoving down, all of it, welled up and poured from my eyes, hot and salty. I replayed Stevie's words over and over. I wasn't blind and I wasn't dumb! I mean, I passed most of my school classes. So what if I did cared about my TV shows? And who didn't pretend to be an Upper every once in a while?

All I wanted was to talk to my mom and have her tell me everything would be okay. I took a deep breath and tried to imagine her with me. When my emotional explosion settled down to a simmer, I heard a sound I didn't expect: the shower running.

I froze. If the shower was running, that meant someone was there. *It must be Roman!* The water shut off. My heart raced as I leapt to the mirror. *UUUGGGHHH*! I looked absolutely, positively horrible. The best I could do was to wipe the snot off my face.

I heard movement in the bathroom. I hopped onto the bed, curled my legs to my chest and tried to steady my breathing.

"Eve? Are you out there?" Roman asked.

"Yes?" my voice cracked. *Ugh, why do I have to be so awkward?*

The bathroom door slowly slid open. I peeked through my tangled hair and my breath caught in my throat as I took him in. Roman stood in gym shorts and a white t-shirt that clung to his damp chest, a towel slung over his shoulder. It had only been a day, but I forgot just how attractive he was. I dropped my face to avoid staring.

He took a step into the room. "Sorry, Gid's room doesn't have a shower and I thought I had time before you got back from...are you okay?"

I focused on the ground. "I'm fine," I said, doing my best to appear strong but failing miserably. My red eyes and shaky voice surely betrayed me.

Roman furrowed his brow but continued, "Ooookay... sorry I haven't been here. I wanted to stick around and help you get acclimated but it's been absolute chaos around here. Ha. No pun intended. I, uh, picked you up some stuff on our scouting trip last night." He reached down and handed me a backpack I hadn't noticed before. "There are some toiletry items. I figured you didn't want to smell like a boy all the time. Some clothes. I had to guess on the sizes. We have an area stockpiled with clothes, but I'd be surprised if there was anything for girls."

I set the bag beside me on the bed. "Thanks."

Roman pulled the chair out from the desk and sat on it backward. "So, how have your first couple of days at the Asylum been? Besides being kidnapped, taken away from your family, and imprisoned by total strangers?"

I smiled slightly. "You forgot being hated by everyone, and ruining the second Chaos."

"Yeah, besides that, how's it going?" He grinned as he dried his hair with the towel.

I rolled my eyes. "It's amazing. Everything I've ever wanted in a radical, child-abducting, anti-government cult."

Roman flashed a flawless smile. "Perfect. I'll let my superiors know we are receiving perfect scores from our abductees."

I giggled again. It was nice to joke around with someone for a change. I knew he was a Kronie, just like the rest of them, but deep down I wanted to believe he was different. My gut told me to trust him.

He reached down and picked up the brown, oblong object I found under the bed. He threw it up in the air and caught it.

"What is that?" I asked

"This?" He tossed it at me. I instinctively blocked my face with my hands. The object bounced off my shoulder and fell to the floor.

Roman laughed. "That is a football. It used to be a sport, but the government outlawed it sixty years ago."

I nonchalantly combed through my hair with my fingers. "They outlawed a sport? Why?"

"According to the O.G., it was too dangerous and caused brain damage, which is somewhat true. But the

real reason they nixed it is because they don't want their citizens involved in any aggressive or violent activities. Just another way OneGlobal controls the world under the pretense of protecting its citizens."

"How do you play football?" I asked.

"Basically, there's a big field and one team tries to get the football to one end while the other team tries to stop them by tackling the person with the ball."

"It *does* sound too violent." I agreed with OneGlobal yet again.

"You just think that because you're used to non-contact sports. Even your version of soccer is much tamer than it used to be, but football's a blast. You'll see."

My stomach let out an embarrassingly loud growl.

"Are you hungry?"

Starving. I shrugged. "A little. I skipped lunch."

"Alright, let's go get you some food." He stood up.

I shook my head. "It's too late. The cafeteria closed already. We have to wait until dinner."

Roman smirked. "You know, it's kind of cute when you act like you know more about this place than I do."

He opened the door and held it for me. I resisted looking at myself in the mirror and stepped into the hallway.

"Being the boss does come with its perks," Roman said as he scanned his band on the cafeteria's door. I followed him as he made his way to the back by the food lines. He buzzed us through another door and we walked into a huge kitchen.

Roman opened the industrial sized fridge and looked inside. "We have to stick to the basics around here. Sorry, we don't have anything fancy. Let's see what we can come up with: leftover spaghetti from yesterday, peanut butter and jelly is always a valid option, or I make one mean grilled cheese."

"I'll take a PB and J," I said, even though I wanted to pick the grilled cheese. "Where's the stuff? I can make it."

"No, I'll get it. You've had a rough day. Pull up a stool and relax."

Rough day? Is it that obvious? Embarrassed, I sat down at the big island in the center of the kitchen.

Roman walked inside a large pantry and came out holding a loaf of bread and peanut butter. "Unfortunately, once again, my time is limited. I have another meeting soon, but I thought this would be a good chance for you to ask some more questions. Re-education is a great class, but it can be overwhelming."

"I think Professor Gray has a personal vendetta against me," I blurted without thinking.

Roman shook his head as he began making my lunch. "Nah. Emily is just very passionate about the U.D."

"If you say so. I just don't get this place."

He furrowed his brow. "Well, that's why I wanted to talk with you and explain anything that I can. I know you didn't come here under the most ideal circumstances. I'd imagine you still hate all of us, myself included, and just want to go back to your old life, which is completely understandable. I wish things had gone down differently, but this is the situation we find ourselves in, so let's try to make the best of it." He slid the completed sandwich in front of me. "Hit me with your first question."

"Can I go home?"

Roman laughed. "Hmmmm. Nice try, but no. Too big

of a risk that you'd run straight to the Docs and bust our whole operation."

"What if I promised not to say a word? I could just show up at the stadium and say I got lost during the fire drill!"

Roman nodded. "I like the creativity. I'll keep that in mind, but no. Still too risky. Next topic."

I wanted to know more about him. He seemed like a nice guy, but he was on the wrong team. "Why did you join the U.D.?"

"Since we're short on time, I'll give you just one reason. My mom was a chemical engineer for OneGlobal. When she discovered all the chemicals they were developing and using in foods to influence the public, she did some research and turned against OneGlobal, hence the mostly basic food here."

"What do you mean using chemicals to influence the public?"

"Sometimes the government puts substances in the food and water to alter people's behavior or feelings. For example, after the first Chaos, your community's water was chock full of chemicals to decrease anxiety and fear. Or after OneGlobal announces some huge change in laws or policy, chemicals are added to make people feel positive and happy. They also load most food with stuff to decrease independent thinking, but we have an inside source that helps us pick out the least contaminated food. It takes a couple of days to get out of your system, but I'm sure you'll start to feel your head clearing up soon."

It was a battle not to roll my eyes. "Why would One-Global do that?"

"They're all about control. They will do whatever they

can to keep people from asking questions."

"Speaking of control, you guys are a bunch of hypocrites." I held up my wrist. "You cut my arm open to take out a 'tracker' only to put a new one on my wrist?"

Roman shook his head. "We don't track you. It's against policy to track any member of the Defiance without their knowledge or consent."

I didn't know if I believed him. I tapped my wrist. I was running out of time and I didn't know when I would have another opportunity to talk with Roman. *Time to act interested in this place.* "Gideon said something about the second Chaos being different than the first. How so?"

Roman let out a big sigh and pulled up a stool across from me. "After the decision was made at Cerebrum to let Oklahoma be the first site of Chaos, some Kronies believed we should mimic the more violent Chaos in Europe to make sure Americans made the association. Others thought we should try to educate the public about the government's corruption and control. After much deliberation, it was decided that the first Chaos would be like Europe, while a second Chaos would be different."

"Which side were you on?" I asked as I finished my sandwich.

"The education side. Violence may be necessary at times, but I think we just need to show America what's really happening in order to make a change. Let people think for themselves and choose a side."

For the first time, a tiny part of me felt the slightest bit guilty for pulling the fire alarm. The second Chaos was Roman's choice, and we would never know if it was the better strategy. I bit my lip and worked up the courage to ask the selfish question burning in the back of my mind.

"So, is that why you used your one Coverture on me? Because you favor education over violence?"

Roman didn't answer immediately. He looked down at the floor as he thought. My nervous hands broke out in sweat as I waited for his answer.

"I didn't think you deserved to die. Even though I was technically in charge of that Chaos, I could tell Gage was really about to lose it. Believe me, I was as mad as anyone that all our work had just been rui...compromised. But, after I heard your story and why you did it...I thought you were brave and I saw potential in you." Roman's face flushed a slight shade of pink. "Anyway, it's almost time for me to go. Anything else you're just dying to know?"

Slightly embarrassed by his compliment, I hurried on with my questions. "Stevie said that you were in trouble with Gage lately. Is that because of me?"

"Honestly...yes. He thought I undermined him in front of everyone when I Covertured you. He thought it was 'blatantly disrespectful,' and that I did it out of pure spite. He was so cocky when the fire alarm went off. He thought I was just getting him back."

"What do you mean?"

"During the planning process we discussed whether we should disable the fire alarms. Gage wanted to shut them down, but I was adamant that we leave them activated for safety reasons...epic fail." He gave me a half-hearted smile as he took my plate to the sink.

I felt horrible. I had single-handedly stopped the second Chaos, ruined the "peaceful" plan, and caused Roman to be in trouble for wanting extra safety measures. It was a good thing I finished my sandwich because I wasn't hungry anymore.

Roman picked up his stool and sat it next to mine. I felt my face warm. Thankfully, he took it only as me being upset. "Listen, don't feel bad for what you did. I'd do the same exact thing if I were in your shoes. You were protecting people and that is the most admirable thing anyone could ever do. I know some people are going to be mean and treat you differently, but just ignore them. If they can't understand why you did it, then they're the idiots. I really hope you can look past all the negativity and appreciate this place for what it really is…somewhere you have the freedom to do what *you* want. And if you don't want to be a part of this…then I understand, but you have to stay here until it's safe for you to go back." He stood up abruptly. "I have to go. I'll walk you back to the room."

I realized I had been holding my breath the whole time he was next to me. Roman went into a pantry and came out with a brown paper bag. "Dinner and snacks, in case you don't feel like getting out again."

We walked through the empty cafeteria. I knew I only had time to ask one more thing. I chose the most important. "Is there any way you can let my family know I'm okay? So they won't worry. I can't stand the thought of them thinking I'm hurt…or worse"

Roman shook his head. "I wish I could do that, but it's nearly impossible. First off, it's very hard to get a message out to people without it being intercepted. The government can easily access all outside communications. I'm certain they are actively monitoring all incoming data your family receives. Sending them a message would put an even bigger target on your family and, trust me, you don't want the government to show more interest in your family. Second, there's too big of a risk that your family would go straight to the D.O.C."

I stopped walking and grabbed his arm. "You can trust my family! If you told them not to say anything I promise they would keep it a secret."

We were in the main hallway by the field. Roman looked around to make sure no one was within earshot. "Eve, I truly wish I could help you out. I really do, but there's no way. Trust me. The less they know, the better."

We continued to his room. I thought I would give it one more try. "You can trust my brother. After the first Chaos, he started researching the U.D., even going to illegal websites. He's also a genius. You could encode some sort of message and I know he would figure it out. Please...I just want him to know I'm alive."

"My hands are tied. If there was something I could do, I would do it. Recently, we had a Kronie reach out to his own family, and it didn't go so well." Roman sighed as he scanned the door and held it open for me. "I don't know when I'll see you again. You picked a very busy time in the U.D. to get kidnapped," he winked, "but if you need me, send a text through your band."

"I picked a bad time? My apologies." As disappointed as I was about my failed attempt to reach my family, I couldn't help but be slightly smitten with him. If he wasn't a Kronie, I would definitely consider submitting my dating application for him. I took my doggy-bag and stepped inside the room. "Thanks for lunch and dinner. Have fun plotting the government's demise."

Roman laughed. "That's the spirit. You're falling for us already. Have a good evening." He let the door shut with a soft click.

I turned, leaned against the door, and slowly sank to the ground. My head spun with new information, causing me to reevaluate my life. Did I feel guilty for pulling the fire alarm even though I still thought it was the right thing to do? Was I starting to believe the government could possibly be a controlling, corrupt system? Did I have a slight crush on the person who kidnapped me? Was any of that as important as getting back to my family?

I knew the answer to the last question. Escape was still my number one priority. I closed my eyes and hit my head against the wall. *You're an idiot, Eve. You wasted your time with him on stupid, selfish questions.* I should have asked about the upcoming Chaos and why had no one mentioned the "master plan" that my mom talked about in her video. Instead, I fished for affirmation about why Roman saved me. Stevie's words echoed in my brain. *Roman deserves better than you.* I took in a deep breath and slowly released it. *Don't think about that. Focus on what you learned today. How can that help you?* I needed to take all the data I gathered and mold it into my own master plan.

I picked myself off the ground and went over to the desk. I took out some scratch paper and a pencil. I attempted to write GOALS on the top of the page but it was surprisingly difficult. I had never actually written anything more than signing my initials on my school tablet with my finger. *This is going to take a while. Good thing I don't have any other plans.*

For the next eight painstaking hours, I wrote out

everything I knew about the U.D., possible escape plans, and accomplices. By the end of my brainstorming session, I listed out four main goals in increasing difficulty.

Goal one: Learn the Asylum. I should have the place memorized as well as the Kronies; each room, hallway, and passage. In case of some type of power failure, I would know the nearest exit route. I toyed with the idea of setting a fire and forcing an evacuation. But the odds of outrunning a large group of teenage boys were basically zero.

Goal two: Befriend Stevie. I was not looking forward to achieving that goal. I knew Stevie couldn't stand me, and the feeling was mutual, but she seemed to know the most about the Defiance. She was also the most influential person in my class. If she trusted me enough to give up all the insight she gained, it would greatly increase my chances of escape.

Goal three: Get a message to my family. I didn't know where to begin, but I needed to let them know I was okay. I couldn't imagine the compounding stress they were dealing with every passing day. The thought of them searching for me in vain made my heart want to burst.

Goal four: Be invited to the third Chaos. I realized that was almost impossible and I had absolutely no idea how I would accomplish it. If I wasn't able to find a way to exit the Asylum on my own, I needed to be taken out. My best strategy was to slowly convince people that I believed the U.D.'s propaganda. Maybe Professor Gray would prove she was a better teacher than anyone thought if she was able to convert me.

If Stevie already knew about the next Chaos, I probably didn't have too much time. Every minute mattered. Every conversation needed to serve a purpose. Every moment alone needed to be spent increasing my knowledge of the Asylum or perfecting my strategy.

I tapped my band for the time: 2146. I stretched out in the chair and looked down at my work. I was actually pleased with my progress. Even Connor would have been proud. I didn't feel any different but maybe my chemical-free diet was helping me think after all.

I folded the papers together and looked around for a hiding spot. My first thought was the box of pictures, but that seemed too obvious. Plus, I didn't know how often Roman looked at them. I tore a small hole in the top corner of the mattress and stored my plans inside. I pulled the sheets back and threw my body onto the bed.

I was exhausted. It had been the longest day of my life, but having some type of strategy pacified my nerves. I quickly found myself reminiscing on how Roman looked after stepping out of the shower and him pulling his chair next to mine. I relived every conversation. "You know, it's kind of cute when you act like you know more about this place than I do." I know he didn't specifically say that *I* was cute, but that's what he meant, right?

I fell asleep with a smile on my face.

CHAPTER 8

KRONIES

My band woke me up at 0800 the next morning. For the first time since my arrival at the Asylum, I felt excited. Rolling my new strategy over in my head, I took a quick shower with my floral scented body wash, then dumped the clothes Roman brought me onto the bed. I looked at the tags to check the sizes and gasped. They were Designer! There were two types of clothes in the world: normal, affordable, All-Mark brand clothes; and Designer brand clothes, worn almost exclusively by the Upper Class.

I bit my lip and weighed my options as I rubbed the plush fabric between my fingers. On one hand, I didn't want to stand out, and wearing something that high-end would definitely make me stand out. On the other hand, Roman must have gone through some trouble getting outfits of that caliber and I didn't want to insult him. Also, it was quite possibly the only time in my life I had a chance to have Designer material touching my skin. I decided it wouldn't hurt to at least try them on. I chose a pair of slim jeans and a gray insulated pullover. Those two items alone were easily worth over 2,000 Credits.

I quickly changed into my new outfit and checked myself in the mirror. From the neck down, I looked like a model. The fit was perfect. I fervently rifled through the other clothes: all Designer, all my size. *Natalie would absolutely freak if she knew what I was wearing. Heck, she may even volunteer to be kidnapped if they dressed her in Designer.*

I bowed to my reflection. "Well, good evening Madam President Mendax. Thank you for inviting me to N.Y.C. Escaping from the Defiance was simple, really." I spun around in the mirror again, awestruck. I would have killed for some makeup to balance out my appearance. I made a mental note to bring up the topic with Stevie since she always wore flawless eye shadow. *Maybe that could be an entry point for our faux-friendship.*

I convinced myself the outfit was comfortable, practical and not too over-the-top. Roman had some great fashion sense. Hopefully looking the part would help me act the part. It was the new me: a bold woman, who took advantage of every opportunity. I laughed at myself as I tapped my band, 0835. I needed to hurry to breakfast before class. I rushed out the door...after taking one last look in the mirror.

I paused just outside the cafeteria and took a deep breath. The possibility of everyone staring at me as I entered made me want to vomit, but I had to integrate myself as part of my strategy. *You can do this, Eve. You're not going to gather intel by standing in the hallway.*

After taking a breakfast burrito tray, I looked around and recognized the younger girl, Hannah, sitting with two other girls. To my relief, Stevie wasn't with them. I knew

I had to face her at some point, but I was completely okay with delaying that goal for as long as possible.

"Good morning, everyone," I chirped as I sat down.

The girls mumbled hello, then an awkward silence followed. I picked at my food, trying to think of what to say.

Hannah spoke up. "I think it's crap what Stevie said to you yesterday."

"Thanks," I replied, a little surprised. "Sorry, I stormed out. I was a little overwhelmed already, and she sent me over the edge."

The girl with long black hair joined the conversation. "I don't blame you. This place is so different than the real world. We are all freaked out, to say the least, but I wouldn't worry about Stevie."

Hannah nodded in agreement. "Charli is right. Stevie doesn't realize she's the only one who chose to be here. Anyway, she's just jealous."

"Jealous? Jealous of what?" I asked, shocked at the idea.

"You," Hannah said as she popped a grape into her mouth.

"Me? Why, because I'm the most hated person in the Asylum?"

Charli giggled. "No, because you're cute and you're Covertured by Roman Dilis."

"So? What does that have to do with anything?" I looked down at my tray to hide my pink cheeks. Just mentioning Roman made me anxious.

Hannah sucked in a breath of realization. "You don't know the connotation with Coverture, do you?"

I shook my head.

Charli explained. "Stevie told us all about it the first night. Basically, it's like picking a girlfriend. Most guys choose someone they find attractive during a Chaos and bring them back to their home base."

"Yeah," Hannah added. "And since they only get one the entire time they are in the Defiance, it's a big deal to pick someone."

I could feel the blush in my cheeks spreading to the rest of my face. "But Roman didn't just pick me out of the crowd. He did it to save my life."

"Either way," Hannah shrugged, "the highest ranking guy in Oklahoma picked you to be his one and only. We're pretty sure Stevie has a huge crush on him."

If I didn't like Stevie before, I borderline hated her after hearing she liked Roman. However, I needed to get the attention off of me before the heat culminating in my head combusted. "What about you guys? Were you Covertured to be a girlfriend?"

Charli went to grab a drink but the girl with short blonde hair nodded. "Yeah, Gunner picked me during the evacuation at the Chaos. He said he didn't know when he would get to go on another mission so he decided to find someone at the last second. Winner winner chicken dinner and here I am. I don't see him very much. I'm pretty sure he doesn't even know my name is Becky."

I turned to Hannah. "What about you?"

"Yeah, I was, but I'm not the normal."

"What do you mean?" I asked.

"I'm the youngest girl to ever be Covertured. Professor Gray pulled me aside the first day and told me she needed to explain some things to me. In order to have the ability to Coverture someone, you have to be a full-fledged Kronie. Most boys don't achieve that status until fifteen or sixteen. But the boy who picked me, Sherlock, is super smart and was inducted early. It's actually kind of funny. He was so excited to be able to pick a girl, he picked the first one he saw…me."

Charli rejoined the table. "No, you've got to tell the whole story."

Hannah smiled timidly. "I was with my mom in line for popcorn, when Sherlock and some boys walked around the corner. He pointed at me and said 'Coverture.' I had no idea what he was talking about. Then all the lights went out and some older boy grabbed me from behind and dragged me into a stairwell. Sherlock kept yelling at them to be gentle. They shoved a bandana in my mouth and told me I would be safe if I didn't make any noise. Sherlock kept apologizing over and over and promising everything would be okay. Then the fire alarm went off and the older kid received a message to evacuate. They carried me to a van, put me in the back, and now I'm here. All the older boys kept congratulating him, but Sherlock felt horrible. He cried the whole way to the Asylum."

"Why did he feel bad?" I asked.

"He said he didn't think about me having to leave my mom and family. He just thought it would be cool to be the youngest boy with a Coverture. Professor Gray said they will look into setting an age limit."

Charli nudged Hannah. "But Sherlock is *the* sweetest. Tell her!"

Hannah flushed. "He checks on me about a million times a day. He writes me notes and gives me a flower every night before bed."

"That's…sweet." I wondered what was normal, for a

Coverture to act more like Gunner or Sherlock. Roman had chosen me under unique circumstances so I couldn't decipher what to expect. "What about Stevie?"

Charli rolled her eyes. "She was recruited by her brother, Gideon."

"What?" I almost choked on my burrito. "Gideon? The one with long black hair? The head of the Engineering Department?"

"Yep," chimed Hannah. "We wondered why he was sitting with you the first day, but now we know Gideon is Roman's right-hand man."

I sat in a fog as the new information rolled over me. Gideon was one of the nicest people I'd ever met. I trusted him, almost considered him a friend, and believed he really wanted me to succeed in the Asylum. Stevie was the exact opposite.

"We better get to class," Charli said as she stood up. "Oh, and by the way, your outfit is adorable. Very fashion forward."

I followed the girls down the hall in a daze, still trying to process that Gideon and Stevie were siblings. I turned into the classroom to see Stevie eyeing me, a vicious smirk plastered across her face. Bile hit the back of my throat, but I choked it down. *Stick to the plan. You need her on your side.* The only thing that made the thought of talking to her bearable was the fact that I was using her. Well, that and knowing she was jealous of me.

I slid into my seat behind her. "Can we talk?"

"About what?" she asked without turning around.

"About yesterday." I paused to make sure the rest of the chatter had died down. I wanted everyone to hear my rehearsed speech. "We got off on the wrong foot. I should have told you what I did when we first met. I'm sorry. I want to get past this and be friends. I really respect you and the passion you have for the Defiance."

I stopped and bit my lip. I had planned on saying more but didn't want to oversell it. I didn't believe one word except that we got off on the wrong foot. But the ball was in her court, and all the other girls knew it. I hoped her desire to be a leader would force her to accept the olive branch.

Stevie twisted in her chair. "Listen, Fire Alarm, yesterday—"

Professor Gray entered the room and cleared her throat. "Good morning, everyone. I'm afraid I have some bad news. There will be no more class."

"What? Why?" Stevie called out.

Professor Gray piled her long hair into a bun on the top of her head. "As some of you may know, the third Chaos is coming up and even though it will not take place in Oklahoma, our Asylum has the opportunity to help out with the preparations. Originally, this was planned for next month but due to complications, our time of planning is significantly decreased. This will be the biggest and most important Chaos yet. It will establish our undeniable presence in America. So, as much as I love this class, I'm sorry to say that I am needed elsewhere and will be unable to continue your re-education."

Hannah raised her hand. "Can someone else teach the class?"

"The people qualified to instruct this class will be working on the next Chaos, and the others…I don't trust. I'm very protective of my girls. Ideally, we would reconvene after the Chaos but that is to be determined."

"What are we supposed to do?" Stevie complained.

"There are several options." Professor Gray fidgeted with her necklace. "You could continue class on your own. Meet together every morning and discuss topics of interest. I've written several papers on the injustices of OneGlobal. You could read these along with your handbook and selections from the library. This class is all about discovering information then forming your own conclusions. Alternatively, you could take a different course offered here at the Asylum. Specks is our class organizer and his office is two rooms down the hall. He can tell you what classes are available. Normally, we have a wide array of classes from True American History and Art Appreciation to Martial Arts and Computer Hacking. However, there may be fewer offerings due to the preparations. Another option would be to volunteer to help the Defiance. This may be too soon for some of you, but if interested, talk to me this afternoon and I can see if we can find a place for you. The last option would be to stay locked up in your room, making the worst of your circumstance and wasting any potential you possess." Professor Gray looked directly at me during her last sentence.

I decided to make another calculated move and slowly raised my hand.

"Yes, Eve?" Professor Gray asked, surprise filling her voice.

"You said the first Chaos was completely covered up by

the media, and I agree. I was wondering what the media said about the second Chaos. Was it recognized at all?"

Professor Gray eyed me suspiciously for a second before answering. "It was easily and completely covered up: a fire alarm malfunction caused an evacuation during a preview of the halftime show called 'Chaos.'"

"So what's going to keep the government from doing the same thing this time?" I set my bait, wanting to draw out as much information as possible.

"Well, this one will take place on live television. We have our top techs working day and night to make sure we *will* be heard and—"

"Will this be peaceful or violent?" I interrupted.

"The demonstration itself will be peaceful, but we will do what is necessary to make sure our message is disseminated to the world. Now, if that's all the questions..." She glared at me as if daring me to ask another. I kept my mouth shut. "I'm needed at Command. I wish you all the best and hopefully, I'll see you helping around the Asylum." She looked around the room once more, then rushed out the door. We sat in silence for several long moments.

"Well," Stevie said as she stood up. "I'm going to go see how I can help. If anyone wants to join me, feel free." She walked out the door, followed by Charli then the rest of the class.

Hannah paused in the doorway. "Are you coming with us?"

"Nah. I'm not sure I'm ready to join the cause just yet."

Hannah nodded slightly. She started to leave then hesitated again.

"You should go," I said. "Keep me updated on what's

going on. Maybe that will help me figure out what I should do."

Hannah smiled and ran after the others.

I sighed heavily and sunk down into my seat. Going with the group would provide excellent information, but may look too suspicious. Plus, one fake interaction with Stevie was exhausting enough for one day. At least I had somehow befriended Hannah and could use her to my advantage. I was surprised at how easily the girls fell in line with Stevie and sided with the very people who kidnapped them. But then again, that's what we had done our entire lives. Do what we were told without question. *Woah, that sounded too much like the Defiance's propaganda.* I shook the thought from my head.

I decided to take some books from the library and wait until lunch to do some more scouting. Maybe if people saw me carrying around old textbooks, they would think I was opening my mind. I walked to the back wall and scanned the shelves. Unfortunately, I didn't find any books about lock picking or how to escape from an underground cult. I decided on a couple of history books, a quilting book, and an art book since I didn't know exactly what "art" was or how to could study it.

I took my selections and meandered to some old bleachers in the corner of the field. To my surprise, the Asylum was pretty busy. Groups of boys hurried up and down the corridors. I wondered if it was that way every morning or just because of the next Chaos.

I passed my morning by pretending to read while observing my surroundings. Twice, I witnessed a small group of boys leave the Asylum through the tunnel to the garage. One set was dressed in dark colors and wore large backpacks. The other consisted of older boys all dressed in Designer and carrying briefcases. I watched longingly as they simply used their bands to escape. I contemplated hiding by the door or developing some way to prevent the door from shutting. Other than that, I didn't gather much helpful information. Several packs of boys stopped to throw a football and Gideon walked through a couple of times, checking his band and shaking his head. *Maybe I could ask him how to get involved.*

A little before lunch, I saw Hannah making her way across the field. I yelled for her to come over. "Well, how'd it go? Did you get some crazy important job in the next Chaos?"

"Ha," Hannah laughed. "Not at all. It was a big flop. Stevie took us to Command and asked for Gideon. He came out looking all annoyed that his younger sister was interrupting him. He told Stevie he didn't know what to do with us and sent us to the cafeteria to wait. After an hour, Professor Gray shows up and says she is thrilled that we want to help out and assigned us all chores."

"Chores?"

"Yes! Apparently, you can't be involved in any of the actual Chaos stuff until you are a full-fledged Kronie. But Professor Gray said we could help the Defiance by taking over the jobs that are vacant while real Kronies are helping in the Chaos. Stevie acted excited about it, but as soon as Professor Gray left, she was all mad saying she should already be a Kronie."

"What are your chores?"

Hannah rested her chin in her hands. "We don't know

yet. We report to the kitchen after lunch to get our assignments."

"Man, I'm so glad I decided not to go with you guys. The last thing I want to do is clean dishes all evening."

"No kidding."

"You gonna go?" I asked.

Hannah shrugged. "I don't know. I don't really want to, but I don't want to be on Stevie's bad side."

"I think it's best not to be on anyone's bad side around here. Although, I can't seem to follow my own advice. Maybe you should go and just see what they want you to do." I sighed heavily and picked up my books. "Want to head to lunch?"

"Sure," Hannah said as she hopped up.

We picked our trays and sat with the girls already at a table. Stevie was in the middle of a rally speech. "I'm telling you, just trust me on this. We have to work our way up. Once they see that we are ready to help with the little tasks, they'll move us to more important assignments."

I thought she was trying to convince herself more than anyone else. All the other girls were zoned out. I realized none of us had interacted with technology in days. When you're used to spending fourteen hours a day on social media, your brain goes into shutdown mode after quitting cold turkey.

Stevie turned her attention to me. "I noticed you didn't volunteer to help, Fire Alarm."

I chose my words carefully. "No, I haven't made up my mind about this place. Some things make sense, but I'm not ready to join yet."

"Give me a break. Everyone knows you hate it here,"

Stevie said, crossing her arms.

"I'm not going to lie, I don't like it here. But that doesn't mean I'm completely ignoring what the Defiance is telling us. I'm also not going to believe everything they say just because they said it. I want to make my own conclusions. Isn't that what this whole big uprising is about? Thinking for yourself?"

Stevie frantically shook her head. "We don't have time for that right now. We need to work our way up as soon as possible. The next Chaos could start at any minute." I could hear the stress in her voice.

As much as I wanted to tell her to calm down since she wasn't that important, I refrained and tried a more diplomatic approach. "I get that, but none of us volunteered to be here. You have been researching and following the U.D. when we didn't even know it existed. Of course, they're not going to give brand new people vital roles in the next Chaos. But I wouldn't be surprised if they came up to you privately to see if you want to be more actively involved, especially when they see you leading all of us."

Stevie opened her mouth to retaliate but stopped. She furrowed her brow for several seconds. "Well, either way, I'm willing to do whatever is needed to help out. I really believe in what the Defiance is doing and I hope you decide to join us...all of you."

That was progress. I needed to keep moving forward. "What's your story? Why are you so passionate about the Defiance?"

Stevie's shoulders relaxed. "Well, I found out about the U.D. through Gideon. He was recruited about two years ago. While they were in discussions with him, I found some of their correspondence letters. I researched the Defiance and fell in love. Ever since I was little, I felt like I didn't fit in with 'the system'. I don't like being told what I have to do and when I have to do it. I know the schools preach all the reasons why the OneGlobal way is superior and OneGlobal only has your best interests at heart, but I never bought it. I started doing an investigation on the darknet Gideon set up at our house, and everything I feared about the government was true. They lie to us. They manipulate us and control us in ways you wouldn't even believe."

"Try me," I challenged.

"We can all agree the O.G. dictates what the media covers and what it hides. You've all witnessed that. But the whole dating system is completely rigged."

"What? How?" Becky blurted.

Stevie smiled at her captive audience, which included me. "The whole dating application and compatibility questionnaire is a sham. Your matches aren't based on who you'll fall in love with. It's who OneGlobal wants you to be with. They have dedicated matchmakers that select your potential matches based on your genetics and loyalty to the O.G. They match someone with a tendency to be more Noncompliant with a diehard OneGlobal lover. Then they mix your DNA to make sure you won't make a baby with some weird genetic defect."

"That's impossible," I scoffed. "We all know how dating works. Once your application is approved, you're set up with multiple people and you both get to *pick* who your True Match is."

"That's exactly what they want you to think. Once they

assign your spouse, they set you up with people that seem compatible at first, but you would never choose as your True Match. It gives you the illusion of choice but it's already selected for you. It's much more complicated than that, but you get the gist."

Stevie's accusations blew my brain. I would have given anything just to talk to Natalie about the subject. She knew the dating system like the back of her hand. She would have been able to find holes in Stevie's story. I brought my focus back to Stevie's continued examples of government control.

"...and don't get me started on the chemicals in the food and water, especially in the school system. Intelligent kids that act and test like they will become model citizens get food to enhance their brain function. Kids that are smart but have the potential to rebel get food laced with drugs to stunt their mental capacity and chill them out."

"No way!" Hannah said. "All the lunches are the same. Everyone gets the same meal."

Stevie shook her head. "They may look the same, but they have different chemicals inside. How did your cafeteria work? How did you get your food?"

Hannah shrugged. "I got in line, scanned my phone and the boxed lunch came out of the automated food slot like everyone else."

Stevie smirked. "That's how they do it. When you scan your phone, it tells the system which type of box to give out. I didn't really believe it either until I hacked the system and looked up my file."

"You looked into your file?" I interjected. "That's highly illegal! You could get kicked out of school or even go to prison."

Stevie rolled her eyes. "I thought the risk was worth it, and I was right. Plus, don't you think it's a bit harsh that it's *illegal* to look at your own file. I asked the school administrator why I couldn't see my file and she told me it may 'interfere with my learning track. If I saw what direction my life was headed too early my own prejudices would get in the way of reaching my full potential.' What's funny is when I broke into my file, I found a note indicating I had been asking about my file."

"What else was in your file?" Charli asked.

"Tons of information. All my test scores, how much time I spent in each textbook, who I sat beside the most, all my internet searches, all my social media usage. You name it, they had it. Finally, there was a big spreadsheet thing with all my information analyzed and packaged together. Turns out, I was at high risk for delinquency and had the potential to carry anti-government sentiments. They sure got that right. Ha!"

"Could you look up our files?" I asked.

Hannah agreed. "Yeah, I would love to find out what the government thinks about me."

"I wish it were that easy," Stevie grumbled. "It took me a good six months to break into mine without getting caught. I would have to start from scratch to look up someone else. Plus, I'm not *that* good at hacking. I had Gideon help me start before he left."

All the girls' bands beeped at once. Charli stood up. "Looks like they already set a reminder for our first volunteer shift. Better get to it."

I smirked. "Well, you ladies have fun cleaning the

bathrooms. I'm going to go take a nap."

The girls slunk toward the kitchen as I headed to Roman's room in a good mood. Just thinking about Stevie scrubbing dirty toilets brought a smile to my face.

After my knocks went unanswered, I unlocked the room and slowly opened the door. No Roman. Disappointed, I set my books on the desk and sprawled out on the bed. Maybe I could try to convince Gideon to look up my file that afternoon.

I tapped my band. "Set a timer for one hour." A dim countdown glowed on the small screen. I cuddled up with Roman's pillow and sighed heavily, ready for a good nap. My band beeped twice, indicating a text. I rolled over to read the message and my heart skipped a beat.

ROMAN: HEY OUR LAST FOOTBALL GAME OF THE SEASON IS TONIGHT AT 1900 IF YOU WANT TO COME. THE FIELD. HOPE YOU CAN MAKE IT.

CHAPTER 9

FOOTBALL

For the next two minutes, I read the text over and over. For the next five I debated what to say back. The three minutes after that I spent replying, then erasing, then replying, then erasing.

I paced the floor. *It's been ten minutes!*

"Reply: Sounds good. Send."

It took you ten minutes and all you could come up with is "sounds good?" He probably thinks you're not even interested if that's all you say. That's practically a pity response.

"Reply: I was going to shut down OneGlobal single-handedly, but I guess I can put that off until tomorrow. Send."

I let out a big sigh and fell onto the bed. *That was a decent reply, right? Not too long, somewhat witty.* I found myself craving Natalie's input once again. She always chatted with guys effortlessly. I, on the other hand, didn't have much experience. It's not that I didn't want to talk to them, but I could never work up the nerve. I looked at my timer. There was no I way I would be able to calm down for a nap.

Beep Beep.

ROMAN: HA. SEE YOU LATER. PRACTICE STARTS
AT 1800.

*Ha – that was good. He appreciated my humor. See you
later – also good. Practice starts at 1800 – what am I supposed
to do with that? Go to practice or just show up for the game?
Did other people show up early?*

I didn't want to be the only person watching practice,
especially the only *girl* watching. But I didn't want to
only show up for the game if he was expecting me at
practice. *Ugh! Why does being a kidnapped cult victim have
to be so difficult?* After multiple imaginary conversations
with Natalie, I finally decided to go at 1830, that way
I didn't look overexcited or indifferent. Plus, since it was
the last game, people may get there a little early to have
a good seat.

Once I made a decision, the minutes crawled. I didn't
want to go into the Asylum in case I ran into someone
and they asked why I was a nervous wreck. I tried looking
through the art book but couldn't sit still. The rest of my
afternoon was mostly spent pacing across the room.

I asked Hannah to come over, but she was "up to her
elbows in detergent" and couldn't talk. At 1700, I had
steadied my nerves enough to venture out to grab a quick
dinner.

When I turned down the cafeteria hall, a thunderous
commotion could be heard. I cautiously approached the
doors and peeked through the glass window. All the tables
had been pushed to the center of the room, dividing the
large area in half. Either side was filled with boys taunting
and yelling at the others across the divide. One group wore

solid black, while the other dressed in red, white and blue. Phrases screamed across the room. I heard, "you're going down," and "regret the day you were born," alongside numerous insults to mothers.

The lights flickered on and off and the volume of the boys doubled. *There's no way I'm walking through that insanity! Looks like I'm eating from my snack bag.* I whirled around and scampered back to Roman's room.

I was staring at my band when the screen turned from 1829 to 1830. I gave myself one last check in the mirror, still admiring my Designer outfit, and headed out the door. When I reached the hallway overlooking the field, my mouth dropped open. The entire Asylum must have been there. Even the second-floor railing was crammed with cheering boys.

I squeezed my way to the edge to get a view. At each end of the field, a group of boys ran about in different formations. I scanned the faces of the boys wearing black, the team closest to me. I didn't see Roman, and there was no way he would spot me on the terrace. Since that was my biggest concern, I decided to take my chances at finding a spot in the bleachers.

I made my way to ground level and walked around the perimeter of the field while scanning the players. Finally, I spotted Roman throwing a football to his teammate. He matched the rest of his team, wearing a red t-shirt with a large American flag on the front. His cut-off sleeves left large holes in the sides, allowing his well defined abdominal muscl—

I collided with a large object and crashed to the ground. The earth spun as I lay on my back. The boisterous laughter around me indicated my tumble did not go unnoticed. I covered my face with my hands and tried to ignore the headache already developing in my temples.

"You okay?" a familiar voice asked from above. My face scorched an uncharted shade of red as I imagined Roman watching my debacle.

"Can I go crawl in a hole and die now?" I asked as I peeked through my fingers to see him leaning over me.

"Come on. I'll help you up." Roman reached for my hand and pulled me to my feet. "I think only about half the Asylum saw you, so nothing to be embarrassed about. Gideon's on the fifty-meter line if you want to sit with him." He pointed midway down the field. I saw a pair of aviator goggles a few rows back.

"Thanks, I will," I said, ignoring the lingering pain on my left side.

"Well, I have to get back to practice. Wish us luck. I'll find you after the game." Roman trotted back to his teammates, a blue fourteen printed across his back.

I made a beeline for Gideon and squeezed my way through the crowd. He scooted over to make room for me. "Hey, Eve. Decide to come watch the big game?"

"Yeah, it was hard to decide between which of the many engagements I was invited to attend tonight, but this sounded the least boring."

Gideon laughed. "Did you make it to the pep rally before the game?"

"Was that the craziness happening in the cafeteria?"

He smiled. "Yep, it's a tradition we have where the fans

from both teams mock and heckle each other. It's great."

"Oh, it sounded like one big room of happiness and rainbows," I said as I watched both teams continue to warm up. "So, I had no idea Stevie is your sister! You must be thrilled to have her here."

Gideon furrowed his brow. "Thrilled is a less than optimal term."

"She told us why she joined and how she broke into her file."

"Yeah, Stephanie is pretty proud of that," Gideon said, keeping his eyes on the field.

"Is that hard to do?"

Gideon shrugged. "Depends…well, yes, it's hard to do without getting caught. Anyway, I try not to associate myself with her."

I felt it was best to change the subject. "Would you explain how you play this football? It's called football, right?"

Gideon hit his face with his palm. "Yes, it's called football. You're familiar with soccer, right? Okay, it's somewhat like that only you throw and run with the ball instead of kick it. This is the final game of the season. We started with eight teams in the tournament. The red team is the Freedom Fighters, your boy's team, and the black team is The Anarchists. A team scores points by passing or running the ball past the goal line and into the end zone. A team can also kick the ball through the uprights to score a field goal…" *That's what I ran into.* "There are twenty guys per team and seven players on the field at a time for each team…"

Gideon droned on and on about the rules and flow of

football. Most of the information went in one ear and out the other. I did learn that Roman was not only the captain of the Freedom Fighters but also the quarterback, who was apparently the most important member of the team. He was in charge of throwing the ball and that's the only position I remembered.

With five minutes left on the antique scoreboard hanging on the south wall, the two teams disappeared into a hallway as the lights went out. The murmur of the crowd built in anticipation.

The scream of microphone feedback made everyone cover their ears. "Is this thing on? Hello? Oh...LADIES, I know not many but still, LADIES AND GENTLEMEN! Ah, who am I kidding, there's no gentlemen here. LADIES AND KRONIES! Are you ready?" The crowd went wild. "Tonight is the final battle between two proven teams." Spotlights lit the hallway across from the bleachers. "First up, we have a group of fierce warriors, known for their tenacity as well as their brutality. It's The Anarchists!"

The crowd cheered and waved black banners as the team made their way onto the field. Gideon leaned over to me. "See the yellow flags around their waists? Normally, the defense stops the play by tackling the player with the ball, but tonight play stops when the flags are ripped off."

"Why?" I asked. Being tackled sounded terrifying.

"Less chance of injury. With the next Chaos so close, Roman insisted they play it safe. Gage fought him on it...of course. Just one more disagreement to add to the ever-growing list."

I turned toward him. "What do you mean?"

Gideon only shook his head.

Again, feedback screeched across the field. "We really need to get that fixed. Now, it's time to say hello to our reigning champions. Last year, they dominated the competition with their skill and strategy. Can they make it a repeat? Welcome your Freedom Fighters!"

I clapped politely as the rest of the crowd roared. I didn't want to draw attention to myself by cheering too much or too little, but in all the craziness it probably wouldn't have mattered.

"The team captains will now meet at midfield for the coin toss," the announcer bellowed.

To my surprise, Gage walked to the fifty-meter line wearing a black shirt. "Gage is the captain?" I asked.

"Well, not originally; we had just started the season when he arrived. He wanted to play so he picked the best team that wasn't Roman's. Not long afterward he became the captain…naturally."

"What's his deal? How is he in charge when he's such a jerk?"

Gideon thought for a second, his eyes scanning the people around us. "My mother taught me if you can't say anything nice about someone, don't say anything at all. So, I will say he is a natural leader and is very passionate about the cause."

I wanted to ask more questions about Gage, but Gideon seemed completely captivated by the game. Roman's team won the coin toss and Gage didn't look too happy about it.

From the first seconds after "kick-off," I found myself excessively enthralled. The excitement of the crowd was intoxicating. None of Connor's soccer games were ever that entertaining…or physical.

Despite the use of the flags to avoid tackling, a large number of boys still ended up on the ground. Roman talked to the referees after each questionable hit but to no avail. The crowd, however, loved it. The announcer had labeled each team correctly: Roman's relied on practiced plays and finesse, while Gage's thrived on raw talent and power. The battle went back and forth between the two sides.

At halftime, the Freedom Fighters were up twenty-one to fourteen. Both teams jogged into separate hallways and a new group of boys ran onto the field.

"What are they doing?" I asked Gideon.

"Setting up for the halftime show. We only do one for the big game, but way back in the day, there would always be a band or performance for halftime. We only have one band though so our options are limited."

I shook my head at the absurdity of the entire evening. "What's the name of the band?"

"Professor Gray and the Specks. It used to be just The Specks before Emily got here since Specks was the guy who started the group. He's the one in the oversized glasses." He pointed to an older boy. "They used to play every Saturday night in the cafeteria, but since the Chaos started we haven't had much free time."

"What's that thing he's holding?" I inquired.

"The guitar?" Gideon asked in amazement.

I stared at him, clueless.

"Wow. It's astounding how different our worlds are even though we live just kilometers apart. Specks is holding an instrument. He plays it to make the music for the songs. Before OneGlobal took over the Arts, people were free to learn any instrument they wanted."

"I know what instruments are," I spat, offended. "I've just never seen one in real life because they're archaic. Synthetic music is far superior to anything humans could do on their own."

Gideon smirked. "We'll just see about that."

The room suddenly turned black. "And now, ladies and Kronies, for your halftime entertainment, I give you Professor Gray AND THE SPECS!"

The crowd's cacophony of screams slowly faded as a single spotlight focused on the middle of the field. Subtle music started as Professor Gray walked into the glow. She wore a full-length evening gown covered in blue and silver sequins. The Designer dress alone was breathtaking, but Professor Gray looked simply stunning. Her makeup highlighted her eyes and lips while her hair piled into a large, braided bun atop her head. When she opened her mouth, the loveliest of notes drifted through the room.

The ballad was slow and haunting, yet powerful. The lyrics spoke about the coming change in the country. The spotlight followed her as she walked to each band member, allowing the illumination to highlight him as well. I was shocked at the amount of talent displayed, not only from Professor Gray, but from the entire band. I didn't understand why they were playing in some underground society when their act could easily win a contract on *Great American Dream*. I watched in a trance as Professor Gray swayed back to the middle as the song ended and the room darkened again.

I expected a roar from the crowd, but the field was silent. The weight of the song seemed to hang in the air for the next several moments.

A single guitar burst through the silence as multicolored light flooded the field. The rest of the band joined, and it felt as if the intense music was inside of me. Professor Gray climbed on top of a newly assembled platform. She belted out a song about revolution as a cauldron of fire was carried in front of her. The crowd joined in for the chorus, and, to my shock, Professor Gray ripped off the gown, revealing shorts and a fitted American flag top. Professor Gray flung the gown into the fire and the audience went berserk.

The second song ended and flowed seamlessly into the finale, an anthem the entire Asylum seemed to know. During the chorus, boys rushed onto the field, pushing and bouncing off each other.

I stood in a mixture of amazement and confusion. "What is going on?" I yelled to Gideon.

"It's a mosh pit. Just stay here."

Not for one second did I think about joining the pandemonium. I watched as the group half-danced, half-fought for the rest of the song. As the last chord echoed across the field, a loud bang shot streamers into the air. Everyone chanted for an encore, including me.

Gideon leaned into me. "Still think synthetic music is superior?"

I tried to hide the smile on my face. "Maybe."

The announcer came back. "Please clean up the streamers as you make your way back to the bleachers. We still have a champion to crown."

Most of the boys reluctantly made their way to the stands, while some of the younger ones had to be dragged back. When the game clock showed less than five minutes, the two teams marched to the field. My eyes locked onto Roman from the moment he walked through the hallway. He motioned for his team to huddle up on the fifty-meter line then looked in our direction. I suddenly became very interested in the floor. I may have heard Gideon stifle a giggle, but I didn't dare look at him to confirm.

After a several seconds, I heard a whistle and knew it was safe to look up. The third quarter played out with the same amount of excitement, but not as much aggression. Gage must have told his team to tone it down. Neither team could make any progress until the last seconds when the Anarchists scored to tie the game going into the fourth quarter.

The teams battled back and forth, but neither was able to score. I bit my lip as I watched the minutes count down to seconds. With time for one last play, the Anarchists threw the ball all the way down the field. The crowd held its breath as Gage bobbled the football in his hands before dropping it to the ground. The clock ran out with the score remaining twenty-one to twenty-one.

I grabbed Gideon by the shoulder. "What happens now? Can it end in a tie?"

"Oh, no. We go to sudden death. First to score wins it all!" Gideon replied.

The announcer called, "The team captains will meet again for the overtime coin toss. The toss is up and...it looks like the Freedom Fighters will have the first possession, a major advantage."

The game restarted with anticipation thick in the air. The Freedom Fighters marched down the field, poised for victory. After two bad passes, Roman completed a play to his teammate, who was stopped just centimeters from the goal line.

Gideon chewed on his fingers. "They're gonna go for it!"

Roman's team lined up while Gage's remained in the huddle. The ref blew his whistle three times before walking into the huddle to make them start the play.

With both teams ready, the ball was hiked to Roman, who looked around to find an open receiver. Out of nowhere, a large body broke through the line and charged toward him. I realized it the same guy who guarded the door to Roman's room when we first arrived. Roman didn't have the time nor the opportunity to brace himself for the blow. The Anarchist latched onto Roman and threw him to the ground. The impact knocked the ball loose and it rolled across the field. The Freedom Fighters were so concerned with helping Roman, who was writhing on the ground, they didn't notice Gage run through the line, grab the football and run to the other side for a touchdown.

The referee signaled for a fair score and both groups of fans lost their minds. The Anarchists shouted in victory as the Freedom Fighters screamed of injustice. Most of Roman's team bombarded the refs with protests, while Roman rolled from side to side, grabbing his shoulder. It took all of my strength to restrain myself from running onto the field to help him.

"I thought you said they couldn't tackle!" I yelled at Gideon.

He shook his head. "They can't. It was an illegal move. They will call it back."

The referees huddled in the middle of the field as the Freedom Fighters helped Roman to the sideline. After five minutes, the crowd grew quiet as the head ref went to the announcer's box to deliver the verdict. "The ruling on the field was a touchdown; however, unsportsmanlike conduct of the defense cancels the play. Redo fourth down."

The crowd erupted again. I leaned over to Gideon. "What does that mean?"

"They still have one more chance to score, but it doesn't look like Roman is gonna be able to play." He nodded toward the field.

The Freedom Fighters lined up for another play, but Roman sat on the bench, cradling his right arm. The new quarterback's legs quaked as he waited for the ball. After the hike, he frantically looked back and forth as the defense closed in. Right before he was overtaken, he took his chance and threw the ball. Time passed in slow motion as the ball sailed through the air. The beautiful spiral floated toward the end zone… and directly into the hands of a waiting Anarchist. The interceptor ran the football past the stunned Freedom Fighters, all the way down for a game-winning touchdown. Fans rushed their field and raised the hero onto their shoulders.

Gideon stood with his mouth hanging open and his hands locked behind his head. The sad sting of defeat settled in my stomach. I felt horrible for the losing team, especially Roman.

The speaker crackled once more. "The Anarchist after-party will commence in the rec center. Thanks for an amazing season and don't forget to tip the waitresses. Good night!"

The celebrating mass of boys funneled down the hall-way, leaving an echoing wake of cheers and screams. Some Freedom Fighter fans slowly made their way back to their rooms, while others sat in the stands in shock. Roman remained on the bench with a couple of his teammates.

"Well, what should we do?" I asked Gideon. "Should we go tell him sorry for the loss or just leave him alone?"

Gideon started down the bleachers. "I think he would appreciate us pointing out how jacked up the game ended."

As we made our way across the field, I noticed some-one jogging from the hallway. It was Gage. He ran up to Roman and whispered into his ear. Roman nodded and looked at his feet. Gage gave Roman a big pat on the shoul-der and Roman winced in pain. Gage threw his hands back as if to apologize, then turned to make eye contact with me. He leaned down and whispered to Roman one more time before trotting back to the hall.

Gideon stopped in front of Roman. "Hey, man. Are you okay? The end of that game was ridiculous!"

"Yeah, I'll be fine." Roman looked up at me. "So, what did you think of football?"

I chuckled. *His team just lost, he's injured and the first thing he wants to know is if I liked the game?* "It was...entertaining, for sure. Sorry, your team lost. I don't know anything about football, but even I know that wasn't right. How's your shoulder?"

"I landed on it pretty hard, but I don't think anything is broken. I'll go put some ice on it. You guys want to come with?"

"Sure," I blurted out, a little too quickly.

"Nah," Gideon replied. "I need to play hall monitor and

make sure no one gets too crazy tonight. It's a big week."

Roman nodded. "That's a good idea. See you at the meeting tomorrow."

"Oh-nine hundred." Gideon started off toward the rec center. "Night, kiddo."

"G-good night," I stammered as butterflies erupted in my stomach. Part of me was excited to be alone with Roman, but without Gideon as a buffer, my nerves kicked into high gear.

Roman stood up and walked us toward the cafeteria, keeping his right arm bent in an invisible sling. He scanned his band to let us inside. "Sorry, your first football game was such a letdown...unless you were cheering for the Anarchists." He winked.

"I wasn't cheering for them!" I snapped as I hit him in the shoulder...his hurt shoulder. "Ohmygosh! I'm sorry. I am so, so sorry. I wasn't thinking."

Roman pursed his lips and breathed heavily through his nose a few times. "It's fine. Pain speeds up the healing process, right?"

"I'm such an idiot. I feel horrible. Let me get you some ice." I was mortified. I rushed to the kitchen and frantically looked for a bag.

Roman sat down on a stool next to the big island. "Ice packs are on the left side of the freezer. For some reason, those are needed quite frequently around here. And don't ever say you're an idiot because you're not."

I was glad I had an excuse to plunge my red face into the freezer. I pretended to search for several seconds before pulling out a large pack. I walked over and handed him the ice. "Sorry, your game ended the way it did. I thought it was totally unfair."

"Oh, I know." He put the pack on his shoulder. "But not surprising. Just because we all have the same end goal doesn't mean we have the same values. But in the grand scheme of things, it's not a big deal. Just a football game, not the end of the world."

I debated which chair to sit in. As if reading my mind, Roman kicked out the one next to him.

I took my seat. "Well, you played great."

"Aw, thanks. But, really it's the team that's good."

"I've never watched a football game so you could be horrible for all I know. So, that wasn't too big of a compliment."

Roman laughed out loud. "Touché. Enough about me. I want to know how you're doing."

"You're too sweet. Caring so much for the incarcerated," I mocked.

Roman frowned. "No, I'm being serious. I really do care about you."

The concern in his voice made my heart skip a beat. *Hold it together. You can reevaluate that statement a hundred times later.* An awkward silence filled the air. I didn't know how deep he wanted my answer so I chose to stick with the superficial facts. "Um, well...no more class, which is probably a good thing."

"Not a fan of our education system?"

I shook my head. "It's not that...well, it's mostly not that. I just think Professor Gray hates me."

"Emily doesn't hate you. Why do you think that?"

"She always seems mad at me."

Roman shook his head. "That's not okay. I'll say something to her."

"No! Please don't. I can handle it. I mean, in her mind, I destroyed an entire Chaos. So, I get it. Plus, I don't have to be around her anymore so it's fine."

"Alright," Roman said, still eyeing me suspiciously. "So, what do you plan on doing with all your free time?"

"I'm not sure. I found an interesting book on quilting. Maybe I should work on that because I've noticed one thing you're short on around here is quilts."

Roman laughed again. "Yes, we are in desperate need of high-quality quilts."

I couldn't keep the large smile from spreading across my face. "What about you? What's happening in the life of the Asylum leader?"

"Too much," Roman sighed. "Unfortunately, I don't see it slowing down anytime soon...I shouldn't say unfortunately. We are making great strides and everything is about to kick into motion with this next Chaos."

Here is my chance. "What is this next big plan of yours?"

Roman smirked. *Man, I love his smile.*

"I shouldn't tell you that," he stated coyly.

"Why? You think I'm going to post it all over social media with all the access I have? I'm just curious." I tried my best at making an innocent but alluring face. I was sure I failed.

Roman leaned back on his stool and thought for a moment. "Alright. I'll tell you, but you have to promise not to say a word to anyone."

"Who am I going to tell?" I smarted back. He raised one eyebrow. "Fine, I promise."

He adjusted his ice pack. "Seriously, this is top secret information that most of the Kronies don't even know about."

"Cross my heart." I mimicked the action.

"Okay." He leaned next to my ear. His cheek touched my cheek. My heart pounded. "Our next Chaos is in Dallas... at The *Great American Dream* semifinal."

My jaw hit the table. "Shut. Up." I almost hit his shoulder again but went for the leg instead. "That is my most favorite show ever. I've seen every episode of every season at least five times."

"Really? I've never seen the show."

"You've got to be kidding me! Did you live in a bubble before you joined the Defiance?"

Roman chuckled. "No, I didn't live in a bubble. I was never really into television."

I couldn't believe what I was hearing. I didn't know one person who didn't religiously watch G.A.D., let alone television. "Oh, man. Natalie and I would live stream it together every Tuesday, Friday, and Sunday, then go to chat discussions every other night of the week."

"Who's Natalie?"

"My best friend from home." I fell silent. Saying it out loud made me homesick. I looked at my feet to hide my watery eyes.

Roman noticed. "Hey, I'm sorry to bring up anything that makes you sad. Let's go back to *Great American Dream*. How well do you know it?"

I had to get back on track. I thought about my goals. "I know *everything* about that show. I know all about the previous winners, the host, how the elimination process works. I cannot believe that's going to be your next Chaos. It's a live show... what's going to stop them from just pulling the footage when you come on stage."

"We've figured out how to hack their systems to make sure they can't take us off for at least ten minutes. It's a lot of technical details that people like Gideon understand, but I don't have a clue about."

"So, you're going to bust into the semifinals, without ever watching one episode to know what's going on?" I asked.

"Actually, I was planning on having a mini-marathon tomorrow evening to get a feel for the show. Would you be interested in joining me?"

"That would be amazing!" The wheels started turning in my head. "The show is very predictable. I know the order of the show, where the cameras will be located, how the backstage is set up, all kinds of stuff…I may be able to help you with the next Chaos."

Roman's demeanor instantly changed. "You don't have to do that. I mean, it would be awesome and I certainly welcome your help. But I don't want to make you uncomfortable."

"No, it's fine. I don't mind."

Roman furrowed his brow. "You don't mind helping out the enemy?"

I rolled my eyes. "It's not like I'm telling you how to break into the O.G. Headquarters. I have an idea this Chaos will happen whether I'm involved or not, and I just want you to be safe. If there's any information I can tell you to make sure you stay that way, then you can pick my brain all you want. Plus, I owe you one for not letting Gage murder me. Let this be my way of saying thank you."

"I'll take all the help I can get. I'm sure your guidance would be invaluable, but seriously, I don't want to pressure you. Promise you'll let me know if you're uncomfortable about...anything."

Anything? Like how my knees give out when he comes within ten meters of me? No way I was telling him that. But maybe he was only referring to the Chaos. *Ugh. One more sentence to pick apart later.* "Pinky promise." I stuck out my fist with my pinky extended.

Roman gawked at my hand. "What's this?"

"You've never pinky promised? It's something Natalie and I did all the time. You lock pinky fingers and make a promise."

"And somehow that makes it more binding?"

"Honestly...probably not, but it does make it more memorable."

Roman chuckled. "Okay." He half-heartedly went through the motions with a smirk on his face. His eyes locked onto mine for several seconds before he suddenly stood up. "I need to go check on the celebration. I'll probably have to shut it down before it gets too crazy."

A trace amount of panic ran through my veins. I didn't want my time with him to end...for multiple reasons. I learned my lesson and didn't want to miss an opportunity to get some real questions answered. "Wait, can I ask you something?"

Roman sat back down. "Sure."

I took in a deep breath. The weight of the upcoming conversation felt like a boulder in the pit of my stomach. "There's been something I've wanted to ask for a while now, since the first Chaos, actually..."

Roman stared at me intently.

"My brother accessed an illegal website that night...and

we saw a video." I paused.

Roman shook his head. "That was probably one of Gage's recruitment videos. We disagreed on how to go about them, but they were effective in going viral. I've actually never watched any of them in entirety, only heard rumors of their absurdity. We did get some Kronies from them but…what was the video?"

"It was…a video of my mother." I bit my lip as tears filled my eyes.

The color drained from Roman's face. "What happened? Was she hurt in any way?"

I tried my best to keep my composure. "They didn't hurt her…not that I could tell, anyway. She was bound and covered in toilet paper. They made her pretend she was President Mendax and asked her about a master plan, but the D.O.C. showed up before she could answer." I paused. I didn't want to tell him any more details. I felt embarrassed for my mom, and continuing would definitely push my tears over the edge.

Roman sat like a statue for several long moments before leaning over and putting a strong hand on my shoulder. His eyes locked with mine. "Eve, I am so incredibly sorry. That must have been devastating to watch. I had no idea how personally involved you were in the first Chaos. No wonder you wanted to stop the second one. You must hate us. I'm sorry you've had to go through all of this." He dropped his hand. "Sometimes, Kronies are so focused on the big picture, we don't think about the impacts on individuals."

I shook my head and wiped my eyes. "I just want to know why. Why did she have to go through that? Why did she have to act so…insane, and what was the master plan?"

Roman slowly rubbed the side of his face. "Oh, where to begin…" He looked at the ceiling, obviously debating what to say. Finally, he inhaled deeply. "Eve, I'm going to be honest with you because you deserve to know the truth, but at the same time, try not to overwhelm you. When planning the first Chaos, Gage wanted to 'teach people a lesson' through violence since he views Dupes as less than Kronies. If it were solely up to him, All-Mark would be just one big crater right now. I, on the other hand, wanted to create anarchy without directly involving the public. So, we came up with a compromise. First, I made it clear that we would not murder anyone. I had the Cerebrum backing me on that. Then, we came to the agreement that we would take over the store, cause as much physical destruction as possible and if people acted stupid, they would be spared from any harm. He even sent some old Asylum prisoners in at the beginning to tell people to act insane. It's weird, I know. He viewed it as a 'philosophical representation of the idiocracy of the American public.' Unfortunately, having your mom wrapped in bathroom tissue and pretending to be the president was Gage's idea of symbolism."

If I thought I despised Gage before, I was mistaken as a new hatred filled my bones. I felt like Mom was humiliated for no reason. "So, OneGlobal doesn't have an evil master plan?"

"We believe they do, but that's a whole different can of worms. Are you up to hearing it? It's like week four re-education material."

I nodded, part terrified of what I would hear and part

relieved that I was finally getting some answers.

"You've learned about the Decimus plague that happened right before the O.G. was founded, right?"

"Of course. It killed millions and millions of people all over the world. The founding of OneGlobal united the countries so we could find a cure. And it worked. The Decimus plague was eradicated within months."

Roman shook his head. "That's what they want you to think, but that plague was actually engineered by OneGlobal in order to kill off the lower class."

"Lower class?"

Roman adjusted his pack. "Before OneGlobal, there were three major classes based on wealth: upper, middle and lower. Much like today, the upper class consisted of the small, wealthy percentage of the population. The middle is where most people lived, and the poorest citizens made up the lower class. Robotic engineering caused the unemployment rate to skyrocket. This, coupled with overpopulation, caused the lower class to grow exponentially which, in turn, deprived the upper class of resources. In order to 'solve' this problem, the founders of OneGlobal decided to eliminate the lower class and bump down the middle class, therefore creating a cushion between the two remaining classes: Upper and normal.

"The fastest and most effective way to accomplish their goal was to create a disease that they could control. They systematically released their nightmare on the homeless, the chronically ill, and in the prison system. Those who opposed a world government were conveniently taken by the disease as well. Once the O.G. economists said enough people had died to ensure the security of the

Upper's lifestyle, the countries united to find a cure.

"The reason they were able to develop a cure so fast was because they already had it. The newly founded OneGlobal looked like the savior of the world and everyone fell in love. Their plan worked and their new class system is still in place. Uppers don't make more Credits than the rest of us. They were just born into their class or invited up. That's why normal people are okay with it. They have a chance at winning a game show or being loyal enough to move up in their station. OneGlobal is..." He stopped and shook his head. "Sorry. I'm getting ahead of myself. Basically, we believe OneGlobal is planning something like that again. I won't get into all the complicated details. It's too much for tonight. I'll explain everything when things calm down around here...after this next Chaos. I promise." He held his pinky finger out to me. I smiled as we shook on it. "Let's get you to bed. It's been a long day."

My head swam with the bomb he had dropped on me. I could have sworn I was ready to hear the "true horrors" of OneGlobal but I understood why they wanted to wait until week four. *Could all of that really be true?* If it was, then maybe the public should know about it. I ignored my thoughts and watched Roman balance the large ice pack on his shoulder with his left hand. "Are you sure you don't need a sling or anything?" I asked.

Roman held the door open for me. "I'll see how it feels in the morning." The faint thump of rock music could be heard in the empty hallway. "Sounds like they're still having a good time."

We walked the rest of the way in silence, but it wasn't uncomfortable.

"Thanks for walking me back," I said as we approached my room. "You didn't need to do that."

"My mother taught me to always see a lady to her door. Plus, I'm almost positive some of the guys snuck in alcohol and I didn't want anyone giving you trouble."

"Alcohol? How would they get alcohol? That stuff is crazy expensive!" I leaned back against the wall, trying to look cute and confident at the same time.

"Well, the Defiance isn't above…I don't want to say stealing. Hmmm. We aren't above borrowing from OneGlobal companies with no intention of returning. But, it doesn't matter since alcohol is illegal at this Asylum."

"Seriously? A bunch of teenage rebels aren't allowed to drink?"

"I'm not sure if you know this or not, but guys are, for the most part, idiots until the age of, like, forty. Since I value the work we are doing here, I thought it was best that we don't have anything around that could contribute to poor judgment."

"That's logical." I paused, trying to think of another question. I didn't want the conversation to end. "I'm guessing you're not forty yet. So, are you an idiot?"

Roman smiled. "I said for the most part. I do not include myself in that category."

"How old are you?" I dared a personal question.

"I celebrated my twenty-first birthday the day of the second Chaos."

I threw my hands over my mouth. "You're joking!"

Roman shook his head.

All pretenses of me pretending to be cute went out the window. I felt horrible once again. "Oh my gosh, I ruined your birthday! I'm so sorry."

Roman kicked at the dirt on the ground. "Ha. I'm not big on birthdays anyway. No harm, no foul."

"I still feel horrible. Birthdays are a huge deal in my family. My brother's birthday is six days before mine, so that whole week is just insane with presents and desserts and games. We would make or buy something for each other every day, trying to one-up each other. Connor would always beat me. He's so creative." I grew quiet, lost in the memories of my family.

"You miss your family a lot, don't you?" Roman asked after several seconds.

I gave him a weak smile and nodded.

Roman looked back and forth down the hall and stepped closer to me. Centimeters separated us. He leaned next to my ear and whispered, "You can't say anything, but I was able to send a message to Connor to let him know you're okay."

My reaction was instantaneous. I closed the gap between us, throwing my arms around his neck and knocking the ice pack off his shoulder in the process. "Thank you," I breathed into his ear as tears ran down my face. "Thank you."

Roman's body relaxed and he wrapped his arms around me. "You're welcome. I can't imagine what it's like to be in your shoes, but I know that's what I would want the most."

I reluctantly let go of the embrace and took a step back, wiping my face with the back of my hand. I reached down to grab the ice pack and handed it to him.

"Oh, thanks," Roman murmured. He looked slightly uncomfortable. I wasn't sure if it was the hug or my crying.

"Um, do you know where the theater is?"

"No," I sniffled.

"Okay, I'll meet you here tomorrow and walk you there," he said as he scanned the door and held it open for me. "Nineteen hundred, okay?"

"Sounds great," I said as I walked into the room.

"Alright, it's a date. Have a good night." He turned around and vanished down the hall.

I let the door fall shut and continued to stare straight forward. *It's a date! What does that mean?* I walked over to the sink and rinsed my puffy face, mulling over the roller coaster of emotions from the evening. What I thought would be just a simple night of football turned into deep conversations and ended with a date. For once, I had made some real progress.

I raced to the bed and pulled out my list of goals. I sat at the desk, pulled out a pen and crossed out goal three. It felt like a weight had been lifted off my shoulders and peace had claimed its spot. Conner knew I was safe. He would be able to protect our parents. I was free to focus on my other tasks.

I crawled into bed feeling giddy. I didn't know what made me more excited; my progress on being invited to the third Chaos, or hugging Roman and possibly being asked on a date. I tried to keep myself grounded in reality. *He may be obligated to call it a date since you're his Coverture. Could he really be into you? Does it even matter? You're supposed to be escaping from him. But...that doesn't mean you can't enjoy the process. Uggghhhh.* I touched my band and turned off my alarm. I knew it would be hours until I fell asleep and I needed my beauty rest for the next evening.

CHAPTER 10

DATE NIGHT

I woke up to my band buzzing from a message. I tapped the screen. HANNAH: WHERE R U? U COMING TO EAT?

Weird. Why does she care if I'm at breakfast? I checked the time: 1238. *What? How did I sleep in this late?*

I quickly replied, "Text Hannah: On my way. Wait for me."

I brushed my teeth, threw on my old t-shirt and jeans, which at some point had been washed, folded, and placed on the desk, then hurried to the cafeteria.

Hannah sat by herself in the middle of the room. I went to the nearest line, grabbed a tray, then sat down beside her. "Hey, sorry. I turned my alarm off and slept in. Did you go to the game last night?"

She nodded enthusiastically. "Yes, it was nuts! I've never seen anything like it."

"Neither have I, but I can't decide if I like it or not. It got pretty violent at the end," I said between bites.

"Did you go to the after-party?"

"Gosh, no! It sounded like another Chaos."

Hannah nodded. "It was."

I choked on my macaroni. "You went?"

"For like two minutes. Stevie talked us into it. She said it would be fun and would help us 'experience the culture.' So, we followed the crowd and music to the rec center. It was so loud you could barely think, let alone talk. And get this! Everyone was drinking! I mean, I guess that shouldn't surprise me, but I've never been around alcohol. Anyway, we made it not even ten meters into the place when guys swarmed us. Thankfully, I had enough sense to text Sherlock on our way. He found us pretty quick and got Becky and me out of there. Charli said she needed to stay to keep an eye on the other girls. It must have been some party though. Stevie didn't show up for breakfast duty. She walked in at lunch and looked like she'd been hit by a FasTrack. Professor Gray stormed in, furious, and asked her to go talk in the hall. I think she's on toilet duty until further notice."

"Yikes," I said.

"I know, right? We have our next work shift in fifteen minutes. I'll try to get the scoop from her."

"Nice..." I needed to get to more pressing matters. "Um, you wouldn't happen to have any makeup, would you?"

"No, but I know Stevie has a ton." She eyed me suspiciously. "Why?"

"Just wondering." I felt my face betraying me.

Hannah pointed her fork at me. "I don't believe you. What's going on?"

I've always been a horrible liar, so I decided to tell her the truth...some of it. "After the game, Roman asked me to go with him to get some ice for his shoulder. We hung out in the kitchen for a while, then he walked me back to my room and...he asked if I wanted to hang out tonight."

I thought Hannah's eyes would pop out of her head. "Shut up! When he says hang out, is it like on a date? Or is it just more of a friend type thing?"

"That's why I couldn't sleep last night. I'm not sure. He did use the phrase 'it's a date,' but we are just going to watch some TV."

"Just the two of you?" she asked.

"I think so."

"That is totally a date, Eve!" Hannah squealed.

"When I say it like that, yes, it sounds like a date. But when I think of the overall evening, I'm really not sure it is. I mean, I highly doubt the leader of this entire Asylum has time to date a captive, even if I'm his Coverture."

Hannah furrowed her brow for several seconds. "Okay, this is going to be tricky. You need to look casual enough so it doesn't look like you expected a real date, but nice enough that you subtly stand out. I'm free after seventeen-hundred. I can come over and help you pick something out."

I reached across the table and grabbed her hand. "I love you!"

Hannah giggled. "You want me to ask Stevie for some makeup?"

"Ugh, I don't know. Yes, I want makeup, but I don't want her asking questions. If she really is jealous about Roman, the last thing I want is for her to know we are hanging out."

"True. I'll see what I can do." Her band beeped. "Duty calls. I'll see you tonight!" She gave me one last cheesy smile before rushing out the door.

I mindlessly picked at my food while devising a game plan for my wardrobe dilemma. *I'll take all my clothes and lay them on the bed, then piece together—* A tray dropped onto the table across from me.

Gideon sat down. "Hey, kid. How's it going?"

"Gideon!" I breathed. "Quit scaring me like that!"

"I'm starving, thanks for asking. Our meeting ran late today, shocker. What have you been up to?"

"Not a whole lot, actually." I thought about my goals. "Hey, are you busy this afternoon?"

"I've got another meeting in a bit, and I'm sure that will last forever as well. Why? What's up?" he asked as he shoved half his sandwich into his mouth.

"Oh, I was just wondering if you could give me a tour of this place. You pointed out some stuff my first day but I don't remember any of it. I've heard about a rec center and Command, but besides the field and cafeteria, I have no idea where anything is. I'd ask the girls, but they're always busy with their new chores."

Gideon chuckled as he stared off into the distance. "Sorry, just the thought of Stephanie cleaning around here makes me incredibly happy. Sure, I can show you around. Let's go right now." He pushed his chair back from the table.

"We don't have to go now. I don't want to interrupt your lunch."

"It's fine." He finished his sandwich in two bites and chugged his drink. "I'm done. Let's roll."

I followed Gideon out of the cafeteria, and he pointed further down the hallway to the gym and recreational areas. We made our way back to the field. "To your right is the tunnel to the garage. Over there," he pointed to the left hallway, "first floor is the communal dormitories. I think that's where most of the girls are staying. Second floor is all the classrooms and instructors' offices. Sorry, I don't have time to walk you around, but there isn't much to see. Above us is Command. Want to check that out?"

"Sure, but only if you have time," I said as casually as possible.

Gideon turned and started up the nearest staircase, to the second-floor platform. "Most of these rooms up front are normally used for gaming." He motioned to the doors as we walked down the hall. "Through Darknet, we are able to play against other Asylums. We used to have tournaments every weekend, but that was back when we had a lot of downtime. This middle area is mainly meeting rooms and this room on the left is the one we use when we have conferences with the Cerebrum – that's like our national headquarters."

"I know about the Cerebrum. I did pay a little bit of attention in class," I joked.

"Finally, this room at the end is what we call the War Room. Hang on a sec." Gideon scanned his band and peeked inside. "All clear, come on."

I followed him through the door and gawked at the technological overload. The room was crammed with state-of-the-art computers, satellite images, and holograms. In the middle of the room stood an enormous oval table surrounded by chairs. Overwhelmed, I turned to a screen on the wall closest to me and tried to decipher the information. I recognized a map of Texas when the display suddenly went black.

Gideon typed furiously on one of the computers. "Sorry, top secret info and all that jazz. Anyway, this table is my pride and joy. I designed her myself; completely interactive with voice recognition and highest quality visual display. The digitally enhanced biometric researching assistant or as I call her, Debra."

"What an impressive name," I laughed.

"I may have spent a few hours on the acronym," he admitted as he placed his hand on the table. "Debra, show me a map of this Asylum."

A sultry voice filled the room. "Anything for you, Master Gideon."

I looked to Gideon, who refused to return my gaze.

"Don't judge me," he commented as a large schematic filled the tabletop. "Whoever is at the table can log in for their own personal screen while the main image in the center is a collaborative view. Great for planning Chaos. You can zoom in and out. Rotate the image and...Deb, give me the three-dee view." The image morphed from a two-dimensional view to a floating hologram. "Still fully interactive and functional. Not too shabby, seeing that I made her from scratch. Anyway, that's the coolest thing here in my opinion, but I'm probably biased. I geek out over this type of thing. Anything you'd like to see?"

"Can it show my house?" I asked immediately.

Gideon thought for a second. "Uh, sure. What's your address?"

"7729 South Madison Place."

Debra confirmed my address and a view of my house filled the table. I fell into the nearest chair as I saw my mother gardening in the front yard.

"Is...is this a satellite image?" I choked out.

"No, the satellite system is too risky to hack without proper preparation. This is from the L.C.F."

"L.C.F.?"

"Local Compliance Feed. Almost every square centimeter of civilian area is covered by twenty-four seven surveillance. I know they tell you they only monitor public places like schools and All-Mark, but cameras are everywhere. These feeds aren't heavily secured, so they are easy to hack. See that drone?" He pointed to the corner of the screen. "That's part of the Additional Compliance Monitoring set up around your family ever since you left. Those are impossible to hack unless you..."

I barely heard him with all my attention focused on my mother.

Gideon slid into the chair beside me. "Your mom gardens? I didn't think anyone did that anymore."

I put my head in my hand and leaned in as close to her as possible. "She says it calms her nerves. She goes out there when she's had a stressful day."

Gideon watched along with me. "Any specific type of flower she likes?"

"Lilies. She had to get special permission from the city council to plant them."

"Why?"

I had never thought about why before. Normally, I would just accept the rules without question, but for some reason it bugged me that my mom needed permission from the government just to plant a couple of flowers in the front yard. "I don't know."

As much as I wanted to sit and watch my mom for

the rest of the evening, I knew she would want me to be productive. It took all my strength to tear my eyes away. "Gideon, some of the girls were saying that it's possible to see our school file. The record OneGlobal keeps on us about our personality and stuff. Is there any way I could see mine?"

He waved his hand and my mother disappeared. "Why would you want to see that?"

"I just want to know what the government thinks about me," I answered honestly.

Gideon leaned back in his chair and crossed his arms behind his head. "Your school file is the basis of your citizen file, which starts after you graduate. So it focuses on your projected future and how much trouble you may give them with Noncompliance. With that being said, you probably don't want to see it."

"Why not?"

"It's hard to see negative comments about yourself. I thought I could handle seeing mine since I already knew I didn't test well. But it was much more brutal than I anticipated."

I rolled my eyes. "I can handle it. How hard would it be to pull up? I don't want to take up your time. I know you're busy with the next Chaos and everything, but I really want to see it."

Gideon rubbed his jaw with his hand. "Actually, your file is already pulled. We do it for all new people that come to the Asylum, so we know who we are dealing with. Normally, we don't show files to the noobs. We want people to discover their own identity before seeing how the government has labeled them. But, I believe that you have the right to see it if you want. It's up to you."

I thought about it for a few seconds, but I knew my curiosity would get the best of me. "I want to see it."

"Alright...but don't say I didn't warn you." Gideon typed on the holographic keyboard. A virtual document appeared on the table. He touched the file and slid it to me. "We only have a few minutes before you need to get out of here. The synopsis is at the top."

I took in a deep breath and beheld the first page of my evaluation.

Name: Evelyn Lily Price
Age: 17.8
Status: Model Citizen
Risk for Insurrection: Low
Incidents of Nonconformity: None
School Performance: Low (Expected/Acceptable)
Final Class Ranking: Normal
Self Worth: Low (Expected/Acceptable)
Potential for Significance: Low (Expected/
Acceptable)
Anticipated Career Path: Service industry for
Upper Class
Overall Progress: On track with planned course

The next page was a complete personality breakdown with a synopsis at the bottom.

Overall Personality Assessment: Subject shows strong loyalty trait - continue to foster feelings of loyalty to OneGlobal and associates. Need to confirm passion for family does not exceed passion for government (especially for brother with higher risk for Noncompliance/insurrection). Betrayal storyline ready if needed. Tendency for sarcasm, attention to detail, and quick thinking worrisome. Keep critical thinking to a minimum. Complete Compliance after January Chaos attack. No concern for loss of discretion.

"We need to hurry up," Gideon warned as he paced the room.

I scanned the next few pages: test results from various classes, list of closest friends, sadly short, with frequencies of how often I text and chatted with each of them, breakdowns of my social media usage, and average time spent watching individual television shows. Next was a complete transcript of my interview with Detective Larkin. Finally, there were countless graphs, charts, and data logs.

"I don't understand," I breathed.

Gideon came up beside me. "It's a little overwhelming. Let me summarize. You do what you're told without asking questions, a.k.a. model citizen status."

I scrolled back to the top. "What's potential for significance?"

"Well, bear in mind that all of this is garbage. You can do whatever you want with your life, but they view you as not having much influence in the world. They don't want you to, either. They want to cultivate your feelings of low self-esteem, so you'll rely on the government to solve all your problems."

"What about my passion for family and betrayal story?"

Gideon sighed. "Their best strategy is for people to

put OneGlobal above all else. If, for any reason, they thought your love of family was a threat to them, they would manufacture some sort of event to create division. If your brother became a danger, they might take him out, then tell you he betrayed the government or something to that effect."

"This is insane," I whispered. "How can they possibly have this much detail on every single student?"

"Oh, you don't even know the half of it."

"Final class ranking? They already know where I'm going to end up in life? I'm just a junior in high school!"

Gideon chuckled. "Oh, it's way worse than that. They already have a short list for your future True Match."

"What? Let me see!"

"Shhhhh," Gideon instructed. Footsteps echoed from the hallway. He waved his hand across the document, and it disappeared. "We need to leave now. Just act natural."

We exited the room to see a tall, slender figure walking toward us. It didn't take me long to realize it was Professor Gray. She eyed Gideon suspiciously. "Hello, Gideon...Eve. What brings you two down this hall?"

"Eve was never given the grand tour. I was just showing her around," Gideon replied.

"You have a really nice facility here," I commented.

Professor Gray continued to stare into my soul. "Yes, we do. I'm so glad you approve. Now, if you would excuse us, Eve, we have a meeting to attend. Gage should be here any moment."

I swallowed hard. The last thing I wanted was to be around that creep. "Thanks again, Gideon." I gave a small wave and rushed past Professor Gray. I couldn't help but notice the smell of the outdoors.

I made it back to my room without incident. I sat down at the desk and dropped my head into my hands. I didn't know what upset me more: the fact that the government had already determined my future, or how freakishly accurate they were in their assessments. If you would have told me a month earlier that I would have a career serving the Uppers, I would have been ecstatic. Just being around Upper Class citizens would make me feel special, but after reading my file, I wasn't sure how I felt.

Out of everything that I read, what bugged me the most was the part about my family. I valued them above everything, and was certain nothing the government could do would ever come between us.

I also entertained the idea that the Defiance had fabricated the entire report just to get me on their side. But if that were the case, why would Gideon not want me to see it? And there was no way for the U.D. to know so much about my personal life.

In my mind, I replayed the video of my mom with her flowers. I missed her so much. I needed to refocus on my goals. I decided to take a long shower to clear my mind and wait for Hannah to arrive. Then, I took all the clothes I possessed and arranged them on the bed. I paced the room and chewed on my lip as the minutes crawled. By 1715, I was ready to lose my mind.

Four minutes later, my band buzzed. "HANNAH: SORRY. LATE. WHERE IS UR ROOM?" I quickly responded with directions and peeked my head out the door. When she appeared around the corner, I motioned her inside.

"What took you so long? I've been freaking out. We don't have much time!" I spouted.

Hannah stared at me for several seconds. "Step one, calm down. We have over an hour. That's plenty of time. Why are you so worked up, anyway? You have a total crush on Roman, don't you?"

"I...uh...no! Okay, well...no. No, I don't. I'm just nervous because he's really nice to me and he's the leader of the Asylum."

Hannah smiled and threw one hand in the air. "You don't have to explain yourself to me. I'm just here to help. But the reason I'm late is because I had to get these." She pulled out a small bag from behind her back and dumped the contents onto the desk. Makeup scattered.

"Where did you get all of this?" I squealed.

Hannah sat on the end of the bed and crossed her legs. "I asked Stevie for some basic stuff. I told her I wanted to start experimenting with makeup, and she was more than happy to help out."

"You. Are. The. Best!" I cried, sorting through my new goodies.

"You seem to be adjusting to this place," Hannah commented.

I stopped my scavenge and thought about my response. She was right. If I was being honest, even I was surprised about how well I was adapting to my situation. If you had told me a month earlier, that I would be kidnapped by a bunch of teenage boys and wasn't crying in the corner twenty-four seven, I'd never believe it. I turned to Hannah.

"I don't know if I would go that far, but I've just decided to make the best of the circumstances. It's weird. I know we haven't been here very long, but it feels like forever." Hannah agreed. "I know what you mean. This isn't how I expected to feel. Do you miss social media?"

"Honestly, I know this sounds stupid, but I've actually enjoyed not having my life filled with technology. I mean... at home I hung out with my family and Natalie, my best friend. But here, it's like I get close to people really fast. Does that make sense? Like you, I would consider you one of my closest friends even though I've only known you for a short time. And Gideon, I know him way better than any other guy at home."

"Yeah. I actually like it here much more than home." Hannah fiddled with a string on the edge of her shirt.

"Why is that?" I asked as I applied foundation.

"I was always alone at home. I'm an only child. My dad works for OneGlobal Energy and my mom works for OneGlobal Gives Back...you know, the charity. They work all the time, but when they are home, all they do is fight. They fight about Credits. They fight about housework. They fight about what to watch on TV. It drove me so crazy that I started doing all the chores and managing the bills myself. They can't cancel their True Match until I graduate and they've completed their 'parental duties'. It's normally so tense, I just stay in my room. They're probably happy I'm gone. Now, they can finally get away from each other."

I felt horrible. I knew we weren't the typical family, but I had no idea home life could be that bad. I turned to Hannah and put a hand on her shoulder. "Don't say that.

I'm sure they miss you terribly."

"I doubt it. Anyway, that's why I like it here, and I'm not planning any big escape like some of the girls."

I dropped my brush. "What? Who?"

"Oh, Adriane and Becky. They've been planning it since we got here. Charli is still on the fence. Sometimes she helps them plan and other times she is convincing them to stay. They asked me to join, but I don't want to leave."

"Interesting. How are they going to get out?"

Hannah shrugged. "Last I heard they were going to steal a band off someone and sneak out. They stopped including me in the plans once they found out I wanted to stay...afraid I'd snitch."

I rolled over the new information in my head. I could team up with them; more people could increase our chances of escape. However, their plan may not be the best, and I didn't want to get caught in a failed attempt. Or what if they wanted to escape that night and I wasn't ready? *Better to stay on target. I can always join them later.*

"Earth to Eve." Hannah tapped my shoulder. "Do *you* want to escape?"

"Sorry, um..." Even though I trusted Hannah, I didn't know how much I wanted to tell her. "I miss my family, but...escaping is pretty much impossible. Right? So, I'm not really considering it."

"Yeah, especially when you have Roman keeping you here." She grinned.

I punched her in the arm. "Shut it! That has nothing to do with it. Help me pick out something to wear."

For the next hour, we picked out my most basic Designer jeans and flowered top, finished my makeup, and put my hair into a stylish yet casual braid. We also talked about our "before" lives, our families, friends, and what we missed. After hearing more about Hannah's home life, it was no wonder she wanted to stay in the Asylum. *Maybe this is the right place for some people.*

At 1830, I stood in front of the mirror and admired our work. "Not too bad, considering what we had to work with."

"Yeah, we didn't have many options on clothes either," Hannah joked as she dodged my punch.

"But seriously…how do I look?" I asked, slowly turning in a circle.

"Like someone who is ready to go on a non-date with a boy she secretly has a crush on, even though he kidnapped her and is holding her hostage in the Asylum," Hannah smarted off.

"Perfect. Exactly what I was going for. Although…are we technically hostages? I mean, they aren't asking for ransom Credits or anything."

"Hmmm, maybe captive is a more accurate term. Anyway, I better scram and get ready myself. Sherlock asked me to hang out tonight. He's going to teach me to play StarStryke."

"What?" I exclaimed. "You should have told me *you* had a date!"

"Oh, I don't think Sherlock would know what a date was if it walked up and smacked him in the face. Text me as soon as you get back. I want *all* the juicy details."

I rolled my eyes. "I'm sure you'll be disappointed, but

I'll let you know."

Hannah whizzed out of the room, leaving me alone with my nerves. I tapped my band every thirty seconds, but time didn't move any faster. At 1852, I decided to brush my teeth one more time just in case the last three scrubs hadn't worked. As soon as I filled my mouth with paste, there was a knock on the door. I stared at my reflection in horror. I rinsed my mouth and raced across the tiny room, my heart beating a million times a minute.

I opened the door to find Roman in a fitted black t-shirt with Designer jeans and neon orange tennis shoes. I tried not to stumble over my words. "Hey."

"Good evening." He smirked. "You have something blue on the side of your mouth."

Toothpaste! I ran back to the sink and wiped my mouth with a towel. "Sorry, I just teeth brushed." *Teeth brushed? Seriously?*

"No worries. Are you ready to watch the greatest television show of all time?" he joked.

"It *is* the greatest show of all time. Just wait. I bet after the first episode you'll be hooked."

"I'm not so sure about that." He held the door open and directed me down the hall. "The theater is on the first floor, past the rec center. I reserved it so we won't have any idiots barging in to give their own commentary."

So, he wants it to be just us. I smiled to myself. "How's the shoulder?"

Roman stretched his right arm in several directions. "Eh, not too bad. A little stiff, that's all. Thanks for asking."

I noticed an eerie quietness had settled across the Asylum as we made our way across the field. "Where is everyone?"

"Mostly on assignments. We're in crunch time and there's still lots of work to be done, especially after that party last night."

"Yeah, Hannah said it was horrible."

"She went to that thing? Good grief. I'm going to have a talk with Sherlock."

"Hannah said he got them out of there before it got too crazy."

"That's good. Someone snuck in some alcohol, which led to some fights and...just a nightmare. They felt the pain this morning, but that's all out of the way. Business only from here on out."

I wondered if our meeting was "business only" as we approached the large double doors of the theater. Roman scanned in and held the door.

I entered into what appeared to be a going-out-of-business sale for a furniture store. There was a wide array of mismatched couches, chairs, and sectionals scattered throughout the large room. To my right hung a huge screen that covered the entire wall.

Roman walked to the middle of the room and sat on an oversized couch with lots of fluffy pillows. He stretched his arm along the back of the seat. "Pick a chair, any chair."

I faced a dilemma I hadn't anticipated. Should I sit on the same couch as him? And if I did, should I sit right beside him with his arm behind me? Of course, that's where I wanted to sit, but that would be awkward. If I sat on the end of the couch, would it seem as if I didn't want to be close to him? I needed to make a decision, so I would stop looking like an idiot just standing there staring at the seats.

I walked toward Roman's couch, but at the last second, I chickened out and sat in a small chair directly in front of him. My back instantly ached. I looked down at my selection. The metal chair looked like it belonged in a modern dining room with its harsh edges and anti-ergonomic supports. It was probably the most uncomfortable seat I could have chosen, but I was too embarrassed to move. I kept my face toward the blank screen in front of me and hoped for the redness to go away.

"How can I get all the top secret information out of you when you're way up there?" Roman asked. I heard movement behind me, then let out a small squeal as my chair lifted into the air. Roman turned and placed my chair next to his couch. "That's better." He returned to his original position.

My face was thoroughly on fire. "You shouldn't have done that with your shoulder."

"I told you it's fine. Now, this isn't a holographic screen. Those are a little tougher to 'borrow' from OneGlobal, but I think it will get the job done. What season should we start with?"

My embarrassment melted away as giddiness welled up in my stomach. I hadn't even looked at a television since the day of the last Chaos. The mere thought of watching my favorite TV show on a huge screen with a hot guy was overwhelmingly exciting.

I thought about my answer. "Hmm, if we were watching purely for entertainment purposes, I would say the fifteenth season, but for research purposes, the last season will be the most accurate."

Roman messed with his band and an episode guide of the nineteenth season popped onto the screen. "We are breaking into, for lack of a better phrase, the semifinals, so should we start with that or go through the entire season?"

As much as I wanted to watch every episode with him, I didn't know how much time we had. "Let's start with the semifinals."

Roman selected the episode and the lights dimmed as the familiar theme song filled the room. My heart raced. I wasn't sure if it was the show, the surround sound, or being next to Roman in the dark.

Roman leaned toward me. "Point out anything that you think will be helpful; where security may be located, where the contestants wait, who the judges are, camera angles, anything."

I nodded. "That's the host, Gavin Starling. He's been doing this show since season ten. Before that, we voted on a different host every season, but he was such a hit that they stuck with him. His signature glasses are actually a teleprompter." We watched the recap of the previous week, with the celebrations of the winners and laments of the losers.

"How many contestants are in the semifinals?" he asked.

"Eight contestants divided into two groups of four. One group for each week of the semifinals, at least that's what it's been like for the past seven seasons. Top four advance to the finals and the bottom four go home."

Roman remained close to me. "Are there ever any variations?"

I steadied my breathing. "Sometimes they'll have a fan favorite from a previous season show back up or have a surprise extra elimination."

We finished off the episode and started the second semi-final. I was so enthralled, I completely forgot about my uncomfortable chair. I made as many helpful comments as possible. I tried to hide my disappointment as the results played on the screen, knowing the night was almost over. "I guess there's no point watching the finale. You'll be long gone by then."

Roman nodded thoughtfully. "Yeah, you're probably right, but...I want to see who wins."

I almost jumped out of my chair. "What? You don't know who wins? Have you been living under a rock for the past year?"

"Actually, yes...technically speaking."

I leaned back in my chair and laughed so hard, I snorted. I gasped as I covered my face and looked at Roman between my fingers. "Ohmygosh. I can't believe I just snorted. I'm so sorry."

"Don't apologize. It's cute." He laughed. "Let's watch the finale before you have a full-blown asthma attack."

We watched the last episode with minimal conversation. Roman appeared more than a little interested in the results. When the winner was crowned, he let out a sigh of disappointment. "Man, I was rooting for the singer. She was way better than the architect."

I shook my head at his ignorance. "It's extremely rare for a singer to win G.A.D. since *Rock the Mic* is an entire series dedicated to deciding America's vocalist for the year. But, I thought you didn't care about these types of shows."

Roman shrugged. "I don't, but I can see why they're addictive. Very suspenseful, but that's exactly why I don't like these things. They make you sit in front of a screen, like a mindless drone, for endless hours instead of enjoying real life."

His words stung and I dropped my gaze. He inadvertently called me out and he realized it. "I'm sorry. That came out wrong." He grabbed my hand. "I didn't mean that *you're* that way. I meant...Eve, you are the exact type of person we're fighting for. You're brave and smart and funny, and I hate to think that all that potential is going to be wasted if you stay on the path planned by OneGlobal."

A million thoughts ran through my head, from the validity of his statements to my concern that my hand may be sweaty. I continued to stare at the floor until I felt his hand under my chin, gently pushing up until I looked him in the eyes.

Sincerity filled his voice. "I'm sorry. That was really insensitive of me. I forget that this is all still new to you. When you've been down here for as long as I have, you lose touch with what the real world is like for normal people. Do you forgive me?"

His eyes set butterflies loose in my stomach. I tried to ignore the fact that we were practically holding hands and focused on his words. "Do you really think that about me? That I have potential?"

Roman leaned back in his chair, dropping my hand in the process. "Are you kidding me? Yes! I wouldn't have asked you here tonight if I didn't think you could help us out tremendously. Do you not see that in yourself?"

His question caught me off guard. "No, well...I guess I've never really thought about it. But Gideon let me see my school file today, and it didn't look like I had much potential."

"I've seen your file too, and that's not what I thought about it."

My stomach dropped. The last thing I wanted was for Roman to read my file and find out how unremarkable I was.

He leaned forward. "First, let me apologize. I shouldn't have looked at your file without your consent, but I needed to know what I was getting into." He winked and lightning flew through my nerves. "Second, I know that, to you, the report looked pretty negative, but that's a good thing. For years, I was the head of recruitment for the Oklahoma Defiance and during that time I scouted countless files. I learned to read between the lines and see the potential in people without ever meeting them. It's almost like…a gift. I picked out the best recruits and every single one has been a success in the U.D."

With one arm he pulled my chair around so I was facing him, our knees touching. "Put yourself in my shoes: you've planned a huge Chaos and it goes nothing like you anticipated. Some pretty girl ruins everything and in order to save her life, you must use your one and only Coverture. You get back to the Asylum, completely in disbelief over everything that's happened. What's the first thing you're going to do? Look up everything you can about this troublemaking girl.

"So, that's what I did. Honestly, I was terrified about what I might find. I sat with your file in front of me for ten minutes before I could read the first line because I knew once I read it, I would know exactly what kind of person I pulled into this whole mess. I closed my eyes, said a prayer, clicked on your name, then—bam—there you were. I started reading: all eighty-seven pages of data, charts, and analysis. Then I bowed my head and thanked God for sending the perfect person into this situation. I couldn't have asked for a better Coverture-slash-kidnappee." He paused and looked into my eyes.

I couldn't believe what I was hearing. It felt like I was dreaming. My voice trembled. "Wha-what did you see to make you think that?"

"It's hard to describe, but I don't think I would tell you if I could, because I want you to discover yourself while you're here."

I shook my head and tried to inconspicuously move closer. "That's the most cop-out answer ever. Come on, tell me one thing at least."

Roman laughed. "Um, okay...you were completely indoctrinated in today's culture, which is a good thing because you would bring that perspective to the Asylum. You're smart, but you don't know it, so you're not cocky. You have the potential to see the big picture. And you love your family more than your government, which is surprisingly rare. If OneGlobal told most people to leave their family and move across the country for no real reason, they would do it without a second thought." He leaned forward as if challenging me to move away. "Is that enough to satisfy you for now?"

"I guess...for now." I couldn't handle his proximity and moved back in my chair. "Thanks again for reaching out to my family. I can't tell you how much that means to me."

"Don't mention it. It's the least I can do." He looked at his band. "Well, I hate to end this lovely evening, but

I have to meet up with Gid to crunch some numbers. Would you be interested in doing this again tomorrow? Say, fourteen-hundred? We can go over the episodes of this season so far. We should probably work on memorizing everyone's names and other details."

"Sure. I'd love to," I responded too quickly.

Roman chuckled. "Great. Let me walk you back to your room."

"It's still *your* room. I'm just staying there temporarily."

We walked back in a comfortable silence. Roman scanned the door and, as always, held it open for me.

I walked inside and turned to face him. "You don't have to 'pick me up' tomorrow. I can just meet you there."

"Are you sure? I don't want to not be a gentleman."

"I don't think you could do that if you tried," I sighed.

We stood there for a few seconds until awkwardness started to fall.

Roman took a small step backward. "Then, I'll see you tomorrow. Sweet dreams."

"Good night," I called after him. I let the door fall shut and turned to look at myself in the mirror. *Wow. What a good night.*

I messaged Hannah that everything went well and that I'd fill her in on the details the next day. She didn't respond, so I assumed she was still hanging out with Sherlock.

I sat down at the desk to complete my nightly ritual of reevaluating my goals. The number one priority was still to escape, but how did I feel about everything else? Was I okay with helping the enemy by providing them with information? The lines defining who was the real enemy began to blur. I justified my actions since I probably wasn't providing *that* much useful information, and it was my best chance at being invited to the next Chaos. I decided to give strategizing a break and focus on the positives of the night: Roman telling me I had potential, confirming he thought I was cute, and inviting me to another night of G.A.D. I brushed my teeth, put on my Designer PJs, set an alarm, and went to bed with another smile on my face.

CHAPTER 11

SKY

The small vibration on my wrist woke me at 0900. I took a shower and planned out my morning. I would start by compiling a list of any helpful information pertaining to the next Chaos. Then, at 1100, I would grab some lunch, talk to Hannah, and get to the theater by 1300. Showing up an hour early would force Roman to choose the seat.

My day was going perfectly to plan, but Hannah's words resurfaced in my mind. I *was* adjusting to my life in the Asylum and if I was being completely honest, I kind of enjoyed my new surroundings. *That's just because you have a purpose, for once, and because some guy has shown a tiny bit of interest in you.* I shook the thought away and got to work.

By lunchtime, I had developed a few pages of notes to take to Roman. I grabbed some food but didn't see Hannah. She messaged me that she was busy doing chores all morning, and we would catch up at dinner.

I went to my room to prep myself for the afternoon. I unlaced my braid and was happy to see my hair actually behaving for once. The waves looked great. I applied some light makeup and picked a more casual outfit. By 1245, I couldn't stand being in my room any longer, so I gathered my notes and made my way to the theater.

On my way, I decided to pick the same couch that Roman sat on the night before, but the real question was *how* to sit on the couch. Leaned back and casual? Attentive and prepared? Lounged and...seductive? *Yikes. Who am I kidding? I could never pull that off.* I continued to argue with myself as I arrived at the large doors and pulled on the handle; locked. I scanned my band and, to my surprise, the door clicked open. I entered the theater and stopped in my tracks. Roman sat on the couch hunched over a large table. He wore a retro t-shirt, casual Designer jeans, and black sneakers.

The door shut behind me, and he looked up from his papers. "Good afternoon. You're here early."

I stood there for a good five seconds with my mouth hanging open slightly. "Uh...so are you." I hesitantly shuffled toward him, internally panicking as I hugged my notes against my chest. When I reached the table, I noticed pieces of paper scattered about. I expected him to hide them from my sight like Gideon did in the War Room, but he continued to focus on the mess of notes.

"What's this?" I asked as I pulled a chair up to the opposite side of the table.

"Paper. I use it to write notes and make plans. For some reason, it helps me organize my thoughts better than doing it electronically."

I rolled my eyes. "I know what paper is! I'm not *that* wrapped up in technology. I meant, what is written on the paper?"

Roman looked up at me and winked. "I was being sarcastic. These are notes I've made about the upcoming Chaos. I like to make lists; what needs to be done, who I put in charge of what, potential complications, yada yada yada."

I scanned over the jumbled sheets and recognized several repeated names: Emily, Gage, and Gideon. There were several other names I didn't know: Bryan, Jonas, and Keaton. I noticed Stevie's name at the top of one sheet with a big question mark beside it. Unfortunately, another piece of paper covered the rest of the page. "How many of you are going to this Chaos since the Dallas Defiance is going to be there?"

Roman stretched his arms behind his back, his large muscles flexing. "Not too many. The other group has been putting in the real work. We're just the extra hands…and talent. It's like how we operated the second Chaos. We had our boys get jobs in the OneGlobal Center of Tulsa and work there for months to get inside information. Only about half of our Kronies live in the Asylum, the others are sleepers, waiting for the right time. Kronies from other chapters have spent years getting positions in the G.A.D. staff as production assistants and security. We even have some in the Dallas Department of Compliance. Those are the hardest jobs to infiltrate."

"Why is that?"

Roman organized the pages into three stacks. "To be in the Department of Compliance, you need a perfect record and unfailing loyalty to OneGlobal. As you can imagine, for us, that was a recruiting nightmare."

"But for someone with your gift, I bet it wasn't a

problem at all," I teased.

He looked up at me and smiled. "I'll have you know, I have a perfect recruiting record. I did find guys for those positions, but I can't tell you how many hours it took. It felt like an entire era of my life was spent in front of a screen scanning through files." Roman leaned back into the couch. "Anyway, what brings you here so early?"

Luckily, an excuse popped into my head. "I came to work on my notes as well." I stuck out my few measly pages.

Instead of taking them from me, he motioned beside him on the couch. I changed seats, leaving a safe distance between us.

Roman scooted closer to me as he grabbed the papers. "And what are these?"

"Papers. It helps me keep my thoughts together when I don't have access to technology."

Roman smacked me on the head with the notes. "Very funny." He wrinkled his face in confusion. My stomach dropped. Roman shook his head. "No offense, but…your penmanship is atrocious. Did you write these in the dark, with your feet?" He pushed into me with his shoulder, letting me know he was joking.

"Give me a break! I've never used these archaic writing implements you keep around here. I had to try my best to mimic what they look like on my tablet. You know, if you really wanted to help, you would provide me with the proper tools."

Roman nodded. "Noted. We'll plan on working on your writing style after this Chaos."

I bit my lip. I liked the idea of him planning our future, but I didn't anticipate being around for that to happen.

Roman scanned the pages. "Anyway, what did you come up with?"

"Just any information I thought may be helpful. I tried to focus on things like security. I know G.A.D. has their own security, so you won't have to worry about the Docs." I looked down at my scribble and suddenly became embarrassed. "I'm sure it won't help you at all. They're pretty stupid, actually." I reached across him for the papers.

He held the pages out of my reach and continued to look over them. "Don't say stuff like that. This is great. Seriously. Thanks." He turned back to me. "You didn't have to do this."

"I wanted to help out. It wasn't a big deal." My cheeks flushed slightly.

"Well, I really appreciate it." Roman's band beeped and he chuckled at the message. "FYI, Gage is going to be here in a couple minutes to give me some data on the next Chaos."

Fear grasped my chest. "Do I need to leave?"

"Of course not…unless you want to. But I don't want you to leave. I was just giving you a heads up." Roman added my notes to his pile.

"He probably won't like me being around all this information."

Roman shrugged. "I really don't care what he likes."

As if on cue, the scanner on the door buzzed. Someone pushed, but the door remained locked. The scanner beeped again with the same result. The door shook back and forth violently but didn't budge. There was a pause and then a pounding knock.

Roman's lips brushed my ear. "I may have had

something to do with that." He placed one finger over his mouth, then walked over to open the door. "Sorry about that. The badge system must be down. I'll have someone look into it."

I stifled a giggle.

Gage stormed into the room. He opened his mouth to speak but stopped when he saw me. "What's she doing here?"

Roman rolled his eyes. "Nice theatrics. Do you have the final numbers or not?"

Gage handed him a file without removing his glare from me. "Yeah. Well, as far as I know. The connection went down, but I got what we needed."

Roman skimmed through the file. "Thanks. Anything else?"

"You know our time frame. Get it done." Gage stomped out of the room.

Roman walked back and sat mere centimeters from me. "I'm sorry. It's so hard to not be a complete jerk to him, but I do find it oddly satisfying to annoy him."

"What's his problem?" I asked.

Roman started to speak, then stopped and shook his head. "In my completely objective opinion, he's just power hungry and doesn't like that I have more pull around here. Anyway, let's forget about Gage. Ready to start this season?"

"I cannot wait!" I had never been so excited to rewatch a season of G.A.D. in my life.

"If we don't watch the preliminaries with all the sucky people, there's over five hours of footage. Can you stand to be around the person who sentenced you to this prison for that long?"

I shrugged. "Good thing I'm not here for the company. I'm here for the show."

Roman laughed out loud. He tapped his band and *Great American Dream* started on the big screen. He grabbed a notebook from under the couch. "Let me know if there's anything that stands out or if I should record parts of the episode to show the team."

We watched the first four episodes straight through, making memos and recording snippets. I didn't know if I paid more attention to the show or Roman's body language. Just when I thought he was intentionally leaning closer to me, he would adjust to a different position. Either way, I was still ecstatic about my situation: binge-watching my favorite show with a guy I really liked. *If only we were in my living room instead of an underground hideout.*

The episode finished as Roman stretched and looked at his band. "Well, it's 1700. I'll have Gid bring us something to eat. What do you want?"

"Whatever's easiest. I know captives don't have the right to complain, but the food around here isn't the best."

Roman chuckled. "Please, complain away. It doesn't taste good to you because it isn't chock full of chemicals and hormones like you're used to. We try to get our food from 'clean' sources with as little O.G. preservatives as possible. Can you tell a difference yet? Does your brain feel less fuzzy?"

I thought about it for a minute. When he phrased it like that, I could definitely tell it was easier to make decisions and think through problems. I wondered if my tiny amount of sympathy for the Defiance was due to the food, the environment, or just Roman. "Yeah, I think so, but it's weird. I don't remember it being fuzzy to begin with."

"That's because they start giving you that crap in middle school after they've mapped out your entire life," Roman said as he typed on his band. "Gid's in a meeting with Gage and I'm sure he's dying to have an excuse to leave."

"How long have you known him?" I asked.

"Gage, about eight months. Gideon, three years. He was my first independent Oklahoma recruit. Before that, other Kronies would look up the guys, then have me evaluate their selections. But I found Gideon on my own. We spoke for a year before I was able to get him in the Asylum. I was so nervous he wouldn't live up to my expectation, but he's blown us all away. Anyway, let us trudge onward."

Twenty minutes into the next episode, the door beeped and Gideon entered with three boxed dinners. "Thank you for getting me out of there! I know we are counting down the hours until D-day but, good gravy, that meeting was ridiculous. Anyway, how's the *research* coming?"

"Only two episodes left," Roman said as he cleared off the table. "Should be able to finish in time. How's everything from a technological standpoint?"

Gideon dropped the boxes onto the table and pulled up a chair. I noticed dark circles under his eyes like he hadn't slept in days. "So far, so good. We wrapped up shooting the promo video this morning."

"Want to join us for this episode?" Roman asked.

"I'll start it, but I have to meet the editing crew in thirty. That's going to take all night," Gideon said as he dove into his cheeseburger.

Roman restarted the episode as we ate. Gideon scarfed

down his food faster than I thought humanly possible and hopped onto a sectional behind us. Within minutes, he was asleep.

"Poor guy," I whispered to Roman. "He must be exhausted."

"Yeah, he's one of the major coordinators for this Chaos. I'm just letting him run with it. He's doing great, but it's so much work."

It surprised me that Gideon was so involved since he never seemed stressed and was always wasting time to check on me. We finished the episode and Gideon remained zonked. During the pause between shows, I could hear his band vibrating constantly. "Should we wake him?"

"Nah, let him sleep. One episode left until we're caught up. Ready?"

"Sure," I said, feigning excitement. I didn't want our side project to end.

Halfway through the episode, Gideon awoke in a panic. "Shoot! I am so late! Why didn't you wake me up? Deuces." He bolted from the room.

"He'll be fine," Roman said as he stretched out on the couch and placed his arm behind me. I tried to remain calm as a new outbreak of sweat appeared on my palms.

We finished the episode, and I jotted down the names of the contestants moving on to the Dallas semifinals. "Well, now we know who will be there during the Chaos."

Roman sat silently for a minute, his eyebrows furrowed. He started to say something several times then stopped.

"What is it?" I asked.

"What do you miss most about the real world...besides

your family? I know that's a given."

His question caught me off guard. "Hmm...honestly, I'm not sure. If you asked me on my first day here, I would have said TV, my phone, or some facet of technology, but that's changed." I tried to think of something, but only my family appeared in my head. Then it hit me. "The sky. I miss the sun and the breeze. I really don't consider myself an outdoorsy type of girl, but—"

"Well, let's go," Roman interrupted as he stood and offered his hand.

I didn't hesitate to take it, and he helped me up. I held onto his grip for a split second after he let go of mine. I quickly folded my arms across my chest and hoped he didn't notice.

We left the theater and walked toward the entrance that we used my first day in the Asylum. He scanned the door and ushered me through. For half a second, I thought about escaping down the long, dark hallway, but then I realized I didn't want to. I told myself it was only because I knew I couldn't *really* escape at that moment.

The lights turned on one at a time as we walked down the corridor. It gave me an eerie sense of déjà vu. I had lived in the Asylum for only a short period, but it felt like a lifetime. We entered the garage with all the vehicles and made our way to the opposite corner to a small elevator shaft.

Roman pulled the gate open using a thick strap. "Ladies first."

I peered inside the dark space. "Is this thing safe?"

"I'm not one hundred percent sure, but that makes it more exciting." Roman waited as I tiptoed into the elevator. The gate slammed shut and we started moving upward at a surprisingly fast pace.

Roman stood in front of me and smiled. "Close your eyes. Trust me. It'll be worth it."

I did as instructed, and pushed my body against the wall for support. The elevator came to an abrupt halt and I heard Roman open the gate. He grabbed my hands and led me into an echoing room. We walked in a straight line for several minutes, then Roman stopped me.

His voice reverberated off the walls. "There's a railing to your left. We are going up a spiral staircase for a bit."

I used the railing and Roman's hand for support as I climbed. The ascent was longer than I anticipated. Legs and lungs aching, I finally lifted my foot up for another step but there was none. I fell forward into Roman's waiting arms.

He laughed. "I'm sorry. I couldn't help myself. We're almost there. Walk straight ahead. No peeking."

My next stride brought the subtle warmth of the sun across my face and the wind pulled at my hair. Roman edged me forward and placed both of my hands on a cold rail. He stepped behind me and whispered, "Look."

I slowly opened my eyes, and the scene in front of me took my breath away. The sun set over the waving grass plains that spread in every direction. We stood on a tiny platform on the side of a spire at least ten stories off the ground. I looked down at the rest of the Asylum sprawled out below and my knees weakened. Roman grabbed my waist to keep me from falling.

I pushed against him to go back inside. "I'm not a fan of heights. I'm going to fall."

Roman chuckled and spoke into my ear. "I'm not going to let that happen. Slow, deep breaths. Here, ease yourself down and sit on the ledge."

He helped lower my shaking body onto the cement slab. As soon as I sat down, I scooted back against the building. Roman laughed, walked to the ledge and sat with his feet dangling. He motioned to the area beside him. I fervently shook my head. He reached back, grabbing my foot, and pulled me to him. Resistance was futile. I wrapped my arms and legs around the iron support.

Roman scooted closer to me. "I'll admit it's a little unnerving at first, but you get used to it. I come out here to clear my head. Plus, you can't beat the view."

I looked across the landscape once more. It was beautiful. "H-how often do you come out here?" I rattled.

"Not too often, nowadays. Too busy. I used to come out here every evening and read. I love the illegal books where the main character overthrows the government and stands up for what's right."

Books can be illegal? I made the mistake of looking down at Roman's dangling feet. I slammed my eyes shut and readjusted my grip. "Aren't you worried about someone seeing you out here in the open?"

"Not after Gideon hooked us up with some amazing drone tracking technology. We've blocked the live satellite images too. So, if anyone tries to see us, it's just a picture of this place years ago." He paused and looked down at me. "I brought you up here for a couple of reasons. I need to run some things by you."

I slowly unwrapped my feet from the pole to let them sway, attempting to mimic Roman. I looked over to see him rubbing the back of his neck as he squinted across the horizon. For the first time ever, he seemed nervous.

He took in a deep breath. "I wanted to tell you the full story of why I joined the Defiance. I don't like to tell people because...well, you'll see why. My story begins eleven years ago. My dad was a geneticist at a research hospital in Oklahoma City, and my mom was a chemical engineer, both at the top of their field. I have an older brother, Luke, who excelled at everything he did. We were the ideal family, on the cusp of becoming Upper Class. The further along my parents advanced in their careers, the more involved they became in OneGlobal. My mom was being 'groomed' for a public office. We loved each other, our lifestyle and, most importantly, our global government. All of that changed when my brother was diagnosed with cancer."

I stopped him. "Cancer? I thought that disease didn't exist anymore. In science class they say that cancer is eradicated and completely curable."

Roman nodded sadly. "That's what they want you to think, but Luke has a very rare form that does not have a cure or treatment. I remember sitting in the physician's office, expecting Luke to simply take a pill and he'd be better in no time. But that's not what happened. They started running all these tests and eventually admitted him to the hospital. They told us everything was normal, but over the following weeks, we were allowed to see him less and less. They talked about moving him to a special facility for a more comprehensive treatment. My mom, brother, and I were all for it, but my dad knew something wasn't right. He started doing some research. Due to his high-security clearance, he was able to pull some files and discovered the unthinkable. Patients with incurable diseases get shipped off to facilities in the middle of nowhere, where they are treated like lab rats for the rest of their lives until the experiments finally kill them.

"That's what they do with convicts too, by the way. Break the law when the government is in need of research participants and you get shipped to one of those facilities. Then, they give you a disease and try to cure you. Or they force you into slave labor, but that's another story. Anyway, my dad comes home after discovering this, and he knew we had to act fast. He made us leave all our electronics, go into the backyard, and fake a picnic. He knew we would be under surveillance. He whispered his discovery and we planned to break my brother out of the hospital. My mom was hesitant at first, but she knew everything the government did to our water since she helped develop the chemicals. I couldn't believe what I was hearing, and as a ten-year-old boy, I couldn't really comprehend it either. They told me if I wanted to save Luke, I needed to do exactly what they said.

"That night I packed my suitcase. I was so upset I had to leave my phone and tablet behind. My mom left a rabbit trail on our computers to send the Docs in the wrong direction. My dad removed our trackers so we could ditch them when the time was right. The next morning, we went to the hospital like normal. Officials were already there waiting for my parents' consent to take Luke. My mom said they would be more than happy to sign, but wanted to take one more walk as a family to the park outside the hospital. As soon as we hit the main doors, we took off running to the parking garage. When we were almost out of the city, we pulled into a car wash and switched cars. We snuck on a Fastrack without using Credits, since that was before all the added security, and made it to Dallas. Once there, we went to the closest coffee shop to regroup.

"By some supernatural means, the owner of the coffee shop happened to be involved in the newly founded American chapter of the Universal Defiance. Long story short, he took us in and we became highly involved. My brother's still alive. Really sick, but alive. My dad is constantly doing research to find a cure.

"Once I learned about all of OneGlobal's manipulation and deception, I dedicated my life to putting an end to the corruption. I want to show people the truth and let them decide what to do with it." He gazed into my eyes. "So, that's why I do what I do. But, the reason I don't like to talk about my family is…my mom is basically the leader of the U.D. in America."

I sat flabbergasted, my mind racing. The story of his brother was heartbreaking, but finding out that his mom was *the* leader of the Defiance blew my mind. Roman had a million other more important things to do, and yet, there he sat beside me, sharing his life story. I took a deep breath and looked at the horizon's dwindling light.

Roman continued. "When people find out who my parents are, they assume I'm in charge of this Asylum because of them. But I worked my way up just like anyone else. I just started at a younger age. I was able to keep my heritage a secret until Gage showed up from the Cerebrum and announced it to everyone."

"Wow," I breathed, trying to form a reasonable sentence from my jumbled thoughts. "I'm so sorry about your brother. That's horrible. It's unbelievable. Not that I don't believe you, but I can't imagine the government treating people like that."

Roman leaned against a rail. "And that's just one tiny example of OneGlobal's horrific reality. See, OneGlobal's system works for you...until it doesn't, until you question them, or fight their control, then it's the worst system imaginable. We want people see OneGlobal for what it really is. But, that's why the Defiance exists, to create a Chaos that puts a wrench in the O.G.'s mechanics. Anyway, that's my story."

I shivered, unsure if it was from his story or the cool darkness that had settled around us. "Thank you for sharing that with me. But, why? If you don't like telling people, why tell me?"

"Because, I hoped it would bring you some clarity about why we are doing all of this, why the Defiance is so important to me, and...because I want you to come with us on this next Chaos."

My heart skipped a beat. I bit my lip to keep from smiling.

Roman turned his body to me. "You've contributed to our preparation and I think you could be a great asset to us. I want you to go because..." He looked up to the sky for a few seconds before making eye contact again. "Because I feel you were meant to go with us. I know it sounds crazy, but I don't believe in luck. You going just feels right. Plus, you'd get to see another side to our cause. It would really open your eyes to the truth. But it's not about what I think or what I want. What do you think?"

I froze. I didn't know how to answer. Emotions rolled through my body like a canoe in a hurricane. Part of me was ecstatic. I was being invited to go on the Chaos! I had accomplished my goal and was one step closer to escape. But, the other part of me, the terrified part, agreed with Roman. It did feel right to go with him on the mission and help the Defiance. But getting back to my family was my ultimate goal. I needed to go for them, and I could sort out my feelings later.

I debated how to reply. If I jumped at the chance to get out, he may become suspicious. If I acted too hesitant, he may think I was still on OneGlobal's side.

Roman sighed, "You don't have to answer right now. I jus—"

"Give me a second," I interrupted him. I swept my wind-blown hair out of my face and decided to go with as much truth as possible. "Thank you for sharing your story. I'm honored that you feel comfortable telling me. And I don't think for one second that you became the leader of this Asylum because of your parents. Honestly, when I first came here, I thought I had been kidnapped by a bunch of crazed psychopaths who were going to lock me in a dungeon for the rest of my life. But for the most part, it hasn't been that bad of an experience. It's hard to believe the horrible things the government has done, but after all these examples, and your story, I see why you guys are doing this. Things need to change. I would love to go with you guys, but I'd just get in the way."

Excitement filled Roman's eyes. "No, you wouldn't! I'd stay with you the whole time, and—" His band beeped. "Shoot, I have to go. Here's the deal, we have a briefing at zero eight-hundred tomorrow in the War Room for the team going to Dallas. I'm leaving it up to you. If you want to go with us, be there. If not, no big deal. No pressure."

He stood and offered me his hand. I breathed in one last look at my surroundings before heading inside. Chills rippled through me as I felt his hand on the small of my back as he led me through the door.

The elevator ride was cool and breezy. I wrapped my arms around myself for warmth. Roman looked a million kilometers away with his thoughts. We made it all the way back to my room before either of us spoke.

I paused in front of the door. "Thanks for tonight, for... everything."

Roman bowed his head slightly. "My pleasure. I'll see you tomorrow, either way. Have a good night." He stood awkwardly for a few seconds, then turned to leave. I watched him walk down the hall, then scanned the door and went inside.

Hurried footsteps echoed through the hall as Roman raced back. "I didn't get your door. Please forgive me." He grabbed my arm and pulled me back outside. He waited until the door closed completely before scanning his band and holding the door open.

"You're ridiculous," I laughed as I returned inside. "Good night."

The door clicked shut. I climbed onto the bed and curled into a ball. I knew I should have been happy about accomplishing my goal, but I didn't feel good about it. I had told Roman the truth when I said I thought the government should be stopped, but I didn't think I should be involved in the process.

I ignored Hannah's messages and decided to do some soul searching. I needed to nail down a firm game plan before the meeting. After hours of pacing the small room, I narrowed down my true feelings. I *did* sympathize with the Defiance. I agreed with their values and hoped they could peacefully spread their message to the world. If the government was a corrupt system, it should be exposed and changed. However, those sentiments did not outweigh the love I had for my family, which meant I would still attempt to escape if the opportunity presented itself.

The question remained of *when* to escape. As stupid as it sounded, I selfishly wanted to sneak onto the set of *Great American Dream*. That was a once-in-a-lifetime opportunity, so I might as well take it, right? The only problem was that I really didn't want to mess anything up for the Defiance. Trying to escape anytime close to the Chaos could put their plan in jeopardy if Roman tried to come after me. Escaping sooner rather than later was probably the best option, but I decided to wait to make that decision until I had more information.

Finally, there was Roman. Admittedly, I had a small crush on him...okay, a medium-sized crush...but it was more than that. I had never met anyone like him. He was gorgeous, smart, funny, family-centered, selfless, and I could be myself around him. I thought about all the times he had lifted me up or encouraged me. No other guy had ever paid me any attention. Leaving the Defiance meant leaving him, and even though the very thought of never seeing him again made my heart feel like shattering, I knew it had to be done. *Just accept it.* But I couldn't leave without telling him how I felt. There had to be a way to say goodbye. Before I could change my mind, I decided to write him a letter, and put it in his picture box, knowing that someday he would find it. I grabbed a pen and paper and began to write:

Dear Roman,
First, I want to say thank you for everything you did for me while I was in the Asylum. Thank you for saving my life and always treating me with the utmost respect and kindness during my time here. You really did change how I view the world, and I am forever in your debt. I will do all that I can from home to spread your message and help your cause. I believe in the Defiance and trust you all will do amazing things for this world.
I know you said you've never been wrong about anyone, but you're wrong about me. I can't stay here. I know you understand, more than anyone, how much I love my family. I could not pass up the opportunity to be with them again. Please don't think I betrayed you. My heart is aligned with your vision, but I'm not the amazing person you saw in that file. I'm not brave or smart or any benefit to the Defiance, but I believe in you. You will lead the Defiance forward.
I'm sorry for any trouble this will cause you and I'm sorry, you wasted your Coverture.
If there's ever a chance you can find me when this is all over, please do, but if you don't want to, I understand.

Thanks again,
Eve

P.S. I apologize for the horrible penmanship.

Tears filled my eyes as I folded the paper and crawled under the bed to place the note inside the box. My stomach turned at the thought of Roman reading it, but by that time I would be safe with my family. I tossed and turned all night until my alarm went off.

CHAPTER 12

PLANS

My nerves fired from the tips of my fingers to the pit of my stomach as I walked to the War Room. I looked down and tapped my band: 0755. The fact that I had made it that far without my knees buckling was a miracle in itself. I leaned into the door and heard jumbled voices on the other side. I needed to sell myself to make sure everyone believed I was completely on board, even though my own feelings wavered from moment to moment. *It's now or never. Do this for your family.* I took in a few deep breaths and held my wrist up to the scanner. It beeped and unlocked.

As I stepped inside, all conversation stopped. The air seemed heavy as I felt every eye staring at me. I quickly surveyed the room. Standing at the head of the large table, Roman smirked, Professor Gray gasped, and Gage fumed. Gideon sat to Roman's right, but I didn't recognize any of the other ten or so guys sitting around the table. I hurried toward the opposite end of the room to an empty chair, but Gage was already on me.

"And just what do you think you're doing here?" he

asked dryly.

I froze. Angry Gage was scary, but calm Gage was terrifying. I needed to sell myself to make everyone believe I was completely on board even though my own feelings wavered moment to moment. I stood, inwardly panicking, and unable to speak. I had practiced my response a hundred times the night before, but all the well-rehearsed gears in my head had locked in place.

Luckily, Roman spoke up. "I offered her a position on the ground team."

Gage casually turned to Roman. "You're joking, right? Right?" Gage realized he wasn't being pranked and his voice escalated. "Tell me you didn't ask the person who single-handedly ruined our last Chaos to go on this one? That's the most absurd thing I've ever heard in my life. There's no way—"

Roman interjected equally as loud, "She's contributed to this Chaos just as much as anyone here. By being my Coverture, she is an automatic member of the Defiance and has every right to be invited on this mission."

Gage pointed at me. "She may technically be an official member of the U.D., but she is *not* a Kronie. We have no idea of her true intentions. She may be planning to sabotage this Chaos, just like she did last time. She—"

"Why don't you ask her?" Roman interrupted again.

I fought the urge to crawl under the table as everyone slowly turned from the action in the front to me. All moisture instantly evaporated from my mouth. It was my one and only shot to convince the group to let me go. Roman had influence, but not enough to overrule the entire room.

I stood against the table for support and clasped my hands together to keep them from shaking. *Focus. You can do this.* "I—" my voice cracked. I cleared my throat and started again. "I wanted to thank you for this opportunity to be here. I know my presence is concerning to most of you. I stopped the last Chaos out of fear for my safety and the safety of my friends. I was present at the first Chaos and did not want a repeat of the horror I witnessed that night. Since the Coverture, my time in the Asylum has changed my point of view. I believe something needs to be done to show the world the truth behind OneGlobal. I would greatly appreciate the chance to make up for my past actions and help in any capacity during this Chaos. Thank you."

Professor Gray eyed me suspiciously. "How could you help us? What can you offer that we don't already have?"

My voice still trembled but only slightly. "I am the biggest *Great American Dream* fan in this entire Asylum and probably within the Defiance. I'm sure you have an excellent plan, but if something goes wrong? If something unexpected happens, what are you going to do? I know that show like the back of my hand. I'd be able to get you out of unpredictable situations. My familiarity with the show is invaluable."

She wasn't convinced. "That may be the case, but you have zero mission experience. We have a full team that has been preparing for months, even years. All I see is a liability."

Roman stepped forward. "I'll train her."

Gage rolled his eyes. "There's not enough time—"

"You underestimate my training abilities," Roman

smirked. "But seriously, it's not like we have to teach her how to hotwire a D.O.C. patroller or hack into a drone feed. I'll take full responsibility for her actions on this Chaos. If anything goes wrong, I'll personally suffer the consequences."

Gage scratched his beard, then pulled Professor Gray and Roman aside. The three became engrossed in a hushed conversation while the rest of the room broke into whispers. I fell into my chair and looked at Gideon, who winked and gave me a discreet thumbs up. I gave him a half-hearted smile, but most of my energy was directed at not puking all over his high-tech table. Roman had put his neck on the line for me. His cards were down and he was betting on me. *How could I possibly bail on him after all he's done?* I talked myself off the ledge. *They haven't even said you can go yet. Worry about one problem at a time.*

I heard movement behind me. I looked over my shoulder to see Stevie sitting in the corner, throwing daggers at me with her eyes. I quickly turned forward, but I could still feel her gaze boring into the back of my skull. *What's she doing here?*

After several minutes, Roman and Professor Gray sat down, leaving Gage center stage. "All non-mission approved personnel, please leave the room," he ordered.

Two boys stood up and made their way to the door. I stole a sideways glance to see Stevie pack her bag. She stormed past me and slammed the door as she left the room.

Gage focused on me. "What are your plans after this Chaos is over?"

I attempted to maintain my facial composure as the

unexpected question rocked my mental fortitude. I had planned examples to show how I may be of use in the upcoming Chaos, but had never contemplated my fake post-mission life. My honest answer was to be back with my family, but I knew that would be a one-way ticket off the mission. I made up something on the spot.

"Well…" I swallowed. "Afterward, I assume we would come back here for some type of debriefing."

Roman chuckled and Professor Gray smiled.

"No!" Gage yelled. "I mean after that, the weeks and months to follow?"

I bit my lip as my brain raced. "After the success of this Chaos, the world will be a different place. The U.D. will no longer be hidden in America. That probably means OneGlobal will try to take us out. Honestly, I'm not sure what the next step is, but that's why we have intelligent people like yourself making those decisions."

Roman beamed. Apparently, I had given the correct response.

Gage, on the other hand, looked more agitated than ever. "You will be allowed to stay in this briefing and proceed in the mission…for now. If at any time, for any reason, *anybody* is suspicious about your involvement in this Chaos, you will be removed from the team immediately. Everything said inside this room is strictly confidential. Is that understood?"

I nodded.

"Good. Let's get started. Gideon, run us through the schedule." He walked to the corner of the room and leaned against the wall.

Gideon stepped to the head of the table. "Morning,

everyone. As you know, tomorrow is the big day; Chaos number three. Initially, we will be infiltrating the recording studio as members of the audience. The live show starts at twenty-hundred hours, so I'm going to walk us through our entire day and answer any questions you may have."

I sat in a state of shock. I couldn't believe that not only had Gage allowed me to stay, but also that I would be escaping the very next day! Thoughts of missing Roman and the Asylum crept into my brain, but I tried to ignore them as Gideon continued. *One thing at a time.*

"Today should be a day of memorization and mental preparation. After lunch, you can pick up your pack of supplies in the theater. In your pack, you will find a pre-planned outfit, phone, alias information, and an individual itinerary. All printed material should be destroyed prior to leaving.

"Tomorrow, you will report to the garage at your appointed time. Check in with Stepha—Stevie, who will approve your clothes, as well as do your hair and makeup if your alias requires it. You will be leaving with your assigned group at different times throughout the morning. If taking the FasTrack, your phone will contain your ticket to Dallas. If your transportation is via other methods, see me after the meeting. Upon arrival, members of the Dallas U.D. will pick you up and escort you to the studio. Deb, show me the *Great American Dream* lot."

"As you wish, Master Gideon." Debra purred.

Gage left his post to join the table. "I told you to shut her off during meetings."

"Sorry, boss. Oversight on my part," Gideon smirked

as a hologram of the studio filled the room. "Your phone is uploaded with your V.I.P. pass to attend the show. You will be moved to a holding area with other audience members. For those of you who don't know, G.A.D. only allows the Upper Class to attend their recordings. After fans arrive, they are taken through the hair and makeup department to appear as normal citizens for the cameras. Outside, the show is broadcast on large screens to non-uppers. We will sneak into these massive crowds after the Chaos for a discreet exit."

That is news to me! I always thought the audience was filled with people just like me, only luckier. If that was true, I had wasted countless hours of my life applying for online lotteries to win bogus tickets.

"One by one, we will sneak out of the holding area using a secret door in this bathroom." Gideon zoomed on the area. "Go into the far stall, move the hidden panel, climb through, and replace the panel. You will find yourself in a small, dark closet. A signal from your phone will alert you to when to exit into the contestants' hallway. Act like you belong or you will blow your cover. The last door on your right will have a purple star. Knock Emily's beat to access the room and we will wait until showtime.

"Emily will be the second act of the night. The program will begin as normal. During the first act, our G.A.D. crew will come and...detain the next contestant. Team Alpha will break into the sound booth, while team Omega escorts Emily to the stage. When it's our turn, Emily will perform her song as our video plays in the background. We are ninety-nine point nine percent certain OneGlobal will be unable to shut us down for at least ten minutes.

That gives us time for the intro video, performance, and a short speech before the show is taken off the air. When OneGlobal has taken back the feed, we will kill the lights, giving you the cue to make your exit. Elevators and doors will remain operational."

I sat in awe of their elaborate plan. I couldn't believe Professor Gray would be performing on the *Great American Dream* stage! She was definitely talented enough, but to think she was *actually* going to do it was astounding. *What I wouldn't give to be able to watch her.* I realized that I had that opportunity if I truly wanted it.

Gideon tapped his band and directional arrows lit up throughout the G.A.D. set. "Speaking of exit strategy, once your portion of the mission is complete, you are to leave immediately. Don't hang around to watch the action. We don't want anyone taken into custody. Your itinerary will tell you exactly when and where to go. For the most part, you will change into the normal clothes given to you by G.A.D. and find the nearest exit. Dallas Defiance members will be stationed at each intersection surrounding the studio. They will be wearing orange shirts that read 'I heart G.A.D.' and will escort you to the nearest safehouse. If you cannot find a Kronie, follow the crowd and try to blend in. There will be a diversion to distract the Docs. Just get as far away as possible. A signal from your phone will let the Defiance track and find you.

"Finally, I want to talk about capture. If you are detained by the Docs, act like a normal citizen for as long as possible in hopes they will let you go. However, if you are placed inside a patroller for transport or there is any indication you will not escape, we cannot let the knowledge in your head be turned over to OneGlobal. They have ways to get inside your mind and learn all of your secrets. They will use torture. They will use chemicals. They will threaten your life and the lives of those you love until you spill everything. Then…they will murder you."

Chills ran down my spine.

Gideon continued. "If you are arrested, dial one-one-one-hashtag on your phone. This will not only wipe your phone's hard drive, but will also dispense a small red pill from a secret hatch on the bottom of your phone." Gideon pulled a phone from his back pocket to demonstrate. "This pill will not kill you, but it will wipe your memory. The dosage will be tailored to you and how long you have known about the Defiance. I know that doesn't sound like fun, but it's better than the alternative. If you are captured, we will do our best to keep track of you, rescue you if possible, and then reintegrate you into our system. Any questions?"

Heaviness settled over the room. I had only about a million questions running through my mind, but there was no way I would open my mouth for the rest of the meeting.

The boy beside me halfway raised his hand. "Can you recover our memory?"

Gideon looked at the floor. "Unfortunately, no. Not at this time."

I swallowed hard, realizing how much of a risk the Kronies were taking. *Thank goodness I won't need to worry about that.*

Professor Gray broke the stillness. "What if we can't get to our phone? The first things the Docs will do is take our phone and handcuff us."

"There will be a backup pill hidden in your left shoe. Look for the secret compartment when you pick up your clothes. Any other questions?" The room was silent. Gideon sat down and Gage took the spotlight.

"Today is the day to tie up any loose ends. Pick up your supply pack and make sure you have everything. Look over your schedule and memorize it. We will not get a second shot at this. Complete all assigned tasks, and if you are a squad leader make sure your men are ready. Tomorrow, our voices will be heard. Tomorrow, our message will be seen. We will not be denied! Let's take back our country! We are the Kronies that will save the world!" Gage rushed out of the room with Emily on his heels.

I clapped my hands, mimicking the rest of the room. The boys stood up and slowly filed out. Roman and Gideon remained seated at the front of the table.

When I approached, Gideon stood, offering me his chair. "I imagine you two have a few things to discuss. Welcome to the team. I'm glad you're coming with us." He held out his hand, but when I went to shake it, he pulled me into a hug. After my initial surprise, I attempted to hug him back, but he was already out the door. I sat down next to Roman and sighed heavily.

Roman swiveled in his chair. "You don't have *any* questions, do you?"

I folded my arms on the table and buried my head. "Nope, none whatsoever. Why would I have questions about a huge mission that I just found out I'm leaving for in twenty-four hours?" Stress sat like a boulder on top of my shoulders. I couldn't decide what aspect of my life freaked me out the most: keeping up the deception of Defiance loyalty to Roman, deciding when I should escape, or the tiny, yet growing, corner of my heart that wanted to go on the mission.

"It's more like twenty-one hours, but…" Roman scooted closer and rubbed my back. Fireworks shot through my body. "It's going to be fine. You'll be with me the entire time. Everything is planned down to the minute. There's nothing to worry about. I mean, what can go wrong? Worst-case scenario, we get caught by the Docs, take the pill, and lose our memory. No big deal."

"You should go into motivational speaking if this whole Defiance thing doesn't work out," I joked as I sat up.

He grabbed my right hand and held it in both of his. "This is a big decision, and I won't blame you one bit if you don't want to go with us. But I promise I won't let anything happen to you." He dropped my hand. "Well, let's hear it. What questions do you have?"

I sat in the warmth of his promise, believing every word. *How can I possibly leave him? How can I turn my back on someone so dedicated to me? Think about your family!* I shook my split convictions from my head. "What made Gage say I could come? I know he hates me. So, why did he allow it?"

Roman grinned. "During our discussion, we decided to test you. Gage would ask what your plans were after the Chaos. If you used the term 'we' or 'us', it would show that you have a team mindset and are on our side. You passed the test." His smile was so big and proud, I felt guilty for passing.

I shook my head. "I don't even know what other questions to ask. I'm slightly overwhelmed. Are you sure I should go? I don't want to mess this up." The honest words flowed out before I could catch them. I shouldn't have given him a way to take me out of the mission and lose my chance at escape.

"I am absolutely positive. With your knowledge, you're a huge resource for us. You're a quick thinker and notice details. What would happen if one of the old judges shows up and we don't know their name? Cover blown. Mission failed. Defiance over."

I giggled. "I'm sure you're way more prepared than you let on, and I don't think this will be the end of the Defiance if this doesn't succeed. At least I hope it wouldn't be." I commented, surprised by the truth in my words.

"We may be a little more prepared than I let on, but I guarantee you this is only the beginning of the Defiance. That's the exciting part! We get to play a role in the start of the biggest revolution in modern history. The world will never be the same because of us. How crazy is that?"

I gave him a feeble smile as my heart and mind tore in half. Part of me just wanted to join the Defiance and assist in the mission. Becoming part of history with Roman would be the most exciting opportunity I'd ever have the chance to take. The other part of me, the practical side, knew the mission was nearly impossible no matter how prepared they were. Plus, I couldn't risk my memory being wiped or never seeing my family again. I had a monumental decision to make and less than twenty-one hours to do so.

Roman misread my nervous expression. "Don't worry. It will be fun. You're going to love pretending to be an Upper. We are traveling first class, only the best for you.

Then, we sneak into a recording studio and become a part of your favorite TV show. What's not to love about that? It's a total adrenaline rush."

"If you say so." The thought of being on G.A.D. did appeal to me.

"I do say so. Well, the clock is ticking. Let's get to training." Roman stood up and offered his hand. "I am an excellent instructor, but the more time we have, the more prepared you'll be."

We left the War Room and my mind ached. I looked forward to spending the entire day with just Roman, but I wasn't sure I could keep up the charade for that long especially with my intentions so unclear.

After reaching the first floor, we walked past the cafeteria and entered the rec center. The large, mirror-walled room played loud music as several boys exercised on the various equipment spread about.

"Sorry, it's a mess," Roman yelled. "They didn't move the machines back after the football party."

The room didn't look that disheveled to me, but I'd never been there before. We walked to one of the many doors lining the back wall. Roman scanned his band and opened one. The smaller room also had mirrored walls, but the blue floor was soft and spongy.

"This is where we have our Jiu-Jitsu and self-defense classes," Roman said.

"What's Jiu-Jitsu?"

"It's an ancient martial art that focuses on unarmed combat."

"Martial art?" I asked, wondering if my training would solely be a vocabulary lesson.

Roman laughed. "I'll show you. Attack me."

I looked in the nearest mirror to see my small frame next to Roman's large figure. Never in a million years could I ever do any damage to him. "You're kidding, right?"

"It's for demonstration purposes. I promise I won't hurt you."

I was more worried about hurting myself. The only fight I had witnessed in my life was in seventh grade when two boys went at it in the hallway. Rumors spread that they both had to take a month-long supplement of anti-aggression pills.

Roman took a step toward me. "Let me help you get started. Step backward with your right leg. Bend your knees. Turn your body slightly." He mimicked his instructions and I followed along. "Good. Make a fist. Bend your elbows. Now, hit me."

I didn't know what else to do. I pushed my fist forward into the solid steel of his arm. Absolutely nothing happened.

He looked down at his unmoved arm. "Wow. That was...unique. Just a few pointers. When you go to hit someone, pull your arm back to increase momentum and put your full weight into the punch. Like this..." He reared back in slow motion then swung his fist forward. "Now, you try."

I took a deep breath and repositioned my stance. As much as I thought the whole process was pointless, I wanted to impress him. I wrenched back my arm and threw my fist forward with all my might. Several things happened in a matter of microseconds.

Roman easily and efficiently dodged my punch. He also somehow managed to grab my arm, twist me around, and take out my legs. I would have crashed to the floor if he hadn't caught me centimeters from the ground.

"*That* is martial art." He winked as helped me to my feet.

"That was insane!" I breathed. "You expect me to learn how to do that in a matter of hours?"

"Goodness, no! I've been training in self-defense for over a decade. And after seeing your combat abilities, I have just one suggestion when it comes to getting in a fight. Run the other way."

I attempted to hit him again but he eluded the blow once more.

"In all seriousness," Roman said, "I wish we had the time to thoroughly go over self-defense training, but we only have one day. So, this morning we will go over some very basic moves, and then this afternoon we will memorize our alias information,, and do some role-playing exercises. After dinner, we can focus on the exit strategy and what to do if we get separated."

He's putting all this work into you and you're just going to leave him to suffer the consequences? The argumentative battle began in my head. *Stop! Focus on the training. One thing at a time. You can't think clearly around him anyway. Wait for a second alone to figure it out.*

I pushed forward. "Let's get started."

For the next two hours, we acted out possible scenarios of security trying to grab me. We went through various pressure points, vulnerable areas, and the "rule of thumbs" to escape someone's grip. I would be lying if I said I didn't enjoy every second of physical contact with Roman.

I may have even asked him to help me escape from his big bear hug an extra time…or two, just to make sure I had it.

I actually thought I was making progress when Roman looked at his band. "Our packs are ready. I'll go grab them and bring back some lunch. Keep practicing."

He looked so happy as he jogged out the door. I finally had a moment to myself. I sat next to the wall and stared at my reflection. *What are you going to do?* I debated between two impossibilities. I couldn't imagine leaving Roman and my new life behind. Ever since being accepted by the Defiance, I was really starting to enjoy myself. My other option was equally gut-wrenching: not seeing my family for an undetermined amount of time. Roman said I couldn't leave the U.D. until OneGlobal was overthrown. How long would that take? Months? Years? Decades? If I *was* going to escape, the sooner the better. It wasn't right to string Roman along if I just planned on leaving.

I weighed the pros and cons of each option. If I chose to escape, there was no way I would be able to contact Roman or be involved with the Defiance after I left. However, if I joined the Defiance, there was a slight chance I could talk Roman into letting me see my family once everything settled down. He had already reached out to Connor once. Why not bend the rules a little more for his one and only Coverture? Plus, visiting the set of G.A.D. was a huge bonus point in the Defiance column. Eventually, I decided to *pretend* I was joining the Defiance for the rest of the day just to see how it felt.

"You okay?" Roman asked behind me.

I jumped. "Oh! Sorry, yes. I was just thinking about tomorrow. I can't believe it's tomorrow."

Roman sat beside me and handed me a boxed lunch. "Originally, the plan was to sneak into the season finale in a couple of weeks, but one of our inside informants learned the location moved from Dallas to Las Vegas. Since the entire city of Vegas is Uppers only, it would have been an infiltration nightmare. So, we stuck with Dallas and the first semi-final. Also, the initial plan didn't include Emily being the talent. They had a singer in the Dallas U.D., but he broke his femur on a scouting mission. Thankfully, Emily was nearby. Just wait until you hear her story."

I nibbled on my pizza, having no idea what a "femur" was. If I was going with the Defiance, I needed as much information as possible. "Tell me about tomorrow. I'm horrible at memorization, so we'd better get started."

Roman smiled timidly. "Not according to your file. But, yes, we should get started." He reached over to the large backpacks sitting beside him while holding his pizza in his mouth. He handed me a small booklet entitled, "CHAOS THREE: Full Briefing."

I skimmed past the table of contents to the alias information. "I will be playing the role of Celestia Westington. Upper names always sound so sophisticated. Anyway, she is traveling to the semi-finals with her fiancé, Xavier Phaeton," I read as heat flashed across my face. "Two chauffeur-slash-bodyguards will accompany them."

Roman smirked sheepishly. "Are you going to be able to pull it off? Pretending to like me for a whole day?"

"You know I like you." The words shot out before I could stop them. *Damage Control!* "I mean, I have to, right? Since I'm your Coverture."

He shook his head. "Not in the slightest. That's the

risk you take by using your Coverture. Some guys spend months doing research, which I personally find a bit creepy, but...I was not afforded that luxury."

"I'm sorry you had to use Coverture under such rushed circumstances."

"I'm not," he stated quickly. He looked into my eyes and didn't avert his gaze.

It was suddenly hard to breathe. I needed to break the tension. "Uh, so when is our True Match date?"

"What?"

"The day we will officially be a True Match. If we are engaged that's the first question people will ask us." I couldn't help but imagine a True Match party with Roman.

He shrugged. "I guess we didn't think about that. You busy June twenty-sixth?"

"Works for me," I laughed. "Who made up these characters anyway? Did you know we would be assigned as fiancés?"

He shrugged innocently. "It wasn't me."

"Then who?" I pressed.

"It's not important. Let's move on. We're wasting time," Roman said as his cheeks blushed slightly. "In the morning, dress in your Designer outfit, then go to the garage to have your hair and makeup done. We will leave with group three, taking an SUV to the FasTrack. Once in Dallas, the Defiance will escort us to the *Great American Dream* set. We will hang out with Uppers in the holding area, which I believe they call the pre-party room, then finally sneak backstage to be with Emily. Once the show begins, you will go with me to the sound booth. Your main focus is to get us out of any unforeseen circumstances. You don't have to worry about anything else.

"The biggest factor in making it to the set is acting the part. Upper Class citizens live differently. They talk differently. They walk differently. Basically, they are entitled and arrogant. If you can act the part, we have a much better chance of success." He stood and went to the other end of the room. "Walk to me."

I was past the point of arguing with any of his instructions, so I complied.

"Perfect," he complimented. "Now, walk back like an Upper."

"What?"

"I know it sounds stupid, but we have to get this down before tomorrow. If you act normal, they will smell you a mile away. You could say you were recently upgraded to Upper Class citizenship, but I doubt they would buy it. Anyway, I'll go first." He took in a deep breath and stepped into his new role. An air of sophistication and superiority emanated from him as he strutted across the room. My knees grew weak as he turned on his heels and winked at me. "Aren't you going to join me?"

I thought pretending to be an Upper would be easy and fun, but testing my acting skills when I was alone with Roman was utterly petrifying. I remained like a statue, my feet glued to the floor.

Roman slowly swaggered back to me. My heart rate increased with every step. He stopped mere centimeters in front of me. "Let's try it together." He slowly reached down, softly grasped my hand, and slid it under his arm. "We'll take it slow."

As we moved across the soft floor, I kept my eyes locked

on my own unrefined reflection. I didn't dare peek at Roman to see how amazing he looked when compared to me.

We reached the wall and he dropped my hand. "Eve, you have to relax. It's just me. I need to know you can pull this off before we leave. As much as I want you to go, I can't risk the mission."

He was right. I needed to get my head in the game. I needed to prove myself.

Roman grabbed the backpack labeled, "EVE," and pulled out a solid white, cropped fur coat and a pair of Designer sunglasses. "Let's see if this helps."

I put on the glasses as he slid the cool fur across my shoulders. He turned me to face the mirror and stood behind me. "Try standing like an Upper." I stood as straight as possible while admiring my new look. He put his hands on my shoulders. "Relax your arms. Chin up. Arch your back a little more." His hands moved to my waist. "Hips slightly turned. There you go. Beautiful."

I blushed and tried to lower my face, but Roman caught my chin. "Don't look down. Never be ashamed, especially as an Upper. I know it's not in your nature to be boisterous and arrogant, but you need to sell it. Want to try the walk?"

I didn't know if it was the clothes or Roman calling me beautiful, but a new sense of confidence filled my bones. It was time to shine. I spun around, pushing past him, and took a few strides forward. I flipped my hair out of my face and looked over my shoulder. "Am I walking myself across the room alone or is my fiancé, Xavier, coming with me?"

Roman smirked as he reached for my hand and

interlaced his fingers with mine. "Sorry to keep you waiting, my love."

I tried to keep my internal freakout in check as we paraded around the room while making small talk about *Great American Dream.* I surprised myself at how well I was acting. Pretending to be Roman's fiancé made the charade much more interesting. I used it as an excuse to flirt with him, clinging to his arm and resting my head on his shoulder. We came to a stop, and I leaned against the glass. I played with my hair while smirking at him. "Well, Xavier, you sure know how to walk around a room."

He faced me and rested his arms above my head. "You're not so bad yourself."

"Oh, that's nothing. I can do much more than walk." I put my hands on his chest.

"Is that so?" he asked as he leaned closer and slid my sunglasses to the top of my head. His green eyes locked onto mine.

I could only nod. His right hand dropped to the small of my back. Heat radiated off his body as the centimeters between us closed. I tilted my chin up and...Roman abruptly pulled away.

I opened my eyes and exhaled the trembling breath I was holding.

Roman paced around the room, his hands locked behind his head. "I'm sorry...I just...got caught up in the moment."

"It's fine," I whispered.

"I'm sorry. We have to focus on the mission. Um, I'm going to go grab some water. Want one?"

I nodded. He left the room and I slid down the wall to the floor. *What just happened? Did I make that all up or did he almost kiss me?* It must have been the latter from the way he reacted. *Roman almost kissed me!* Having a crush on him was one thing, but to know he had feelings for me changed everything. I took in a long, slow breath to steady my heart. *Can you really leave him now?* I asked myself as I wondered if the last five minutes had made an impact on my decision. *Don't make an emotional choice. You still have time.* I placed the coat and glasses back into my bag and laughed when the reflection of two full water bottles caught my eye. I dropped my head to my knees as my mind ripped in half; one part analyzing every second of our interaction and the other deciding my fate in the Defiance.

At least thirty minutes passed before Roman returned empty handed. He sat on the opposite side of the room. "Sorry, it took so long. I just needed a couple of minutes to myself. Again, I apologize for my actions. Do you mind if we proceed with the training?"

"Of course." I desperately wanted to know what was going on in his head. But like he said, we needed to focus on the mission.

Upper training restarted in a tense and awkward fashion, but after me tripping a few times and several jokes from Roman, we settled back into a relaxed routine. Over the next few hours, I learned how to interact with servers, D.O.C. officers, and normal citizens from the filter of an Upper. I didn't like viewing other people as less than myself, but Roman insisted it was necessary.

He checked his band. "I have a dinner meeting with the Dallas Defiance in fifteen minutes. Afterward, I'll meet you at our room to go over what happens after the Chaos, okay?"

My stomach flipped at the term *our*. "Sounds like a plan."

He hoisted our bags onto his back and motioned to the door. "Ladies first."

"Roman, wait." I was ready to make a decision, but there was still one issue I had to address. "I really appreciate that you've risked so much for me to go on this Chaos. I'm honored, actually. But there's something I need to ask you."

He set the bags down and walked to me. "Anything."

"I know you broke the rules and reached out to Connor, and I am eternally grateful for that. But is there any way *I* can speak to my family, all of them? Or any way I can see them? Not right now, of course, but after this Chaos. I just...miss them. I can't bare the thought of not knowing when..."I trailed off, trying to keep it together.

"Eve, I will never make a promise to you that I cannot keep. I wish there was some way for you to see your family while you're in the Defiance. Recruited Kronies know temporarily losing their family is the price they have to pay. Unfortunately, you didn't get that option. Allowing you to contact them will only put your family in danger, and I can't let that happen. I want them to stay safe." He wiped the tear from my cheek and sighed. "I promise I'll look into it. Maybe I can talk to my mom and see if she can pull some strings. But that doesn't mean she can. And none of this will occur until the dust settles from this Chaos. Deal?" He stuck out his fist, pinky extended.

A large smile spread across my face and I locked his pinky with mine. "Deal!"

He walked me to the cafeteria and then disappeared up the stairs. It was a little early for dinner, but I hoped Hannah would be there. I decided to spill my guts to her:

the escape plan, the crush, the almost-kiss, everything. I was going insane keeping all my thoughts to myself. I trusted her enough to keep my secret and help me sort out my feelings. I opened the door and walked inside. If I thought being captured by a crazed anti-government cult was an emotional ride, I was about to step onto the largest roller coaster known to man.

CHAPTER 13

CLARITY

The cafeteria swelled with more people than normal. I casually made my way to the food lines wondering how many of them knew the third Chaos was the next day. I reached for my tray as someone grabbed my arm. I whirled around. It was Hannah.

"Where have you been? I haven't seen you in forever!" she exclaimed.

"Actually, I've been crazy busy. We have a lot to catch up on." I noticed Charli waving us over to the girl's table. I sighed in relief when I didn't see Stevie.

Hannah sat down across from me. "What have you been soooo busy doing?"

I didn't know how much information to give away in front of the other girls. "Well, I've been...more active around here. I've decided to help out the Defiance. I thought—" Hannah wasn't looking at me anymore. Her huge, frightened eyes gawked past me. I turned around. Stevie charged toward me with her hands balled into fists.

"Is it true?" she spat as she approached. "IS IT TRUE?"

"Is what true?" I asked.

"Are you seriously going with them?" Tears gathered in her eyes. "ARE YOU REALLY GOING ON THE NEXT CHAOS?" Stevie's shrieks silenced the room, making us the center of attention.

Fire burned in my cheeks, but I tried to keep my voice low. "Stevie, can we talk about this in private?"

"TELL ME!" she yelled as the dam broke and tears streamed down her face.

I didn't know what to say. She obviously heard I was going, so lying to her wouldn't help the situation. But, I didn't want to encourage the conversation by admitting the truth. "I'm not getting into this with you." I turned my back to her.

Stevie continued her rant. "That was my spot! You took my spot! You think you can fake your way out of this place. You don't deserve to go. I'm the one who has been working day and night for this. I'm the one who has been fighting for the Defiance for years. You come in here, bat your eyes at Roman, throw a couple of pieces of information at him, and now you're special enough to go?"

My temper rose with every word she spoke. I had enough to worry about without her berating me in front of the whole cafeteria. I couldn't take her antics for one more second. I stood up and faced her. "Let me make this simple for you. What I've been telling the Defiance is none of your business. You have no idea how much I've helped or the strategy I've provided. I had absolutely no say in whether you went on this Chaos, so you can't blame me. Who knows? Maybe an outburst like this is the exact reason you're not going."

Stevie's face morphed from anger to shock to rage over the course of my reply. "How dare you assume what I know! I know *exactly* what you've been telling the Defiance. Not only that, I know the original plan and it did *not* include you going on this Chaos."

I decided to put her in her place. "You're just jealous because I'm a Kronie now, and you're going to be stuck here on clean-up duty. You're jealous that Roman trusts me and—"

"Let me finish!" Stevie interrupted. "I didn't get to tell you everything. I know that it was Roman's designated mission to butter you up and get information out of you. He was *assigned* to be your friend. Bet you didn't know that. Did you?"

My breath caught in my throat. "Wh—what?"

Stevie crossed her arms and continued. "Yeah. Gage instructed Roman to get to know you, flirt with you, do whatever it took to get information about the show. You think Roman was hanging out with you because he likes you? Don't you think it's odd that he wants to spend so much time with the person who ruined the last Chaos; *his* Chaos? Isn't it suspicious that you, the person who is the most absorbed in OneGlobal culture and knows the most about *Great American Dream* is the person the Asylum director suddenly wants to get to know better? Think about it. The night of the big game, Roman, being the great leader that he is, didn't go console his team. Instead, he hung out with you because Gage told him to. And your little 'training session' today, it was all an act... all of it. What do you think about that?"

The room suddenly became very small. It was difficult

to breathe. "I...I..."

Stevie smiled victoriously. "That's what I thought. Seems like you don't know everything after all. You're nothing special. He just used you for information and he'll do the same thing during this Chaos. As soon as it's over, he'll—"

I couldn't stand it anymore. I fled the cafeteria in tears, a repeat of my second day in the Asylum. I ran to my room and threw myself on the bed, my heart shattering into pieces along the way. If what Stevie said was true, then the Defiance was just as big of a lie as OneGlobal, and I didn't want any part of it. Out of all of the mess, one aspect became clear: I was more determined than ever to escape the Asylum.

After ten minutes of sobbing, a knock at the door broke my thoughts. "Eve, are you okay? It's Hannah. Can I come in?"

I didn't want anyone to see me in such a disheveled state. "I just want to be alone."

"Don't believe what Stevie said. She's just a bully. If it makes you feel any better, Professor Gray stormed in and ripped her apart in front of the entire Asylum...text me when you're ready for company. We'll break into the cafeteria and steal some ice cream or something. I don't know how, but I'll work on that."

I smiled feebly to myself. "Thanks. You're a real friend. I'll text you when I'm ready."

Silence settled in the room and a new wave of sobs crashed down on me. I relived every word Stevie said over and over. *How did she know about the football game, and the training session? She said all of it was fake. Did that include the almost-kiss?* After what felt like a lifetime of crying, the tears dried. I took a shower to refocus and crawled back into bed. Unfortunately, the more time that passed, the more believable Stevie's words became. I was stupid to think an amazing guy like Roman could ever have a thing for me. But then again, he was just using me, so he wasn't that amazing after all. *He means nothing to you and you need to move on! Focus on what's important.* I didn't think it was possible to feel any more stress, but I needed to concentrate on my escape. I needed—a small knock at the door made me jump. I pretended not to hear it. The knock came again.

"Eve. Can we talk?" It was Roman.

"Go away," I called back.

"Eve, please let me in."

"I don't want to talk to you."

"I heard what happened...Stevie had no right—"

"Stop." I cut him off. "I don't want to talk about it."

Roman sighed heavily. "Alright. I'm going to wait outside the door until you feel like talking. Just let me know when you're ready."

I pulled the blanket over my head and began to cry again. Just hearing his voice reopened the wound. Deep down I knew I should let him explain, but I didn't have the energy to hear his lies. My resilience lasted almost an hour. I dragged my blankets to the door and sat down. "Are you there?"

"Yep."

"Just answer me one question. No lies. Did Gage tell you to get to know me in order to get information?"

"I need to explain my answer. When—"

"Yes or no? That's all I want right now."

Roman stalled. "Then, yes, but—"

"Stop. That's all I wanted to know." I breathed hard to hold back the tears. Stevie was right. I set my sights on my crystal clear goal. "You can leave my bag by the door, and I'll see you in the morning."

"You still want to go?" Roman asked. I could hear the surprise in his voice.

"I'm not going for you. I'm going to help the Defiance. Is there anything I need to know about tomorrow?"

"Five minutes. Just give me five minutes." After I didn't reply, Roman sighed. "You should know that all squad leaders have a kill switch."

"What does that mean?"

"It means if they think anyone is acting suspicious or jeopardizing the Chaos, they have the power to deactivate their phone and kick them out of the mission. If that happens, you are to report to the Asylum as soon as possible."

"Anything else?"

"Everything is in your pack. There's a lot of stuff I'd like to go over with you...can you please open the door?"

My resistance didn't waver. "Leave the pack and go away. I'll go over everything by myself." I huffed, mad at myself for not wanting him to see my puffy face.

Roman's firm voice responded. "I told you I'm not leaving until you talk to me."

"Well, it's going to be a long night then." I marched over and hopped onto the bed, hoping he could hear the squeaky springs.

Somehow, I fell asleep. I awoke to tears still leaking from my eyes. I looked at my band, 0315. *I wonder if he's still outside.* I crept to the door, opened it slightly and peeked out the crack. Next to the door was my backpack. Beside that Roman slept, using his backpack as a pillow. I cautiously seized my pack and pulled it inside, taking one last look at Roman sleeping. My heart ached as I eased the door shut.

I set the pack on the bed, took out the fur coat, and looked underneath. I inhaled sharply as I pulled out the most gorgeous white lace top, embroidered with intricate gold accents. Next was the typical, skin-tight Designer jeans, only with shiny, gold stitching. The shoes looked handcrafted, a delicate sandal with a small heel. I examined the left shoe to find the hidden compartment that contained the memory pill. I set them to the side and removed out the last item: a Designer handbag. I opened the bag to find a small box labeled, accessories. I carefully poured the contents onto the desk. There was a set of dazzling crystal earrings that probably cost more than my mom's car and a set of beautiful silver and gold cuffs. But what really caught my eye was the enormous engagement ring! The intricately cut sapphire was surrounded by countless delicate gems. I held my breath as I slid the ring onto my finger, a perfect fit. It couldn't possibly be real, but it shimmered radiantly even in the dingy light of the room.

As upset as I was, I couldn't wait to wear the outfit. Natalie would have lost her mind if she saw me dressed in something that posh. I made a mental note to take the outfit with me as a parting gift when I escaped. I spent the next hour going over the first section of the schedule to decide when to make my exit. No need to waste my time learning what would happen after I left. I decided my best chance to make a break for it would be at the FasTrack station. I could sneak off to the bathroom, change clothes, and then make my way home. As much as I wanted to visit the G.A.D. studio, it would be harder to make it back from Dallas. Plus, the sooner I got away from Roman, the better.

At 0419, I crept back to the door and peeked out. He was gone. As I shut the door, it hit me that Roman had access to the room. He could have unlocked the door at any point, but he chose to give me space instead.

I shook the thought from my mind. *Don't sympathize with him.* I refocused and began to dress for the day. The Designer outfit fit perfectly. *I* almost believed I was Upper Class. After running through my plans step-by-step, I took one last look around the room, knowing I would never see it again. All the positive memories were overshadowed by Stevie's bombshell. I grabbed my purse, packed with my new phone and getaway outfit, and noticed the huge engagement ring still sitting on the desk. I ignored it and reached my band toward the door. A small knock froze me in place.

After several seconds the knock came again. Slightly louder. Panic rose in my chest. I wasn't ready to face Roman. I knew I couldn't avoid him forever, but—

A third knock echoed in the room. "Eve? It's Hannah. Are you there?"

Relief rushed over me as I quickly opened the door. "I'm so glad it's you! Get in here!"

Hannah stood in the doorway with her mouth hanging open.

"What?" I asked, confused.

"You look beautiful!" she exclaimed as she entered the room. "I didn't know going on the Chaos meant you got to wear Designer. The other girls went to do makeup for the Chaos team, so I thought this might be able to catch you."

"Hannah, I don't have much time." I grabbed her by the hand and we sat on the bed. "I'm pretty sure I know the answer, but can I trust you to keep a secret?"

"Of course." Her eyebrows furrowed.

I took in a deep breath. I was grateful for the opportunity to say goodbye but didn't exactly know how to do it. "First of all, I want you to know that your friendship has meant the world to me. I don't know how I would have survived this place without you. I'm happy that you like it here, and I respect your decision to stay. But, this isn't the place for me. I need to get back to my family. So, on our way to the Chaos, I'm going to escape." I bit my lip and waited for her response. Even though I had no reason, I half expected her to run out the door to tell someone.

Hannah nodded thoughtfully to herself. "I'm going to miss you, but if that's really what you want to do... I support you."

I wrapped my arms around her and squeezed. "I'm going to miss you, too! Who knows? Maybe after all of this, we can meet up sometime." I knew how unlikely it was even as I said the words.

Hannah smiled weakly. "I just want to know, did you decide to do this because of what Stevie said? Or were you planning this all along?"

I regretted not being completely honest with her from the beginning. "Well, I always wanted to get back to my family, but after what Stevie said...it made the decision a lot easier."

"Have you talked to Roman about it?"

I shrugged. "In not so many words. I just asked him if it was true that Gage assigned him to get to know me and he said yes. That's all I needed to hear. Plus, everything Stevie said makes so much sense."

"I'm not telling you what to do, but I don't know if I would put much stock in what Stevie says. I've been around her a lot more than you, and she likes to make it appear as though she's really high up with the Defiance. But Charli says she is starting at the same level as all of us. I think she's just jealous since you've gotten way more attention than her. She was expecting to be placed on a pedestal since she is the first voluntarily recruited female in Oklahoma. I just don't want you to make a decision you'll regret."

"Well, I'm not going to regret being with my family." My band beeped: **REPORT TO THE GARAGE ASAP.** "I have to go. I'm sorry this is such a rushed goodbye. Are you really going to stay here forever?" I pulled her into a tight hug.

"I'll wait and see how things shake out after this Chaos. And I've been hanging out with Sherlock more. He's really sweet." She blushed slightly.

I felt like a total jerk. I was so consumed with my own situation, I hadn't asked Hannah about her life in the Asylum. "When I get home, I'll have my brother figure out a way for us to communicate. He's a genius."

We walked to the field together. I gave her one more hug. "What are you going to do now? You don't want to come and watch Stevie do my makeup?"

Hannah laughed. "As tempting as that is, I'll let you handle that can of worms on your own. Sherlock is in charge of security monitoring for the Asylum. So, I'll be watching all the action from a screen. Take care of yourself, Eve. I'll be waiting for your message." She smiled and trotted toward the War Room.

I watched her disappear, then joined the small group of boys headed to the open doors of the exit. I noticed more than one of them giving me the up-and-down. I held my chin high and rushed through the long tunnel.

The garage was a flurry of activity. Beauty stations lined one wall, their bright lights filling the area with warmth. I noticed Stevie, Charli, and several other girls doing makeup.

I walked down the row, gaped at each guy in the chairs. They looked Hollywood Upper Class, like the kind I saw on television. I had never been in the actual presence of an Upper since we didn't have many in Oklahoma, just high ranking political figures and other OneGlobal elite.

My band buzzed. "PROCEED TO STATION ONE."

My stomach sank as I continued down the row and realized that was Stevie's station. *This will be the last time you ever have to deal with her. Suck it up. Act like she doesn't bother you. You are the one going on the mission, not her!* My self-pep talk actually worked. I strutted over to station one and plopped into the chair.

"Look straight ahead. Chin up, please." She tapped on her tablet without looking at me. "First, I need to take your facial measurements." Her hand shook slightly as she pressed a large pen to different points on my face. "Close your eyes."

I followed her instructions, and she ran the pen across my eyelids.

"You can open. It will take a few minutes to calibrate. We don't have an auto-styler so I have to do your hair by hand." She turned my chair away from the mirrors.

Stevie worked in silence, twisting and knotting my hair. After ten minutes, the tablet beeped. She walked in front of me and handed me a plastic mask. "Put this on your face, eyes closed and don't move. Hold it against your skin until it beeps, then you can relax."

I stared into her eyes, but she refused to look at me. I gave up glaring at her and followed her instructions. I felt a slight pressure against different areas of my face for thirty seconds until the small machine finished. Stevie continued to work on my hair for the next half an hour while I counted down the seconds until I could leave her presence.

"All finished," she said as she spun my chair around to face the mirror.

My jaw dropped. I recognized myself, but I looked amazing. My hair twisted and weaved into a perfect bun on the top of my head. My makeup was precise, even and flawless. I legitimately looked Upper Class, but even better was the fact that I could leave Stevie.

"Thanks," I spat as I grabbed my purse and turned to leave.

"Eve, wait." Stevie played with a string on the edge of her shirt. She took a deep breath and looked me in the eye. "I apologize...for yesterday. I was out of line and upset and...I'm sorry."

"I'm glad you're sorry." I didn't care what Stevie had

to say. I turned my back on her and rushed toward the middle of the garage as my itinerary instructed.

Chairs filled a central holding area. Boys sat scattered in the seats waiting for their group to be called. I picked a seat and pretended to look at my phone. I could check Stevie off my list, but I still had to face Roman. I casually looked around the room but didn't see him.

Gideon walked in front of the chairs and spoke into his band. "GROUP TWO, PROCEED TO YOUR VEHICLE," his voice boomed throughout the facility.

Several of the boys stood up and made their way to a line of Upper SUVs. Gideon noticed me and walked over. "You look legit."

"Thanks." I smiled slightly. "Why aren't you all fancied up like the rest of us?"

"Not my style. I'm using a more…unconventional way of getting on set." Gideon sat down in front of me. "I'm really sorry about yesterday. Maybe now you can guess why I don't get along with my sister. Anyway, I'm really glad you're still coming. We need people like you. I gotta go make sure everything's still on track, but I'll catch you in Dallas, kid." He gave me a fist bump then trotted off.

Suddenly, a large backpack slammed down in the chair beside me. I almost jumped out of my skin. I looked up to see Roman standing over me.

"You ready?" he asked as he finished buttoning his shirt.

It took several seconds for me to register what he said. I was too busy gawking at how impressive he looked. His hair was braided into a tight, dapper ponytail with the sides freshly buzzed. I noticed a large, antique watch on his left wrist as he adjusted his jeweled cufflinks. His Designer shirt modeled a crisp pattern of varying blues. The shirt was slightly too small, accentuating every muscle in his upper body. This was tucked into grey, pressed slacks with a thin, black belt. Sleek, black shoes completed the outfit. My eyes made their way back to his face. I realized he was staring at me just as hard.

"You look astonishing," he whispered.

My heart fluttered, but then I remembered everything that happened the day before. "Did Gage tell you to say that?"

Roman balled his hands into fists and shook his head. He pulled a chair in front of me and sat backward. "I know you hate me right now, and as much as I would like to sit here and hash it out, we don't have the time. When we are in public, we must act like an Upper Class couple. If for any reason we can't pull it off, I'll take us both off the mission. Deal?"

I crossed my arms. "Deal."

Roman unzipped his backpack and removed a small silver rectangle. "May I see your band?" I stretched my wrist toward him, and he attached the box to my band. After several seconds, the small metal bead holding the ends together released, and the band fell into Roman's waiting hand. "I'll get rid of this." He walked to the nearest Kronie and started a conversation.

I turned my back to him, willing my eyes not to tear up. It was incredibly frustrating that I could be so mad at him and, at the same time, be craving his attention. *Just get through this. Just ignore him and focus on escape.* It didn't help that, dressed in Designer, he was easily the most attractive man I'd ever seen in my life. I stole a quick peek in his direction, only to see him peering directly at me. I promptly averted my eyes.

Gideon's voice echoed through the room. "GROUP THREE, PROCEED TO YOUR VEHICLES."

Roman walked past me and motioned with his head for me to follow. We walked toward a fully loaded SUV. Roman opened the back door for me and I hopped inside. I marveled at the top-of-the-line interior.

"You forgot this." Roman dropped the fake engagement ring in my lap then closed the door. I hesitated, then put the beautiful ring on my finger as he slid in beside me.

"You're not sitting in the front? What if someone needs to emergency drive?" I asked.

"Uppers don't ride in the front and this isn't a self-driving vehicle. OneGlobal can control all self-driven vehicles, so we take that out of the equation," he replied. As if on cue, both front doors opened and two older boys wearing black suits and sunglasses entered the car. "This is Agent Davidson and Agent Ross. They will be our bodyguards for the day. Let's roll, gentlemen."

My stomach knotted as we drove silently into the large elevator. Darkness engulfed the vehicle. It felt like years since I had made my descent into the Asylum. I couldn't believe I was leaving. I had accomplished my goals, and in a matter of hours, I would be back with my family.

The elevator came to a stop as the building's door squeaked open, the morning light kept out by the darkly tinted windows. We passed the buildings I had last viewed from the spire. I found it crazy how different I felt about Roman then.

Agent Ross turned on the radio to the G.A.D. preview

station. It played a synopsis of the remaining contestants as well as recaps of the judges' critiques. "Don't miss the Dallas semi-final. Text in your guess of tonight's mystery judge. Winners will be entered into our finale ticket drawing!" I looked over at Roman. His head leaned back against the seat, eyes closed and lips moving silently as if rehearsing a script.

I wiped my sweaty palms on my jeans and wondered when the best time to bolt would be. The sooner I left, the less chance of something going wrong. For the first time, I wondered if I still supported the Defiance after what I learned about Roman. I knew I lost any respect I had for them, considering they would do whatever it took to get what they wanted. Which was the less of two evils? I didn't feel bad about bailing on them since I didn't really think I could add anything to the mission.

I chewed on my lip as we entered the outskirts of civilization. Roman's knee bounced up and down. After several minutes, I recognized buildings as we approached the downtown area. By the time we arrived at the terminal, I officially felt nauseous. *Don't be nervous. There is no way Roman will run after you in public. All he cares about is the Chaos, he won't abandon that for you.* A gate blocked our path into the glass-encased Upper Class FasTrack parking area.

"Here we go," Agent Davidson said as he rolled down his window. He held his phone toward the scanner and the gate opened briskly. "Looks like the phones are working."

I had never been in the Upper section of the station. Usually, we parked far away and went through multiple security checkpoints. But as an Upper, we drove right up to the platform and parked. I could see hundreds of people milling about on the other side of the tracks. The FasTrack pulled into the station and separated us from the normal area. I surveyed my surroundings, no bathrooms to sneak into. I mentally crossed "plan A" off my list. A few other elite cars were scattered around the lot. Not the crowd I had hoped for to hide my escape. I could either make a run for it or wait until the train doors opened and try to make my way to the other side.

I had to make a decision. The longer I waited, the more my courage evaporated. I needed to do something before the boys had a chance to realize what was going on. I took a deep breath, shifted my weight against the door, grabbed the handle, and squeezed.

CHAPTER 14

FLIGHT

A strong hand gripped my shoulder. "Don't get out on your own. Let the guards get your door. Upper Class, remember?"

I froze. Every nerve in my body fired, except the ones that made my body move. I don't think I was even breathing.

Roman recognized the terror in my eyes. "Hang on, I'll come help you. Get my door first, guys."

I heard the driver exit the vehicle and open Roman's door. Adrenaline coursed through my veins. I needed to bolt as soon as my door opened, but I didn't know if I had the guts. Roman casually walked around to my side and one guard helped him put on a blazer. He adjusted his collar as he waited for the other guard to open my door. I closed my eyes and willed my body to the nearest exit.

I fell out of the car with the release of the door. Of course, Roman was right there to catch me. I immediately sensed a change in his demeanor as he stood me upright.

"Oh, Celestia, clumsy as always. I told you that was too

much to drink this early in the morning." He grabbed my hand and placed it on the inside of his bicep.

I looked up at him and he winked at me. *Ugh, why did he have to be so good looking?* I pulled my arm from his grasp. *Two can play this game.* "I am perfectly capable of walking by myself. Thank you very much." I snapped as I stormed off toward the train.

I glanced cautiously around me. To my right, the empty lot stopped at a cement barricade. *No escaping that way.* To my left waited a group of Uppers and beyond them a few other smaller groups. There was no way I could make my getaway with Roman so close. In two seconds, he would seize me and be alerted to my intentions. As much as I denied it to myself, I didn't want to put the mission in jeopardy. I just wanted to go home. I pretended to play on my phone. My thumbs hovered over the screen as I realized that, for the first time, I had a real, working phone in my hands. I could threaten to call the D.O.C... or I could call home.

"The doors should open any second now," Roman stated behind me. He wrapped his arms around my shoulders and buried his head into my neck, sending lightning bolts through my spine. *Why does that still happen when I'm so mad at him?* Roman whispered in my ear. "Just FYI, our phones cannot call any government agency. Plus, your family's phone lines are being monitored. Any unknown call to them only puts them in jeopardy."

I spun around. "How did you know?"

He shrugged. "That's what I would do."

I turned back to the train and chewed my lip as I assessed my circumstances. Our bodyguards stood at attention behind us, making a foot chase impossible. My best bet was to wait until the doors opened, then make a beeline for the other side. I took a slow, deep breath and balled my hands into fists. *It's go time. Suck it up and run.* I shifted my weight from foot to foot, willing my body to behave. Suddenly, the doors flew open. I lunged forward, but Roman's hands pulled me back against him.

"I read your letter," he confessed. "Ride with me on the train. Let me explain everything. If you still want to leave, you can ride back and never have to deal with me or my friends again. Deal?"

Shock hit me like a ton of bricks. I had completely forgotten about the letter. I could only nod and let him guide me onto the train. He knew I was planning to escape all along. *Why hadn't he—*

"Ticket, please," an automated voice chimed as I entered the train.

Mechanically, I placed my phone on the scanner. It flashed green and I watched Roman do the same. We stepped into the social hall of the train, restricted to Uppers. It was the first time I had ever been in an Exclusive Area, so I tried not to gawk at the extravagance of it all. Several people laughed around a stainless steel bar, while others lounged on plush, oversized couches. Decadent mini-chandeliers hung from the ceiling and large holographic TVs covered the walls.

"This way, my love. I booked us a private room." Roman took my hand and led me down the hallway. I realized I hadn't even looked for the exit. We stopped at the door labeled C3. He pulled me in for a hug and murmured, "Follow my lead. Act asleep. As soon as the train starts moving we can talk."

He tapped his phone against the door and it slid open automatically. The room was simple, yet elegant: a small table in the middle with a couch on either side. Through the large window, I could see the hundreds of common people in line to board the train. I was a mere three meters from freedom.

Roman took off his blazer and hung it in the closet. "I don't know about you, love, but I'm beat."

I sat on the couch. "How long until we get there?"

"It's about a thirty-minute ride to Dallas. Should be enough time for a good nap. Do you mind if I close the window?"

I took one last look at the oblivious bystanders. "That's fine." I curled up on the couch and was immediately taken aback with its luxury. It was ten times more comfortable than my bed at home. If I wasn't so stressed, I would have fallen asleep immediately.

Roman strode over to the window and touched a panel. A dark shade dropped as small lights surrounding the perimeter of the ceiling created a soft glow. He walked over to me and opened his palm to show a small green pill.

"What's this?" I asked, skeptical. I didn't think he would drug me, but I knew how much the Chaos meant to him.

"It's your nausea pill. I don't want you puking all over this very expensive cabin." He pleaded at me with his eyes.

I hadn't even thought about my motion sickness. As much as I was over Roman, I didn't want him holding my hair back as I emptied my guts into the trash can. I swallowed the pill and Roman stretched out on his couch.

After several minutes, musical notes chimed throughout

the cabin and the screen covering the windows morphed into a three-dimensional stewardess. "Hello, and welcome to FasTrack, the fastest and safest way to travel the country. We will be arriving at our destination of Dallas, Texas in exactly thirty-three minutes. Enjoy the ride, and if there is anything we can do to make your trip more pleasurable, don't hesitate to call your personal attendant." She blew each of us a kiss then disappeared.

My heart raced as the room rocked gently with the train's departure. Roman took off his watch. He played with the dials, then set it in the middle of the table. He threw himself on the couch and pretended to fall asleep. I closed my eyes and did the same.

The minutes passed by slowly as I longed to take advantage of the lush sofa and just fall asleep. But my mind raced with anticipation of what Roman had to say. *How could he possibly explain his actions?* I couldn't imagine any scenario where I would forgive him. I took solace in Roman's promise of returning me to my family after the ride.

After what felt like an eternity, I heard Roman stir. I opened my eyes to see him bring a finger over his lips as he sat up. He examined the watch. "Okay, it's safe to move and talk now, but it's still best to keep our voices down."

"What do you mean?" I whispered.

"You have to remember that everywhere, and I mean *everywhere,* in public is under constant surveillance by the government. In order to have a private conversation, we must set up safeguards."

"Safeguards?"

He pointed to his watch. "That is a Looper. It loops the feed so it appears that we are sleeping the entire time if anyone happened to peek into our video footage. It also blocks audio devices, so our conversation cannot be recorded. We have limited time to talk, so do you care if I start?"

I nodded and hugged my knees up to my chest.

He crossed the small distance and sat on the end of my couch. "First of all, I want you to know that I have never lied to you about anything. Every conversation has been genuine and sincere. The first night in the Asylum, after I took you to my room, I knew I had to face Gage. To put it lightly…he was livid. He felt I completely degraded and humiliated him in front of everyone. I apologized for making him feel that way, but I used my right. I didn't want someone to die for doing what they believed to be the right thing. I promised him I would look after you and make sure you would not be a burden in any way. We parted that night still not seeing eye to eye, but he didn't look like he was going to murder me anymore.

"The next morning, I had a meeting with the Dallas Defiance, so I asked Gideon to keep an eye on you. Gage found me and asked what I thought about your file. I was honest. I told him you had great potential and could be a huge asset to our side. I hoped you would be open to re-education, but didn't think your personality would mesh with Emily at first. Especially since she…wasn't too fond of you at the time. Gage then told me that you were my next mission; that I was to get to know you and gain your trust by any means necessary, so you would tell me information that may benefit the next Chaos."

My heart dropped in defeat. Stevie was right. I realized a deep part of me still hoped it was all a lie. I bit my lip hard to try to keep the tears from overflowing. I didn't want him to see how much he meant to me. I tasted blood.

Roman continued. "At first I told him no way. I would not unethically manipulate you for information. He reminded me that he was technically my superior and was giving me a direct order. So, I agreed, with the following stipulations: I would try to get to know you, but if it was unnatural or you didn't want anything to do with me, I would leave you alone. I would accept information, but only if it was offered freely and willingly. I did not want to force or coerce you in any way. Gage said he didn't care how I accomplished my assignment as long as I did it.

"I hope you know that I would not do something if I believed it was wrong or immoral. The only reason I agreed was because I really wanted to get to know you. I mean…you're my Coverture and some people may not value that, but I do." He scooted closer, leaving the gap between us mere centimeters. "So, what Stevie told you was true…partially. Gage did technically 'assign' me to get to know you, but that didn't matter. I would have done the same thing if Gage told me to avoid you completely. Every conversation, every episode of *Great American Dream*, every moment came from what *I* wanted to do. I've truly enjoyed each second we've spent together, and I wouldn't change anything about the second Chaos because it brought you to me. The only thing I regret is not telling you about Gage's assignment, but I wasn't following it in my heart, so I didn't think it mattered. I'm sorry about how you found out. Stevie had no right to maliciously attack you in front of everyone. I'll do whatever it takes to make it up to you. I'm sorry, Eve." He leaned back and sighed deeply. "That's what I needed you to know. Now, it's your turn. What questions do you have for me?" His knee bounced up and down as he waited for my response.

I sat in the fallout of his response. I desperately wanted to believe every word, but things still didn't add up. "What about the night of the football game? Afterward, I saw Gage talk to you, then he looked directly at me."

"He wanted to remind me about my assignment. He was worried I felt obligated to console my team and not take an opportunity to pull information out of you."

"So, that *is* why you hung out with me?" I blurted.

Roman shook his head. "Not at all. Honestly, I was torn between hanging out with you and being with my team. I felt a responsibility to be with my players. That game meant a lot to them, and the way we lost was just ridiculous. On the other hand, I knew we wouldn't have many more opportunities to hang out with just the two of us. I weighed my options and decided what I thought was more important in the long run." He never diverted his eyes.

My skepticism continued. "How did Stevie know about it? About the football game and the training?" I blushed, wondering exactly how much of the training Stevie knew about.

A look of frustration flashed across his face. "Emily found me after my meeting and told me what happened in the cafeteria. She had no clue about my 'assignment,' so I knew it wasn't her. This morning I found out it was actually Gage himself who spilled the beans. Conveniently, he had already left for Dallas, so I couldn't talk to him about it. But I'm betting he did it to get me back for saving you in the first place or in hopes that you would decide to bail on the mission. Either way, after this Chaos, I will personally find out why he did it and will rectify the situation." Roman smiled slightly, in what I imagined to be thoughts of smashing Gage's face in.

His explanation made sense. If he was just doing what *he* wanted to do the entire time, then maybe I could forgive him. I wished I had longer to decipher my feelings. I needed more information. I decided to go broad with my question and see where he went with it. "Is there anything else I don't know about?"

Roman furrowed his brow. "Let's see. Your first night in the Asylum, Gage told me he wanted you tracked at all times. I told him that was illegal since it's against Defiance policy to track any member of the U.D. without their consent. He said you weren't a real Kronie, so it didn't matter if we had consent. I said you were my Coverture, which gave you all the rights that I have. We left agreeing to disagree but understanding that you would not be tracked. The morning after we first watched G.A.D. together, Gideon told me that he discovered Gage was tracking you. Not only that, he had intercepted all communication through your band. I wanted to go straight to his room and take his head off, but Gideon talked me out of it. Let's just say we had a heated discussion, and from that moment on you were no longer tracked."

I nodded and smiled slightly, thinking about Roman standing up for me. "Anything else?"

He shifted his weight on the couch and rubbed the back of his neck. "There's something else I've been debating telling you…about your family. It may be difficult for you to hear."

A new fear settled in my stomach. "What?"

"After you told me how 'involved' your mother was in the first Chaos, I did some research. When she was released from the hospital, did she act a little different? Like the Chaos never occurred?"

"How did you know?" I whispered.

"I had Gideon hack into her medical records. OneGlobal had her memory erased. When the D.O.C. arrived at All-Mark, your mom was physically fine. She was taken to Central and interrogated. Once they got all the information they wanted, the decision was made to wipe her memory of that night. Unfortunately, what she went through was too traumatic to be erased by a simple pill like we have. She required stronger IV medication. That's why she was admitted to the hospital."

The idea of my mom being pumped full of chemicals made my heart break and rage at the same time. "Why didn't they erase my memory too?"

"Several reasons, but I'm betting the main one is that you had information they didn't want you to forget. That way if another Chaos occurred, they could question you again. The really sad part is that made her agree to do it, had her sign a consent form and everything. The reason she complied," he took a deep breath, "is because they told her it was best for you and Connor. They said having too many traumatic memories in the household would create anxiety, mistrust and paranoia that could lead to Noncompliance. It was either her or you, and after hearing all the side effects, she agreed to do it. They were going to do it either way, but now they're covered if anything were to go wrong."

I sat, numbly disgusted, imagining everything my mom had gone through.

Roman put a hand on my shoulder. "I'm sorry, Eve. I probably should have told you the second I found out, but I didn't want to upset you with everything else going on."

"Thanks for telling me. It makes sense." Believing OneGlobal had hurt and manipulated nameless people was one thing, but knowing they had messed with my family was another. A new passion burned in my belly. "Is that everything?"

"I think that's about everything. Well, all the bad stuff, anyway."

I furrowed my brow.

A slight smile spread across his face. "I may have given your brother periodic updates on your well-being."

"What?" I yelled.

"Shhhhh!" He covered my mouth with his hand. "I've been talking to Connor quite often. I wanted to tell you, but I needed you to be able to play dumb if I was caught. He's a pretty cool little dude. Can you forgive me?"

Tears raced down my face as I threw myself at him. His strong arms locked me in place. I'm sure Roman was saving that ace up his sleeve, knowing my family was the way to my heart, but I didn't care. All was forgiven.

I hugged him as hard as I could. "Thank you, thank you, thank you! You have no idea how much that means to me."

"I'm so sorry about everything, Eve. I'll never hide any-thing from you again. Please forgive me." He squeezed once more then let go.

I leaned back in my seat, trying to cover my

embarrassingly snotty nose with my hands. "I forgive you. I'm sorry I didn't let you explain earlier. I was too upset."

"Completely understandable." Roman handed me a handkerchief from his back pocket. "There is one other thing I would like to discuss...the letter."

My smile faded as my nerves came back to life. Once again, I had completely forgotten about the letter. "I...I..."

Roman wiped my tears. "I'm not mad. I'm actually honored you thought about me."

"I didn't mean for you to see it until after the Chaos. When did you read it?"

"This morning, right before we left. I always go through my family photos before something big like this. When did you write it? I mean...when did you decide you were going to escape?" Roman asked as his eyes pierced my soul.

I hated to admit my plans to him, but I had to tell the truth. "Over the past few days, I've wavered back and forth. After the War Room meeting, I really was excited to go but then after the whole Stevie incident I was done. But, I guess since we are being completely honest..." It was my turn to share secrets. "I was always planning to escape. From the moment I arrived, I calculated ways to break out. I decided I wouldn't make it out of the compound by force or stealth, so my best shot was being invited out. When I heard about the next Chaos, I looked for opportunities to be an asset in the hopes of being invited. I..."

Reality hit me like a ton of bricks as I said the words out loud. *I'm a complete and total jerk.* I was so upset at Roman for "manipulating" me when I had been the one doing the manipulating. He had never given me a reason to doubt him, but I didn't even give him a chance to explain. On top of that, he had done nothing but defend me and look out for me. He put himself at risk over and over, while I was planning on betraying him the entire time. I felt just as immature as Stevie. If Roman had any respect for me before, he surely lost it after he read the letter.

"I'm so sorry, Roman. I was deceiving you just to try to get what I wanted. How could you ever forgive me? I guess my letter was true after all. I'm not the amazing person you saw in the file. I'm horrible." I hesitantly looked up to gauge his expression. To my surprise, he was beaming. "What?" I asked.

Roman chuckled softly, "That's what I saw in you! That's my girl; resourceful, determined, calculating. It proves your letter wrong. You may think you're not good enough to help us but I *know* you are more than enough. You're the exact reason I'm fighting. I want every person on the planet to be able to reach their full potential, and that's only possible through having freedom and truth. Eve, only you have the power to choose your fate, no one else should be allowed to do that for you."

The sincerity in his voice overwhelmed me. He truly believed all the wonderful things he said about me. I opened my mouth, but no words came.

Roman continued. "I'm so sorry you've had to go through all of this. You never asked to be in this situation, yet...here you are and I don't think it's by accident. Now, I stand by my word. If you want to turn around and go back to Oklahoma, I'll make sure you are safe. But you *can* help us. It's completely up to you. Unfortunately, we don't have much time."

I felt like my emotions were a roller coaster and my

safety harness was busted. The day had been a whirlwind, and we hadn't even gotten to the hard part. All along my goal was to be reunited with my family, but looking into Roman's eyes, I couldn't imagine leaving the new adventure behind. Plus, after hearing what OneGlobal did to my mom, maybe it was in my family's best interest for them to be shut down. I wanted to make what Roman saw in me a reality.

"I'll help." I said as relief washed over his face. "But I need to know: is there any way my involvement could hurt my family?"

"Only if you were to get caught, and I promise I won't let that happen." He stuck out his fist with his pinky extended.

I laughed as we sealed the promise.

Roman's eyes lit up. "Out of Chaos, revolution is born. Eve, today we change history and we'll have a fun time doing it." He took back his handkerchief and walked over to his watch. "Time to get back into character. In five minutes, the Looper will turn off and we will be back in the real world. Try to get back into the same position you fell asleep in. Follow my lead when we get there and stay close."

I cuddled up on the couch and closed my eyes in disbelief of how one FasTrack ride could change in my life. I felt excited, yet terrified. I had no idea what to expect, but I trusted Roman to get me through it. In what seemed like seconds, I felt a small shift in the cabin and the melodious notes overhead signaled our arrival. It was time for me to join the Defiance.

CHAPTER 15
GREAT AMERICAN DREAM

That time, I waited for my door to be opened as we parked in the back lot of *Great American Dream*. I tried to force my nerves into submission, but internally, I was freaking out. Roman had told me to not think about the Chaos, but to focus on being an Upper on the set of my favorite TV show. I adjusted my fur coat as I stepped into the early evening breeze.

"Are you ready, my love?" Roman asked with his chin high. He had regained his air of superiority as he waited for me. For some reason, I found his smugness charming, probably because his real personality was the complete opposite.

I strutted over to him and slid my hand into his. Since I was back to crushing on him, I wanted to take advantage of every opportunity. I chose to ignore my awkward, sweaty palm and hoped he didn't notice.

We fell in step with the others strolling down the covered walkway to the entrance. I had never seen so many Uppers in one place at the same time. *I would score*

sooo many points if I was playing the Upper game with Mom!
I tried not to stare, but I didn't think anyone would notice
since every eye was glued to a phone. I couldn't help smiling as I surveyed my surroundings. Every single person
was decked out in Designer. Uniformed servers weaved
through the crowd offering drinks and hors-d'oeuvres
on silver platters. Clips from earlier episodes played on
the holographic televisions above our heads. *Maybe this
will be fun after all.*

As we joined the end of the security line, a girl wearing
a dazzling, sheer, pink dress turned to us. "What is taking
so long? This is ridiculous to make us wait outside!" She
threw down her empty glass. A server raced forward to
pick up the shards.

Roman didn't look up from his phone. "Beats me."

A guy behind us joined the conversation, his metal
fedora reflecting the bright lights of the walkway.. "Probably the extra security. I heard they doubled up for this
recording."

I squeezed Roman's arm as my stomach dropped.

A girl in a turquoise jumpsuit spun around with her
jaw hanging open. "You mean none of you've heard yet?
It's because of tonight's guest judge. Erikson Mendax!"

I couldn't believe my ears. Talk about worst case scenarios. Mr. Mendax was the only child of President Victoria
Mendax. If we thought security would be an issue before,
Erikson being on set complicated everything a hundred-
fold. I looked at Roman. I could tell by his expression the
news was a surprise to him.

The girl in pink let a squeal. "Get out! How did we get
so lucky? Do you think he'll stick around for the after

party? He's only the most eligible socialite in the world!"

The server returned with a new round of drinks, which seemed to pacify the group since they returned to their phones. I couldn't believe Erikson would be at the recording. The fangirl inside of me was absolutely freaking out. *Natalie would give up G.A.D. forever just for the chance to take a selfie with Erikson.*

Roman wrapped his arm around my shoulders. "We should have known about that. I guess it just makes tonight more exciting."

Exciting was not the word I would have chosen as regret washed over me. *I shouldn't have gone on this mission!* I could barely stand without shaking, let alone pretend to be an Upper while secretly infiltrating a building that housed the President's son. We slowly shuffled forward as I focused on maintaining a vertical status. When it was our turn, a security officer waved me forward.

Roman hugged me from behind. "You got this. You're an Upper," he whispered into my ear.

Great. I knew he meant to boost my confidence, but I could only think of the disappointment I would cause him if I screwed up.

"Pass, please," the officer droned without looking up from his tablet. I looked at his badge: Tyler, *Great American Dream* Security, Level 1.

I stuck out my arm to give him my phone. My hand shook noticeably.

Tyler slowly looked up and eyed me suspiciously. "You nervous or something?"

"No!" I responded too quickly. *Pull yourself together, Eve!* "Just crazy excited. This is my first live recording experience."

He nodded. "Oh, that explains it. Well, Miss…Westington, I hope you enjoy your experience. Through these doors is a standard body scanner, then you will head to the pre-party to receive your locker."

"Thank you!" I rushed forward.

"Miss?"

"Yes?" I turned around.

"Your phone." He smiled warmly, holding my phone in the air.

"Oh, yeah. Sorry." I grabbed my phone and glanced at Roman. He discreetly shook his head and smirked sheepishly.

I rushed through the automatic door; the frigid air hit my body like a wall. I heard the door shut and lock behind me. In front of me stood a large, clear tube, attached to countless wires with—

An automated drawer nudged my hip. "Purse and shoes in the container, then step into the scanner." I jumped at the voice.

I looked to my left. Two D.O.C. officers sat behind a large window. The voice carried through a speaker in the wall. "Please hurry, Miss Westington. We have many people to get through."

I froze. I didn't expect the Docs to be there, even with Erikson present. I knew G.A.D. personally selected the security that patrolled the set, but I'd never, in any season, noticed a D.O.C. presence. Reality crashed down. I wasn't playing a game of sneaking onto my favorite show. It was serious and I was in too deep to turn back. I stood, gawking at them, my feet glued to the floor.

"Miss Westington. Are you okay?" he asked. Both

officers stood to evaluate me.

Relax. You're not caught yet, but you will be if you keep acting like this! I attempted to swallow, but my mouth was sandpaper. "Um...yes. Yes. Sorry, excitement and...stuff."

I shoved my belongings into the small container. It silently moved away from me and into the room with the officers. One of them emptied my purse onto the counter and rifled through my belongings. The other continued to eye me suspiciously. I rushed into the tube, suppressing my panic as best as possible.

"Hands against the glass," the officer instructed.

I had been in a security scanner before, but never one that high tech. I followed his instructions and the machine warmed my hands. My vital signs instantly displayed in the glass. *Those have to be severely out of range! I should have paid more attention in Basic Science.*

The words "checking background" flashed in front of my face. I wondered how much it would slow down the screening process if I puked in the tube. To my relief, the name "Celestia Westington" popped up. I had never been so excited to see anything in my life. I sighed and dropped my head.

"Miss Westington? Are you okay?"

Knowing my alias had worked gave me a new confidence. "Perfect! I just can't take it any longer. In a matter of hours, I'll be face-to-face with Gavin Starling! Are you done yet?"

The officers instantly relaxed. "Yes, and we will get you to him as quickly as possible. But, can you explain these?" one asked as he held up my getaway clothes.

I forgot I had stowed my "plan A" escape outfit in my

purse. I had to think fast. "I thought we dressed like norms for the show. Has that changed?"

He laughed. "G.A.D. provides your costumes. Would you like for us to hold on to these?"

"Gross, no! Why would I want that garbage? Trash them."

"Perfect. The rest of your belongings will be on the other side."

I smiled and turned to leave, ecstatic that I made it through security. *I may be able to pull this off after all! When they see—* I tripped on the edge of the tube and stumbled out. My attempt at a smooth exit failed. The officers chuckled as the next door opened automatically.

"Welcome!" A bubbly, young adult with bright pink hair motioned me forward. "Pass, please."

I grabbed my belongings and hurried toward her, awkwardly lacing my sandals as she scanned my phone.

"So glad to have you with us for the first time, Celestia! Your locker key has been uploaded to your phone. Down the hall is our pre-party holding area. Feel free to hang out and enjoy complimentary refreshments as you wait for the show. Lockers and stylist stations are along the far wall to your right. Inside your locker, you will find your 'normal' wardrobe for the show. You need to be changed and checked off by our stylist by seven p.m., then you will be escorted into the filming set. All areas beyond holding are restricted. Accessing these will result in immediate expulsion from the facility, as well as a permanent ban from future recordings." She smiled enthusiastically. "Any questions?"

I perked up, trying to match her energy. "No. I don't think so. I'm just ready to get this started!"

"That's the spirit! Well, if you need anything at all, our Comfort Associates will be scattered throughout the room. Enjoy!"

I proceeded down the long hall, fighting the temptation to look behind me to see if Roman followed. Life-sized holographic portraits of previous winners waved to me as I walked by. I hesitantly waved back, my inner fanatic wanting to break free. I approached a large black door and pressed my phone to the scanner. The door opened to complete darkness. I turned around and looked at Ms. Peppy. She casually leaned against her podium and motioned for me to continue forward. I took a deep breath and stepped inside.

The door closed behind me, plunging me into pitch black. I stretched out my arms but felt nothing. My stomach dropped as the room ascended rapidly. "Celestia..." a techno voice surrounded me. "Welcome to the pre-party!"

Suddenly, the room flooded with multi-colored light as the *Great American Dream* theme song blasted through the tiny space. The door in front of me flung open to reveal a crowd of cheering Uppers. I hesitantly walked forward as shouts and whistles welcomed me.

"Looks like we have a first timer, boys!" someone yelled.

A girl around my age rushed forward and grabbed my arm. "We *must* get you a drink!"

She dragged me toward a bar in the center of the room. Her tight brown curls bounced with every step. I let her direct me as I took in the extravagance of the room. The place made the Upper FasTrack car look like a dump. Gigantic chandeliers drones floated majestically every few meters. The walls and floors changed color in time with the loud music as holographic models posed throughout the room. I turned my attention to the girl. Her skin-tight black dress flowed up into a beautiful, blue peacock. Its neck wrapped around her shoulders gracefully, but it made me appreciate my comparatively modest top and more practical jeans. She tapped furiously on the digital bartender.

The last thing I needed was a drink, especially since I'd never tasted alcohol before. I tried to stop her. "Oh, no thank you. I really shouldn't. I'm a lightweight and I don't want to appear drunk on camera." I yelled over the music.

The girl burst into laughter. "Appear drunk? You crack me up. I like you already. Didn't you bring your detox pills?"

"Detox pills? Um, no, actually…I knew I was forgetting something."

"No worries, babe. I always bring extra." She reached into her jeweled purse and pulled out a small orange pill and pressed it into my hand. "Take it right before six-thirty and you'll be completely sober by show time." Our drinks appeared, hovering beside us.

I held mine up. "To team Crystal!"

"I'll cheers to that!" She lifted her glass then downed half the drink, as I pretended to sip mine. "Name is Androm-eda. I wish it was my first time again. You'll be an addict before you know it. These pre-parties are *the* best thing ever! Except if you count the after-party. Those get crazy insane. So where are you from?"

"Oklahoma City."

"Oh, so that's why it's your first time. They never shoot out here in the middle of the country. But, can you blame them? This is, like, normal people America. I can't stand being around so many of *them*. Most of us here are from the coasts. I flew in from New York. I didn't think many Uppers lived in Oklahoma."

I fake sipped again, the liquid burned my lips. "No, and I wouldn't either if I had a choice."

The girl laughed hysterically. "You. Slay. Me." She finished her drink as she ordered another. "Celestia, right?"

"How did you know?"

"It shows above the door as you enter. The name is displayed in green if it's your first time. We like to welcome noobs properly with a drink...or two."

I nodded and scanned the room for Roman. *He must be in here by now.* There were so many people I couldn't even see the entrance.

"So, Oklahoma, may I ask you a question?" Andromeda ran her index finger around the rim of her glass.

"Um, sure," I replied, still searching the crowd.

She leaned over and pressed her lips against my ear. "I heard those crazy anti-government people showed up in Oklahoma and tried to blow up an All-Mark." She leaned back and stared at me intently. I could see the concern in her eyes.

How do I play this off? I burst into laughter. "You're joking, right? You mean those psychos in Europe?"

"Shhhhh." She forced her fingers over my lips. "We shouldn't be talking about it. I just heard a rumor."

"Well, it's not true," I whispered. "I would have heard about something like that. With so few of *us* in the state, that would be big news. Don't you thi—"

A strong hand grasped my shoulder. I saw Andromeda's eyes widen as her mouth parted slightly.

"There you are, my love. Some welcome, right?" Roman slid his arm around my waist. "Who's your friend?"

"Andromeda," the girl interjected as she stuck out her hand. "And the pleasure is mine."

Roman brought her hand to his lips and kissed it. "Thank you for showing my fiancé to the bar. Now if you'd excuse us, I believed I promised her a dance."

Andromeda reached past me and grabbed Roman's arm. "Fiancé? Well, your not True Matched yet. You have the rest of your life to dance with her. Why don't you take me for a spin while she finishes her drink?" She slinked past me and pressed her body against Roman.

I sat, stunned in the wake of her brashness. My anger triggered as I leapt to my feet. "Excuse you! He's...I, uh..." Even though we were theoretically in the same class, I couldn't bring myself to threaten an Upper.

Andromeda smiled coyly. "It's okay, babe. I won't damage him too much." She turned toward the dance floor, Roman's arm still in her clutches.

I tipped over the edge. *How dare this entitled, arrogant, narcissistic Upper touch my fiancé!* That was when I grabbed her shoulder a little too forcefully, ripped the delicate embroidery and promptly snapped the peacock's neck.

I stood horrified as Andromeda scrambled to keep from having a severe wardrobe malfunction. She slowly spun to face me. "Please tell me you did not just destroy my fifty thousand Credit dress."

"I'm so sorry!" I gushed. "It was an accident."

Andromeda lunged at me with pure hatred filling her eyes. Roman stepped in front of her back. "Let's just calm down, everyone!"

She struggled against him. "I will have you banned from here! Do you know who I am? I—"

"Andy!" a deep voice called from behind me.

I turned to see a young man in a sleek blue suit walking toward us. He wore dark sunglasses and a warm smile. "How we doing? Having a good time?"

Roman visibly relaxed while Andromeda perked up and smiled brightly. The newcomer embraced Andromeda and kissed her cheek. "Andy, beautiful as always. How long has it been? Oh, what happened to your dress?"

"It's nothing," Andromeda replied as she batted her eyes. "It's just a small tear. No big deal."

"Well, we can't have that. I'll tell you what. Sit here and have another drink, since alcohol fixes everything, am I right, and I'll have one of my personal stylists fit you for something even more beautiful. If that's even possible for such an exquisite specimen as yourself. Let me order that drink for you." She instantly followed his instructions while he typed on the bar. "There you go, darling. Now, Xavier, Celestia, please follow me."

I threw Roman a questioned look, but he only winked and followed our new friend. We came to a booth at the far end of the room. He bowed as he indicated which seats we should take. "You make friends quickly," he commented, as he placed his sunglasses on the table.

Roman shrugged. "What can I say? People are just drawn to me."

The man stuck out his hand to me. "Introductions are in order. I'm Braxton Ryan Nexius, but you can call—"

"Bryan Nexius?" I interjected. "As in, *the* Bryan Nexius, one of the five executives of *Great American Dream?*"

He smiled. "The one and only. You know your stuff. Part of my job is to make sure everyone, especially newcomers, are having a great time. Is everything as you expected? Is there anything I can do to make your visit better?"

Roman shook his head. "Everything is amazing. But I did hear people in line mention an increase in security. Is that normal?"

Bryan rolled his eyes. "I told the execs that was completely unnecessary, but what do I know about safety issues. I assure you, it shouldn't interfere with any activities tonight." He winked at Roman.

I started to realize Bryan was one of our inside informants. I wanted to play the game too. "Is it true that Erikson Mendax is the guest judge tonight?"

Bryan nodded slightly. "You know I can't be telling secrets. I don't even know who the guest judge will be until the day of the show. But, I will say that if you see the Department of Compliance roaming around, that may have something to do with it. Again, I assure you this will not interrupt your experience."

Roman slid his arm around my shoulder, sending goosebumps down my spine. "My fiancé and I are beyond excited to be here. You must be a busy man. Thanks for taking the time to meet with us."

Bryan stood and adjusted his tie. "My pleasure. If you need anything tonight, here is my personal business card." He pulled a small square from his pocket and slid it across the table. "Hopefully, I'll be seeing you around more often. Especially you, Celestia." He reached for my hand, brought it to his lips, kissed it lightly, then disappeared into the crowd.

Natalie will flip when she finds out that not only did I met Bryan Nexius, but he also kissed my hand! I turned to Roman, "Is he...?"

"Yes, I think that was really him." He squeezed my shoulder. "Looks like he left his sunglasses. Think you should hang on to them? For safekeeping, of course."

I took the glasses and slid them into my purse. Whether Bryan was on our side or not, I couldn't pass up taking them as a gift for Natalie.

"Are you ready to dance?" Roman asked, motioning to the mass of bodies in the middle of the room.

Fear bubbled up inside me. "Um, no. I do not want to dance. Nobody wants that. I'm a horrible dancer. One look at me and G.A.D. security would escort me off the premises."

"You just haven't had the right teacher." He winked. "As much as I would love that honor, it's time for other activities. Plus, I can't risk you picking fights with anyone else. Let's go change into our costumes."

I punched him in the arm before exiting the booth. As we walked past the bar, I noticed a sleeping Andromeda sprawled across the counter.

Most people in the holding room were living it up in their elegant outfits, but some had trickled over to the lockers. A group of Uppers gathered around one girl, who had changed into her All-Mark clothes. "That outfit is absolutely hideous! Do you see this cheap fabric? How do people live like this?"

I had always been in awe of the Upper Class, but after seeing them in person, I felt disenchanted. I thought pretending to be an Upper would be the best part of the mission, but it quickly became the worst.

I scanned my phone to my locker and took out the clothes: t-shirt, jeans and sneakers, all in my size. Even my "normal wear" was nicer than anything I owned. I turned to Roman. "Do you want to go first or should I?"

"Or we could go together," Roman responded as he tapped his watch.

After waiting for the bathroom to clear out, Roman set the Looper and we snuck into the last stall. The small, secret door released with a small hiss. He held the door open and I ducked inside.

I stood up and felt the closet door in front of me. *There's no way both of us will fit in here!* I heard Roman moving behind me and tried my best to scoot forward.

I barely heard his hushed voice, "Drop the clothes here. We wait until our phones buzz." Roman's chest pressed into my back as the door shut, plunging us into complete darkness.

I didn't want him to feel uncomfortable by our forced proximity, but I didn't know where else to go. "I can try to make more room," I whispered.

"No, it's fine," Roman quickly replied. He placed his hands on my shoulders and my body tensed. "Calm down," he chuckled.

Roman's hands slid down my arms and took hold of my hands. In the silence of the small room, I was certain he could hear my heart beating out of my chest. I attempted to steady my breathing and relaxed into him. I wanted to stay in that moment forever. The worry and stress from earlier in the day melted away. Roman had everything under control. He always did. I could trust him, even when I couldn't trust myself. I silently promised to prove myself in the mission, and make up for my mistakes.

In the middle of my internal discussion, I realized we were just standing there...in the dark...holding hands. My heart rate spiked again.

As if reading my mind, Roman dropped my hands and placed them on the closet door. "Get ready, we are going to move fast. If you see anyone, act natural, but don't enter the dressing room. We can't risk it."

I could feel him tense. A few seconds later, my purse buzzed and a bright light blinded me as I was pushed into the hallway. We walked as quickly as possible without looking completely conspicuous. I took a risk and peeked over my shoulder. To my relief, the hall was empty. We reached the dressing room with a purple star. Roman knocked in a unique pattern and the door flew open. He threw me inside and closed the door behind him.

I leaned against the wall, panting. Emily sat in front of a large mirror, finishing her makeup. Her long hair cascaded down her back in soft curls. Gage stood beside her texting furiously. Gideon sat in the corner with a laptop and headphones. He gave me a casual wave like we were in the middle of study hall. Several other large boys lined the room in security uniforms.

"It's about time you showed up," Gage snapped without looking up from his phone. "Eve got flagged."

"Names!" Roman hissed.

Gage pointed to a spinning orb hanging in the corner

of the room. "That Looper is the best in the world. We're safe in here."

Roman stepped toward Gage, his voice raised. "It's a good thing because there are some things I would like to discuss."

Emily finished her lipstick. "If it doesn't have to do with the current Chaos, then this is neither the time nor the place."

Both men glared at each other as an awkward silence filled the room.

"What's flagged?" I asked.

"It means you're a suspicious person." Gage put down his phone and walked toward me. "I knew you couldn't pull this off. You've endangered this mission already and we haven't even started the hard part."

Roman stepped in front of me, his muscles flexing with restraint. "She's here, isn't she? No thanks to you. I suggest you worry about yourself and—"

"Children, children." Emily put down her brush and spun around. "Can we put our differences aside for a moment? Roman is right; everyone made it here safe. Phase one is complete and it's onto the next. Gideon, what's our status?"

"Soundcheck in progress and they are moving the audience into the auditorium. Rome, did you get the codes?" Roman handed him Bryan's business card. Gideon tore off one end of the card and pulled out a tiny strip of paper. "Then we are a green light in all areas. Gage, what's the security status?"

"By now, I'm sure everyone knows that Erikson Mendax is on set. This, along with the D.O.C. presence, complicates things."

Roman interjected. "When we spoke with Bryan, he indicated this shouldn't change anything for us."

"Nevertheless, we should hedge our bets." Gage smiled slightly. "I think Eve should be on the ground level with Emily and me."

Roman shook his head. "Absolutely not. We stick to the plan."

"Hear me out. Eve is a much more valuable resource getting Emily on stage than taking over the production booth. Plus, with the extra security, you'd just be putting her in harm's way."

Roman looked to the ceiling for several long moments. "Fine. But if anything happens to her, I'm holding you personally responsible. Look out for both of them."

Emily looked at me and winked. "Oh boys, we are perfectly capable of taking care of ourselves."

Gage continued his breakdown. "Alright. In approximately fifty minutes, Gideon, Roman, Keaton, and Tank will make their way to the production booth and secure the area. While the first act is on, Emily, Eve, and myself will make our way to the stage. Intro video will play. Em will give her speech, and yada, yada, yada. Chaos three is a success. As soon as the lights go out, follow your evacuation route. Use a backup route if needed. Avoid getting caught, but if you are...you know what to do."

Silence fell over the room and I tried to reign in my panic. Not only did I not go over my exit route beforehand, but Roman wasn't going to be with me.

Finally, Emily spoke up. "Well, I don't know about you guys, but I'm pumped! Who wants a shot of Clarity?"

She reached into a bag and took out a small bottle and tiny plastic cups. She filled the cups with a bright blue liquid and passed them to each person. I sniffed mine. It smelled like a cleaning solution.

"Just so everyone is aware," Roman announced, "this is a mind and body enhancer. It will keep your mind sharp and your body in top condition for the next couple of hours. Everyone has the option not to take it since we aren't OneGlobal. Full disclosure, the Defiance is against all chemical enhancements or restraints, but I don't think they would mind under the circumstances. Cheers."

Everyone in the room downed the drink before I could even look at mine. I didn't want to be the only non-enhanced member of the team, so I quickly followed suit. I coughed harshly as my eyes watered from the horrible taste. I looked up to see Roman smirking at me.

"Now, it's a party!" Emily cheered. "Gideon, play us some tunes."

Music I'd never heard before filled the room. Everyone appeared to relax a little and went back to their previous distractions. A warm sensation filled my stomach and radiated outward. Roman walked over to Gideon, received a small black pouch then motioned toward the couch.

I sat beside him. "You said we would be together the entire time! I don't think this is a good idea."

"I don't like it either, but Gage is right. It's the safest and most effective plan. He may not like me, but there's no way he would put you in danger, especially with Emily watching."

I bit my lip. Discussing my exit strategy seemed like priority number one. "Well, I need to tell you something."

He smiled slightly. "You didn't study how to evacuate?"

"How did you know?"

"No reason for you to worry about the exit strategy when you're not planning on being present for it. Don't worry, your route is pretty straight forward. But if you get lost, I'll walk you through," he replied.

"How? You won't be with me."

"With this." He handed me the pouch. "This is a closed communication system, just you and me. Full disclosure; it is a tracking device, but that's the point. Wear this earpiece and I'll be able to talk to you the whole time. Put some pressure on it to talk to me. I thought about making it a one way channel, so you wouldn't be able to talk back, but…" A smirk spread across his face.

I punched him in the shoulder. "How is it you're always one step ahead?"

He only winked, then leaned back into the couch. "Time to focus." He closed his eyes and put one arm behind me, fingers barely touching my shoulder. His face appeared calm, but his knee bounced up and down.

I tried to relax and lose myself in the beat, but calming my mind was utterly impossible. The more I hoped for time to stop, the more the seconds raced. It felt like only five minutes had gone by when Gideon stopped the music. "It's go time."

Roman turned and placed his hand on my knee. "You'll be fine, I promise. Just think, an hour from now we will be on our way back home. Let me help with your earpiece. I'll be on radio silence until we secure the production booth." He placed the tiny bud in my ear then leaned in close. "If things do go south, get out as quickly as possible and I'll find you. Remember, I'm always one step ahead. Oh, and keep those sunglasses close. They may come in handy." He tucked a piece of hair behind my ear, then stood up. "Emily, break a leg out there. You'll do great. Gage, I look forward to talking to you when this is over."

And with that, he was gone.

CHAPTER 16

CHAOS THREE

I dropped my head into my hands. I was not prepared to handle the Chaos on my own. Without Roman keeping me on cloud nine, the reality of the situation hit me like a ton of bricks. I was about to put my life on the line for a cause that I had believed in for a few measly hours. I thought about how each person on the team had spent years training and preparing for that very moment. And somehow I was in the thick of it all by sheer luck. *Breathe, just breathe. You have the least involved role possible. Roman will keep you safe...even though he isn't with you? Uuuugghhh.*

I felt the cushions move beside me. I looked up to see Professor Gray. I hadn't noticed her dress before that moment, a stunning shimmer of red, white, and blue. The evening gown cascaded over one shoulder into a sleek train with a high slit.

"You look beautiful," I said.

"Thanks. It is lovely but not very functional. Listen... I know I was hard on you in class. Honestly, when you first arrived, I didn't like you very much, and I didn't keep that a secret. Roman always stood up for you and tried to make me see things from your perspective, but I was too upset. It wasn't until Gideon pointed out how close-minded I was being that I realized I wasn't giving you a chance. That was very unprofessional of me. I was wrong and I apologize. Do you forgive me?"

Never in a million years did I ever imagine Professor Gray asking for my forgiveness. I could only nod my pardon.

She continued, "It's been…interesting to see you grow since you've been with us. I'm not your instructor any-more; today I'm your colleague. I'm really proud of you for being here. There are a few things I need to tell you before the Chaos." She took a deep breath. "I know that out of everyone, I'm the least likely to make it out of here."

Gage jumped up. "Don't talk like that!"

"I'm being realistic." She turned back to me. "We need more people like you in the Defiance. You stood up for what you thought was right because of your love for your friends and family. You wanted to protect people and I'm sorry I didn't see that in the beginning. The Defiance *will* change this world and we need to change it from a place of love. Not greed or power or selfishness. Love needs to be the driving force."

"Oh, for cryin' out loud." Gage paced the floor. "First of all, you're going to be fine. Second, your hippy side agenda should be the last thing on anyone's mind, especially yours. We need to focus on the Chaos."

"Shut up, Gage. This is my time and I can spend it dis-cussing whatever I choose. Maybe things would have been different if you'd taken some of my advice. Anyway, I love the Defiance and you'll see why shortly, but remember, no organization is perfect. Healthy groups need continued growth. If we win the battle tonight, we will start a war, and I need you there fighting for what is right."

"We *are* fighting for what's right!" Gage snapped. "Right here. Right now. You need to stop looking fifteen steps ahead and get your head where it needs to be instead of up in the clouds."

"Yeah, you arguing with me is exactly what I need right now," Emily quipped.

Gage threw his head back. "You always do this. I'm just trying to help you and you spin it to make me the bad guy."

I watched the volley of words with curiosity. It was obviously not the first time they had this disagreement. I wanted to ask Emily for more details, but I never had the opportunity. Gage's watch beeped and all conversation stopped.

Emily rose to her feet. "Let's go."

Thankfully, my quivering legs were still able to hold the weight of my body. "If I throw up on your dress I apologize in advance."

Emily chuckled, then closed her eyes as she waited. A security officer opened the door and motioned us through. We walked down the empty hallway toward an elevator labeled Stage Door One.

As I stepped inside, a small beep in my ear nearly made my heart stop. "Hey, it's me." Roman's voice filled my head. "Sorry for the long silence. We ran into a couple of snags, but we are good to go in the production booth. We can see you getting on the elevator. When you arrive you'll be directly behind the stage. Follow Gage. By the way, he doesn't know about this earpiece. So, don't talk back right now. Does he have that stupid-angry look on his face?"

I laughed out loud and everyone turned toward me. "Sorry, nervous laugh."

Roman continued. "Alright, you're approaching the stage floor. I'm going to stay quiet until phase two is complete. Stay with Gage. I just text him that if he didn't keep you safe, I'd personally smash his face in."

The elevator came to a gentle stop. Gage suddenly turned to embrace Emily, then let go just as fast. The doors slowly opened to thunderous applause, and I could see the first contestant bowing through an opaque screen. Two stagehands ran toward us. One pulled Emily toward the stage as the other dragged Gage and me to the side. I expected backstage to be a flurry of activity, but I only saw a few security officers.

I looked toward the crowd and my knees weakened. From that angle, I could see the entire stage, audience, and there at the judge's panel sat Lazlo, Heiress and Erikson Mendax! *Natalie would kill to be here!* I couldn't imagine being Emily and having to stand in front of everyone, much less perform. Emily wrung her hands as a stylist primped her hair. I gave her a weak thumbs-up as the previous contestant whisked by me.

"I nailed it! America *has* to vote for me," I heard her say as she stepped onto the elevator.

The lights dimmed and the host, Gavin Starling, sauntered into a single spotlight in the front of the stage. He recited the Defiance's infiltrated script without a second thought. "Our next act may come as a shock to most of you. She's an underdog with a very intriguing story. Please welcome our first twist of the semi-finals, surprise contestant Emily Gray!"

The lights dimmed as a shot of Emily walking through an empty city played on the side screens. I recognized part of the Asylum as her voice filled the auditorium. "My name is Emily Gray and I'm not your typical teenage girl. When I was twelve years old, my mother passed away from leukemia. I know most of you think that disease doesn't exist anymore, but some cancer is alive and well. My dad couldn't handle our loss and was declared mentally incompetent. With his parental rights revoked, he was forced to sign me over to the government. I was sent to live at OneGlobal's Children Research Academy. I remember having my blood drawn the day I arrived. They took so much, I wondered if I would have any left."

I stood in awe at the powerful imagery of the video; flashbacks intertwined with the present day. Whoever directed it deserved an O.G. Honor.

"I lived at the facility with other girls my age. We took classes together, ate our meals together, and shared a bedroom. Occasionally, one of my classmates would suddenly disappear. We were told her family had arrived to take her back home. It always made me sad, because I knew my dad would never come for me.

"One morning, when I was fourteen, I was called to the Dean's office and informed that my father had completed grief counseling and was ready to be reinstated as a parent. I was escorted to the back of the facility where a limousine waited. Once inside, a nice woman told me she was my assigned counselor to help with the transition. She offered me a pill for my nerves and...I took the pill.

"I woke up to beeping in a cold, bright room. In a haze, I looked down to see a hospital gown and an IV in my arm. The medication keeping me asleep had run empty. I stumbled to the door, but it was locked. I yelled for help. There must have been a mistake. A young orderly walked by my room. He used his badge to unlock the door and said, 'follow me if you want to live.' We escaped out of the hospital and into the safety of the Universal Defiance. I later found out I was in a donation center. Some bigwig Upper needed a new liver and I was a perfect match. That was the day my eyes were opened and today I share my story to the world."

The screens faded to black as white lights illuminated Emily in the center of the stage. I always thought she was beautiful, but under the soft glow, she was absolutely breathtaking. Smoke rolled around her feet as the music began, the same haunting ballad she crooned at the football game. If she was nervous, you couldn't tell. Every note was so full of emotion, you could feel the melody in your soul.

As Emily sang, the screen flashed documents proving her story: her dad's signature to waive his parental rights, the Title of Bodily Acquirement to OneGlobal, the medical records showing the transplant request and the matching lab work. The music faded as the screen zoomed in on the name of the requesting recipient. A small gasp left my mouth as the name Gavin Starling appeared on the screen.

The song ended and Emily yelled to the silent crowd. "Mr. Starling, you tried to end my life by buying my organs, but I was rescued. However, that wasn't the case for this boy. Mitch Alexander." The picture changed to a boy,

Conner's age, wearing a soccer uniform. Emily started to tear up. "He was placed in a Research Academy two days after my escape because his parents both died in a car accident. Coincidence or convenience? Countless children have had their lives taken from them in order to be harvested for the Upper Class."

The screens flipped through hundreds, no, thousands of pictures. Emily cried openly, "Mr. Starling, how do you answer for these crimes? The government must be held accountable!"

Suddenly, *every* light in the auditorium turned on. I winced from the brightness. A voice in my ear whispered, "That wasn't us. Things may start to get dicey. Get ready to bolt."

"Wow," Laszlo, the chief judge remarked. "I've seen some crazy things in my day, but never anything like this. How dare you come in here with some insane conspiracy theory just to get votes. I've seen sob stories, but to make up lies, and not just lies, but horrible fabrications about our honorable government is ridiculous. This is a family show and you've crossed the line. There might be crazy anarchists in Europe, but I will not let you be the first in America. Your voice may be amazing, but I know this country will not vote for you or support what you stand for. Heiress, what did you think?"

"Oh, I completely agree." The gorgeous judge with snow white hair shook her head violently. "I hope this actually opens the eyes of America to see the threat people like you present. But I'm here to judge your voice, not you. When it comes to pitch..."

Emily stood on stage looking as confused as I felt. My

ear beeped. "What is going on? This was not the reaction we expected."

I scrambled for an explanation. *Why aren't they freaking out? They must know this isn't part of the show.* Suddenly, it clicked in my head as Erikson began his assessment of Emily's voice; they were treating her like a contestant. They were pretending she was part of the show to keep the audience from panicking and to discredit Emily. I looked at the crowd. Some seemed confused, but no one looked concerned about the information that was presented.

I realized the Defiance's fatal mistake. They were talking to a crowd of Uppers. Not only did the audience have their minds completely shut off to any outside viewpoint, but they were the people who would avidly choose to ignore the injustice to preserve their way of life. They were just like I used to be only a hundred times worse. Viewers at home would base their reaction from the "everyday" audience and the Chaos would accomplish nothing. *I can't let my friends fail like this.* I had to do something. I racked my brain to think of what would make "the before" me stop and realize what was happening.

I took a deep breath and walked onto the stage. The third Chaos ended and my Chaos began.

CHAPTER 17

MY CHAOS

"Eve? Eve...what are you doing? EVE! Turn around! Get off the stage!" my ear hissed.

I squinted against the blinding lights as sweat beaded across my brow. I took in my new perspective. The three judges were mere meters away! I couldn't believe I was actually standing on the *Great American Dream* stage! *If only Natalie could see...*

Roman's voice brought me back to reality. "Eve! Get off the stage! Run! Think of your family! They'll find out—"

I slid the earpiece into my back pocket. I couldn't focus with Roman yelling about what a horrible decision I had made. I knew that already. Emily gawked at me as I came to her side.

"And who might you be?" Erikson asked, obviously thrown off by another twist.

Erikson Mendax is talking to me! I ignored the butterflies in my stomach and grabbed Emily's microphone. "My name is Eve...Eve Price."

The judges whispered to one another. The crowd

murmured as the tension grew. A scuffle broke out in the back of the auditorium as D.O.C. officers pushed their way forward. The place was about to erupt. I had to act fast.

I took a step forward and pointed at Emily. "She is not a contestant! This is real! This really happened. It's not some ploy or trick to get votes. This is the true story of her life!" The blank stares from the judges and the increasing volume of the crowd told me I was failing.

"I'm confused," Erikson said. "Now, who or what—"

"Shut it! There's no time! The rumors are true. There have been two attacks by the Universal Defiance on American soil. I know this because I was present at both of them." Silence fell across the room. *Now, I have their attention.* "The explosion at the OKC All-Mark was the first Chaos and there was a second attack attempted in Tulsa, but I stopped it by pulling a fire alarm. The Defiance exists and it's in your backyard. The government is trying to hide it, but they can't hold it back anymore.

"Not long ago, I was just like every single one of you, living in ignorance, being a 'good citizen' by doing what I was told without question. Then, the Defiance kidnapped me. They showed me the truth. The government controls every aspect of your life. They pollute your water with mind-altering chemicals. They use cancer patients as lab rats. They use orphans as living organ donors. To some of you, this may not make sense, but I would guess most of you watching at home have had something in your life not add up. You've had the government tell you to keep your mouth shut and ignore something. In OneGlobal, you don't have rights. You don't have freedom. I know that sounds crazy, but please just consider what I'm saying.

Make your own decision! Don't just believe what you're told. Don't believe what I'm telling you. Research the U.D. websites. You owe it to your family, your friends, and yourself because you never know when you will be in the crosshairs of this world government. They don't care about you. They—"

All the lights shut off and goosebumps rose on my arms from the drop in temperature. "Hello?" My microphone no longer worked. Someone grabbed my shoulder.

"That's our sign. We have to leave now," Emily whispered in my ear. She used her phone as a flashlight and dragged me to the side of the stage.

I didn't realize I was shaking until I tried to put my earpiece back. "—of there. Now! They are taking over the booth. Follow Gage. If you get separated just get out and hide. I'll find you."

I heard a scuffle then silence. The crowd's murmur grew louder and louder. Someone screamed. In Emily's dim light, I saw someone running at us. I took a defensive stance that Roman had taught me. Relief washed over me as I realized it was Gage.

He pushed us toward the elevator. "Turn that light off," he hushed. The room was so dark I couldn't see in my hand in front of my face.

A small ding signaled the elevator's arrival. I felt my way inside and searched for the buttons. Suddenly, the room lights flashed back on. I looked up to see Gavin pointing at us. "There they are! Grab them!" Gage smashed the close door button and we descended into the belly of the set.

"Shouldn't we be going up?" I screeched.

"There's a secret escape hatch to the sewers on the bottom

level. Here, Em." Gage handed her a large pocket knife.

I watched in horror as Emily brought the knife to her neck. She twisted her hair into her fist, then cut through the knot.

"What are you doing?" I gasped.

Emily dropped her hair to the floor and began to cut up the slit in her dress until it fell off, revealing a tight aerobic outfit. "Making myself less recognizable. I'd do the same for you, but we didn't plan on you being recognizable." She offered the knife to me. "Unless you want to run around in your skivvies."

I followed her lead and loosed my hair from the bun. I took off my coat but that's all I dared to remove.

Gage stepped into my face. "What were you thinking out there? You could have ruined everything. All you ever do is—"

Emily stepped between us and shoved him. "She saved the mission. They weren't responding to me. If it wasn't for her, we—"

The elevator came to a screeching halt.

Gage pushed the button for the lower level repeatedly, but nothing happened. "This can't be good."

Our phones buzzed simultaneously. I pulled mine out and saw a text from Gideon: CONTROL OF PRODUCTION LOST. EVACUATE IMMEDIATELY. DISTRACTION IN 30.

"What does this mean?" I asked.

Emily read the text. "It means the Chaos is compromised. Deactivate your phone, so it can't be used to track us."

I punched in the emergency digits. The screen darkened and the small compartment containing the memory pill popped open. I quickly snapped it closed and hoped I wouldn't need it.

Gage reached for the elevator doors and attempted to pull them open.

I grabbed his arm. "What are you doing? What if they are out there?"

He shook me off and continued. "They know we are in here. They saw us. The best chance we have is to get out as soon as possible."

Suddenly, a dull rumble in the distance grew louder and louder. The elevator shook slightly as dust fell from the ceiling. After several seconds, the noise and vibration subsided.

"What was that?" I gasped.

Gage opened the door a few centimeters. "The distraction. It will be true chaos out there now. This is our best time to make it out."

With Emily's help, Gage managed to open the door completely. We had stopped directly between two floors. Gage bent down to look into the bottom one. "Looks like the lower floor is the one we want." He slid out of the elevator. "Let me clear the area."

After seconds that felt like an eternity, Gage returned. He reached his hand inside toward Emily. As Emily bent down, the elevator jerked violently and rose in the air. Gage barely had time to pull his hand out.

Emily looked at me, horrified, as we slowly ascended. Floor after floor passed by the open doors. "We have to get out before we reach them!" She yelled. We looked at each other for a split second, then jumped.

Thankfully, we landed in an empty office space. "What

now? Do we try to get back to Gage?" I panted.

"No, he'll continue to the exit route. They'll be watching the security cameras and will find us soon. We need to keep moving," Emily stated as she made her way down the corridor.

I pressed my earpiece. "Roman, are you there?" Silence.

I jogged to catch up with her. "Do you know where you're going?"

"Not a clue. You would think someone would have planned for this."

"WAIT!" I yelled and rummaged through my purse. I pulled out the sunglasses. "Would these help? I got them from Bryan and Roman said to keep them close."

Emily gasped as she grabbed the glasses and put them on. "Eve, you're a genius. These glasses are fully integrated with the G.A.D. set. I only have to choose a destination and...we now have our exit route." She sprinted down the hall.

"We can sneak back through the secret door to the pre-party room. Hopefully, we can blend in with whoever is left," Emily instructed as we arrived at the dressing room hall.

I grabbed her hand as she reached for the closet door. "Wait, I have an idea." I rushed down the hall with my eyes on one thing: the fire alarm. I pulled it as hard as I could. Immediately, strobe lights and sirens filled the area.

I raced back to Emily, who stood unimpressed. "Are you kidding me right now?"

"You still underestimate the power of the fire alarm? It

adds to the rush to get out. Contributes to the chaos. Isn't that what it's all about?" I asked.

"You're fitting in way too easily."

Thankfully, I had way more space in the closet with Emily than I did with Roman. I tripped over something on the ground. *The clothes we dropped!* I reached down and whispered. "Here's the shirt I left. I won't stand out as bad now."

Emily sighed. "That's great and all, but we don't know what we are getting into out there. We could be walking right into the hands of the Docs."

"We may not be as blind as you think." I pushed my ear. "Roman, are you there?"

After a few seconds, he replied, "I'm here. We made it to the sewers. Are you out yet?"

"Not exactly. Emily and I are hiding in the hidden closet."

"Wait, what? Why are you there?"

"Long story," I whispered. "We are going to sneak out through the pre-party room."

"No. Wait there. I'll come and get you. Give me a couple—"

"Roman, there's no time. It's too risky. You'll just get caught too. Is there anyway to see if it's safe out there?"

"Hang on. Gideon, yes you, get over here...." Several agonizing moments later, "Okay, there are still people in there. Looks like they are being evacuated for a...fire alarm? Your best bet is to try to blend in with them. They did not go to the taping, but it was playing on the monitors. Hopefully, they won't recognize you."

"What if they do?" I asked.

"Don't worry about that. Eve, you can do this. If

something happens just let me know and I'll be there. Promise?"

"I promise."

I explained the plan to Emily. Together we pushed on the secret panel and fell into the bathroom, which was thankfully empty. Emily ran to the door and peeked outside. "Everyone is crowding around the elevator. There's not many left though. We need to hurry."

We crept to the back of the small mob, keeping our heads down. I wrapped my arms around my body to keep from shaking. It didn't take me long to realize most of the people around us were intoxicated.

The group of Uppers didn't seem too happy. "What is taking so long? If they are going to make us stand around and wait, they might as well open the bar back up. My dad paid good Credits for my pass and I'm barely drunk."

"What even happened? Was there a bomb or a fire?

"A bomb caused the fire!"

"No, that one contestant did really bad, and then some crazy took the stage."

"I wasn't watching. All I know is this is unprecedented and we should not have to deal with this. I have rights!"

I pulled out my nonfunctioning phone and tried blend in without looking around every three seconds. Finally, we crammed onto the elevator like a can of All-Mark sardines. We were almost free.

The G.A.D. theme music started to play and a bubbly voice sounded overhead. "We hope you had a great time during your stay with us. Remember to tune in tomorrow for the live results show. We look forward to seeing you next time on *Great American Dream!*"

I couldn't help but laugh at the absurdity of the message, given the situation.

A new batch of nerves gripped my stomach as the doors opened. A long line of Uppers filled the hallway. Four D.O.C. officers had replaced the girl at the welcome booth. One of them carried a megaphone. "For you newcomers in the back, please stay in line. We are doing a security check. Have your phone ready. No need for alarm. This is standard procedure. Everything is under control."

We fell into step with the others. Emily leaned into my ear. "We need a plan, our phones don't work, so we'll never get past security."

We edged forward in silence. With each step, a new band of sweat broke out across my forehead. One look at me and the Docs would know something was up. I couldn't think of a single scenario to make it out. I had run out of fire alarms, even though the sirens and strobe lights continued.

Halfway through the line, Emily pulled me toward her. "There's no way both of us can make it out of here. When we get near the front, you make a big scene and point out who I am. The guards will be distracted and come after me. I'll run the other way while you rush the exit with the masses."

I thought the plan over in my head. It had potential, but there was one way it could be improved. "It's probably our only option. But let's reverse roles. You yell and I'll be the distraction."

Emily shook her head. "No, you've already gone way beyond the call of duty. You—"

"Stop. Think about it. You are barely recognizable and

I'm exactly the same. You are worth way more to the Defiance. Everything you told me about carrying on if something happens to you...I don't know how to even begin any of that. You are the future of the Defiance. They need you safe."

Emily thought for a second. "What about you?"

I shrugged. "I'll get captured, take my pill, and forget all of you stupid Kronies."

Emily wasn't convinced. "Are you sure? I'm completely willing to take this one."

"Yeah, I'm sure." I wasn't really sure.

Emily furrowed her brow. "I wish I could come up with a better argument. You know, if you pull this off, you'll be in the Defiance Hall of Fame."

"That exists?"

"It will after today."

I believed everything I told Emily, but I also secretly believed I had a better shot of being let go than she did. I still thought my spotless reputation with OneGlobal would somehow protect me from punishment, especially if I couldn't recall any of it. Plus, the sacrifice would absolve me of any guilt for manipulating Roman.

I discreetly pushed my phone against my ear. "Roman?"

"I'm here. Are you out?"

"Almost, but I have a question. You said you could track me, but can I track you? Like, can I use your signal and just find you?"

"No, well, you can but not without a phone. Don't worry about that. Just let me know when you're ready and I'll come pick you up."

"Okay," I whispered, not wanting to think about my

immediate future.

"Are you ready for this?" Emily asked as we neared the end.

I inhaled deeply. "As ready as—"

"IT'S HER! IT'S HER! THAT GIRL WHO STOPPED THE SHOW!"

If Emily planned to catch me off guard, it worked. Everyone in my near vicinity slowly backed away as Emily continued screaming like a crazed lunatic. The Docs cautiously started in our direction. I turned and sprinted back to the elevator. I looked over my shoulder and smiled. Not only were the officers running after me, but the rest of the line was running straight through the security doors. Emily would make it out.

I reached the elevator and placed my hand to my ear. "Roman, if you're there. I'll miss you. I hope this makes up for all of my mistakes. Maybe you were right about me after all."

"Eve? What are you talking—"

A ton of bricks slammed into my back and pinned me to the ground.

CHAPTER 18

CAPTIVITY

I opened my eyes to a sideways world. It took a good ten seconds for me to regain my bearings. My hands and shoulders ached from the weird angle of the cuffs and the knee in my back.

"We have the culprit! I repeat. We have the culprit in custody!" a voice yelled behind me.

Panic welled up in my throat, but I had to stay focused. I scanned the ground furiously. Thankfully, my eyes locked on the target. My earpiece rested in the far corner of the elevator.

"Alright, up we go." An officer hoisted me to my unsteady feet. "You are officially under arrest. According to the One-Global Criminal Entitlement Act, your injustices have waived your rights as a citizen. You—"

I jerked away from the officer. The sudden movement caught him off guard as I stomped on the earpiece, smashing it to bits. Relief flooded over me. They wouldn't be able to track Roman.

I accomplished my mission but not without a price. The

air in my lungs escaped my body as a heavy fist buried itself in my side.

"You want to do this the hard way?" the Doc yelled.

I fell to my knees, gasping for breath.

The Doc leaned in next to my face. "Try something like that again and you won't be able to stand back up. I promise you that. Let's go."

I didn't put up a fight as the officer dragged me through the empty hall. We went straight through the body scanner and into the bright lights of the walkway. Docs stood at attention along both edges, while a full camera crew waited directly in front of me. They filmed my parade down the aisle to the waiting D.O.C. patroller. I had one foot in the van when a yell stopped me in my tracks.

"Cut!" screamed a man behind the cameras. "Let's do that one more time. I want a wider shot. Boys, can you walk a little faster and...let's try one with the cuffs in the front and Eve...It's Eve, right? Don't look around so much. I want a guilty-slash-terrified look. So, keep your head down and occasionally glance up. From the top."

"What?" I gasped, as my hands were released and cuffed in front of me. "This is insane!"

The director jogged to me. "No, this is production at its finest. Don't expect to blow up a Hollywood-grade studio and not be asked for the perfect shot. Listen, the more you cooperate now, the easier things will be for you later. Chop, chop everyone!"

In a haze of disbelief, we reenacted my capture. I guess I did better on the second take because they loaded me into the patroller and shut the door.

I felt trapped in a real-life nightmare. *Wake up, Eve!*

I pinched my leg but it only hurt. I knew what should come next. *Just do it. Suck it up and do it. Take the pill and forget all of this mess. They won't be able to convict you if you don't know anything. You'll be able to go home and be with your family. Right?*

I leaned my head on the seat in front of me and stared at my shoes. Centimeters separated me and amnesia. I felt the enhancement shot I took earlier slowly slip from my body. I was mentally and physically spent. *Just reach down and take the pill and be done with it. You owe it to him. He would want you to protect the Defiance.* I had never been so torn in my life. The thought of forgetting Roman and everything I'd been through was unbearable. Tears fell to the floorboard. I weighed my options. What would Roman do? I tried to imagine him sitting in the back of a D.O.C. patroller but couldn't even picture it. He wouldn't have allowed himself to be in that situation. *Where is Mr. One-Step-Ahead when I needed him?*

After several minutes of arguing with myself, I hit my breaking point. I reached for my shoe and opened the secret compartment. The small pill rolled across my hand as I stared at it, unable to bring it to my lips. The sweat from my palm started to dissolve the pill. I gasped in disbelief. *It's now or never.* I opened my mouth and—

The van door wretched open to reveal a Doc. "Good news. You're headed home."

He pointed a small gun at my arm. I barely felt the pinch before I fell asleep.

I awoke, slumped in the back of the dark van. My head

pounded as if someone had hit me with a hammer. My memory slowly regained focus, pulling in images of the past twelve hours. I looked into my empty palm. No trace remained of my event-of-capture "plan A." I pushed my sluggish body to a sitting position and took in my surroundings. No one else was inside the patroller. I looked outside and did a double take. I'd been there before, but in a different life. I was back at the underground entrance of the Oklahoma City D.O.C. Central Headquarters.

About twenty armed Docs surrounded the vehicle. Standing in front of the entrance were several men in Designer suits speaking with the officer who arrested me. They shook hands and my arresting officer walked toward the patroller.

He opened the door. "Alright. It was fun while it lasted, but this is where we part ways."

Still in shock, I let him pull me from the van. Another Doc headed toward me with a smirk on his face. He looked familiar.

"Evelyn Price. We meet again. You may not remember me, but I was in charge of handling your family after the first incident and I'll admit...I never pegged you for a terrorist."

My memory flashed back to the night of the first Chaos; Connor being torn away from me so I could spend hours in a room with him. I glanced at his badge: Detective Larkin.

He put a hand on my shoulder. "I requested to personally oversee your case here in your hometown. Usually, they handle these sorts of things in New York, but this is unprecedented. We are going to get to know each other really well."

He motioned to one of the guards, who grabbed my cuffs and led me inside. We went through a maze of corridors, security checkpoints, and locked doors. At one point I was allowed to go to the bathroom to change into my standard issue convict attire, which did nothing for my hips.

We finally arrived at Interrogation Room 2. Larkin unlocked the door with his badge and pushed me inside. The first thing I noticed was the size of the room. It was about three times as large as the room I was interviewed in last time. My second observation was the girl sitting at the lone table, her back to me. The door slammed shut and she whirled around. It was Natalie!

Even with no makeup and messy hair, she still looked beautiful. She ran over and threw her arms around me. "Eve! You're safe! I've been worried sick. Where have you been? We all thought you were gone forever. I'm so happy you're okay. Are you okay?" She squeezed me tight, then pulled back. With wide, gold-speckled eyes, she waited for me to speak, but no words came. I was completely shocked by the presence of my old friend. Tears blurred my vision as she pulled me in for another hug. "Oh Eve, what did they do to you? You're safe. You're safe, now. Come sit down."

Natalie dragged me to the table and pulled the other chair next to me. She held my hands in hers. "Are you okay? Minus that hideous outfit."

I snorted through my tears. "Yeah, I'm okay. I mean, no. I'm probably not okay, but...I don't know what I am, to tell you the truth."

Natalie stroked my hair. "Ever since the night of the

Comet's game, I thought I'd never see you again. Then last night, I'm watching the semifinals of G.A.D. and you come walking out on stage! I couldn't believe it. I started screaming at the TV like a complete psycho. Mom thought I had lost my mind. I just pointed at your hologram and kept yelling 'It's Eve! She's alive!' I immediately contacted the Department of Compliance and told them my missing best friend just showed up on TV and is talking all crazy. I knew they must have drugged you or something. The Docs said they would put their best team together to rescue you and they came through like always! They called me early this morning and told me to come see you immediately...so, what really happened?"

I opened my mouth to speak but caught myself. I looked around the room. In each corner was a discreetly placed camera. *They almost got me.*

"I can't tell you."

Hurt shot across Natalie's face. "Eve, it's me...your best friend since the fifth grade. You can tell me anything."

"I can't...it's not safe." I knew telling her anything would only put her in danger. It was best to keep her completely in the dark.

Natalie leaned forward. "Eve, *you are safe.* You're back where you belong. OneGlobal will take care of you. You have nothing to worry about. I know those guys brainwashed you, so none of this was your fault. I just want to hear your story. Were you really with the Defiance the whole time?"

I realized Natalie was just bait to make me comfortable enough to tell my story. I sighed. "I really don't want to talk about it. Could we please just talk about something

normal? My brain is beyond stressed out. Please, just...
tell me something that's going on with you. Anything?"

I couldn't help but notice Natalie's glance to the corner
of the room as she pulled away from me. "Um, okay.
I finally submitted my dating profile."

"Aaannnddd?" I prodded.

She couldn't stop the smile from spreading across her
face. "I'm meeting my first match next month!"

"Shut up! No way! That's so exciting!"

"I know! And want to hear something even crazier?
He's an Upper! Can you believe I matched with an Upper?
We've chatted a little bit but nothing too in-depth. I don't
want to come across as clingy. He's from Tulsa. Graduates
when we do...will you still get to graduate on time?"

The simple conversation made my heart happy. I hadn't
realized how much I had missed my best friend. All I
wanted to do was walk out the door with her, grab a
pizza, and come up with potential dating scenarios. "I
don't know. Hopefully, but there's a lot of other stuff to
worry about. Anyway, what's he like?"

"Well, he—"

Someone knocked on the door. "Time's up."

Natalie wrapped her arms around my neck and whispered. "Are you sure you don't want to tell me anything?
I'm here to help you. Just tell them what they need to
know and they'll get you out of here. You're the victim.
Do the right thing."

I gave her one last squeeze. "Thanks, Natalie. I've missed
you so much. Your friendship means the world to me."

Detective Larkin stepped into the room and ushered
her outside. He turned back to me. "Your family is now in

custody. I suggest you become a little more cooperative."

He slammed the door as I leapt to my feet. "MY FAMILY HAD NOTHING TO DO WITH THIS! LEAVE THEM ALONE!"

I banged my fist on the door, but only silence followed. I sat back down and realized Roman was right to avoid contact with my family. It was too late for Connor, but he was smart. He would know to play dumb.

I paced back and forth for hours. I played out every possible scenario I could imagine about what might come next, but nothing happened. I sat alone forcing my eyes to stay open while debating what to say to the camera to make someone come talk to me. Eventually, exhaustion overwhelmed me as I rested my head on the table.

The sound of a man clearing his throat jarred me away from my dream sanctuary. Reality came crashing down as the man fidgeted with the cufflinks of his Designer suit. I eyed him suspiciously as I sat upright.

He was attractive for an older man, but years of stress showed on his face. His sandy blonde hair gave way to gray on the sides. His casual posture gave a certain air of confidence like he was used to getting his way.

"Ms. Price. Is that correct?" he asked, smiling with only half of his mouth.

I nodded.

"I must apologize for the delay in my arrival. I was in New York when I received word of your...predicament."

"And who are you?" I asked.

"Chancellor Montgomery Ashburn, Chief of Homeland

Security, but friends call me Ash." He stuck out his hand. When I refused, he smirked to himself. "I know you've been through a lot this year. More than anyone should go through in a lifetime, let alone the brief seventeen years you've been on this planet. But, I'm not going to sugarcoat it. You're not in the best situation right now. Based on what I've seen, we could charge you with nineteen different counts of treason and criminal mischief. But, I want to know the real story and for me to know that, you are the one who has to tell it."

He poured us both a glass of water from a pitcher I hadn't noticed. He offered me the glass. My parched throat longed for the liquid; however, all I could think about was the mind-altering chemicals it probably contained.

"No, thank you," I croaked.

"Suit yourself," Ash chuckled softly. He clasped his hands and leaned on the table. "The way I see it, you have two options. You could choose to cooperate with us, staying true to your government, your family and your society. You can tell your story, answer our questions, and help in any way we see necessary. This would be taken under deep consideration when the courts look into your criminal case. Or you can choose to not cooperate. This would force us to use any means necessary to keep our country and citizens safe.

"I don't know about you, but I don't want to go down that road. Before you make your decision, I want you to know all the facts. It's very important to me, personally, that you know what's really going on with both parties before you side with one. Is that fair?"

I nodded, not quite sure where he was going.

"Let's start with what we both know. Set up a basis for everything." He reached into his jacket pocket and pulled out a pair of reading glasses. After adjusting the fit, he pulled a tablet from under the table and began to scroll. "You were in the OKC All-Mark when the first attack happened. You escaped safely while your mother suffered injuries requiring hospitalization. Seventeen people were murdered during that attack." He paused for several seconds before continuing. "The government decided that in order to keep peace and minimize fear, this information was not shared with the general public. At the time, we thought this was a small band of teenage boys trying to copycat other parts of the world. We continued our research and, to be honest with you, they had us fooled. We had no idea they were planning another attack. We made a mistake in underestimating them, but, trust me, that will not happen again. We are prepared to through our full resources at them and it's only a matter of time before we end this madness. Anyway... they decided to have another go in Tulsa. It took us days to decode their hacks and when we viewed the security footage, we discovered it was you who pulled the fire alarm. You have been reported as missing since that night. I've always wondered what made you pull that alarm. Care to enlighten me?"

I considered keeping my silence but didn't see any harm in telling him my reasons. "I knew what was coming. I didn't want anyone hurt, so I had to do something to get everyone out. I saw the fire alarm and I went for it."

He put down the tablet and whispered across the table. "That was very brave of you, saving all those people.

OneGlobal thanks you for your courage. We can only hope to develop that type of self-sacrifice and community stewardship in our citizens. I commend you." He gazed intently into my eyes. "Later that night, we discovered that the whole stadium was rigged with explosives. They were going to blow the whole place sky high. You did the right thing...we then saw you carried down to the basement; however, the footage from inside the room was unable to be recovered. We assume they were discussing what to do since you ruined their plan."

I nodded suspiciously. *Rigged with explosives? Roman would never stand for that...unless Gage did it behind his back.*

Ash picked up his tablet to show me a video from the parking garage. I suppressed a smile as I watched Roman run after me and toss me over his shoulder. "We saw you thrown into a van and driven off into the night. At this point, we knew we were dealing with serious terrorists who had access to not only weapons of mass destruction, but also highly sophisticated technology. You were declared a Global Hero and we did everything to track you down, but we were unable to find you."

"Because they took out my tracker," I replied automatically.

Ash furrowed his brow. "Took out your what?"

"The tracker in my arm that was placed with my hormone therapy."

Ash shook his head slowly and began typing on his tablet. "There's no such thing as a tracker."

"Then why would they take it out?"

He pursed his lips together for a few seconds. "Pardon my brashness, Ms. Price, but my best guess is that they did it in hopes of getting you pregnant in order to raise up children in their anarchist cult."

My face burned as I regretted my question. I bit my lip and decided to keep my mouth shut from that point on.

"I didn't mean to offend you, just being honest. I believe being honest with each other is the only way to get through this," Ash paused and sipped his water. "On a side note, the fact that you stopped this attack will not be ignored. In fact, that is why I personally wanted to oversee your treatment while in custody. Anyone who does not know your history may assume the worst. Anyway... next, we tried to dig deeper into who this group was and what they stood for, but as I said, they're good. We've gathered information on some of the culprits and traced their origins to terrorist groups in Europe. We believe that most of these guys are good people who just got mixed in with the wrong crowd of conspiracy theorists. That brings us to the events of yesterday. They put a block on our production feed, so the entire ordeal was broadcasted to not only all of America, but also to most parts of the world. Did you hear any explosions while you were on set? Any bombs?"

I nodded once more.

"That's because they set off quite a fireworks display... before they destroyed the entire set. After their stunt was taken off the air, thirty-seven government buildings were bombed across the country. The official death toll hasn't been released because the number keeps climbing. Did you know about that?"

I looked down at my feet and shook my head.

"That's what I'm talking about. I want you to know exactly who you're dealing with here. For example, we were able to pull files on Emily Gray. Her story lines up until the part where she stepped into the limo. She was being taken to a reconciliation center to be reunited with her father. In the limo, she ate a peanut-filled candy bar that was offered to her by the chauffeur. Since Emily is deathly allergic to peanuts, this sent her into anaphylactic shock. She passed out immediately and was admitted to the hospital. She was kept in a coma for two days while the swelling in her throat subsided. During that time, a young orderly was noted to be lingering around her room. When Emily woke up, the orderly kidnapped her and flew her to Europe to completely brainwash her in the Universal Defiance, much the same way you were. We've found out that this young man's name is Charles Buckley and he goes by the alias Gage Levison."

I couldn't hide the shock in my face.

"This Gage character…you know him. Don't you?" I kept my silence. "Well, we didn't have to dig very deep to find information on him. He was, what we call, a 'frequent flyer' with the Department of Compliance. His injustices include burglary, criminal mischief, conspiracy, and kidnapping. Not to mention his tendency of anger and aggression that led to his dismissal from school. The orderly position was part of his last chance rehabilitation program before he became a permanent member of the criminal system. I could go on and on about the criminal history of the guys we have associated with the U.D. but that's not what I want to focus on today. I want to focus on you and your future.

"You mentioned that the government," he peered down at his tablet, "'uses cancer patients as lab rats.' That's a pretty harsh statement. Cancer is ninety-nine point nine nine percent eradicated and there is a big difference between using promising experimental treatments and just poking and prodding at someone who is dying. All patients with terminal illness are treated with dignity and respect in our hospitals, receiving only the medications they *request.* We make scientific advancements every day by trying new strategies. How do you think we cured cancer in the first place? But we *always* get consent. That brings us to the concept of 'the greater good.' Can you indulge me for a couple moments? Will you please state the OneGlobal Pledge?"

I didn't want to participate in his antics, but I knew we probably wouldn't move on until I complied. "I pledge allegiance to OneGlobal and to uphold the ideals of its foundation. To seek the unity of all mankind, to be committed to the greater good, and strive to be a productive member of the international society. I devote my life to the well-being of the world and will put its needs before my own, no matter the cost," I recited apathetically. Saying the words out loud felt...weird. Never had I ever questioned what I quoted every morning before school. I just automatically believed it for so long.

Ash smiled warmly. "Perfect. Does any of that sound wrong to you? Corrupt? Evil?"

"No," I answered honestly. "It's very idealistic."

"I agree. And why shouldn't it be? We want to leave this world a better place than we found it. And just between you and me, we are considering adding that to the pledge. But, I want to focus on 'the greater good'. What is your interpretation of that motto?"

The answer flowed from my mouth like I was reciting for an economics test. "It is one of the main pillars of the OneGlobal community. It's the idea of making personal sacrifices if they benefit the collective whole."

Ash nodded. "Very good. I want to get your opinion on something. Say there's an individual who is the very definition of Noncompliant. This person has been given every opportunity to change their life—counseling, rehabilitation programs, education—but they still continue to hurt other people. That person deserves to be in prison, right?"

I nodded.

"So, they would be sent to jail for the opposite of the greater good, for taking advantage of others for their own personal gain. Say that, while in jail, we give him the opportunity to rectify some of those wrongs by giving back to the greater good. This could be through things like community service, building projects with manual labor, or it could be by volunteering to participate in ethically approved scientific experiments.

"That is where your friends in the Defiance got their facts wrong. We don't force this on anyone. Not only that, but physicians have saved thousands and thousands of lives with the research conducted on these willing individuals. So I ask you: what is justice? To test a new vaccination on needy children in Africa, or on a willing criminal who has forfeited their rights, but wants to give back to society?"

I chewed on my lip, overwhelmed with the barrage of ethical scenarios that I wasn't equipped to handle. Ash made too much sense.

He continued, "We don't share these concepts with the general public because it would cause them unwarranted stress and anxiety. Men and women who have dedicated their lives to the study of morality make these decisions. We are fixated on the wellbeing of our global community.

"Eve, we could sit here all night and I could explain to you in depth the reasons why we do what we do. But I can assure you of this, everything focuses on the greater good; what is best for the most people. Is the greater good a small group of teenage boys destroying property and murdering for reasons that don't even exist? That's for you to decide over the next twelve hours. Think about your life before the kidnapping…were you happy? Were you safe? Did OneGlobal ever wrong you in any way?

"I want you to be completely informed, so let's talk about consequences. If you decide not to help us, you will be declared an enemy of the world. You would lose your OneGlobal citizenship and your friends and family would suffer from the consequences of that stigma. If you choose to help us, you and your family could live freely." Ash took another drink of water. "You're probably wondering why we would allow someone who just declared on global television that the government is a bunch of sadistic, power-hungry maniacs that don't care about the public off the hook? There is a catch. By agreeing to help, you would become the champion of this new war on Noncompliance. By publicly explaining your kidnapping and brainwashing story, you would help expose these anarchists for what they really are. You said it yourself in the speech. You were just like everyone else, and they got to you. That proves the danger we are up against. We need you to help the greater good.

"You have an opportunity not many individuals have... to right your wrongs. By helping me in this room, you are helping the entire world. You hold the key to ending the violence, brutality, and bloodshed. I'm asking for your help, but I want it to be because you chose to do the right thing, not because you were forced. You were told the government controls every aspect of your life, and that you have no say in anything. I'm going to prove that theory wrong."

Ash paused dramatically, then sighed. "You must be exhausted and hungry. I know I am. Detective Larkin is going to escort you to your room and get you a decent meal. You have my word that it contains no trace of secret mind-altering chemicals. We will reconvene tomorrow morning to record your official statement about all this mess."

The door behind me clicked open to reveal Detective Larkin. Ash nodded in his direction, indicating I was free to go.

I stood to leave, then hesitated. "Can I see my family?"

Ash thought for a few seconds before answering. "I really want to say yes, but I don't think it would be best for them to see you until you've made your decision. I don't want them to influence you to take their side and help the community. I want that decision to be completely up to you."

I turned in defeat and left Ash behind.

After several long, twisted hallways, we entered Holding Area: Level One. Detective Larkin shoved me into my room. "This is just a holding cell, so don't get too comfortable. Actual criminal cells make you regret bucking the system. I hope you know your family is staying in one of these tonight because of you."

He attempted to slam my door but it only clicked shut. My cell was a narrow room with only the necessities. I looked around and did a double-take. On the small nightstand sat a to-go sack from Burgerz, my favorite fast-food restaurant. I raced over, ripped opened the bag, and tore into the double-burg with cheese. I melted onto the bed and breathed in the juicy aroma. *Yes! They even got me a large fry!* I crossed my legs, leaned against the wall, and savored every last bite of my meal. I didn't realize how much I missed the food.

It took some effort to hoist my satisfied, yet distended, stomach off the bed to see if anything was in the nightstand. I opened the drawer and my heart skipped a beat…a tablet. I held my breath and touched the screen. The device lit up, unveiling every social media and television app I could ever ask for. I quickly learned I was denied access to any news or media outlets, so I simultaneously watched my favorite sitcom as I scrolled through my social feed and email. A sense of connectedness that I hadn't felt in a long time filled my body.

Natalie had emailed me every day. Tears filled my eyes as I saw her thoughts progress from "this isn't funny, where r u!?!?" to "I'm really scared I'll never c u again." The later emails updated my ghost on her day-to-day life, focusing mainly on her new dating profile. I tried to send her a reply to thank her for coming to see me, but a pop-up informed me I was blocked from sending any correspondence.

Connor had sent a few messages, but they were difficult to understand. They seemed like a garbled mess of random thoughts. The most I could decipher was that the family missed me and hoped I was safe.

I checked the time: 12:23 a.m. Without realizing it, I had wasted hours on the internet. I knew I needed to focus on the task at hand. I put the tablet away and crawled into bed. I massaged my temples as I tried to piece together all the facts. When it came down to it, both sides accused the other of horrible lies and transgressions. I had no definitive proof to lean one way or the other. I knew that Roman believed in the Defiance with all of his heart, but was he tricked too? All I wanted was for him to be in the room to talk through everything. He would know what to do, always one step ahead. Well, except for my capture, but I went rogue on that decision.

Before talking with Ash, I was completely for the Defiance. But everything he explained to me made sense. He had a perfectly logical explanation for Emily's story and I totally believed Gage could have kidnapped her and brainwashed her in Europe. Even the part about testing medications on willing prisoners was unexpected but not utterly insane. Even if what the Defiance said was true, was it that bad if it helped more people than it hurt?

Then I thought about all the personal stories: Roman, Gideon, Emily, and even myself. Knowing the type of destruction OneGlobal caused in my family alone was reason enough to fight them...but then again, the government wouldn't be involved in my life if the Chaos had never occurred.

And then there was the topic of consequences. I groaned in frustration and closed my eyes. My brain felt like it was being ripped in half by arguments for both sides. With all the stress and a full belly, I finally succumbed to exhaustion and collapsed into mental darkness.

The sound of an alarm woke me. In a groggy haze, I fumbled to find the source. It was the nightstand. I pulled out the tablet to see a flashing memo informing me the time was 7:30 a.m. and my statement would begin in thirty minutes. I sprang from bed in a panic. I hadn't decided one thing during the night. I washed my face, then brushed my teeth as I tried to make a pro-con list in my head.

By cooperating with the Docs, I would betray the Defiance and put Roman in jeopardy. By not cooperating, I put my family and myself at risk...and possibly the entire world, if Ash was to be believed.

I paced the small room. If my family was my top priority, being a snitch was the way to go. Maybe I could tell my story but leave Roman out completely. But could I really betray the others? Gideon, Emily, Hannah. I had grown close to them faster than I thought possible. Even if I tried to protect my friends, who was to say the government would hold up their end of the bargain. Would they punish us all no matter what I did?

My thoughts continually returned to Roman. If I was being honest with myself, I truly believed everything he had told me. Was that just because I had a major crush on him or did I really believe the government would do evil things to people just to keep everyone in check? I swayed one way then the other about fifty-seven times when a knock at the door stopped me in my tracks.

Officer Larkin opened the door. "It's time."

He placed me in handcuffs and escorted me down the hall like some sort of trophy. "Can I offer you some advice? Think of how your decision is going to affect the next fifty years…for you, for your family, for society. You only get one shot at this. Don't screw it up."

We arrived at the same interrogation room. Larkin closed the door behind me, leaving me alone with my thoughts. I sat in the chair and dropped my head into my hands. After several tense minutes, I realized I would have to play the waiting game for Ash again. I used the time to continue my internal debate. I thought about Roman, then I thought about my mom.

Suddenly, I heard the door open behind me. My legs shook uncontrollably as I bit my lip and stared at my feet. I couldn't bring myself to face Ash since I was about to betray someone I couldn't imagine my life without.

"There's been a change of plans," said a voice beside me as a watch slid across the table.

CHAPTER 19

PROMISES

The voice reverberated in my head as the officer walked around the table. Roman stood in front of me, dressed in full D.O.C. uniform. I sat stunned, in complete denial, unable to move or think.

Roman smirked as he straightened his badge. "Sorry for the wait, Ms. Price. I usually pride myself on punctuality."

With wide eyes, I slowly turned to stare at the door then looked back to him. He was miraculously still standing there. I opened my mouth several times, but no words came.

Roman spoke instead. "I made you a promise and I intend on keeping it."

"What..." I breathed. "What is going on? How are you here? WHAT IS GOING ON?"

"All in good time, my love." He winked. "Let's just say we are operating in a different time zone than the rest of Oklahoma right now. Therefore, Ash is going to be a little late for his meeting. But, as you can imagine, we are on a bit of a tight schedule. First things first, do you want to be rescued?"

I nodded enthusiastically.

"Perfect. Let us begin." He reached into his back pocket and placed a tiny box between us. I took the box and opened it. A small pill sat perched in the center.

"What is this?" I asked.

"It is a memory jogger. The opposite of the memory eraser. Disclaimer: I am morally opposed to chemical enhancements of any kind—"

"But when necessary..." I interjected.

He chuckled. "When necessary, I can see their benefit. Obviously, with all the security checkpoints, we can't just walk out the way you came in. But, thankfully for us, you've been here before and exited a different way."

"Through the hospital," I realized out loud.

"Exactly. Think about that time, take the pill, and you will remember everything in perfect clarity. I will escort you out of the facility, as my prisoner, of course. We will rendezvous with the rest of the team to take us off the grid and into safety. Any questions?"

I stood on wobbly legs and grabbed the box. "Let's get out of here."

He stepped around the small table and pulled me into a bear hug. "Eve, I'm so sorry for everything you've had to go through over the past thirty-six hours. I shouldn't have let them take you off the set. I'll never put you in danger again. But I'm so proud of you."

Completely caught off guard and having my hands cuffed in front of me, I just stood and soaked it in. I wasn't sure about ninety-five percent of my life at that time, but I was sure about Roman. He was genuine, loyal, and I knew in my gut that going with him was the right thing to do.

He leaned back and placed his hands on my shoulders, as his eyes sparkled. "Are you ready for the most epic jailbreak in history?"

I nodded and brought the small box to my lips.

Roman grabbed my hand. "Word of warning: it's going to be a little...trippy."

Cautiously, I swallowed the pill. I waited a few seconds but felt the same. "I still don't remember anything." I tried reel in my panic, worried I had somehow messed up everything.

"It will take a minute. Follow me at first, then once your memory returns take the lead. If we run into anyone, I'll handle it." Roman put on his watch, took a deep breath, and gave me one more smile as he opened the door.

The hall was empty. We walked past doors and doors of interrogation rooms. I had never been so scared in my life. I wondered if my light-headedness was the medication or just my nerves. The sight of a Doc rounding the corner snapped me back to clarity. My stomach dropped as I realized it was Detective Larkin.

"Cry," Roman whispered.

I dropped my head and bit the side of my cheek until I tasted blood. Tears filled my eyes as I looked up to see Larkin rushing toward us.

"What is going on? This is *my* prisoner! No unsanctioned movement is to occur without my knowledge or—"

Roman interrupted him. "Detective Larkin, just the man I was looking for. Chancellor Ashburn had an emergency that required his immediate attention. He asked me to deliver Ms. Price to you to give her statement."

Officer Larkin eyed Roman suspiciously. "Who authorized—"

"Chancellor Ashburn requested that you personally oversee this situation. He didn't trust anyone else to do it. If you don't feel comfortable, I can take her back and—"

"Of course, I'll do it! It's about time he left her to me. It was my case to begin with…" Larkin trailed off.

"Any of these rooms work?" Roman nodded to his right.

"Certainly." Larkin turned and scanned his badge.

As soon as the door clicked open, Roman kicked Larkin hard in the back. He fell forward into the empty room. Roman jumped on top of him and with one swift punch, Detective Larkin was no longer an issue.

I stood in the doorway, staring in disbelief as Roman moved the limp body into the chair. "What the heck was that?" I hissed.

"Neutralizing the threat. I'm not gonna lie…there may have been some pent up aggression behind that." He looked at his watch. "We should probably get going."

As we walked into the hall and the lights seemed brighter. I shook my head. Suddenly, I could remember every detail from my first visit to Central. It was like I was living in two realities at the same time. It was a couple degrees colder this time, or maybe that was from my prison garb.

"This way," I whispered, and restrained myself from running down the hall.

I led Roman through the maze of hallways without a trace of doubt. I couldn't believe how well the pill had worked. We ran into a few other officers, but I kept my head down and no one gave us a second glance.

Finally, we made it to the skywalk. I remembered how different the situation was the first time I crossed, but many emotions were the same: anxiety, fear, and a small amount of excitement.

"When we get to the hospital, act sick," Roman instructed.

"That won't be hard. I already feel like I could puke at any moment."

My mind enhancement led us to the check-in area, and to my surprise, the same elderly woman in pink sat behind the counter. I closed my eyes and mentally zoomed in on her nametag, Dorothy.

"I have a prisoner to be evaluated in the med bay," Roman said as he flashed his credentials.

"What's the name?" Dorothy asked as she smiled politely.

"Joan Arkadia."

She typed on her screen. "One moment, please."

I gave a few dry heaves for dramatic effect. The anxious sweat beading down my forehead didn't hurt my case either. I glanced up at Roman. He looked completely confident...and also smoking hot in his uniform.

Dorothy inhaled sharply. "Possible quarantine? Minimize exposure? Um...continue to exam room five. Quickly. please."

She buzzed us in and we entered the hospital.

Roman kept a firm hand on my shoulder. "Now, think about the last time you were here. Where could we change into surgical scrubs?"

I closed my eyes. I could see myself being escorted into Waiting Area 3, then running down the hall when— I crashed into the scrub cart! "There's a laundry room down this way!"

Roman used his badge and we dashed into the room, thankfully finding it empty. The smell of detergent filled my nose as Roman unlocked my handcuffs. He walked down the rows of laundry and threw me a pair of scrubs. "You're not a prisoner anymore. You're a patient. We have a sleeper agent in the scanner wing that will get us out."

Roman had already changed his shirt and was about to drop his pants. I had just enough time to turn my body before he could see my bright red face. I knew time was of the essence, but I could not bring myself to change in front of him.

Roman noticed. "Shoot. I'm sorry. I get tunnel vision on missions. I won't look, Kronie's honor."

I made sure he wasn't peeking and quickly changed clothes. "Okay, I'm ready."

Roman turned back to me. His arms barely fit in the sleeves. It was crazy how he could make any outfit look good. He walked to the door and peeked out the window. "First empty bed we see, jump in and I'll push you to my friend."

"How will we find him? This is as far as I went last time."

"He works in the imaging department. There should be signs. Ready? Let's go."

We slipped down the hall and found an empty bed in the third room we checked. I hopped over the railing and nestled under the covers. After several aimless turns, we found signs pointing to the imaging center.

The automatic doors opened to an empty waiting room. Another set of doors at the far end of the room read, RESTRICTED AREA AUTHORIZED PERSON-NEL ONLY. Roman walked over to the young girl at the check-in desk. "Good morning...Abby P. I'm here transporting patient Arkadia."

The girl's eyes widened when she looked up to see Roman. She smiled brightly. "Oh, okay. Let me check... um, I'm not seeing anyone on the schedule by that name. Are you sure you have the right department?" she asked as she batted her eyes.

I was torn between panic over the snag in our escape plan and the desire to sit up and yell at the girl to just do her job and stop ogling Roman.

He leaned forward across the desk. "Ugh. I could have sworn they said imaging. I am so bad at this job. It's only my second day and I've gotten lost three times. Could you do me a tiny favor?"

"What?" the girl breathed.

"Could I take the patient to an empty bay until I get this straightened out? If I take her back to her room my supervisor will know I screwed up again. Also, that may give me enough time to find your dating profile."

I coughed loudly.

The girl blushed. "I'll see what I can do."

Roman gave her a wink. "Thanks, babe." He turned to look at me as the girl typed furiously on her computer. I shook my head subtly. He innocently shrugged his shoulders and mouthed "what?"

"Oh," the receptionist exclaimed. "Somehow your patient magically appeared on our procedure list. I wonder how I missed that the first time? I guess you should take her to bay four."

"You're amazing," Roman replied as he pushed my bed through the open doors. "I'll message you."

Roman backed my cart into the small holding area. He pulled the curtain closed and sat on the end of my bed.

"What was that all about?" I hissed.

Roman chuckled. "Just meeting my objective. What? You're not...jealous, are you?"

"Why would—" The curtain drew back, cutting off my words.

A man in a white jacket stood in the opening. He walked in and embraced Roman. "It's been a while. Man, it's good to see you."

"I just wish it was under better circumstances." Roman turned to me. "Eve, this is Physician Crawford. He assisted in my brother's care and is a dear friend."

Crawford stood beside me. "Pleasure to meet you, but we need to hurry. Eve, I need you to think back since the time of your capture. Did they inject anything into your arm or leg?"

I closed my eyes and let the drugs take me through the past thirty-six hours. "No, at least, not while I was awake."

"Do you have any small aches that you didn't have before? From a possible shot?" Crawford asked as he examined my arms.

I shook my head. "Just the one that knocked me out."

Crawford pushed on my abdomen. "Did you eat while in their possession?"

"Yeah, I had some fast food last night."

He let out a frustrated sigh. "Well, let's do this the hard way. If it's there, we don't have much time. Once they discover she's missing, it's all over."

Crawford took off down the hall. Roman helped me out of bed and we rushed after him into Procedure Room 1. In the center of the room stood a long table with a monstrous looking machine hanging directly above it.

"Lay flat on the table and lift up your shirt," the physician instructed.

"What is going on?" I asked.

Roman swept me off my feet and placed me on the table. "They probably put a tracker in your food. The quicker we get it out the less likely they will find us."

"WHAT? Get it out? How? Ash promised me there were no chemicals in my food!"

Crawford sat behind a glass window and spoke through a microphone. "Well, this isn't a chemical. Lay back for the scan."

I flattened as a large tube passed over my entire body.

"Yep," Crawford said. "There it is, small intestines. Usually, we sedate people for this, but we don't have time. I'll put in the calculations and…Roman, you may want to hold her down."

"Hold me down? What? Wait! Roman, I don't think—" I tried to sit up, but he held my body against the table.

"I'm so sorry, but we have to get it out before they know you're gone. Do you trust me?" His green eyes pleaded with me.

As much as I didn't like it, I didn't have another option. I begrudgingly nodded and attempted to relax on the table.

Crawford came over the microphone. "Try not to move. This will only take a minute."

Roman laid one arm across my collar bone and the other across my hips. I didn't think I could even move, much less escape, no matter how hard I tried.

The ceiling robot lowered, then stopped centimeters

above my body. Several arms expanded and hovered over my abdomen. I gripped the sides of the table as a cold solution poured over my stomach.

"That was antiseptic," Crawford explained. "This next part is the worst. An injection of antibiotics and local anesthetic. After that, you will just feel pressure. Deep breath in and blow it all out…and I suggest not looking."

I tried to hold still, but my body shook violently. Roman squeezed my shoulder. "Hey, it's going to be okay. Look at me."

I took a deep breath and locked onto Roman's eyes. *Man, I missed him.* I exhaled slowly as Crawford counted down from five. On two, a searing hot pain stabbed into my abdomen. I attempted to scream, but all my breath had escaped my body. I writhed under the weight of Roman's arms. My vision wavered as the sharp pain morphed into a deep ache that traveled all the way to my spine.

"Breathe," Roman reminded me. "Worst part is almost over. Focus on me. Focus on getting out of here."

His words calmed me and I realized the pain was slowly slipping away. I made a critical mistake and looked down to see my intestines peeking out of a small hole in my torso. I threw my head back as nausea rolled over me. On the brim of passing out, I felt two hands cradle my face.

"It's out! It's over. Stay with me." Roman continued to stroke my cheek as the robot glued my wound shut.

Crawford came back into the room. "Success. I already tubed the tracker back to Central, so hopefully, they will start looking for you over there. Now, let's get you guys out of here."

Roman picked me up and carried me out of the room.

"You're amazing. You know that, right?"

"Whatever. I'm average at best."

"I wish we had the time for me to explain how very wrong you are."

I shook my head as I leaned against his chest. Crawford ushered us inside a small room with an Out of Order sign on the door. On the far wall stood a metal hatch labeled Biohazard Waste. I didn't like the looks of where we were headed.

Crawford punched a code into a panel and the hatch opened to reveal a metal crate almost as tall as me. "Ninety percent of the hospital's trash is destroyed by the incinerator, but we send our biohazard waste off-site."

"Load me up," I stated.

"Really?" Roman scoffed. "No questions or concerns about crawling into a biohazard receptacle and plunging into the unknown?"

I shrugged. "At this point, I figure there's no use."

Roman chuckled as he helped me inside the crate. He turned to Crawford and embraced him. "I can't thank you enough."

"Anything for the cause, brother."

"You need to get out of here now. Get Casey and the kids and go into hiding."

"Don't worry about us. We'll be fine, I have—" Crawford's phone beeped obnoxiously as alarms sounded in the distance. He read his text, "Dangerous convict escaped from Central. Be on alert. Contact the D.O.C. with any information." He flashed the phone to us, my latest school identification photo appeared.

"Best be on our way." Roman climbed into the crate and

we maneuvered for both of us to fit.

"Good luck," Crawford said as he closed the top of the crate.

Darkness enveloped us. I heard the metal door close. Roman wrapped his arms around me. "Do you like roller coasters?"

"Wha—" My stomach flew into my throat as we were suspended in free fall for what felt like an eternity. The crate tipped onto its side, throwing Roman onto his back, and me onto Roman, as we slowed to a halt. I struggled to catch my breath as automated mechanics echoed around us. Suddenly, the floor dropped from under us. Roman braced me as our crate crashed to the ground with a large thud.

The soft ting of raindrops echoed off the container. I could hear traffic and distant thunder. *We must be outside the building!* A small rhythmic beep slowly drew closer. Loud hydraulics shifted the crate to an upright position.

"What's going on?" I yelled over the noise.

"We are being loaded onto the truck." Roman held me tight as a soft hiss indicated our release and my gut shifted as the truck picked up speed.

"Now what?" I asked. "I think it's time I found out the rest of the plan."

Roman released his arms from around my waist. I didn't notice how tightly he was holding. "The truck takes us over a sewer entrance, not visible by government cameras. Gideon will weld a hole in the bottom of this crate. We hop into the sewers, meet up with the guys who developed this escape plan, and then ride off into the sunset."

"Wait, you didn't come up with the plan?"

"Ha! I wish. I'm not nearly smart enough to pull off something this elaborate on such short notice. Don't get me wrong. I helped as much I could, but this took more collaboration and talent than you'll ever know."

I shook my head in the dark. "Why? Why go through all of this just for me?"

"Well...setting personal reasons aside, you stood up for the Defiance. You saved the last Chaos. You put us on the map, and we protect our own. If you never helped us again you've already done enough."

The brakes of the truck squealed as we rocked to a stop.

"What about your personal reasons?"

I could feel Roman smile behind me. "That's a question for another time."

A loud bang on the floor of the crate startled me.

Roman kicked back in response. "Move your feet to the edge and don't look down."

The crate filled with heat and light as Gideon carved our escape hatch. After a minute or two, I looked down to see Gideon pop his head through the hole, his trademark aviator goggles perfectly in place. "You guys just gonna stay here and spoon all day or what?"

"Shut it, Gid," Roman said as he helped lower me into the sewer opening.

Gideon offered me his hand as I climbed down the last few rungs of the ladder. "Welcome back to the dark side, kid."

I threw my arms around him. "Thank you for... everything."

He laughed. "Just doing my duty. Thanks for not ratting us out."

I looked over his shoulder to see Emily waiting for her turn. "Emily! What are you doing here?" I released Gideon and grabbed her.

She tossed her short hair out of her eyes. "Self-driving trucks don't drive themselves to hidden places. Plus, I owed you one."

I stepped back and watched Roman slide the manhole cover into place, plunging us into darkness. Gideon passed out small flashlights and turned to lead us through the sewers.

I looked around at the ancient brick walls. "I had no idea any of this was down here."

Gideon directed us down another tunnel. "It's not utilized anymore. If I had a Credit for every time I've escaped down here, I could buy a whole—"

He stopped short when Roman grabbed both our shoulders and slammed us against the wall. "Don't move a muscle," he whispered as he pointed at two shadowy figures headed in our direction.

CHAPTER 20
NEW BEGINNINGS

My heart raced as the two shadows continued toward us. I looked to Roman and he brought one finger to his lips. He maneuvered himself in front of me, hiding me between the brick wall and his stone body.

The distorted voices of the strangers echoed off the walls, making it impossible to decipher what they were saying. Gideon scooted closer to us and whispered, "Is that who I think it is?"

"We're about to find out," Roman replied, as he stepped into the middle of the tunnel. "Identify yourself!"

The figures froze. "The mastermind. Is the package delivered?"

The voice wasn't at all what I expected. It sounded very... youthful. Roman took my hand and started toward them. I breathed a sigh of relief. As long as it wasn't the Docs, I didn't care who the mastermind was.

"The package is here now," Roman called.

One body took off in a dead sprint toward us. Instinctively, I moved behind Roman for protection. Roman only smiled down at me. "Don't you want to know who came up with this whole crazy scheme?"

I peeked around his bicep. The "mastermind" was only meters from us. He raced around Roman and slammed into my torso.

His arms clutched around me as he picked me up and spun. "YOU'RE OKAY! You're really okay! You made it! We did it! I can't believe we did it. I mean, I knew we could, but we did it!" he cried.

Worlds collided as I recognized the voice. I started to tremble as he put me down and I stood face-to-face with my younger brother, Connor.

"Connor! What? How?" I gasped as I pulled him in for another hug.

We clung to each other as tears streamed down my face. Somehow, it felt like he had grown in our time apart. I looked to see a lanky shadow joining the reunion. It was Isaac, Connor's best friend. A rolled-up red bandana held his hair out of his face as he bowed dramatically in front of me.

Gideon cleared his throat. "I hate to break up this beautiful moment, but we are currently fugitives on the run, and we aren't doing much running."

Roman nodded in agreement. "If we don't get on the move we're going to miss the helicopter."

"Helicopter?" I gulped. I had seen them in movies, but my feet had never left the ground. The very thought of being thousands of meters in the air made my stomach drop.

Roman winked. "We're big time now. Only the best for you."

Gideon navigated our group through several twists

and turns. I linked arms with Connor and pulled him close. "How did all of this happen? The D.O.C. said you were in their custody."

"It's a long story, but basically Roman and I have been communicating ever since your 'disappearance'. I did my research and told him I wanted to join the Defiance, but he said it wasn't the best time with all the upcoming festivities. Then, Roman told me to stay away from our house on *Great American Dream* semifinals night. He said to watch the show and if something crazy happened, fall off the grid and they would find me."

"Always one step ahead," I murmured.

"So, I told Mom and Dad I was going to Isaac's house. Isaac said he was coming to our house. Then we both went to the downtown G.A.D. watch party. Easy to blend in there."

Isaac interjected, "You should have seen Con's face when you popped up on the big screen. I couldn't believe it either. We figured that was our signal, so we went to an arcade ran by Defiance members and they took us in."

Connor finished the story. "I wanted to contact the parentals, but it was too much of a risk. We were supposed to wait to be contacted, but I knew you were probably in D.O.C. custody. So, I reached out to the guys, they told me you were locked up and we started some 'critical thinking' to bust you out."

I didn't like Connor calling Defiance members "the guys," but I chose to ignore it. "What about Mom and Dad?"

"I'm already working on a plan for them, but Roman was insistent we focus on rescuing you first. Are you guys like girlfriend, boyfriend or something?"

"No!" I hissed, intently grateful for the shadows to hide my red face. Leave it to Connor to embarrass me in front of everyone.

"Geez. Sensitive much?" Connor mocked. "Well, you must be pretty important in the Defiance for them to go through all this trouble. I can't believe we're back together...and both Kronies! This is so awesome."

I stopped in my tracks. "You two are Kronies?"

Connor stood tall with pride. "Oh yeah! Roman had us say the pledge and everything."

"Pledge?" I had never heard of Kronie pledge. I looked to Roman, who smiled sheepishly. I did not like the idea of Connor and Isaac being a part of the Defiance. Heck, I didn't know how I felt about being in it myself. "Connor, I don't know if you should be involved in all of this. I mean, I can't thank you enough for rescuing me, but this isn't one of your video game missions. This is real life and it's dangerous."

Connor rolled his eyes. "Oh, don't go all big sister on me. I'm old enough to make my own decisions. I've done all the research. I know all about the horrible stuff One-Global is doing and I want to put an end to it. I can help!"

I wouldn't get anywhere arguing with him, at least not moments after he planned my successful escape. I decided to let it go and discuss the matter privately with Roman. We stopped in front of a ladder leading to a grated manhole.

Roman faced the group. "Okay, when you get to the top, the chopper will be about twenty meters in front of you. Run for it and hop in. Gideon, take the lead and I'll wrap up the end."

Gideon ascended the ladder and Emily followed.

Roman motioned me toward the drain. "Alright, Eve, you're next."

I shook my head. "Connor and Isaac first."

Roman disagreed. "You're our main objective. You go next."

I crossed my arms and leaned against the wall.

Roman sighed loudly. "Connor, Isaac, up you go."

"That's not the plan!" Connor whined.

"Up! That's a direct order. We'll be right behind you."

The familiar feeling of nervous anticipation filled my body as I watched them scurry toward the circle of light, leaving only Roman and me.

He slowly walked over and put his hands on my shoulders. "Are you okay?"

I shrugged. "I'm not sure yet."

He wrapped his arms around me. "You're safe now. Connor is safe and I promise we will get your parents out soon."

I breathed him in as I rested my head on his chest. He was simply amazing. "I know. I can't thank you enough. That's twice you've saved my life."

Roman chuckled softly, "Let's hope you won't need it a third time. But if you do, I'll be there. I'll always be there."

Hearing those words filled me with peace. In those dark, damp sewers, I knew in my gut I was doing the right thing. I looked into his eyes and my pulse quickened. He smiled down at me and stroked my cheek with his hand. "We have to go," he whispered and released me from his grasp. My heart flooded with disappointment as I turned and took hold of the cold ladder.

Dark clouds covered the sky as I reached the surface. In front of me sat a large, rusty egg with blades circling overhead. I hesitated. *What is that thing? It isn't a helicopter. It's a piece of garbage!* I could see Connor sitting in the middle of the junk pile, motioning me to him.

I decided to just go with it and ran through the rain. I jumped inside and sat down beside Connor, who handed me a headset. I put them on as Roman came in behind me and shut the door. He made a spinning motion with one finger and we lifted into the air. Emily sat beside the pilot, who was the oldest member of the Defiance I'd ever seen, probably mid-forties.

Connor reached toward me and pulled down a microphone from my headset. "You can talk into this."

"I thought you said we were taking a helicopter?"

Connor laughed. "This *IS* a helicopter. Just a really old one, so it can't be tracked. It has no computer technology."

I put on what I took to be my seatbelt. "Is it safe?"

Gideon shrugged. "Eh. It will get the job done."

We lifted off the ground with a violent jerk. I clutched Roman's arm, knowing any second we would plummet back down to our deaths.

Roman only laughed at my misery and put his arm around my shoulders. *I guess I can put up with this mode of transportation if it means being this close to Roman.* He reached into his pocket and held out a small green capsule. I smiled and swallowed the nausea pill.

"Won't they just follow us? This thing isn't very inconspicuous," I asked as we reached the top of the buildings.

Roman answered, "We have Kronies on the ground taking out all cameras and drones in the area. Once we get over the clouds we'll be off the grid."

I knew that between my brother and Roman all possibilities were covered, but I still couldn't believe they had pulled it off. I looked down onto the shrinking city. It made my heart ache thinking that my parents were somewhere in the middle of that mess because of me. I noticed a growing cloud of smoke on the west side of the city.

"What's that?"

Isaac smiled menacingly. "A distraction. Very effective."

Connor nudged me in the ribs. "So, what happened over the past thirty-six hours?"

I looked to Roman, who nodded in agreement as he texted furiously on his phone. I sighed heavily and began my story when the lights shut off on the *Great American Dream* stage. I retold the account of being stuck on the elevator, using Bryan's glasses, making it to the pre-party room, then Emily's brilliant plan to save at least one of us. I told them about almost taking the memory pill but being tranquilized in the van. Roman was *very* relieved I didn't take follow through since their rescue mission had panned out. I described my arrival to Central and the Docs bringing Natalie to see me.

"I didn't tell her anything because I wanted to keep her safe. I really wanted to spill my guts…and almost did, but I knew they were just using her. What would they have done to her if I talked?"

"Memory pill," Roman replied. "They probably did that to her anyway. She'll wake up this morning with no recollection of ever talking to you."

I hated thinking about Natalie being drugged, but at least she was safe. My entire body ached from mental and physical exhaustion. I placed a hand over my stomach and realized the anesthesia was wearing off. "Enough about me, I want to hear your story. How did you two come up with this crazy scheme?"

I listened in awe to the intricacies of how their plan came together. In short, Connor and Isaac hacked into Central's database, causing it to revert to an archaic system called "daylight savings time." This jumped every clock ahead one hour except for Ash's since his phone and watch were a part of the national database. Roman snuck into Central via a sleeper agent and zipline. Conner knew I could get us out of the building once I took a memory jogger. I always knew my brother was way smarter than me, but to hear him think of minute details blew me away. He was a mastermind for sure.

Roman spoke up after the explanation. "Your brother is one brilliant guy. Isaac's not too bad either. They are going to be a huge asset to the Defiance."

The boys beamed across the helicopter, but my heart sank. *Maybe they can help the Defiance behind a computer screen.*

Roman grabbed a backpack from behind his seat and passed out meal bars. "We have a few hours until we arrive, so I suggest we all get some rest. It's going to be a nonstop chaos once we land. Ha. No pun intended."

"Where are we headed, anyway?" I asked.

"To the Cerebrum. We'll be meeting with the high council to discuss our next steps."

I noticed Emily reading the packaging on her snack, then handing it to the pilot.

Isaac had already downed his meal bar. "What are our

next steps?"

"Don't worry about that now. Just get some sleep." Roman messed with my headset, then his own. "Private channel."

Good, I thought as I bit my lip. I needed to ask Roman some private questions. "Hey, I need to tell you something. When I was in custody, they told me a lot of horrible things about the Defiance."

"Of course they did. That's one of their main tactics, discredit the enemy. I'd be surprised if you didn't start to question the Defiance. Am I right?"

I nodded sheepishly. "What they said made sense. I'm not saying I don't believe you, but it's just hard when I haven't seen much with my own eyes."

"When we get to the Cerebrum I'll show you all the proof you need."

I nodded. "They also told me after the last Chaos, many government buildings were destroyed."

Roman shifted his weight. "Yes, we needed to send a message. Make our presence known to the public. Show we are serious. All of our targets were part of OneGlobal administration or buildings the Defiance has deemed Unconstitutional."

"Unconstitutional?"

"Way back in the day, the American government had a written document that stated their fundamental laws, basic citizens' rights, and what was fair or unfair. It was called the Constitution. The U.D. has reinstated that concept for each country independently. It's how we decide what is right and wrong. Unconstitutional buildings are places that manipulate the public like chemical engineering labs, OneGlobal news stations, the online matchmaking centers."

I did feel a little better knowing the Defiance wasn't picking random buildings full of people. "How many people died in the explosions?"

Roman shrugged. "We did our best to make sure most of the buildings were empty."

"Most?"

Roman sighed. "I hate violence as much as anyone, but we have essentially declared war on the world. There's going to be loss of life on both sides. My personal goal is to minimize that as much as possible, but it's a rough road ahead of us."

The weight of his words settled in my stomach. *Declared war on the world?* I looked at Connor and Isaac already sleeping. They were too young to be involved in a war. "I just want my family to be safe."

"I understand and we will do everything we can to keep them safe...but for now, stop worrying and rest." He motioned to his shoulder.

I leaned against him and breathed in his scent. "What about the others? Everyone at the Asylum? Is Hannah safe?"

"I think Gage made it back, but I don't keep tabs on him. The Asylum is on lockdown until we can make sure there is no chance of O.G. infiltration. They will be going through emergency exit drills in case the base is discovered. And I wouldn't worry about Hannah. Sherlock will do everything in his power to keep her safe."

Hearing that everyone was okay filled my heart with happiness. Mentioning Gage sparked my memory. "Oh, I forgot to tell you. Obviously, the D.O.C. knows about

Emily, but they know Gage too—his real identity. But they didn't mention you."

"Well, that's good news...what's Gage's real name?"

"Charles Buckley."

Roman threw his head back and laughed. "No way! That is great. Chuck Buck. I'm actually looking forward to seeing him now." He leaned back in the seat and closed his eyes. "Get some sleep, Eve."

A million questions floated around my head, but I followed his instructions and closed my eyes. It took several minutes for my mind to slow down and the new baseline of adrenaline to quit coursing through my veins. I smiled to myself as I thought about sitting in Professor Gray's class and swearing to myself I would never fall for the Defiance's propaganda. I still wasn't sure what I fell for more—the Defiance or Roman—but it didn't matter. I had chosen a side, and there was no going back. I had no idea what the future held, but I knew it would be with Roman. I let exhaustion overtake me and fell asleep on Roman's shoulder.

EVE'S STORY WILL CONTINUE.

Until then, here is a preview of what is to come at the
Cerebrum…from Roman's perspective.

I knocked on the cold, metal door. It opened automatically, and I walked into the large office. It had been years since I'd been to the Cerebrum, let alone her office. While the rest of the facility made me feel like I was living in a space station, her room made me feel like home with its oversized couches and colorful paintings. My mom sat behind a large oak desk. She smiled weakly. *This isn't good.*

She motioned to a chair. "Take a seat."

I cautiously followed her instruction. "What's up?"

"No 'nice to see you, Mom? It's been a while. Let's catch up. How's the rest of the family?'"

"You're stalling." I knew my mother. She wanted you to feel comfortable before she dropped the bomb.

She sighed, "Alright. There's no good way to go about this, so I'll just say it. Eve's a match."

My heart dropped as sweat broke out across my forehead. I decided to play dumb, hoping I was wrong. "What are you talking about?"

She could see straight through my charade but played along anyway. "You know our next major goal is to overthrow the American branch of OneGlobal then assist the other countries in their take over. We have several avenues to move forward; plan A, B, C, etc. The fastest and most effective way to accomplish our goal is Project Jubilee. You're familiar with the project, correct?"

I couldn't believe my ears. "Absolutely not. Eve is not doing that. It's too dangerous."

Mom furrowed her brow. I could almost see the internal battle of Mom vs. commanding officer. "We will present the scenario to Eve and let her decide."

Hope returned to me. "Well, that's great, but I can tell

you right now there is no way she will go for it. She's not ready...physically, emotionally, or mentally."

"We will prepare her."

I stood up and shook my head. "I will not let her go through that."

"Roman, sit down."

The commanding officer was winning the battle. I reluctantly followed her order.

She leaned across the desk. "Look, I know you care a lot for this girl, but—"

"Eve," I interrupted. "Her name is Eve."

"I know you like Eve. She is your Coverture and that means a great deal. *I* like Eve. She saved the last Chaos from complete disaster. She defended the Defiance when she could have sold us out. That's why I think she's the right girl for the job. I need you to take a step back from all your personal feelings and look at the big picture. You know her better than anybody. Do you think she could do it?"

Mom was right. If Eve was a match, she was obviously the right selection. I nodded, unwilling to verbalize my agreement.

"What would it take for her to say yes? Be honest with me. I'll know if you're lying."

She wasn't bluffing. She could always tell if I was lying. Sometimes, I really hated my mother being the leader of the Defiance. I'd rather her be one or the other.

I took a deep breath and thought about what Eve needed. "Her highest priority is her family. She won't agree to go on any mission until her parents are safe."

"We can't wait for that. We will send our top Kronies

on a rescue mission while she goes through training."

I shook my head. "That isn't enough. She doesn't trust the Defiance with something that big."

"What if we sent you to do that?"

"I'm not leaving her," I huffed.

Mom nodded. "Alright. Who else would she trust?"

My stomach knotted as an idea formed in my brain. "Gideon…and Connor."

"Perfect. We will equip them with whatever they need. They can start planning immediately. What else does she need to say yes?"

I smiled to myself as I envisioned Eve in the helicopter. So many questions, yet trusting me at the same time. "She needs to have more proof of how evil OneGlobal really is. Whatever doubts she has about their true motives need to be erased."

"That will be easy. What else?"

"I'm going with her."

Mom sighed. "I was afraid you would insist on that, but you are too involved. You can supervise her training, and we will send our top security—"

"I am going with her," I stated as calmly as possible.

Mom chewed her lip. "Fine. You have until zero eight-hundred tomorrow to show her the proof of One-Global's crimes. I'll contact Gideon and get him started on his mission. Do you want to present Jubilee to Eve or would you like me to do it?"

"I'll do it. She's more likely to agree if it comes from me."

"Perfect. Then, you're dismissed." She raced around the desk and pulled me into a hug. "I'm so sorry to put you in this position. I wouldn't do it if it wasn't our best shot at taking our country back." The commanding officer had left and she was just my mom again.

I half-heartedly returned the hug. "I know, but I still don't like it. It's too much, too fast."

Mom leaned back and smiled. "But that's the exciting part. Just think about all of this being over and we will have our freedom. Go talk to Eve. I need to check on your brother."

She rushed out the door, leaving me alone with my thoughts. I sank into the plush couch and dropped my head in my hands. *What did I just set in motion?*

ACKNOWLEDGEMENTS

First, I would like to thank God for literally and figuratively giving me this dream. I've had so much fun developing this world and growing closer to Him through the process. Thanks to my amazing husband, Michael, for loving me and providing so much laughter in my life. To my parents and family, who have always supported me through thick and thin, I wouldn't be where I am today without you.

To my pro bono editor Natalie, who has spent countless hours fixing my thousands of errors and improper use of em dashes, thanks for believing in my book from the second you heard about it.

To Charli, the first to finish my book (and in record time), thanks for rereading every draft and for your encouraging reviews. Thanks to Hannah for all the invaluable input and all your "critical thinking." Thank you Emily for starting this crazy journey with me at ABER summit.

Thanks to all my test readers: Becky for your wise guidance, Dani for your contagious passion, Angela for your motivational push, and Don for your calculated foresight.

I would also like to thank my design team Vika V and Bobby Ross. You truly blow me away. Victoria, your hard work and research made my dream beautiful. Your excitement for this project overwhelms me. Bobby, thanks for taking a risk on me and perpetually thinking of new ways to make my book a success.

Thanks to my dog, Jagger, for spending countless hours

on the couch with me as I created Chaos. (Even though you'll never read this or have any concept of what a book is.)

A special thank you to my Grandma Owen, who loved books and didn't get mad at me when I read the last page of your mystery novel and ruined the ending. I hope you can read this is Heaven.

Thanks to all the friends who knew about my secret project and didn't say "you're doing what?"

And finally thank you to you...the reader who bought my book and took the time to read this acknowledgement page. You're seriously amazing!

I love you all and can't wait to see where this chaos takes us...

ABOUT THE AUTHOR

Aubrey Ballard is a self-proclaimed nerd, board/video game connoisseur, and laughter junkie. She is a proud, native Oklahoman, where she lives with her husband, Michael, and her dog, Jagger the boxer.

What started as a literal dream, sparked an idea for how to raise money for IVF, then blossomed into the Chaos Theory Initiation novel. She has a passion for the next generation, which is the driving force behind Chaos Theory. She wants to encourage youth to dream big and help open their minds to the exciting possibilities of life. She looks forward to connecting with readers and listening to their stories.

See her full story at TheAubreyB.com or drop her a line at hello@TheAubreyB.com.